New York Times Bestselling Author

HEATHER GRAHAM

ANGEL OF MERCY

D0047619

H **HARLEQUIN**®BESTSELLING AUTHOR COLLECTION

ISBN-13: 978-0-373-53782-2

Angel of Mercy

Copyright © 2017 by Harlequin Books S.A.

The publisher acknowledges the copyright holders of the individual works as follows:

Angel of Mercy
Copyright © 1988 by Heather Graham Pozzessere

Standoff at Mustang Ridge
Copyright © 2013 by Delores Fossen

Recycling programs for this product may not exist in your area.

This edition published by arrangement with Harlequin Books S.A.

For questions and comments about the quality of this book, please contact us at CustomerService@Harlequin.com.

® and TM are trademarks of Harlequin Enterprises Limited or its corporate affiliates. Trademarks indicated with ® are registered in the United States Patent and Trademark Office, the Canadian Intellectual Property Office and in other countries.

Printed in U.S.A.

www.Harlequin.com

New York Times and *USA TODAY* bestselling author **Heather Graham** has written more than a hundred novels. She's a winner of the RWA Lifetime Achievement Award and the Silver Bullet Award. She is an active member of International Thriller Writers and Mystery Writers of America. For more information, check out her websites: theoriginalheathergraham.com and eheathergraham.com. You can also find Heather on Facebook and on Twitter, @heathergraham.

USA TODAY bestselling author **Delores Fossen** has sold over seventy novels with millions of copies of her books in print worldwide. She's received the Booksellers' Best Award, the RT Reviewers' Choice Award and was a finalist for the prestigious RITA® Award. In addition, she's had nearly one hundred short stories and articles published in national magazines. You can contact the author through her webpage at deloresfossen.com.

CONTENTS

ANGEL OF MERCY

Heather Graham

1

The car fishtailed and spun crazily. Brad compressed his lips in silence to bring the Chevy under control again. If he went off either side of the two-lane road, he would crash straight into swampland, into the endless "river of grass," a hot and humid, godforsaken hell on earth. He was heading west on Alligator Alley—a road that offered a weary traveler just about nothing at all except for the miles and miles of mud and muck and saw grass, the occasional cry of a bird and the silent, unblinking stares of an abundance of reptiles.

No phones here. No fast-food stands, no gas stations. Just miles and miles of nothing but the Florida Everglades.

Brad hated swamps.

Not that it mattered much now.

He straightened the car and quickly looked into the rearview mirror. Michaelson was still after him. Glancing ahead, Brad noted that steam was pouring from the old Chevy's front. Hell, he hadn't even managed to steal a decent automobile. And now here he was in the middle of nowhere, the object of a hot pursuit, cruising in an old rattletrap of a car that was about to die on him.

Sweat beaded along his brow. Without the car, what would he do? He hadn't seen a call box for miles and miles. There was only the narrow, two-lane road, stretching through this eternity of swamp. He wouldn't stand a chance on foot. He'd be a sitting duck. They'd shoot him down in a matter of seconds.

Something popped and whizzed in the engine and a cloud of steam billowed out, obscuring Brad's view of the road. He squinted; there seemed to be some kind of a dirt road up ahead, to the left heading southward. Another glance in the rearview mirror told him that Michaelson was almost on him. He had to take the chance.

With a sudden, vicious swing, Brad veered to the left. The wheels bucked as the car bolted and groaned. It was a road—of sorts. Saw grass slapped against the body and windows as the car plunged along. Brad could hear the eternal drone of the insects, even above the groan of the Chevy's overheated motor.

The car pitched into mud. Brad wrenched hard against the steering wheel. In growing desperation he tried to floor the gas pedal, hoping to bounce out of the mire. The wheels spun; the Chevy remained stuck in the mire.

Brad slammed out of the car. Black mud oozed over his leather shoes and knit socks, soaking his trousers up to his calves.

He paused, listening.

He could hear the motor of the approaching car—Michaelson's car. Following.

There was a sharp retort in the air. Gunfire. A bullet whizzed by Brad's ear. The sharp retort sounded again. Another bullet. Closer. *Whish.* Nearly nicking his ear, making a sick, plopping sound as it embedded itself in the swamp.

Brad turned and ran. His gun was back at the site of the drop-off, along with Taggart's body. Damn, he couldn't even go down fighting. There were three of them with Magnums and sawed-off shotguns, and there was him, without even a nail file.

What a bloody stupid way to go down. Running, unarmed, in an infested, insect-laden, swarming, sullen, putrid swamp.

The mud sucked at his feet with every step he took. He hadn't gone twenty paces before he had lost both shoes. Running was agony. There was nowhere to run to, anyway. Nothing but saw grass and rattlers, coral snakes and gators, water moccasins and mosquitoes… and swamp. Every time he put his foot down, he wondered what he would land on next.

Another bullet zinged by, close to his face. He felt the air rush against his chin. He was dimly aware that night was coming. The song of the insects was growing louder; the horizon had turned red, bloodred. Turning around to look behind him, he could see nothing but grass, tall grass, like needles, raking against his hands, raking against his cheeks. Saw grass. River of grass…that was what the Indians called this place, this Everglades. And it was. An endless river of grass, for as far as the eye could see.

Another bullet whined and whizzed by in a deadly, speeding whisper. Brad inhaled sharply and felt a stab of pain. His lungs were bursting, his hands were cut and bleeding, but he kept on running, always running. Suddenly he sank, plunging into a canal. Kicking and thrashing, he came up, sputtered and staggered onto higher land. He turned, resting his hands on his kneecaps, struggling for breath. All he could see was the grass. Were they still following him?

"Think we hit him?"

He heard the faint voice. Probably Suarez—he was the bloodthirsty one.

Someone snickered. "Does it matter? If we did not get him, Old Tom Gator will."

There was a spate of raucous laughter, then Michaelson, who never laughed, never even twisted his lip in the facsimile of a smile, spoke quietly.

"Keep still. Listen. See if we cannot lodge a bullet in his brain. I do not like leaving fate to Old Tom Gator."

Brad groaned inwardly and straightened, inhaling again for all he was worth to run once more.

The landscape had turned red, the setting sun casting a crimson pall over the flat swamp waters and the few trees straggled out upon the distant hammocks. Red...it was the color that seemed to fill his lungs as he gasped against the humid air, struggling to breathe. It was the color of the saw grass, the color of the single egret that perched in a distant tree, balanced upon one leg.

Rat-a-tat. Bullets flew by him again.

Then he felt a pain, sharp and piercing, stinging his temple. Instinctively, he reached up to touch his head, then stared at his fingers.

Red. It was the color of the night. It was the color of blood—his blood, seeping over his fingers.

He had to keep going. The hum of the insects seemed louder as he staggered along. He could hear no whispers from behind him, no laughter, no words. He gazed up at the sky and saw that the sun was falling. A coolness was descending. The breeze picked up.

Chills shot through him.

Red would not be the color of night. It would be black here—pitch-black. Florida Power and Light did not call upon the snakes and the reptiles and the birds and the wild orchids. Night would descend, and with it would come a blackness like ebony, sleek and impenetrable.

In truth, the horizon was still streaked with pinks and golds and burning reds. Yet Brad could no longer see them. His mind was sinking into the ebony darkness, just as his body was slipping into the oozing muck. All sounds around him were fading to a soft, lilting drone.

He was losing consciousness. He couldn't allow himself that luxury; he knew that. If he fell here, he would not survive the night. He would drown in the mire, become easy prey for the predators of the swamp, provide endless fuel for the bloodsuckers.

He could not fall.

But he couldn't go any farther. Besides, there was nowhere to go. Staggering, he paused. Everything blurred before his eyes.

He heard a humming sound. More bugs. Hell, he'd never seen or heard so many damned insects in his life. They were coming after him now; a herd of them, flying, floating together, in mass.

They were almost upon him. The noise suddenly cut off. Brad pitched forward, certain that he was crashing straight into the horde of insects.

But he fell against something hard. And he was dimly aware that something soft touched him.

Then the red landscape was completely enswamped by the ebony darkness.

Wendy screamed at first sight of the man. For several frozen seconds, after she had squinted against the mirage and cut the motor on her airboat, she simply stared at him.

He resembled the creature from the Black Lagoon. He was an apparition, a giant pile of black mud, rising before her.

She was accustomed to alligators and snakes and any number of slimy beings, but gigantic mud creatures were not indigenous to the Florida Everglades.

It didn't take her long to realize the figure was that of a man. A tall one, nicely built. Heavily built, she decided, grunting as she tried to drag him onto the airboat. Once she had him there, she paused again, panting for breath, trying to discern the place and extent of his injury. She checked his pulse first. Fortunately, he was still alive.

She slipped a hand into the water of the canal and tried to clean away some of the mud from his face. Against his temple she found the wound—a small gouge, still bleeding. What had he done? Tripped and fallen against something? She shook her head, and a rueful, somewhat contemptuous smile curved her lips. City slicker. It was written all over the man. Beneath the mud she could see a fashionably cut three-piece suit, silk tie and cotton shirt. No shoes at all—probably lost in the muck somewhere. She sighed, shaking her head again. When would these people learn? A swamp was a place to be respected. It was not welcoming to the unwary. And now, what to do with him?

She sat back on her heels, lost in the dilemma. He wasn't seriously injured, so he probably didn't need to be in a hospital. She had no idea where he had come from, so she couldn't really return him anywhere.

She couldn't leave the fool lying in the swamp. It would be tantamount to murder.

Wendy sighed. Maybe he should be in a hospital, but even so, she'd have to take him home first and call Fort Lauderdale for an ambulance or conveyance of some sort. Since her car was up in the garage, she couldn't take him too far herself.

"Well, sir, would you like to come home for dinner?" she murmured to her prone form, then she laughed with dry amusement. It was the first time she had ever asked a man to dinner. Well, except for Leif, and that had been different. They had never exactly asked each other to do anything; tacit consent had always seemed to rule between them.

Putting aside memories of Leif, Wendy settled the mud creature onto the boat, then started the motor and headed into the swampland. She turned on the lights; it was growing dark, and night fell quickly in the swamp.

Two miles inland, she came upon a high hammock and switched off the motor. She docked the boat, then stared at the huddled form again, trying to determine once more what to do. She was beginning to worry because he didn't show signs of coming to. Concussion? Maybe. She needed to clean him up, then she could give his condition a more professional assessment.

After a moment of hesitation, she decided to leave him while she went inside for a stretcher. He was simply too big for her to move without one.

Her house was little more than a cabin, but it was self-sufficient, and she had made it home. A generator provided electricity, and though she bought most of her drinking water, she had a purification system, too. The house itself was a square frame structure with two bedrooms, a living room and a big, eat-in kitchen. Her furniture was Early American, and her windows were dressed in earth-toned gingham drapes. It was possible to sit in the house and imagine that next-door neighbors could be found twenty yards away instead of twenty miles.

Wendy hurried through to the second bedroom and dug beneath the bed for the canvas stretcher. She had no problem carrying the stretcher out to the airboat; it was not so easy getting the man onto it. He was not only tall and very well muscled, he was unconscious, and therefore deadweight. Grunting and panting and working up a sweat, she at last managed to pull him onto the canvas.

His clothing was going to have to go before she brought him in. Not all of it, but she could strip him down to his briefs. Although Wendy lived in the swamp, she tried to keep mud out of her house. She wondered briefly what would happen if he regained consciousness while she was stripping him of his clothing, then shrugged. If he came to, he could damn well help her, and he'd better do so pleasantly. He could have been dead by then without her.

His socks peeled off easily. His suit coat proved to be a problem. She could not lift his shoulders high enough to pull the jacket away.

Wearing thin, Wendy sat back panting. Realizing that his wardrobe was ruined, she decided to cut his clothes away.

Wendy scampered back into the house in search of scissors. In the kitchen, she decided to bring out a bucket of soapy water and a washcloth. Once she had determined a plan, she set about it with a certain energy and will. Although she was handling a complete stranger, it was a little bit late to be reticent about the situation.

She hurried back outside and began cutting away his clothing with a vengeance. She rid him of his jacket, vest, tie and shirt and gently washed away all the muck and mud on his face and his shoulders. She sat back then, studying him and experiencing a shaft of acute discomfort as she did so.

She had thought his complexion was darker; it had only been an illusion created by the swamp muck clinging to his sandy-colored skin. His hair was a tawny color, the type that lightened in sunlight and grew darker in winter. He had a nice-looking face, a ruggedly handsome, masculine face. His nose was long and straight, his brow was high, and his well-defined cheekbones rose above a hard, square jaw. Even in repose, he had a determined look. She wondered how old he was, then guessed that he was between thirty and forty.

He'd been heavy and difficult to lift because he was composed of muscle, sinewed and taut. He was bronzed, as if he spent time in the sun, and he was hard, as if he spent time working with his body. Yes, it was a nice body.

Wendy recoiled quickly from touching him. She gave herself a furious shake, refusing to believe that she could be thinking this way about a stranger's body.

She searched his jacket for a wallet but found nothing except a piece of spearmint gum. When she tried to reach into his trousers' pockets, she found them glued together by dried muck. Determined, she stood, loosened his belt and tried to slip his trousers off. At first she couldn't budge them. Then they suddenly came free and she fell back, landing on her own hind end with the breath knocked out of her and more than his trousers in her hands.

His briefs had come free, too. The man was now stark naked on the canvas stretcher.

Wendy blushed profusely, then froze in a panic as the man stirred and let out a soft groan.

She hadn't been wrong to try to help him, to clean him or cut away his clothing. But she hadn't intended to go this far. What if he awoke now? What was he going to think? How could she ever explain this?

"Damn!" she swore to herself. She rose quickly, rubbing her derriere and thinking that she needed to procure a sheet before the stranger woke up. She tried to run past the man without looking at him, but something wayward within her soul tugged at her, tempting her to take a peek.

He really was a nice example of the human male.

Muscled, trim and lean, with a broad chest tapering to a slim waist and hips and long, muscular legs. His chest was furred in a mat of tawny, red-flecked hair, which became a thin line at his waist and broadened into another thick mat that nested his sexuality. Despite her usual restraint, she felt her heart plummet and hammer, and for the briefest moment she couldn't help thinking that he was, indeed, built very well. She'd been alone for such a long time...

Slightly horrified at her wandering thoughts, Wendy gave herself a shake. It hadn't been that long, and staring at an absolute stranger in such a way seemed so wanton and disrespectful. Strange, but she hadn't even thought about sex in the longest time, and now, just the sight of a man's body had made her mind start playing tricks.

Hot, fiery tears burned her eyelids and she realized she hadn't even had a good cry for a long, long time. But there was no time for that now. She needed to get a grip on herself, get inside the house and get the man a sheet.

"What the hell…?"

Too late. He was awake. The man blinked and struggled to raise himself. His gaze raked over his naked body, then he looked up, and his eyes caught hers. His eyes were tawny, just like his hair. They were neither brown nor green, nor even hazel, but a shade that combined all the colors and became tawny gold.

Tawny eyes, misted in confusion, anger, wariness— a wariness so acute that it frightened her. She took a step back, swallowing, not sure whether to be embarrassed or scared, suddenly wishing that she had left him stuck in the mud.

"Who the hell are you?"

His voice was raspy and deep and not in the least reassuring. The sound of it added another layer to the myriad emotions playing havoc in Wendy's heart. It inspired a certain fear inside of her; it also incited a definite anger.

"Wendy Hawk. Who the hell are you?"

"What?" The wary look shone in his eyes again.

"Who the hell are you?" she repeated irritably. He continued to stare at her, so she nervously went on. "I live here. You fell face forward into my airboat. I've been trying to help you."

Amusement flickered across his face, leaving a smile in its wake. And when he smiled, he was very attractive. "You were helping me—by taking my clothes off?"

She sighed, blushing furiously despite herself. "I didn't mean to—"

"They all just fell off?" he inquired politely.

"No, of course not. You were wearing half of the Everglades. I can't help it if your clothes were so tight that everything came off with one—oh, never mind. I was about to get you a sheet and drag you inside, but apparently you can—" She broke off, gasping as he hopped to his feet. It was one thing to stare at him while he was lying on the ground and unconscious; it was quite another now that he was towering over her, striding toward her with little self-consciousness. "You can walk," she murmured. "Would you stop, please? Haven't you a shred of decency? I'll get you a sheet—"

"I'm sorry," he said pleasantly. That easy grin was still in place and Wendy suddenly realized that his smile was duel-edged. He wasn't sorry one bit. "Frankly, I assumed you'd already had a good eyeful of everything."

"Wait!" she commanded, racing back into the house, spilling half of the things out of the linen closet in her haste to bring him a sheet. He accepted it and wrapped it around his waist.

"It is rather strange, waking up stark naked in the middle of a swamp," he said. His voice was still very deep, the kind of male voice that swept into the system, penetrating. Wendy trembled slightly. Perhaps it was just the night breeze, coming to dispel the dead heat of the day.

"I'm sorry. I was trying to help you."

"I noticed." He laughed, pulling the sheet tighter around his body. "Really. I was just wondering how you would have felt if it had been the other way around."

"Pardon?"

"Well, if I had been trying to help you, and you were the one who had woken up without a stitch of clothing."

"This is ridiculous," Wendy said, wondering if she should have left him in the mud. "There is no comparison. I'd never be in your foolish position. This is swampland. You were wandering around near quicksand pools! If I were you, I would just be grateful for my life."

"Oh, I am grateful. Very grateful," he said softly. He indicated the door behind her. "Were you really going to invite me in?"

Wendy hesitated, uncertain then. She hadn't felt threatened when she'd first dragged him home. Now he seemed dangerous. He might have been out of his element in the swamp, but this man was no fool. He was sleekly muscled and toned as if he were accustomed to taking on physical challenges. And there was an air of tension about him, as if, even when he smiled, he were wary and alert, ever watchful of his surroundings.

"Hey," he reminded her, as if he had read her mind. "I didn't touch *your* clothing. You were the one undressing me down to the buff."

Wendy groped behind her for the doorknob. She opened the door and went in, waiting for him to follow. When he didn't, she paused and looked back.

He'd been examining his clothing. He stared at her with reproach, holding up the bedraggled pieces of his shirt. "I would have stripped on command, if I'd known it meant that much to you," he said.

"I was worried about your life!" she snapped.

He nodded, hitching up his sheet to follow her. "Thanks."

As he came through the doorway he looked around, taking in the cool comfort of the air conditioning and the squeaky-clean butcher-block pass-through to the kitchen. He didn't seem to miss much. His gaze swept the hooked rug and the rocker, the deep, comfortable sofa and the cherry-wood coffee table. When at last he looked back at her, Wendy was glad to see the wary confusion in his eyes once again. His question was very polite.

"Where are we?"

"The Everglades," she replied sweetly.

"But—where?"

"East of Naples, northwest of Miami, almost dead-set west of Fort Lauderdale."

A tawny brow arced high. "We're in the middle of the swamp. And you *live* out here?"

"Yes, I do." Wendy smiled pleasantly again, glad to feel that she had the advantage once more. She walked around him to the kitchen. Although she wasn't sure if she wanted a glass of wine, she needed one. And producing vintage wine suddenly seemed like the right thing to do. It would only baffle him more.

She took a bottle of '72 Riesling from the refrigerator and fumbled in a drawer for the corkscrew. Suddenly, she heard his voice behind her.

"Please, let me."

She was startled enough to oblige, letting the corkscrew slip into his hands while she backed against the counter. A tingling warmth swept through her as he brushed by. His chest was still bare and smelled of the soap she had used upon him.

"You still haven't told me your name."

"Bill. Bill Smith."

He was lying. She wondered why. Only criminals lied about their names. He couldn't be a criminal.

Why not? asked a little voice in her head.

The man could very well be a criminal. She had found him facedown in the swamp.

"What were you doing in the swamp?"

The cork popped out into his hand. He lifted the bottle to her and she nervously turned around, searching for glasses. They clinked together when she handed them to him. When he took them, they didn't make a sound. He poured the wine and raised his glass to hers.

"Cheers. I was lost. A fool, just like you said. I'm afraid that I don't know much about this area at all."

Wendy was determined to pry some truth from him. She lifted her glass politely but did not let her eyes waver from his. "A swamp is a strange place to suddenly lose oneself."

"My car broke down." He lifted the bottle and studied the label. When he looked at her again, his voice was soft. "I am grateful to you for helping me. Thank you."

Wendy nodded, unsure of herself. "You should take care of the gash on your forehead."

"Gash?" He frowned and touched his temple. "Oh, right."

"You probably need some stitches."

"No, I'm sure it will be all right. I'm pretty tough."

"I can at least clean it out for you," she offered.

"I'd appreciate that." He touched the wound again, then ran his fingers through his hair. "I'm still pretty muddy."

"Well, you can take a shower for yourself now."

"Is there one? May I?"

"Down the hallway, second door on your left. Please, Mr. Smith, go right ahead."

"Thanks." He handed her his half-consumed glass

of wine and strode down the hallway. Wendy heard the door close.

She gnawed on her lower lip for a moment then walked down the hallway, heading for her bedroom. After a moment's hesitation she knelt down and pulled out the bottom drawer of her dresser. She dug around for several seconds and came up with a T-shirt, jeans and a pair of briefs. This man was only a little bit taller than Leif, and they had similar builds.

Back in the hallway, she could hear that the shower was still running. She tapped on the door. "I've left some clothes for you out here. I think they'll fit."

Wendy returned to the kitchen and thoughtfully sipped her wine again. Was she crazy to be helping him? No, of course not. She had known that she couldn't just let him die in the wilderness.

And yet she was wary, concerned by the effect he'd already had on her. Reluctant to think about it, she opened the refrigerator, idly picked out some vegetables and began to slice them. By the time he came out of the shower, clean and dressed with his hair still wet and slicked back, she had added diced chicken to the vegetables and was stir-frying the lot of it in a huge skillet.

He leaned across the counter. "Smells delicious."

"Thank you."

"Does it mean that I'm invited to dinner?"

"You have no choice. I don't think I can get you out of here today."

"Why not?"

"My car is in for repairs, and the garage closed at five. All I have is the airboat. Well, actually, I could take you back to the road and you could hitchhike—"

"I'd much prefer the dinner invitation," he said hastily.

By way of response, Wendy dished the vegetables and meat onto a platter and handed it to him. "Mr. Smith, if you'd set that on the table...?"

"Certainly."

Wendy took brown rice from the stove, emptied it into a bowl and joined him at the kitchen table, which she'd already set for two. He pulled out her chair, then retrieved both their wineglasses and the bottle before sitting down across from her. He smiled at her, and her heart gave a little thud again—she did like that smile.

"Thanks. For everything."

Wendy nodded, almost afraid to speak.

"Whose clothing?"

She swallowed tautly. "My husband's."

"Oh." His eyes narrowed warily. He was silent for a moment then gestured toward the table. "We're eating without him?"

"He's dead."

"Oh. I'm sorry."

Wendy nodded again. Strangers couldn't really be sorry. They couldn't really care. Especially this one. He was more relieved than anything else, she was certain of it.

"You live here alone?"

It was the question she'd dreaded. She was a prime target. And the more she saw of him, the more she became certain that he wasn't as innocent as he wanted to appear.

But her instinct told her she could trust him, that he would never hurt her. It was a foolish thought, a false sense of security, she told herself. Still, it was there, and she couldn't shake it.

"Yes, I live here alone."

"Wendy," he murmured. "Wendy Hawk." He leaned forward and reached out. Before she could think to protest, he'd curled a strand of her hair around his finger. "A five-foot-two, blue-eyed blonde named Wendy Hawk who looks like an angel and lives in this sultry pit of hell. Am I dreaming, or did I die and make it to heaven?"

"I'm almost five-four, my eyes are gray, and not even the most avid nature lover would ever compare this place to heaven."

Wendy gently tugged her hair from his grasp. Unable to stay at the table any longer, she picked up her wineglass and backed away, feeling as if a tempest were brewing within her.

"We need to do something about that gash," she murmured.

"You haven't eaten."

"I was just keeping you company. I had dinner with a friend before I found you." It was almost the truth. She had been coming from Eric's and she had eaten lunch with him earlier. "Please, go ahead, though."

She smiled a little weakly and turned away, sipping her wine as she moved into the living room. She turned on the television and ambled back to the sofa, vaguely noticing that the news was on while reproaching herself for abandoning a guest at the table.

He wasn't really a guest. She didn't know anything about him. When he had finished eating, she would do what she could for the gash in his forehead, then return him to the road.

The word *Everglades* suddenly caught her attention, and Wendy stared at the television with interest. She frowned, trying to catch up on the story; she had come in on the middle of it.

A violent confrontation had erupted over the illegal transport of drugs. The FBI had been involved; also the Drug Enforcement Agency and the local authorities. An agent had been killed, and the drug runners were still at large. A man's photograph flashed on the screen, then Wendy's vision was suddenly blocked.

Bill Smith stood directly in front of the picture. Without turning around, he flicked off the television.

Wendy straightened, glaring at him. "I was watching that."

He stared at her intently for a moment. His chilling look made her shudder, and she wondered again if she hadn't been a fool, bringing him into her home.

Then she realized that she wasn't trembling with fear, but with a strange warmth. He was wearing Leif's clothes. He was Leif's size, she knew that, and in the darkness, in the heat of passion, he might be very much like Leif.

No. He wasn't like her husband at all.

He was arresting and appealing all in his own right, and he was stirring up long-buried desires and emotions within her, feelings she was afraid to face.

And yet he was in her house. It was going to be a long night.

"The television," she reminded him. "I was watching the news program."

"I'm sorry. I needed your help."

"For what?"

"This gash. Would you mind? Have you got some peroxide or something?"

"Sure." Wendy went into the hall, pausing to flick on

the television again. The news was already over, and a game show had begun.

Wendy hurried to the bathroom for the peroxide and Mercurochrome. When she opened the medicine chest, she flinched, surprised to see his reflection in the mirror. He was standing right behind her, his eyes intense as he watched her. "Where do you want me?" he asked.

She shrugged. "You might as well sit right here."

He did. Wendy poured peroxide on a cotton ball and gingerly sponged it over his temple. Although he didn't move, she winced at the sight of the wound. Whatever he had struck had caused a deep gash. She knew it had to be painful for him.

After she had finished with the peroxide, she hesitated.

"What's wrong?" he asked.

"This stuff is going to hurt."

He nodded. "That's okay. Do your damage, please."

Blushing, she took the medicine bottle from him. Although she dabbed at his head repeatedly, he remained stoically silent. She bit her lip, dabbing carefully. "I can't imagine what you hit," she murmured. "It's almost as if the flesh were spooned out...."

"Strange, isn't it?" he murmured. He took the second cotton swab from her, tossed it into the trash can and smiled again. "I feel better already."

"I'm glad."

"Can I make you some coffee?"

She shook her head. "No. But I will have tea."

Wendy followed him into the kitchen, where he filled the coffeepot and she filled the kettle. The man had a nice manner about him. He was able to be helpful and yet not seem intrusive. She was acutely aware of him, of every move he made. She was aware of too much. His smooth jaw…he had shaved that morning, she was certain. His scent…a musky odor that mingled with the clean smell of the soap. His eyes…tawny and alert.

She was so accustomed to being alone that the mere presence of another human being heightened her awareness. Wasn't he just a normal man? A lost city slicker?

No, this man was special. This man was arresting and alluring.

"What do you do?" she asked him as they waited for the water to boil and the coffee to perk.

"Do?" he said blankly.

"Yes. For a living."

"I'm in—pharmaceuticals."

"Salesman?"

"Er—yes."

"You were heading toward Naples?"

"Yes. Yes, I was."

"Do you live in Fort Lauderdale?"

"Well, actually, I live in New York. I was just—transferred down here."

The water boiled. Wendy turned off the burner and poured the water into the teapot. When she felt him watching her, a warm sensation surged through her blood. So this was it, she thought. This was the way it felt, that spark of attraction. She wasn't sure if it was right or wrong, or if it was painful or pleasant. He was a pharmaceuticals salesman from New York whose name was Bill Smith. He'd literally stumbled into her life, and she was feeling alive for the first time in years.

She spun around. He was studying her, his eyes warm, sparkling with a strange tenderness. He shook his head, smiling. "How did you get here? Do you really live here all the time? What do you do for a living?"

"Once upon a time, I was a nurse. Then I met Leif. He was an environmental scientist. This was his home. I came out here to be with him."

"And you've stayed?"

"It's home. I love it."

"How the hell can you love the swamp?"

"There's much more here than swamp, Mr. Smith."

He cleared his throat. "Someone who has seen me in less than briefs is still calling me Mr. Smith?"

She flushed but kept her chin high. "This is a beautiful place, Bill. You haven't looked. If you spent time here, you'd see the magic, and you'd understand."

He didn't believe her, not for a minute. He hated this place: the quicksand, the reptiles, the stinking insects. And yet, there had already been magic in the night. The fact that he was alive was a miracle in itself. He had awakened to see her standing above him, blond and petite and beautiful, an angel of mercy, protecting him from the darkness.

Now it was time for another miracle: getting his man, and getting out of here alive. He sobered quickly, hoping that Michaelson and his men had really given up. He needed to see a newscast, without Wendy around.

Wendy. He even liked the name. It suggested the clean coolness of a breeze, the exciting rush of a storm. A fitting name for this tempestuous angel.

Whoa. He couldn't let his mind wander. He had to find out what else had happened that day. He didn't think that Michaelson could have followed him here, into the thick of the marshy wilderness. Michaelson wasn't any good at navigating the swamps. But still, he'd have to be careful—very careful.

If he could just keep her away from the newscasts, he would be in a good position.

He reached out and touched her cheek. It was as soft as silk, golden tan against the nearly white halo of her hair. "Are you going to let me stay here?" he asked her softly.

"Once I picked you up, there really wasn't much choice," she told him. She cleared her throat. "There's—there's a spare bedroom next to the bath."

"Maybe in the morning you'll show me why you live here," he said. "Good night."

Wendy watched as he retreated into the dark bedroom, his words an echoing whisper that stirred and rustled in her heart.

2

When he slept, he dreamed of her.

It was probably natural. His last conscious thought was of her, of those beautiful, silver-blue eyes, sparkling with determination when she'd sent him off to the guest room. She'd stared at him with a blunt honesty and self-assurance that he had found admirable. She wasn't a coy woman; she wouldn't play games. She lived here alone, she was damned vulnerable—and he knew it. But hers was a calculated risk. If she hadn't assessed him quickly and decided that he was a trustworthy character, he wouldn't be here. She would have invited him back into the airboat and right now he would be standing on the roadside with a bandaged forehead and an upturned thumb.

And of course, she was perfectly safe with him.

But that didn't stop him from dreaming.

Sweet dreams.

She was an acre of heaven in a godforsaken wasteland, a diamond among pebbles, a bolt of silk among bales of burlap. He didn't know what it was about this woman that had seeped inside him so deeply, so quickly, but she had penetrated his world.

Even her voice was music—a smooth, lyrical melody, accented with tenderness, infused with laughter. In his dreams she walked to him, and he watched her, fascinated anew by the easy sway of her soft blond hair, hypnotized by the sparkling beauty of her eyes. He smiled and he reached for her, imagining how her supple body would feel in his arms. She moved in a night mist, a dusky fog that reminded him he was dreaming.

For now, a dream would suffice. She would be perfect, with a slim waist and smooth breasts that just filled his hands, firm breasts with dark rose nipples. Her hips were rounded, too, slightly flared beneath his hands. They didn't know each other very well, but they knew the really important things about each other, things that couldn't really be said but could only be sensed in another person. He wanted her, and he wanted her just this way—in tacit understanding, in sweet, ardent, mutual yearning.

She moved closer, and he exhaled. His entire body tensed and he reached out to touch her. He felt the bed sink as she curled her long, supple legs beneath her and sat there, staring at him. He could almost feel the warmth of her breath against his face.

Suddenly the subconscious realms of dream gave way to reality.

He wasn't imagining the weight at the foot of his bed.

Slowly, still struggling against the enticing darkness of sleep, Brad opened his eyes.

For the longest time he lay still, awake but perfectly still—and absolutely amazed.

There was a creature at the foot of his bed. It wasn't Wendy; it wasn't a woman at all. And it was certainly not the stuff of dreams.

It was some kind of cat. An enormous, fierce-looking cat.

At first, Brad thought of a tiger, but he knew that tigers weren't indigenous to this swamp. The creature had tawny gold fur and menacing yellow eyes. It stared at him for a moment, then curled back its lip and let out a bloodcurdling noise.

His blood seemed to congeal, but he remained perfectly still, staring at the hundred-pound monster. Great! He'd eluded Michaelson and escaped the perilous reptiles of the Everglades, only to become catnip for some giant feline.

"Bill?"

He heard Wendy's voice just as light flooded the room.

"Wendy, no! Get out—and shut the door!" he warned her. Standing in the doorway, with her hair a soft, golden cloud about her fragile features, she even resembled an angel. Her eyes shimmered with concern.

He wasn't about to let her become cat food.

Brad sprang up on his knees, ready to meet the teeth of the animal, ready to grab for its throat. He'd never come across anything quite like this in his training, but what the hell, a man couldn't live forever. If he could get to the cat before the cat got to her...

"Baby!" Wendy chastised, striding into the room.

"Wendy! I said—"

"I'm sorry, Mr. Smith." She marched in, heading straight for the animal at the foot of his bed. "Baby has her own little door in the back of the house. She comes and goes as she pleases. Guess I forgot to warn you about her."

Crouched by the pillow and clad only in the borrowed briefs, Brad arched a brow. Wendy sat down by the cat, scratching the animal's ears, flushing ruefully as she glanced Brad's way. "I am sorry. Did she frighten you?"

"Uh, no, not at all," Brad lied blandly. "Baby, huh?"

"She's a Florida panther. An endangered breed."

And she should be! Brad thought, but he didn't think that Wendy would appreciate the sentiment. Slowly he slid back under the sheets and pulled them up to his waist.

"Baby, huh?"

"Well, she was just a cub when I found her. Someone had made an illegal game hunt of her mother, leaving her an orphan. We kind of called her 'the baby,' and the name just seemed to stick. She's really very affectionate and very, very sweet."

"I'm sure," Brad agreed.

Baby let out another sound that was something between a roar and a purr, and Wendy flashed Brad another of the smiles that seemed to cascade into his libido—and his heart.

"Honest. She's gentle, I swear it."

Tentatively, Brad stretched out a hand to pat the cat on the head. "Nice kitty."

Baby licked her chops. Brad decided that Baby's teeth could have belonged to a saber-toothed tiger.

But she didn't nip at him. She merely stretched out on her back, thrusting all four paws up in the air.

Wendy laughed. "She likes to have her stomach scratched." Brad watched her slim fingers move over the silky pelt and he longed to tell her that he liked to have his stomach scratched, too. The very thought of it made a certain heat suffuse his veins. He wondered if his thoughts were revealed in his eyes. With one glimpse, Wendy blushed and pulled at the cat, hauling her down from the bed.

"Sorry," she murmured. "Come on, Baby. We should let our company sleep awhile longer."

When the door closed softly behind her, Brad exhaled, realizing just how damned tense he had been, and just how knotted and hot he still felt. His fingers were curled into fists, and the sheet didn't provide much cover for his body. Maybe she had noticed more than the message in his eyes.

Groaning softly, Brad tossed away the covers and rose. A soft stream of pink was filtering into the guest room through the soft cream-colored curtains. Brad walked over to the window and pulled them open.

The early-morning air seemed to be colored by the sunrise in shades of glittering gold and fairy-tale pink. From the window he could see that they were on a rise of higher ground, that trees and flowers and a little fenced-in garden surrounded this side of the house. The sun reflected off a pool of water beyond the trees, though, and Brad imagined that they were probably on a hammock that stretched out perhaps an acre before giving way to the canals and muck and saw grass of the swamp.

The view from the window was pleasant, though. Wild orchids grew in profusion over the cluster of trees, in shades of lilac, yellow and pink. Closer to the house, there was a garden of roses and a bougainvillea. The flowers provided an aura of silence…and a curious sense of peace.

Brad gave himself a mental shake. The last thing that surrounded him, he reminded himself bitterly, was any semblance of peace. He had to get dressed and get moving and decide what the hell he should be doing.

With that thought in mind, he quickly donned his borrowed clothing and stepped out of the bedroom.

A glance down the hallway told him that Wendy was already in the kitchen. She was wearing denim shorts and a tank top, socks and a pair of sneakers. Her blond hair was pulled back into a simple ponytail that fanned over her shoulder as she poured water into the coffee machine.

Brad smiled at her as he ducked into the bathroom. "You could have gone back to sleep!" she called.

He stuck his head out and grinned. "Naw, I'm awake now."

He washed his face studiously and used the tooth-brush she had given him. Then he stared at his features. The gash in his head was ugly, but he could arrange his hair to fall over it. He probably should have had a few stitches, but he wasn't going to die from the lack of them. With a shrug, he splashed water over his face again. He had to know what was going on. He probably needed to act, but he didn't know what he should be doing. He really needed to talk to the boss. Hopefully, Wendy would take him to civilization, where he could make a phone call and find out what the hell was happening.

A little hammer seemed to slam against his heart.

Well, then, that would be it. His blond angel of mercy would drop him off, and that would be all. So much for dreams. So much for sweet images of her coming to him in the night, smiling, reaching out to touch him...

So much for dreams of reaching out and cradling

the fullness of her breast in the palm of his hand, of tasting her lips.

"Damn!" he muttered out loud, shaking his head, dousing his face again in the water. He had to break this spell, get away from this woman.

But he still needed her help.

He turned off the water and combed his hair back with his fingers, carefully pulling a lock over the ugly reminder of the gash.

Outside the kitchen, the aroma of cooking bacon filled the air, and the scent was making him ravenous.

Baby was nowhere to be seen and Wendy was poised by the counter, looking out to the living room. Brad saw that the television was on, tuned into one of the popular, national news shows. National news...

Was he safe? he wondered. He hoped so.

She turned away from the television to greet him. "Hi. Sorry you were woken up."

He shook his head. "I'm not a late sleeper anyway."

She smiled at him, and again, he liked her lack of guile. "Want some coffee?" she asked.

"I'd love it. I'll help myself."

As he stepped into the kitchen, she brushed past him, going to the stove while he headed for the coffeepot. There was a beautiful scent about—something clean and fresh and light. He was tempted to grab her, sweep her into his arms, bury his face in the perfume of her hair.

But if he did so, he thought, grinning, he would probably end up wearing his coffee rather than drinking it. He poured himself a cup, then contented himself with leaning against the counter to watch her. He studied the golden hair that played over her sun-browned shoulders, the natural sway of her hips, the easy grace that seemed to rule her every motion.

Sensing his thorough observation, she turned to face him. "How do you like your eggs?"

He grinned. "I always feel lucky if I get them cooked," he told her.

She grimaced. "Scrambled, over easy, sunny-side up?"

"However you have yours," he said firmly.

With a shrug, she cracked an egg into a frying pan. He was having his eggs sunny-side up.

"As soon as we've eaten, I'll take you to the garage. There's a phone there. No use rushing, though. The phone is inside, and the garage doesn't open until nine."

"I'm not in any hurry," he said softly.

Wendy not only heard his voice, she felt the timbre of it. He hadn't really said anything, yet his words seemed to wash over her in a gentle, beguiling caress.

Nudging an egg with the spatula, she wondered why he had such an effect on her. She couldn't forget that he was lying about his name. And men just didn't lie about their names without a reason.

But her initial instincts had been right. She had trusted him in her house, and he had proven that he deserved that trust.

Face it, Wendy! she taunted herself. You don't know a damn thing about him, good or bad. The real truth is that you're attracted to him, and though you're incapable of going about a simple sexual relationship, you just want to hold on to him and think about the possibilities....

She swallowed, trying to ignore her unhappy thoughts. The eggs were done. She strained them with the spatula and slipped them onto plates. Her guest was right beside her, ready to take them from her.

Glancing his way, she couldn't help but admire the planes and angles of his face. He was handsome, but a far cry from pretty. The texture of his skin was masculine, as were the muscled structure of his sinewed form and the calluses that lined his strong palms. Idly she wished that she could have him unconscious again. Now she would be fascinated just to explore him from head to toe.

To touch him.

He set their plates down on the table a little too sharply. Wendy frowned, aware that the television had drawn his attention.

And then she heard it.

The newscasters were still reading the national news, but it seemed that her small part of the world had gained national attention. Wendy forgot her guest for a moment, trying to concentrate on the words of the announcer.

She and Brad both rushed toward the television set at the same time.

"Stop!" Wendy ordered.

For a moment, he paused and glared at her. Wendy could feel his eyes boring into hers.

Danger emanated from him, hot, desperate danger, sweeping around her, encompassing her.

Yesterday, there had been a shoot-out. "A violent exchange of gunfire," according to the Fort Lauderdale police. A federal agent had been killed, and law-enforcement officials were still looking for the gang of men involved, a gang of drug traffickers, arms dealers and murderers.

"You don't want to hear this."

He tore his gaze from Wendy's and strode toward the television. She began to protest, but when her mouth opened, a horrified gasp escaped instead as Brad's picture suddenly flashed upon the screen.

There were five men in the picture. One tall, blond man, three medium, darker men and Wendy's guest—Mr. "Alias" Bill Smith.

"Son of a bitch!" he swore. Too late, he turned off the television.

Wendy stared at him, her gaze wide and brilliant—and condemning.

"Wendy…" He lifted a hand to her imploringly. He wished he hadn't lied to her. The whole ordeal was going to be difficult to explain. Even worse, the look of betrayal in her eyes was going to be impossible to soothe. Those shimmering, beautiful, silver-blue eyes of hers, gem hard with hatred and reproach.

And fear.

He raked a hand through his hair, wondering how to explain. "Wendy—"

She spun around, ready to escape. He couldn't let her do that. He couldn't let her leave him stranded here, and he didn't dare let her risk a panicked run back to civilization.

God only knew who she might run into.

"Wendy, please wait!"

But Wendy had already begun to flee. She was at the door, tearing it open.

Freedom, she thought. Another second and she would be free. All she had to do was fly out the door and reach the airboat. She didn't need much of a head start. The swamp would slow down the unwary man, the one who was unprepared.

She threw open the door.

It was abruptly slammed shut before she could begin to get out. Acting on reflex, she swung around to face Bill Smith—or whoever he was! Now his handsome features bore a chilling countenance. She was frightened. This man was an impostor, a liar. The way he had slammed the door had proven his speed, strength and agility. He would be a powerful adversary.

"Wendy—"

She ducked beneath his arm and raced down the hall to her bedroom. Perhaps she could escape through a window....

All the while she could feel him behind her, following close. Gasping, she flew through the door to her bedroom, slammed it shut, locked it and leaned against it, panting.

Her heart caught in her throat as she felt him try the knob. "Wendy! You have to listen to me—"

"Stinking bastard—liar!" she retorted...her eyes surveyed the room. If she was lucky, the screwdriver would still be by her dresser, where she had left it after trying to fix a brass handle that had come loose.

"Wendy, I admit that I lied to you, but you have to give me a chance to explain."

The screwdriver was there, right on the carpet. If she could pull out a screen, she could escape through one of the large windows above her bed. She just had to keep him talking for the time it would take her to do so.

"So go on! Explain!" she snapped. Carefully, silently, she moved away from the door. She picked up the screwdriver and approached the window. "Explain!"

she shouted back at him as she jumped up on the bed and set to work.

"Wendy, I'm not a bad guy. Honest." She heard his voice, coaxing, sincere, from the other side of the door.

Yeah, sure.

He'd fooled her once already. He must be thinking that she was the most naive creature this side of the Mason-Dixon line.

The first screw fell away in her hand. Holding her breath, she started on another. Her fingers shook. Oh, God. The FBI and the DEA were after him. An agent had been killed. This was serious business; her house-guest was a member of a drug mob.

"I should have told you the truth from the beginning. I was trying to protect you, and at first I didn't know whether I could trust you or not. I lied about my name to protect you. I was afraid of what the media would be saying. You've got to understand. The boss can't give out the real information because he assumes that I'm still with Michaelson and his group. But they found me out when they caught Jim. Jim is the one who was killed."

What the hell was he rambling on about? Wendy wondered. The third screw gave way in her hand and the screen came careening down. She caught it as it crashed against the wall. It was harder going now. She had to hold the screen and unscrew at the same time. Concentrate! she berated herself.

She probably deserved this. If she wasn't so frightened, so close to tears, she would laugh at herself. Maybe she shouldn't have stayed here, holed up alone in the Everglades. Maybe she had spent too much time mourning the past and licking her wounds. Because right out of the blue she had picked up a stranger, admired his face and form—lusted after him, Wendy girl, admit the truth! she chastised herself in silent reproach—trusted him and made a complete fool of herself. If she'd stayed a little nearer civilization, she might have been smart enough to smell a rat beneath her very nose.

The fourth screw finally gave way. He was still talking, but she had been too breathless to hear him. She set the screen down carefully, then silently hiked her rear up on the sill. With a groan the glass pane eased open, allowing her to slip through the window and fall onto the soft grass below.

"Wendy, do you understand?" Brad pleaded softly. There was no answer. Too late, with sudden, definite clarity, intuition warned him that no one was listening.

He slammed a muscled shoulder against her door. The flimsy lock gave way instantly and he stepped into her room. There was only a screen leaning against the wall and curtains that billowed in the gentle breeze from the open window.

Bolting across the room, he leaped onto the bed and propelled his body out the window. He fell to the grass and rolled.

On the path below, Wendy was running as fleetingly as a young doe, trying to reach the airboat.

"Wendy!" He tore after her, catching her just as she neared the water.

Caught by the arm, she flailed and kicked like a trapped animal. Her small, clenched fist caught him in the shoulder. Then she delivered a blow to his right eye, a punch that hurt like hell.

Now he was probably going to have a shiner to go with the cut in his temple.

Then she landed a hefty kick. He could only be grateful that she had aimed for his shin.

"Wendy—"

She wasn't listening. He was pleading; she was swearing. Brad ducked low, sweeping her over his shoulder. He ignored the hands that pounded against his back and the nails that scratched him through his borrowed shirt. Striding quickly, he entered the house by way of the front door. He had to calm this woman down.

He didn't stop in the living room, but proceeded to her bedroom at the end of the hallway, where the door with its broken lock hung open. He barged into the room and unceremoniously dropped her on top of the bed. Her fists were still flying and her hair tumbled over her shoulders in a golden cloud.

"Damn you, I'm not trying to hurt you!" Brad cried.

"And how am I supposed to believe that's not just another lie?"

"Wendy!"

There seemed to be only one way to calm her. He crawled over her, straddling, pulling her arms high over her head and securing her wrists. Her hair fell in front of her face; she tried to blow it away, growing silent at last but continuing to stare at him with a look that could definitely kill.

"You liar!" she shouted.

"I lied about my name. I'm sorry. It's Brad. Brad McKenna."

She lay still for a minute. Her body relaxed slightly, but the suspicion never left her eyes. They seethed up at him with simmering skepticism.

His heart ached for her, for the feelings of betrayal she was suffering. He still liked her, so damned much. And he was still so entranced by this silver-eyed angel. Her breasts rose and fell with agitation, and he could feel her warm body caught between his own thighs.

"Honest. Give me a chance to start over. Mrs. Wendy Hawk, meet Brad McKenna. Oh, Mr. McKenna, so nice to meet you. The pleasure, Mrs. Hawk, is completely mi—ine! Hey!"

She wasn't amused, not in the least. She bolted against him in a powerful surge that almost sent him flying, despite all his well-trained reflexes.

"Wendy!" He laughed. "Please, give me a break!"

"I gave you a break! I plucked you out of the mud and I brought you here and I fed you—"

"And bathed me," he supplied.

Her eyes narrowed and she barely skipped a beat. "Fed you and clothed you and gave you a roof over your head! I should have left you for a reptile feast!"

Brad inhaled and exhaled slowly. Deep inside, he was in anguish. What the hell difference did it make? he asked himself bleakly. So, she hated him. So what? She was going to take him to a phone, and she would never see him again anyway.

There had never been anything for him here at all. An undeniable attraction wasn't always worth pursuing. He didn't indulge where he couldn't turn his back and walk away with a clear and easy conscience.

It would be difficult to walk away from this silver-eyed sylph. But it would be devastating to know he'd caused her pain. And right now, she was hurting because of him. She had to understand. He didn't want her hating him.

"Wendy, please." He eased his hold on her arm. "I know I don't deserve your trust, but I really need it. I need it badly."

She didn't say anything; she didn't fight him. She stared at him defiantly. And for a moment, her mind wandered. She saw the familiar comforter on her bed and the walnut, antique dresser sets she and Leif had stripped and repolished themselves. She saw the daylight streaming through the cream curtains, and she felt the man above her.

Once she had lain like this, and laughed. And the man above her had been no threat. He had been her husband, and she had loved him. And now a stranger straddled her as Leif once had, asking her to trust him. It seemed a sacrilege.

Yet even with that thought, she realized that the panicked beat of her heart had slowed. Despite herself, despite everything she had seen on the news, she wanted to believe him. He couldn't be lying to her, not here.

And he couldn't be such an awful criminal. He could have already killed her if he'd wanted to. He could have strangled her easily, and there were plenty of sharp knives in the kitchen. There was even a double-barreled shotgun hanging on the wall.

She twisted her face aside, not wanting to look into the tawny gold eyes that pleaded so eloquently with hers. More than his words, more than the tenor of his voice, his eyes swayed her. His gaze poured into her, like a liquid warmth, promising honor and truth and even security, when there should have been none.

She swallowed and spoke softly. She couldn't have him touching her. She didn't want to feel the power in his thighs as they locked around her, and she didn't want to feel the warm whisper of his breath. She didn't want his hands so gently but thoroughly locking her own.

"If you don't want to hurt me, then let me go."

He hesitated, then unwound his fingers from her wrists and moved away.

Quickly, Wendy edged away from him, absently rubbing her wrists while she stared at him. He idly sat at the end of the bed and met her gaze.

"Brad McKenna?" she said doubtfully.

He nodded gravely. "I'm with the DEA, I swear it. My partner—the man who was killed—and I were working undercover. We had infiltrated one of the roughest gangs running cocaine, marijuana and hash-ish out of South America. This area's a target zone for us—especially since the drug traffic has increased. It's hard to stop—there are just miles and miles of coast-line and an endless supply of pilots willing to risk their lives for the monetary rewards of bringing in one big supply. Anyway, Michaelson—the head honcho in this little group—caught on to us. He meant to perform a quick execution, but we'd gotten some word in about our location. We'd assumed that he was planning an exchange with the buyers. It all came down too fast." He hesitated, locking his jaw and swallowing painfully. "Jim was killed. I was next in line, but I stole a Chevy and took off down the Alley. The engine died on me, and Michaelson and his boys almost finished me off. But you found me instead."

She stared at him. "Pharmaceuticals?"

"What?"

"You told me that you were a salesman. Pharma-ceuticals."

He shrugged. "I'm telling you the truth now, I swear

it." He wanted so badly to reach out and touch her. He wanted to assure her.

He wondered if that look of contempt would ever leave her eyes. "Wendy, for God's sake, I'm telling you the truth now. Please, can't you believe me?" He reached out to stroke her cheek, but she twisted away.

"If you're telling the truth," she demanded, "why were you in that picture with the smugglers?"

He sighed. "I told you, I was working undercover. They can't reveal my identity at the office until they know for sure that my cover has already been blown." He paused. "Michaelson is wanted for first-degree murder as well as drug smuggling. If he gets a chance, he'll kill me."

Her arms were locked around her legs defensively, and she observed him warily from narrowed, long-lashed eyes.

"Wendy! You've got to believe me!"

"Why?"

"Because," he told her quietly, "I still need your help. I have to have your help."

She kept watching him in silence. He held his breath, then expelled it slowly. "Well?"

"I don't have much choice, do I?"

He lowered his head, smiling. "Thank you," he murmured. He reached out to stroke her cheek with his knuckles.

"But don't—don't even think of touching me again!" she said vehemently. Slipping away from him, she rose from the bed and strode, slowly and regally, from the room.

3

Are you coming?" Wendy demanded coldly. She was waiting for Brad in front of the house.

Brad closed the front door, eyeing her suspiciously. Where was that drat cat, Baby? He had forgotten about the animal when he had chased her outside. Baby was probably more useful against unwanted prowlers than a pair of well-trained attack dogs.

"I'm not sure that I trust you, Mrs. Hawk."

"You're not sure that you trust me?" she demanded indignantly. He didn't answer her. "Well of all the nerve!"

"Where's the panther?"

"Baby?"

"Your deadly kitty cat."

"How on earth should I know," she replied sweetly. "Any cat is difficult to find, and as you might notice, Baby has a big backyard!"

Brad issued an oath at her sarcasm. Forgetting that he had promised not to touch her, he grabbed her wrist and pulled her close. Her body was warm and soft against his. He felt the taunting fullness of her breasts against his chest, the smooth silkiness of her golden tanned skin. When he inhaled, her fragrance was clean and sweet, more haunting than any tormented dream.

Afraid that she could sense his heated reaction, he wanted to drop her wrist and push her away. And he wondered what she was thinking, for she didn't fight, she simply cast her head back and scowled at him with that unique silver magic in her eyes.

Brad gritted his teeth. "What I want to know, Mrs. Hawk, is if that cat of yours is slinking around somewhere, poised to attack."

She hesitated just a minute. "No."

"Are you sure?"

"What do you want—a sworn statement?"

"Yes!"

"Dammit, I'm the one who deserves one of those!" she protested.

"I asked you to trust me."

"But you don't trust me!"

He wanted to kiss her. He wanted to know if the heat that raged in her eyes would warm her mouth and fuse their lips together. The temptation was ungodly. His fingers trembled with the desire to snake into her hair, his body shook with the very force of his longing. Maybe it was the wild, primitive appeal of the ground he stood on. Maybe it was the defiant challenge in her beautiful eyes. He had never wanted a woman more. And he had never wanted one so passionately, so suddenly. He closed his eyes, praying that God would get him out of the swamp and grant him some sanity.

Then he released her. "I'm sorry, Mrs. Hawk. You're right. I am asking a lot of you. Forgive me. Shall we go?"

For a moment she stared at him in silence, then she turned with squared shoulders and started for the airboat.

Brad followed her onto the vehicle, releasing the secure rope she kept tied around a tree. As she started up
the motor, Brad let the sights and sounds of the swamp
fill his senses. The day was bright now, and growing
hotter. He could hear the drone of insects again. A light
breeze caused the distant saw grasses to bend beneath
it, and the vista did, indeed, appear to be a green sea,
with ripple after ripple of wave listing through it. He
heard a ruffling sound and turned to see a long-legged,
awkward-looking crane soar to beauty and elegance as
it took flight from the ground and entered the arena of
the powder-blue sky.

Wendy seemed to be deep in thought, staring straight
ahead. He smiled; she seemed so small and fragile on
the airboat, like an angel driving a two-ton semi.

What kind of a love had kept her here, in the deserted
marshes, all alone? Could anyone, man or woman, be
so self-sufficient that he or she needed nothing but the
earth and sky to survive? The land, the air—and memories?

He quickly realized that she knew this land well.
Having been unconscious, he hadn't seen where he had
come from last night. He could determine their direction
from the sun, but he'd be damned if he understood how
anyone could navigate a swamp with no distinguishing
landmarks. Or were there subtle, natural landmarks,
evident only to those who sought them? A clump of
trees that bowed at an angle there, old trees that had
surely survived countless storms. A wide vista of the
grass, to the right, and to the left, a sudden profusion
of color where a hammock rose from the swamp to provide a home for scores of wild orchids and tall, blue-
toned herons.

Birds burst out of the foliage before them—the airboat's motor was loud. He didn't know how fast they were going—maybe thirty-five miles an hour, tops—but still the breeze became a wind that whipped by them, fierce, challenging, invigorating. Brad closed his eyes, savoring the feel of the wind on his face while the sun beat down on his back. The scent of the swamp that had repulsed him yesterday now seemed rich, redolent.

When Wendy slowed the airboat, he thought they were idling near another hammock of high land. On closer inspection, he could see that strands of high grass hid the planks of a series of small, weather-beaten docks. Wendy tossed him the rope, and he secured the airboat.

Wisps of blond hair had escaped Wendy's neat ponytail. They played about the soft contours of her face as she squinted toward the small building.

"Thank you," he said quietly.

Her hands were on her hips as she continued to survey him. "The phone is inside the office," she said simply.

They crossed a groomed lawn—regular grass that had actually known the touch of a lawn mower—and just ahead of them Brad could see a bright, whitewashed rectangle of a building that sported a few gas pumps outside.

As they approached, an old man in overalls stepped out to meet them, staring curiously at Brad. He wiped grease from his bronzed and wizened hands, and his flesh wrinkled around a pair of light green eyes as he narrowed them upon the newcomer.

"Hi, Mac." Brad didn't realize that he was holding his breath, worrying, until she spoke. "Mac, this is a

friend of mine. Brad McKenna. Brad, Mac Gleason."
Mac arched a brow but reached forward to shake Brad's
hand.

Brad reciprocated the gesture. "Hi, Mac."

The old man nodded, but kept staring at Brad. "You
own that old Chevy that's all torn up near the Alley?"

"Uh—no, I don't own it," Brad said. That much was
true. Some irate owner was probably making a claim
with his or her insurance agent over the car right now.

"Brad needs to use the phone," Wendy said. "How's
my car doing?"

"Car's all ready to go when you are, Wendy. Local
call, son?"

"I—uh—I don't know. Fort Lauderdale." He started
to fumble in his pockets, then he realized that they
weren't his pockets and that he didn't have any money
anyway.

"I didn't ask you for money, boy," Mac said indignantly. "I just asked you where you was calling. You
want Lauderdale, you dial a one first, ya hear?"

Brad nodded. "Thanks. I appreciate it."

"Up in the office. Take your time."

Brad turned and headed for the office. He wanted
to look back, but he didn't. He wondered if Wendy was
whispering to the old man, sharing her suspicions that
he was a murderer and a drug smuggler. Maybe the
old man had a shotgun handy. Or maybe Brad would
be greeted by a pair of pit bulls when he opened the office door. Here in the swamp, people were isolated, a
breed apart, and they often had their own way of dealing with things.

Don't, Wendy, please don't. Don't betray me, he silently pleaded.

The office was cool and air-conditioned inside. There was a desk with a blotter and an old swivel chair to the right of the door. Against the wall stood a Pepsi machine, another machine that dispensed chips and candy, and a large glass globe full of ice water. Brad poured himself a paper cup of the cold water, drank it down and peered out the window.

Wendy was laughing at something the old man had said. Her hands were on her hips, her head was tossed back. When she glanced up at the shop and saw him, her laughter faded.

Brad walked over to the desk and dialed the emergency number. Gary Henshaw answered first. Brad smiled, filling with warmth as he heard Gary scream out in relief that he was alive. "Where the hell are you, buddy? No, never mind, let me get the boss."

Two seconds later Brad was talking to L. Davis Purdy, the man in charge of their operations in south Florida—the Boss, as he was known with respect and affection by his men. Purdy was no pencil pusher. He'd worked the streets for years and had gradually risen through the ranks of the agency. There were few tricks he didn't know. Michaelson was one of the toughest nuts Purdy had ever tried to crack.

"You're alive," Purdy said. The words sounded matter-of-fact, even a little cold.

"Yeah." Brad leaned back in the chair.

"Thank God." Purdy meant it. "Jim is dead."

Brad closed his eyes. "I know. Michaelson got wind that we were both DEA."

"We figured that much out." Purdy hesitated a moment. "Your town house was firebombed last night."

"What?" Brad sat up. His home here was gone? His

collection of rare forty-fives, his stereo equipment, his lumpy old recliner, his college football jersey…little things that meant a lifetime. They were all gone.

But he was still alive, he thought soberly. Jim wasn't so fortunate.

"We're going to have to get you in under protective custody. Brad, you're the only one who can put Michaelson away now. He wants you dead, and usually Michaelson gets what he wants."

"Doesn't sound good at all," Brad said gruffly.

"You know the ropes. You're lucky to be alive now. Where the hell are you that he hasn't gotten wind of you? I'm trying to bring him in, but you know the man, and you know the system. He's as slippery as an eel, and his kind of money can buy all kinds of favors."

"I'm in the swamp."

"The swamp? You're out in the Glades?"

"Yes. I don't really know exactly where. That's probably why he hasn't found me." Brad hesitated, sitting forward. "Come to think of it, at the moment, this is a fine place to be." He started at a sudden sound.

He was slipping, he realized, slipping badly, letting down his guard.

Wendy Hawk entered the office. She sat at the edge of the desk and stared at him expectantly.

"Purdy, will you talk to someone for me?" Brad said. "That picture that came out over the news last night almost did me in."

"We sent that out before your home was hit," Purdy explained. "Who do you want me to talk to?"

"A concerned civilian who kept me alive last night," Brad said dryly, watching Wendy as he spoke. "Now she's afraid she was aiding a hardened criminal. Say something, will you?"

"She?" Purdy murmured.

Brad gritted his teeth. In the background he could hear Gary repeating the word, then embroidering upon it. *"She?* Leave it to Brad. Even in the damn swamps he can find himself a woman."

"Tell Gary to put a lid on it," Brad said with annoyance. "I'm putting on Mrs. Hawk."

He thrust the receiver to Wendy. Curiously, she took it. "Hello?"

"Hello, Mrs. Hawk? My name is Purdy, ma'am, and I'm with the DEA. I understand that you helped one of my men last night, and I'm exceedingly grateful. Brad tells me that you saw the news. I'm sorry about that. We had to take all precautions."

Wendy was silent. Brad, listening in as best he could, realized then that there was still no definite proof of his innocence. He could have called anyone, and the voice on the other end of the phone could be spinning lies as easily as he had.

He groaned softly, slumping back in the chair. Well, she'd believe him when they sent out a car for him.

No. Abruptly, he sat back up. No, the agency couldn't send anyone near here. That would put Wendy in danger. She was safe here in her swamp, because no one would think to come here.

Unless they followed someone in, someone coming for him.

He jerked the phone out of her hands.

"Boss—"

"We'll get a couple of cars out there with our best—"

"No! No, listen to me. I'm going to get out of here by myself."

"Brad—" He could almost imagine Purdy frowning. His brow would be furrowed, and his sharp blue eyes would be squinting.

"Really, Purdy, this plan is safer. I'm calling from a gas station with an old man, and I've been staying at Mrs. Hawk's home. And, Boss, I mean, I am deep in the marshes. There's no way that Michaelson can stumble on me here. It's just impossible. This place is a watery jungle. You need a map to go from tree to tree. If I get myself out, then Michaelson won't think to go after anyone who might have helped me. I'll start wending my way out this morning."

Wendy watched him, her eyes widening. She didn't know how or why she believed in this man, she just did. For all she knew, he could have phoned the Florida State Penitentiary; the man giving her the assurances could have been working on a chain gang.

But she trusted him. She was relying on instinct again.

Her heart was beating just a little too fast; her breath was coming just a bit too quickly.

Perhaps she should simply wash her hands of the man, then and there. She owed him nothing.

But before she even knew what she meant to do, she leaned forward and gently caught Brad's hand. "Maybe you should stay here."

"What?" Startled, he stared at her.

She hesitated, wet her lips, then elaborated. "Some guy is looking for you, right? This Michaelson character. Maybe you're as safe as you can possibly be right here."

"Wendy," Brad said softly, staring into the soft mystery of her silver eyes. "This guy is tracking me down to kill me. I am the only one who can testify against him."

She nodded. "I know. But you just said that he can't possibly find you here."

What was the matter with her? she wondered desperately. She didn't want him here! This man made her feel dazed and irrational. But she wasn't afraid of him. Even when he had held her, when he had pinned her beneath him, she hadn't been afraid. She had been aware—painfully aware—of his build, of his warmth, of his strength. She was captivated by the man, and it had been okay because he was leaving, but now…

Now she was sitting here, suggesting that he stay. Why?

Her heart seemed to skip a beat, slamming mercilessly against her chest. It was foolish, it was all so foolish. But suddenly all that she could remember was the sight of blood, all the blood that had once spilled over Leif's chest. She could hear her own scream, echoing against the corridors of her heart.

Her memories ruled her now. She couldn't let the same thing happen to Brad. The swamp was her refuge; she knew it well, backward and forward, and it was a good hiding place. The Indians had discovered it years ago, but few men had charted it since. The Everglades could shield a man. The swamp was a tough and rugged mistress, but when her secrets were learned and respected, she could embrace and protect a man, an ideal—an entire people.

Conflicting emotions flickered across his face. He set his jaw in a hardened twist. "Wendy, I can't just hide here with you. Running is my forte—my job."

"No one has a job that says he has to get killed foolishly!" Wendy snapped. "Do you think you'll make it out of this wilderness in one piece? Don't be a fool. The law doesn't want heroics. The law needs you alive—"

"But I can look after myself—"

"I imagine that might be true in the big city," Wendy interrupted coolly. "Were you trained to elude a gang of murderers in the Everglades?" She crossed her arms over her chest.

"Brad! Brad!" Purdy was calling him, in an aggravated voice.

Still watching Wendy's eyes, Brad spoke into the receiver again. "I'm here—"

No matter what happened, Brad was due for some painful inactivity. Suppose he did make it out of the swamp? He would have to hide out in a safe house. He'd be locked up with a group of agents guarding him day and night. Brad would be in seclusion until they managed to catch Michaelson.

He groaned, holding the phone away.

Wendy snatched it from him. "Mr. Purdy, can you prove to me that Brad is innocent?"

"I can release the details to the news media," Purdy told her. He cleared his throat impatiently. "Will you please ask Mr. McKenna to remember that he works for me—and put him back on the line. He's going to be on a forced hiatus for even longer than he thinks if he doesn't stick with me this time."

Wendy smiled. Brad noticed that she had the smallest little dimple in the center of her chin. He took the phone back from her. "I've got an idea, Boss. It will keep me safe, and her safe, too. I'm going to lie low right here."

"What?" Purdy was screeching.

Brad moved the receiver away from his ear while Purdy went on and on about the lack of control in the situation. Brad was miles from civilization; there was no help nearby.

"That's right," Brad said quietly. "I am miles from anywhere. No one knows where the hideout is, and no one can squeal. Boss, think about it."

Purdy changed his tactics. "You're going to stay out in the swamp for a good week or more?"

Brad laughed. "Can't you boys do any better than that? Come on—I'll supply the proof. All you home militia have to do is rope in the target!"

Purdy swore. But then he paused. Brad knew Purdy. The Boss was always willing to throw "standard procedure" out the window if another solution seemed to be better.

"All right, McKenna. Now you listen to me for a minute, and listen good. You might be right. Michaelson is a smuggler and a killer, but he sure isn't any Daniel Boone. Sitting tight could be your best move. But remember, he'll have men on both ends of the Allcy, and I'm willing to bet he gets some air coverage of the swamp, too. I want you to check in if you see anything, and I don't want you making a single move without my approval. Got it?"

Brad's muscles tightened. He hated the swamp. What the hell was he doing?

He inhaled. He was trying to live the dream. He wanted to go back to the house and lie in the bed, and so help him, he wanted to make love to the woman. He wanted to touch and taste her flesh, to explore the breasts that were so firm and full in his dream. He wanted to see her mercury eyes above him as passion filled them. He wanted to kiss her, to drown in her...

Purdy was still talking, but Brad couldn't hear him anymore. He stared up at Wendy, and he wondered if his own features had gone as ashen as hers. What was she thinking now? Was she regretting her impetuous offer? It was a mistake. He didn't know how to sit still; he hated to sit still. What the hell was he going to do in the swamp for all those hours?

Except to lust after his silver-eyed angel of mercy.

He swore softly and rubbed his temple. "Hey, Boss—"

"Not a move, Brad, unless you talk to me. They've run a trace on the phone number, so we've got your co-ordinates. I'm going to get my men out there to nail Michaelson. You do your bit—stay alive, huh?"

There was a dull buzz. Purdy had hung up on him.

He didn't put the receiver down right away. He swallowed, staring at Wendy. She was still so damned white. At last, Brad exhaled, slamming the receiver down. "You look as if you had just invited the Indians in for a scalping. I can see that you still don't believe in me. Maybe you should have kept your mouth shut."

She hopped off the desk and her hands rode her hips. "Ingrate!"

"Finished with the phone, son?" Mac, the old-timer grease monkey interrupted them.

Brad shook his head, and a slow smile came to his lips. Mac was perfect for the place. His hair and beard were clean but shaggy, his manner abrupt but well-meaning. It was evident that Mac was Brad's friend as long as Wendy vouched for him. And it was equally evident that the old man would defend her come hell or high water. "Yes, I'm finished all right," Brad said.

Mac nodded serenely. "Wendy, you want to take your car now? Or did you just come to use the phone? Is he going to drive the car while you take the airboat?"

"Uh—we just needed to use the phone."

Mac nodded. "Maybe someone will get a chance to drop it off later." He walked over to the old percolator on the counter and poured himself some coffee, not taking his eyes from Brad. "Coffee?"

"Yeah, thanks."

Mac poured him a cup. The brew was hot and strong. Brad had just taken a sip out of a stoneware mug when Mac said casually, "You got anything to do with those men running around in the big black sedan?"

He nearly spit coffee all over the floor. Instead, he swallowed and glanced from Wendy to Mac.

Mac smiled, enjoying Brad's reaction. "Yep, those boys were here wanting some gas last night. Can't rightly say I liked the looks of them, myself. They asked about the Chevy, and for some dark reason, I told 'em I'd never seen the thing. They were really looking for a man—a buddy of theirs they said they'd lost in the swamp. I told them that most things that get lost in the swamp stay lost. Why, I reckon, too, that if they come back, I ought to tell them that it's true—if they're still looking for a man, they oughta count on the fact that he's lost, deep in the darkness of the Glades, huh?"

Brad reached out and shook Mac's hand. "Thanks," he said gruffly. "Thanks. It's—it's really important. I don't know how I can prove it to you, but I'm really a decent man. And those guys are looking to stir up trouble."

"A man don't need things proved to him," Mac said. "And there's all kinds of good guys and bad guys in this world. Instinct, boy, that's what counts."

He nodded to the two of them and walked outside. When the door closed, Wendy glanced briefly at Brad, then hurried out after Mac. Through the dusty window, Brad watched Wendy give the old man a fierce hug and a kiss on his weathered cheek.

They were old friends, good friends. Brad felt a sudden stab of envy. The old man knew Wendy Hawk well. He knew the details of her life. He probably had shared her past, had listened to her dreams of the future. And Brad didn't really know her at all. He knew only that he wanted her, that she intrigued him, haunted him.

Perhaps he ought to be hiding out from her instead of from Michaelson. Michaelson wanted his life. Wendy Hawk would steal his heart and his soul.

He followed her out. She waved goodbye to Mac, then climbed onto the airboat. For a moment the breeze rustled by, and they sized one another up silently. Then she walked past him and released the tie line.

The engine came to life; its powerful roar filled the air. Birds squawked and flew before them.

Wendy stared straight ahead.

Brad sighed and settled down on the boat. They were going home, to her home, together. The die had been cast. He watched as the sun danced along the golden highlights of her hair. Light, light, ethereal gold. As he studied the bronze of her shoulders and the feminine line of her body, he remembered holding her.

How long were they destined to be together? he wondered bleakly.

Maybe time didn't matter. They both knew it already. There was something between them now, simmering and steaming, wild and explosive.

They were heading home; fate had thrown them together. He suddenly knew that he would have her, would touch her, would love her, just as surely as he knew that the sun would set in the west. Despite their individual dreams and fears, their shared destiny was inevitable.

She turned to tell him something, to point out some landmark, but when her eyes met his, her words seemed to freeze in her throat.

Their eyes remained locked together, silver melding with gold, and surely creating some ancient alchemist's magical treasure. Or perhaps it wasn't magic at all. Perhaps it was a simple pattern of nature and life, as basic and raw as the need of a man for a woman.

When she found the strength to turn away from him, neither of them cared that some vague thought was forgotten. Among soul mates the pretense of words was unnecessary.

4

The house seemed smaller. Brad didn't know how, but the house had shrunk, closing in around them.

Wendy threw out the breakfast that they hadn't eaten and started cleaning up the kitchen. He would have offered to help her, but he was certain that she didn't want his assistance now. The kitchen had gotten smaller, too.

Brad turned on the television. It was nearly noon. He tried different stations until he found one of the major networks. A soap opera seemed to be in the midst of its final, anguished, tear-jerking scene of the day. Brad hunched down and waited. He swallowed, realizing that he was watching the soap Jim used to watch. His partner had never known quite how and when he had gotten hooked, but he had. And whenever things were slow, whenever Jim and Brad were stuck on surveillance, sitting for hours and hours, drinking coffee and waiting for something to happen, Jim would dramatically recount all the latest episodes. Of course, he had missed the soap's broadcast most of the time, but he videotaped the show religiously.

Jim wouldn't be watching any more soaps.

They hadn't worked together long. Not even a month.

Brad's old partner, Dennis Holmes, had left the DEA when he'd married the college sweetheart who had waited for him for ten long years. He was teaching in Boston now. Funny, Brad thought, he and Dennis and Jim had all agreed on one thing—their line of work and marriage just didn't mix.

But Jim would never have a chance to marry. The thought cut Brad to the quick. Jim had been shot down in the prime of his life. Damn Michaelson! He would pay for Jim's life. Like a cowboy in the Old West, Brad would give his eyeteeth for a walk down a long and dusty path, and the simple chance to best the man. But this wasn't the Old West. He couldn't meet Michaelson that way. The law needed Brad alive to testify. Then the judicial court system could determine Michaelson's fate. Brad knew the rules. But for once, he'd relish the opportunity to take justice into his own hands.

Brad started, aware that the images on the screen in front of him had changed. The soap opera was over; the news had come on. He tensed, then relaxed as the personable blonde went on in grave tones about the Michaelson smuggling case.

First Jim's picture was flashed onto the screen. Brad smiled even as a bitter sadness pierced his heart. The picture had been taken at a Labor Day picnic. Jim was wearing an old football jersey. His hair was all mussed up and he was smiling unabashedly for the camera. He looked so young—far too young to be dead.

The pretty blond newscaster announced that his body would be returned to his hometown in Delaware for burial.

Then Brad's picture flashed on the television screen.

The photo had been taken the same day. He was wearing a football jersey, too, and cradling a football in his arm.

In his other arm, he cradled a buxom redhead.

Where the hell had Purdy come up with these pictures? What would have been wrong with a simple ID photo showing him in a blue suit and tie, a stoic, mugshot expression and combed hair?

Leave it to Purdy.

In this snapshot, he looked like one of the good old boys. You could almost see the beer cans in the background. His hair was tousled and his eyes reflected the sultry laughter in the pretty girl's gaze.

Funny, but he couldn't even remember the redhead's name.

The reporter explained that Brad and Jim had been working undercover and that the previous incorrect information about Brad McKenna had been released to protect the agent's cover. However, it was no longer necessary. Brad had been found out. According to the newscast, Brad was missing, and authorities feared that he was dead. But Purdy had been true to his word to exonerate him—at least he was presumed dead as an agent rather than presumed dead as a drug smuggler.

The picture left the screen. The blonde came back on to state that the police and other government agencies were searching for Michaelson.

Brad realized that Wendy was behind him. He heard her exhale in relief. He was aware that she had been believing in him on instinct alone. Still hunkered down on the balls of his feet before the television, he looked up at her. Now, at least, her instinct had been somewhat vindicated.

"See, I am legit," Brad told her with a mild note of reproach.

Her gaze flicked down at him.

"Now I don't know what to think," she murmured. "They can say anything they want on the news, and we're obliged to accept the information." She smiled sweetly, and went back into the kitchen.

He rose slowly and turned the television off, suddenly feeling very awkward. What the hell was he going to do here—except try like hell to keep his hands off her?

"Hungry?"

The question came from the kitchen. He almost answered it with a sexual innuendo, yes, hungry like you'll never know, hungry for you. Instead, he forced himself to smile casually. "Yeah. Sure. We never did get to breakfast."

An accomplished cook, Wendy didn't seem to mind being in a kitchen. She flashed him a quick smile and reached into the refrigerator. Brad assumed that she was reaching for the makings of sandwiches or the like. She brought out an opaque white container and handed it to him. He frowned, then opened it up. A bunch of broken shrimp stared up at him sightlessly.

"What—"

Wendy smiled, turning away. "Let's go catch lunch." She opened the closet near the refrigerator and pulled out two fishing reels. "It's our bait."

Brad looked blankly from the fishing gear to his hostess. He grinned slowly. Thank God, they were going to get out of the incredible shrinking house. Fishing. It sounded great. "All right. In the airboat?"

She shook her head. "There's a little canoe around

back. We'll try for some catfish. I've got a great Cajun recipe. You like spicy food?"

They were staring at each other again. Wendy flushed, walked past him and started digging beneath the counter. "I've a cooler in here somewhere," she muttered.

"I'll get the ice," Brad offered quickly.

In another ten minutes, they were ready. The cooler was filled with beer, ice, a block of cheese and a stick of pepperoni. Wendy had decided that they might get hungry while waiting for the meal to come along. Besides, when the meal did come along, it would more likely be closer to dinnertime than lunch.

The canoe was out back. When they walked around, Brad saw that the road was just barely discernible behind a patch of tall saw grass growing on the opposite side of the canal.

"How do you get to your car?" he asked her, puzzled.

"I take the canoe."

"You have to take your canoe to get to your car?"

Wendy laughed. "Yes. It isn't that difficult. And I don't drive that often. Most places I want to go around here are easier to reach by airboat."

"What a way to live," Brad murmured.

Wendy paused, cocking her head as she watched him with a musing smile. "It's really not so bad, city slicker. Everything that I could want or need is very close."

She stepped past him, carrying the fishing rods over to the canoe. Brad stared across the water to the saw grass and the road, trying to memorize the area and achieve a sense of direction.

Suddenly, Wendy screamed. By reflex, Brad spun, reaching to his waist for his Magnum. Then he remembered that it wasn't there, that it was lost. Without it, he felt naked. And Wendy was screaming...

He ran to her, ready to protect her with his bare hands. But even as he neared her, she was sitting back, laughing.

"Wendy, what happened? What the—"

"Baby!" she sputtered.

The great panther rose from the floor of the canoe, growled, then stretched against Wendy like any of her smaller feline cousins, seeking affection. Wendy scratched her ears, then shoved her away. "Baby, get out of here! You scared me to death."

The cat crawled out of the canoe. When she shimmied past Brad, he petted the panther's sleek coat. His heart was still pounding crazily.

Still laughing, Wendy looked up at Brad. He was not amused. On the contrary, he appeared a little gray and cold, and the contours of his face were hard-set.

"Is that shotgun the only weapon you've got?" he asked her brusquely.

She hesitated.

"Is it?"

Wendy shook her head. "I've got a police model Smith & Wesson .38 in one of the dresser drawers."

"When we get back, I want it," he told her. He lowered himself into the canoe beside her, shoving off in a fluid motion. For several moments, they drifted in silence. Wendy stared at Brad from beneath the shelter of her lashes, and she wished studiously that she had never told him the truth. She hated guns, hated them with a passion. She wished that Baby had not startled her so, and she wished that she hadn't screamed.

And she nervously wished that she had never, never

suggested that she bring Brad McKenna back home. It was awkward already, and she had a feeling that it was only going to get worse. He didn't seem to understand that she had brought him back here just because her house was so damned isolated. No one could find him here; there was no danger here. He didn't need a gun.

The sun beat down on them. For miles the only sound seemed to be the dip of Brad's paddle against the water. Wendy realized he knew something about canoeing. His strokes were slow, steady and even. He'd rolled up the sleeves of the shirt, and with each of his movements she could see the muscle play of his arms beneath the bronze flesh. Deep in concentration, his face was handsome, but harsh.

It had been different in laughter, she decided. In the photo they had shown on the news, he had seemed young, and easygoing. He had appeared happy and relaxed. And ready, able and willing, she finished dryly. Who had the redhead been? The sudden thought chilled her.

"Brad?"

"Yeah?" He had been paddling strenuously, becoming accustomed to the land around him, the river of grass, the calls of cranes and loons and herons. He was growing acquainted with the stillness of the swamp, punctuated by the occasional, startling cries of the birds.

"We've gone plenty far," she said. He set the paddle inside the boat. They were drifting idly. Balancing herself from years of experience, Wendy reached forward and grabbed her pole. She checked her weight and hook and secured some bait from the white bucket. All the while she could feel him watching her, silently, broodingly, watching her every movement.

"Live shrimp are much better bait," she murmured. "But these will do, I'm sure." With a skillful arm, she cast her line.

Brad took his time setting up his fishing rod. After his line hit the water, he reached into the cooler for a beer. "Ready for one?" he asked.

Wendy shrugged. "Yes, I guess so."

He popped open the can before handing it to her. She hadn't realized it was quite so hot out until she sipped the icy cold beer. It tasted good, but it hit her stomach with a churning swirl. She remembered then that they hadn't eaten anything.

She glanced across the canoe at Brad, who was staring at the water, pole in one hand, beer in the other. He wore Leif's jeans and denim shirt well, she thought. She would never forget how she had found him, not a full day ago, struggling through the swamp. A lot had passed between them since then.

Nor could she forget the way he had caught and held her this morning. She realized that her emotions were alternating between gloom because he had interrupted her peaceful life, and elation, because he excited her so. He was making her feel again. He was making her blood whistle and sing. Maybe it was wrong since he was such a stranger, but she didn't know whether she wanted to fight it or not. In one way, she felt the gravest sense of security around him. Brad McKenna would never take anything from a woman that she didn't intend to give—wholeheartedly.

But then she met his gaze and her mind grew wary, her heart raced in fear. He'd been thinking about her— physically, sexually—and that scared her. She could almost read his precise thoughts, and awareness of those desires caused her to tremble and burn deep, deep inside.

"Brad." She was startled by the huskiness of her own voice, dismayed by the sensual undertone of it. But she had a question that had to be answered.

"You're—" This was ridiculous. She had to moisten her lips to keep talking, and the breathless quality would not leave her voice. She shook her head, then she smiled in a rueful confession, because he was staring at her again, seeing into her, penetrating her thoughts. "You're not married, are you?"

He looked at her for a long moment, then shook his head. "No."

"Who was the redhead?"

Again he paused. A dry, pained smile crossed his features, and he winced. "Honest? I don't remember. I think her name was Chrissy."

"Oh."

He set his beer on the seat beside him and wedged his pole beneath a thigh. Reaching forward, he caught her face between his palms.

She couldn't move, and she couldn't breathe. She could feel his callused touch against her flesh, and it warmed her from head to toe, just as the sound of his voice seemed to feather inside of her, touching her everywhere.

"I'm not married, Wendy. And I'm never going to be. Do you understand?"

She wanted to jerk back. Hurt and confusion raged in her heart, and still she couldn't move. The sensations that warred against her flesh would not leave her, and she sat dead still. A mocking, chilling smile curled her lips. "Well, now, McKenna, I do remember asking you if you were married. But I do not remember going so far as to ask you if you wanted to change your status."

She was glad to see that he flushed slightly. "Wendy, it's just that you have been married."

"That's right," she drawled softly. "Have been, past tense. And I don't intend to marry again, Mr. Mc-Kenna."

Suddenly the atmosphere between them was tense and explosive, and hotter than the midday sun that beat down mercilessly upon them. He still touched her, held her with his hands. Their knees brushed, their breath mingled.

"Why is that, Wendy? Was the experience too good— or too bad?"

"Too good, McKenna. It could never, never be matched."

Silence swept and swirled around them, as stifling as the shimmering heat.

"Well, remember that, huh?" Brad murmured. "I wouldn't want you forgetting it in the future."

"I doubt if there's a chance of that."

"Really?" His lips moved closer to hers. "You'd better be careful. Very careful. I wouldn't want you to care too much." He moved his thumb, drawing it in a slow, sinuous line over her lower lip.

"And maybe you had better be careful, too, Mc-Kenna. I wouldn't want you to care too much. I wouldn't want you to get hurt."

"Watch out for your heart, Wendy." And then his lips touched hers.

Bold and brash and commanding, the sensual, intimate contact was still as gentle, as tender as a brush with morning dew. His touch was sure and steady. Wendy wondered if making love came naturally to him.

The ultimate effect was devastating. Wendy didn't think about the words that they had exchanged, nor did she think about what he did for a living, nor did it even occur to her that she had known this man for less than twenty-four hours.

All she could think about was his kiss. All that she could feel was the sweet, subtle, sensual pressure of his lips against hers, his mouth, artfully claiming her own. The tip of his tongue explored her mouth, plundering the richness of it, filling it. She savored his lips and the smooth surface of his teeth, and every little nuance of passionate movement.

His kiss evoked feelings deep inside of her, where he did not touch her. She felt warmth invade her like showering rays of the sun. Passion curled and undulated in the center of her being, steaming through her limbs, sweeping into her breasts and hips and thighs. This was desire, liquid and sweet. She longed to drop everything and throw her arms around his neck. She yearned to press her body against him and feel the length of them touch and duel, as did their mouths.

Just in time, she remembered his words of warning. And she remembered that when she loved, she loved very deeply. Even if she sometimes felt desperate to reach out again for a pale facsimile, a pretense, of what she had known, this was not the time or the place.

And this cocky, overconfident city slicker probably wasn't even the right man.

His lips parted from hers. She opened her eyes and stared into the sharp, questing depths of his. Their breath still mingled. And, she noted with some satisfaction, his breath seemed to come faster than her own. Did the thunder of his heart outweigh the tremor of her own?

He arched a brow. She smiled as sweetly as she could. "Well, McKenna," she said softly, seductively, "I think my heart is safe. Quite safe."

He was quick, she noted, but not quite quick enough to hide his surprise at her words. His hands fell from her cheeks and he sat back, watching her. "Oh, yeah?"

"Yeah."

Then he laughed, and she found herself laughing, too.

"I must be slipping," he teased.

"Happens to the best of us," she agreed consolingly.

He picked up his beer and took a swallow, still watching her. Wendy kept her eyes evenly set with his, though she couldn't control the small, wicked grin that continued to ghost her lips.

He leaned forward once again. "I'll have to try harder next time."

"You're really going to have to be careful," Wendy warned him, her eyes growing innocently large. "If you have to try so very hard, you might find yourself tripping and falling on your own effort. Could be dangerous."

"I'm a big boy, Mrs. Hawk. I do know how to take care of myself."

Wendy smiled flatly. "And I'm a big girl. Far better able to take care of myself in the present circumstances, I think."

"Next time, Wendy," he warned with a devil's grin.

He had passed the first forbidden door; he had touched her. Now he flexed his fingers to stop the tense tremors that had claimed them.

"Is there going to be a next time?" There was nothing coy to the words, nothing demure. It was a blunt, direct question, voiced with an open, amused interest. She was still smiling, and the smile lighted up her eyes to a silver-blue so bright and alluring that Brad felt himself begin to tremble all over again. His muscles were hot and tight—everything was hot and tight—and he found himself grateful that denim jeans could hide a multitude of sins.

"You bet," he promised her pleasantly through gritted teeth.

Just then, his pole dipped in the water and dug into his buttocks where he sat upon it.

"You've got something!" Wendy cried delightedly.

He had something, all right, Brad decided.

He wasn't a bad fisherman. Although these rods were a bit different, he'd grown up near Lake Erie and had done his share of fishing.

He gave the fighting fish a little space, then reeled it back. Once more, he gave the fish a little line to play itself out, then he reeled in. Meanwhile, Wendy reached for a net.

"Do we need that?" he asked her.

"You get stuck by a catfish, and it hurts like hell," she warned him. "We don't have to have it, but it would be kind of foolish to need medical care now for something stupid." She offered him a rueful grin. "I got stuck once and needed ten stitches."

He smiled. "By all means, haul out that net. I'll play macho some other time."

"Oh. Like 'next time'?" Wendy taunted, but then she bowed her head quickly, wondering what on earth was goading her.

Finally, Brad caught the line, and Wendy thrust the net out over the water. He deposited his squirming catch in the net, letting out a pleased holler. It was a hefty catfish, which would definitely rate as a dinner fish. They could even invite company over and have plenty to spare.

"A pretty damned good fish, huh?" he demanded triumphantly.

Wendy nodded serenely. "Yeah. Pretty damned good," she acknowledged. But she couldn't resist adding, "For a city slicker."

Brad conceded the point. He sat back, watching supremely as Wendy put on a glove, then carefully freed the hook and line from the fish's mouth. He enjoyed watching her. She still seemed like an angel with those silver-mist eyes and all that near-platinum hair and her slim, fragile form. But she was capable, lithe and quietly self-assured.

But like hell his touch hadn't affected her!

She tossed the fish into a bucket in the rear of the canoe.

He reached into the cooler and offered her a new beer. "You deserve it," he assured her solemnly.

"What a sport."

"Yeah, I'm a sport. I'm going to do all the paddling back, just like I did all the paddling here. And, my dear lady, you will recall, I am the one who caught the fish."

"The first fish," Wendy said.

But she never did catch anything. When the second beer made her dizzy, she decided it was time to cut up some of the cheese.

To her chagrin, Brad caught another fish, a second

catfish, bigger than the first. To console her, he assured her that he had gone fishing many times before.

Sunset was coming when they headed back. The canoe streaked through the water in silence, and Brad found himself mesmerized by the beautiful surroundings once again. Gold and pink highlights fell upon the soft white of a crane, giving the bird the hues of a rainbow. The water reflected the glow of the dying light, and the waves of grass dipped to the soft, cooler breeze of the coming night.

As Wendy sat facing him, she did not see the alligator when Brad first sighted the creature. It was so still, he thought that it was a log at first.

And then he realized that it was a giant reptile.

An enormous, grotesque creature. About twelve or thirteen feet long, with a snout full of evil teeth that seemed to be a third of the length of the body.

It was ugly, incredibly ugly, Brad thought. His body tensed as he stared at the prehistoric creature.

But he wasn't going to give her another chance to call him a city slicker. He had to start getting accustomed to the creatures that roamed here. He'd been ready to battle the big cat with his bare hands, only to discover that the panther was a beloved pet named Baby.

What did she call the alligator? he wondered dryly. Junior, maybe? Spot? Rover?

He swallowed and tried to relax. When they drifted by the alligator, Brad was going to be casual—even if it killed him.

He slid the canoe up on the embankment, shoving his paddle into the muck to bring the canoe up high and secure. He started to rise, but Wendy caught his hand.

"Wait!" she said tensely.

"Wait for what?" he drawled laconically. "Oh—the gator? I saw it already."

"You saw it!" Her eyes flew to his, rounded. She grabbed his hand and pulled him back down to the seat. "Then sit still and let him go first, you idiot!"

"What?"

Wendy stood, carefully. There was a small fallen branch nearby. She picked it up and threw it hard at the alligator. The monster with the evil yellow eyes just stared at her. She tossed another one. It plunked the alligator right on the head, and the animal slunk back into the water and glided away. A moment later, it disappeared into the darkness.

Brad stared at Wendy. "You mean it isn't a pet?"

She shook her head, frowning at him as if he had lost his mind. "Who in God's name would want one of those monsters for a pet? That thing was about twelve feet long. He could have consumed both of us in one gulp. They're dangerous. I mean, you're all right if you avoid them. But I'd sure as hell never want to befriend one. They're vicious in the water if they're hungry, and bear in mind, they can move about forty miles an hour on land, too."

She smiled and rose, grabbing the pail with their fresh catch of the day. Brad remained in the canoe, watching the fluid, languid sway of her buttocks as she strode toward the house.

He smiled. Okay, so only that TV cop kept an alligator for a pet. Panthers were surely more popular. He'd learn. Surely, he'd learn.

Brad rose, collecting their gear. He'd seen a hose outside. He found it again and rinsed off the fishing gear. Then he brought the gear back into the house.

Wendy had been a quick worker, too. The catfish were already headless and well on their way to becoming fillets. She smiled up at him, then finished her task, dropping the fillets into a bowl of marinade when she was done.

"I'm going to hop in the shower. Turn on the television, have some wine, make yourself at home. I'll be right out."

He leaned against the refrigerator, popping open another beer. "Want company?"

"No, thanks."

Brad shook his head sadly. "Couldn't handle it, huh?"

She paused, rising to the taunt. "I think that time will tell, city slicker, just who can handle what around here."

He lifted his beer can to her in a toast. Wendy saw that his lashes fell lazily over his eyes, and that beneath, he surveyed her in a long and leisurely fashion.

She'd seen Baby look at birds in much the same way.

But the look warmed her, causing a hot flush to rise and tint her cheeks. Maybe he was right. Maybe she was out of her league. Maybe she couldn't handle anything that was happening to her at all. He'd given her every chance to retreat. He'd warned her that she couldn't be anything more than a friend. She didn't want to end up like the redhead in the photo; he'd remember the color of her hair, but he wouldn't remember her name.

Wendy spun around. "I'll be out shortly," she murmured.

Brad stared after her, wondering what had caused the change in her.

In the bathroom, Wendy stood beneath a warm spray and trembled with the chill that had seized her.

Perhaps she didn't want him remembering her name.

She just wanted him to touch her, because she had been so lonely, and because it would feel so good to be touched again. But darkness and anonymity held a certain appeal.

The water cascaded around her. The sound cocooned her.

She wondered how he would feel if he really knew the truth. Yes, she wanted him. The chemistry was right; the attraction was strong. They had both felt it. And there had been more. They'd had the chance to know that they both delivered in certain values in life, maybe in a certain sense of honor. They didn't know much about each other, but they knew the important things.

And so maybe it would be all right.

Except that he just wasn't the kind of man to stand in for another. Wendy was quite certain that if Brad Mc-Kenna even guessed that she wanted him only in darkness, as a substitute for another man, his smile would fade and his sensual suggestions would fall silent.

There was just something about him... Even if he intended to have a woman only once, he'd want her to know damned clearly just who she was with.

Wendy bit her lip. Yes, there was just something about him. And that unusual quality was drawing her closer and closer to the edge.

She jumped suddenly, hearing the bathroom door open quietly, then close.

"Brad?" she whispered. "Brad!"

There was no answer. The sound of the water cascading over her naked form and onto the tile was all that filled the room.

5

"Brad!" Panic rose high in her voice.

"Shush!"

There was a heated whisper at last. Wendy didn't have much time to worry about the fact that the man had interrupted her shower. She pulled the curtain against her body and looked out. Brad wasn't even glancing her way; he was standing at the small window over the commode, looking out into the right side of the yard.

"What is it?" Wendy whispered. He stood at the window, tense and silent as a wraith. "Brad, what is it!" she insisted softly.

At last she had his attention. He stared at her pensively, then strode toward her. He didn't touch her but came close, so that their eyes met amid the steam that poured around them.

"There's someone out there."

"If you heard something," Wendy said with a relieved smile, "I'm sure it's just Baby."

"No, no it's not."

"Really, Brad, I understand your circumstances, but we are tucked so far into the swampland. I'm sure you're just imagining—"

"I don't imagine," he said, cutting her off bluntly.

Wendy tightened her hold on the shower curtain and swallowed uneasily. He was, after all, still a stranger. He'd entered her shower without the decent grace of a quiet tap against the door. And right now he was so solidly implacable and assured that it was like talking to a rock. He had changed. He was a bundle of tension. She could see it in his eyes, in his stance, in the constriction of his muscles.

And it was frightening.

"Can you shoot?" he asked her tensely.

"Come on now, Brad—"

"I asked you if you can shoot!"

"Yes."

"Stay inside, but load that shotgun of yours and be prepared to defend yourself. Do you hear me? Stay here, and if something should go wrong, have the shotgun in your hand."

He spun around and left her. The bathroom door closed quietly in his wake.

Wendy turned off the water and hopped out of the tub, longing to call him back. There wasn't any danger out there—there just couldn't be! She had to catch him.

But she couldn't go running after him stark naked. She dried off with a lick and a promise and stumbled into her clothes. She came charging out, then paused. There was nothing out there, but maybe, just maybe, she should load the shotgun.

She raced to get it down from the wall, then she panicked when she couldn't find the shells for the gun in the box in the closet. Pushing things around, she finally found a second box. She loaded both barrels and started down the hall. Brad, she knew, was already outside somewhere. But where? There seemed to be an eerie silence about the place.

But then that silence was shattered. "There you are, you son of a bitch!" a male voice grunted out.

"I've got you now!" a second man swore.

"Oh, no!" Wendy breathed, recognizing both male voices and realizing what must have happened. She ran down the hall to the front door and threw it open. "Stop!" she screamed. "Stop!"

She was ignored, so she raised the shotgun, and barely aiming, she squeezed the trigger. The kickback of the shotgun nearly sent her sprawling as the explosive sound filled the night—to be followed by complete, stark silence.

Brad didn't know how he knew that someone was outside, he just knew. He hadn't really heard anything, just the whisper of the breeze, the rustle of foliage, all natural things.

And yet he had felt it, sensed it.

They were being watched. Someone was watching them, watching them carefully, in stealth and silence.

That surprised Brad. Michaelson was the type to come striding right in. If he had made it to a place like this, he could quickly ascertain that he was far more powerful in terms of manpower and ammunition. And he didn't make it a habit to tease, taunt or torture—he assessed things quickly, and just as quickly he relieved himself of excess baggage.

No, this didn't feel like Michaelson.

But then, who the hell else could it be?

Dusk had fallen when he finally slipped out the front door. He locked it behind him, intending to buy Wendy a little more time to get prepared just in case the trouble turned out to be serious.

Shadows fell all around him, and the lights from inside the house made them all the worse. Brad flattened himself against the wall, straining to see against the darkness. He could hear the sounds of the night, the chirps of crickets, the occasional grunt of a frog, the wind, slight and rustling in the trees, in the long grasses that bowed low before it. Nothing seemed out of the ordinary.

But someone, he knew, was near.

Brad began to move around the house. He probably should have taken the shotgun himself, but then he didn't know where she kept the ammunition, and he had wanted the element of surprise to be on his side.

Puzzled, Brad realized that although he was still certain that someone was on the hammock with them, he didn't know how he had gotten there. The airboat was still secured where they had left it that morning, and when he came around the house, he saw that the canoe, too, was exactly where they had left it. There were no other boats of any kind on the land, nor out in the nearby water.

He heard something, and he froze. He didn't know what it was, or where it had come from, but he had heard something. He came around the corner, squinting, flexed and ready, poised on the balls of his feet. He kept moving, certain that his quarry was just ahead of him. At last he reached the front of the house again.

Suddenly, he felt a whoosh of motion. He looked up just as a heavy weight fell on him from atop the roof. Falling and tumbling beneath his attacker, Brad swore at him, and the man instantly responded.

"I've got you now!" the man returned.

And he did, Brad thought. The man was straddled over him, and he was agile and powerful. His hold was nearly merciless. Brad strained with all his might, shifting his weight, throwing his attacker.

But the man was fast—damned fast. He spun around in the darkness, a fist flying. It caught Brad cleanly in the jaw.

He responded, slamming into the man's stomach. It was like shoving against steel.

A blow struck his shoulder; Brad responded by ducking his head and butting into the stranger, a move that brought them both careening and rolling and bitterly wrestling on the ground again. Poised over his attacker for a brief moment, Brad stared down and gasped in surprise.

The guy had green eyes, but his hair was pitch-black and long against his neck. A headband kept it from falling into his eyes. He was wearing jeans and a denim shirt, but his features were strikingly bold.

Just as another blow reached his chin, Brad swore and slugged back. No, it wasn't Michaelson. It sure as hell wasn't Michaelson. He was being attacked by an Indian.

"Son of a bitch—" Brad began, but then he was thrown, and he had to gasp for air to strain against the new hold on him.

"Stop!"

Vaguely, Brad heard Wendy's voice. "Stop!" It didn't really mean anything—not to him, not to the tight-lipped man above him. Somehow they had gotten too involved in their exchange of blows. The fight had become too serious.

They were evenly matched, yet each man was determined to win.

But then it sounded as if the whole earth had exploded around them, and simultaneously, they fell back, startled.

Brad twisted around, staring in stunned surprise at Wendy. She was sitting on the ground, with the shotgun resting in her lap.

"Stop it!" she insisted, gasping for breath. "Both of you, do you hear me, stop!"

Panting, Brad stared over at the man who had attacked him.

The Indian was stretched out on the ground, pushing up on an elbow—and panting from exertion.

Brad stared back at Wendy. "Who the hell is this?"

"Who the hell am I?" the man retorted, his voice sounding much like a growl emanating from the back of his throat. "Who the hell is this guy?" he demanded of Wendy.

Brad pushed himself to his feet, staring at Wendy, and then at the Indian, who wasn't about to accept Brad's vantage point. He stood, too, placing his hands on his hips. The hostility between them still seemed to crackle in the air.

"Wendy! Who is this?" the Indian demanded.

Leaning against the shotgun, Wendy came to her feet. She hurried over to position herself between the two men. They barely seemed to notice that she was there. Their eyes were locked and she could feel the hatred that radiated from the two of them, spilling over to her. What was it with these two? Men! Let's Punch Each Other Out First seemed to be their motto.

"Brad McKenna, this is Eric Hawk. Eric, this is Brad McKenna."

"So who is Brad McKenna?" Eric said flatly, maintaining his wary glare at Brad.

"Eric! He's a friend of mine."

Brad spun on Wendy. "*Hawk?* I thought you said that your husband was dead."

Wendy saw Eric's jaw clamping even more tightly and the line of his mouth drawing into a grim scowl. "Leif is dead. Eric is my brother-in-law."

Brad kept staring at the other man, wondering why the hell it was taking him so long to assimilate it all. "He's an Indian. You were married to an Indian?"

"Well, Wendy, this is one bright boy you've got here," Eric drawled sarcastically.

"What's it to you?" Brad returned.

Fists were going to start flying again, Wendy thought in dismay. She placed a hand on each of the masculine chests, as if she could push the men apart.

"I mean it, stop it! Or both of you can get the hell off my property right now!"

They both gave her a wounded look.

She breathed a little more easily. For another long moment she waited, watching them both warily. They still stared at one another with open hostility, but at least they were silent.

"Shall we go in? Are the two of you capable of behaving decently to one another?"

Brad shrugged and inclined his head accusingly toward Eric. "He was the one stalking around the house as if he were out on a scalping party."

"Brad!" Wendy snapped.

"What was I supposed to think?" Eric asked her innocently.

"Well, Eric, you could have knocked," Wendy insisted.

Eric wasn't going to accept the blame any more than Brad intended to. "I saw Muscle Man here slinking around the windows. I was afraid for you, Wendy."

"Okay, okay!" She turned away from the two men and started toward the house. "You want to beat each other up? Fine—go to it. Tear each other apart. Just don't come here for ice packs when you're done!" She swung around and retrieved the shotgun, mumbling to herself. "Honest to God, but they deserve one another!"

Wendy stormed back into the house. Brad surveyed the man he'd been wrestling. They were almost exactly the same height, and had similar builds. A real even match. He could feel his left eye puffing up; the other man had a trickle of blood coming from his lip down his chin.

"Leif and Eric?" he heard himself query.

For a moment, the other man was silent. Then he cast his head back and laughed, and Brad felt a smile creasing his own features. "Well, I don't know who you are yet, and I'm still damned curious. Wendy seems willing enough to defend you, so I guess you're all right, but it doesn't seem that she's told you very much about herself."

Brad shrugged. "No. I guess she hasn't," he admitted. "You are an Indian, right?"

Eric grinned. "Seminole through and through."

"Leif and Eric?"

"Mom is Norwegian."

"Of course." Brad lifted his shoulders. "Norse Seminoles. Why the hell not." Suddenly it was as if the hostility had disappeared, dissipated into the evening sky. He liked the man with the sharp features, strange green eyes and rueful smile. And he felt the same respect in return. "Want to go in?"

"Yeah, I guess we should."

Eric led the way. Another little tremor seized Brad as he realized that Wendy's brother-in-law was very comfortable in her home. Eric hopped up on the counter, smiling at Wendy as she soaked pieces of fish fillet in batter before dropping them into a skillet.

Wendy kept her lips pursed in disapproval. "Are you staying for dinner?" she asked.

Eric cast a glance Brad's way. "Am I welcome?"

"We've plenty of fish," Wendy said.

Brad kept silent. He'd been worried about being alone with Wendy, but now that their privacy had been taken away, he wanted it back.

Eric watched Brad, and his grin deepened. "Well, Wendy, you know how I just love your Cajun catfish."

Wendy nodded, her eyes on her task. "Eric, would you fix yourself and Brad a drink?"

"Sure." He slid off the counter and turned to Brad. "Name your poison."

"Jack Black on the rocks, if it's available."

"You got it. Wendy? A glass of wine?"

Wendy dropped a fillet into the sizzling oil, then looked over at her brother-in-law. "Tonight? Nooo... I think I'll have bourbon, too, please."

"Your wish is my command, Wendy. You know that." He looked at her so innocently.

At this point in her life, Eric was probably her closest friend. When Leif died, Eric had mourned beside her. No one could understand her grief more than Eric, because the two of them had suffered a loss together. For the longest time, they had been each other's only salvation.

It had all happened two years ago, but she knew that seeing her with another man like this had to open old wounds for him. But then again, Eric had always encouraged her to get back out in the world again.

That had been before he had actually found a strange man in her house.

Eric handed her a Jack Black on the rocks. She sipped it quickly, savoring the sweet, burning sensation.

Brad lifted his glass to hers. "Cheers."

She nodded and started to take another sip.

Oh, what the heck! she thought. Wendy cast back her head and swallowed the entire contents of the glass. Dinner threatened to be a long and nerve-racking affair.

In the end, it really wasn't so bad. Brad remained silent at the beginning, adding a bit to Wendy's uneasiness. But Eric talked about the family and Wendy was grateful that he kept to easy topics. After a few minutes, he even included Brad in the conversation. She told Eric that Brad had caught the fish and that she hadn't been able to hook anything. Then the two men entered into an enthusiastic discussion on fishing.

However, things were bound to get sticky. They did so when dinner was over, when Wendy started to rinse the plates and load the dishwasher.

Both men went to make coffee. This time, Eric deferred to Brad, but they were both scrutinizing each other suspiciously. Sensing the tension, Wendy decided to serve some brandy and Tia Maria along with their coffee. Just as she gripped the brandy bottle, Eric asked Brad what he did for a living.

The bottle slipped from her fingers and fell to the floor. The glass bottle shattered, and the sticky liquid flew everywhere.

Both men stared at her. Wendy smiled weakly. "Slippery fingers, I suppose." She knelt to start mopping up the spill.

"Let me help you," Brad said, hunching down before her. She cut her finger on a piece of glass and absently sucked upon the wound as she stared at him in a growing panic.

"Wendy—" Brad frowned at the state of her finger.

"Did you cut yourself?" Eric demanded, concerned.

"No, I—"

"Yes, she did," Brad said. He helped her to her feet, sticking her hand under the running water at the sink. It wasn't serious, but Brad started muttering about antiseptic and Eric said he'd get some peroxide and Band-Aids.

"Brad," Wendy murmured. His arm was around her as he held her hand beneath the faucet. She smiled slightly, admiring the planes of his face, noticing the concern he showed. She was surrounded by the heat of him, and the subtle male scent that suddenly seemed to tease her mercilessly.

"Hmm?" He was still concerned about her cut.

"What do I tell Eric?"

He looked into her eyes, understanding her question. "Do you trust him?"

"Of course. I'd trust him with my life."

"That's all that matters," Brad said softly. Then he shrugged. "Tell him. Tell him the truth."

He finished speaking just as Eric returned to the kitchen. "Just peroxide—it won't hurt," Eric told Wendy, taking her hand. Brad backed away while Eric cleaned and bandaged her cut with a tender care that probably outweighed the seriousness of the situation. Brad bent down and picked up the rest of the broken bottle, soaking up the spilled brandy with paper towels.

When Brad finished rinsing his hands, Eric confronted him again. "Well? Did you decide whether to tell me what you're whispering about or not? Wendy, I hope you didn't cut your finger just for my benefit."

"No!" she gasped quickly.

"DEA," Brad told Eric.

Without flinching, Eric kept his eyes on Brad, then nodded. They all stood in silence for a moment. "I thought you had to be with some branch of law enforcement," he murmured.

"Yeah?"

"Well, you were ready for me, and I'm pretty good at stealth. It's that 'Tonto' blood in me, you know."

Brad laughed and clapped Eric on the back.

Wendy decided that they were both crazy. She turned around and started to pour coffee.

"You're involved in that Michaelson deal that went bad?"

"Yes."

"And you're hiding out here?"

Wendy had been dropping shots of Tia Maria into the coffee. Now she tightened her trembling fingers and set the bottle down. She didn't need any more alcohol on the floor.

"Yes," Brad said at last.

Noticing Wendy's hesitation, Eric grabbed the Tia

Maria bottle and added another shot to each of the coffee cups. He took a sip of his coffee, then muttered, "That's dangerous for Wendy. She shouldn't be so involved in this sordid business."

"Eric—" Wendy tried to interrupt him.

"Where did you meet? How did you meet?" Eric probed.

"Eric!" Wendy protested again. She loved her brother-in-law. And it had been nice to have him care for her, to be protective. It had been nice to know that he had been close, that there was still someone out there who loved her enough to risk life and limb for her. But he was prying into dangerous territory.

"It's all right, Wendy," Brad said. "Michaelson chased me out on Alligator Alley. My car blew a gasket or something after I'd taken a side road. One of his bullets nicked me in the forehead—Wendy found me facedown in the mud."

Eric nodded slowly.

"Couldn't we have coffee in the living room?" Wendy murmured. When they both ignored her, she decided to ignore them. She took her coffee cup into the living room and considered turning the television on. Tonight, some soothing music might be a better bet. She turned on the system that Leif had so painstakingly set up and slipped in a Beatles disc. As music filled the room, Wendy sat on the couch and closed her eyes, warming her hands with her cup.

Despite the music she could still hear them talking in the kitchen, their words growing louder.

"Excuse me!" she called. "This is my house, you know. I am the hostess, you are the guests. Want to come on out here and behave?"

They both appeared, slowly. Although they apparently hadn't been able to restrain their anger in the kitchen, now they had nothing to say.

Brad wandered over to the far side of the room, studying the titles of the books that lined the shelves. With a grimace, Eric sat down beside her on the couch.

At length, he sighed. "Wendy, it's dangerous—"

"He's right. I think I should go," Brad interrupted.

"Dammit!" Wendy exploded. She slammed her cup onto the butcher-block side table and flew to her feet, spinning around to face Eric, then Brad, then Eric again.

"Eric, if you really love me, trust me enough to know that I'm not a fool. And no one knows better than you do how deeply hidden we are here!" She turned back to Brad. "If I didn't feel that I could safely help you, I'd never have asked you here. I'm a grown woman, capable of making my own decisions. Don't try to run my life—behind my back!"

Brad picked up the TV guide and began to idly leaf through it. He cleared his throat. "Wendy—"

"It wasn't behind your back," Eric said.

She glared at them both. "Oh, hell!" she groaned, falling back onto the couch in mock defeat.

"This is great," Brad said, suddenly changing the subject. "Do you get TV out here?"

She smiled slowly. "Yes, I have satellite TV."

"Ten o'clock, *No Way Out* is on! I've been trying to see that movie for over a year."

Wendy got up and turned off the Beatles disc. "Go ahead, turn on the television."

Eric rose. "Got any microwave popcorn, Wendy?"

"In the top cabinet over the stove."

Brad turned on the television; Eric went into the

kitchen and found the popcorn. By ten-fifteen they were huddled together on the couch with Wendy in the middle, crunching away on popcorn.

It was strange, Wendy thought. Very strange.

But then, she thought that it was nice, too. It was as if they had all known each other for ages. Considering their precipitous introduction, Brad and Eric seemed to be getting along very well.

When the movie ended, Wendy yawned. Brad stood and stretched, picking up the popcorn bowl.

Slightly uneasy, Eric stared at Brad.

Wendy lowered her head. Although Eric knew that Brad was staying here, she sensed her brother-in-law's reluctance to depart, leaving this stranger behind. "Do you have to work tomorrow?" she asked him.

"Yeah, I do."

"Do you need me?"

He shook his head. "No. It's probably better if you just lie low. I'll drop by again in a few days."

"How did you get here?" Brad asked Eric, baffled.

Eric laughed and winked at Wendy. "You've got to show him where the stones are."

"The what?"

Wendy grinned. "There's a place in the canal where Leif set boulders into the water. The depth there is only about a foot—in the dry season, you can see them. Eric drove here—his car is right behind the saw grass."

"I see." With good grace, Brad grinned. The two men shook hands. Wendy felt that Brad sensed Eric's discomfort. "Well, I'm going to call it a day. Wendy, Eric, thank you both."

"Take care," Eric warned him softly. Brad nodded, strode into the guest room and closed the door.

"I'll walk you out?" Wendy said to her brother-in-law.

He set an arm around her shoulder and ruffled her hair. "Sure."

Outside in the darkness, Eric said, "I like him, Wendy. I mean, not that it matters. You're a mature woman, and you have the right to make your own decisions. But I have to admit, I like him."

Her lips trembled when she tried to smile. "Eric, nothing has hap—"

"Wendy, don't encourage me to act like a surrogate parent. I know you've needed to get out. Hell, *I've* been out. I've been out a lot," he said bitterly.

Yes, he had, Wendy thought, but she didn't voice her agreement. They'd had their different ways of coping with the pain after the horrible night when her husband and his wife had been killed together. For Wendy, it had been a complete withdrawal. For Eric, it had been a near fall into a world of reckless delusion.

But they had both survived, she thought.

"Good night, Wendy. I'll tell the folks hi—"

"I'll be in to see everyone soon." She paused. "Think I can bring Brad to the folks?"

"Yes, I think you can."

She smiled at Eric. The breeze picked up his sleek raven hair and moved it in the darkness, and for a moment, her heart caught in her throat as he reminded her of Leif. He kissed her on the forehead, and then he disappeared in the night.

Wendy went back into the house, locking the door behind her. When she reached the guest-room door, she knocked lightly.

"Yes?" Brad responded after a moment.

Wendy pushed the door open. Brad was still in jeans,

but he had taken off his shirt. The room was dark, but light seeped in from the hallway. It gleamed bronze upon his bare shoulders while his features remained hidden in shadows.

"I wanted to thank you," she said.

She could sense his confusion. "For what?"

"Eric is a good friend."

"I noticed. You're close."

"Yes, we are, but not like that. I mean, we could never be involved. He's really like a brother in the truest sense. Since I haven't dated since Leif died, you see, and—not that we're dating or anything—but I think it was just hard for Eric to leave with you and me here alone. And, well, the way you made a point of coming in here, I…" As her voice trailed away, she stood there, wishing to God she didn't feel quite so foolish.

"Or anything?" he queried softly.

"What?"

"We're not dating, or anything?" he repeated, and she noticed a rueful smile on his face. "Come on, Wendy, we're doing *something* together, aren't we?"

She smiled, glad that he had a way of making her feel comfortable.

"Hey. Come over here," he said softly.

Slowly, she began to walk toward him.

She paused when she reached him. The light was still shielding his eyes, while it played over the rippled muscles of his bronze shoulders. There was a rich spattering of tawny hair covering his chest. She wanted to touch it.

She did.

She laid her palm flat against his chest.

And that was when he kissed her. Threading his fingers through her hair, he lowered his head over hers.

For the longest time his breath seemed to tease her lips. Tentatively, she gazed into his eyes, soft gold and fascinated as they searched her. Then his lips touched hers, very gently. Her fingers curled into his chest as she felt the force of his mouth upon hers broaden, sweeping her away. His tongue bathed her mouth in a sweet, warm invasion.

Even with her eyes closed, she saw the man, knew the man. She felt his hands, and his kiss.

A delicious weakness overcame her. It would be so easy. So easy to give way to the liquid in her knees and fall. He would catch her, she knew. He would catch her and sweep her away to bed, where she could surrender to the darkness of night.

His lips parted slowly from hers, hovering above her. She felt the golden probe of his gaze again.

"Wendy..." he murmured.

They were spellbound, locked in a magical moment. She used her free hand to smooth the tendril of hair that had fallen over his forehead.

He inhaled, and then exhaled, shakily. With stony resolve, he lifted her hands and kissed her palms. "Go to bed, Wendy," he told her.

She lowered her eyes, nodding. Neither of them was ready. "Good night."

She started walking to the door.

"Wendy!"

In an instant he was beside her again, and she rushed into his arms. This time he kissed her with passion and fire, and then his hands slipped deftly beneath her oversized shirt, finding her bare breasts beneath it. As his palms caressed her nipples a jagged sob escaped her lips beneath the sweet and savage force of his kiss.

And then, just as she had imagined, he swept her off her feet, heading with purpose for the bed that loomed huge and enticing in the shadows of the night.

6

With grave tenderness, he eased her down upon the bed. She could feel the urgent hunger in the heated length of his body as he lay down beside her. His kiss continued to sear her, and his touch lingered upon her. His hands were everywhere, holding her face, stroking her shoulder, caressing her bare back. He was staging an onslaught against her senses, and she wanted desperately to hold on to each feeling, to each nuance of emotion and reaction. He was awakening sensations she had forgotten, feelings she had forsaken when Leif died.

His passionate assault was like the sudden surge of the tide; swept into that tide, she found that thought was difficult. She explored his chest with her fingertips, marveling at the warmth of his flesh, the tension in his muscles. She loved the coarse feeling of the short, whorling hairs that teased her fingertips, and most of all, she loved the evocative feel of his body over hers, so much of him eclipsing so much of her.

She seemed to drown in his kiss, for it was never ending, although it evolved. Fiercely, he claimed her lips...then pulled away to press his mouth against the pulse in her throat, or the hollow of her collarbone. The inner circle of his palm fell gently against her breast, and his fingers closed slowly around the full weight of it, exploring and caressing sensitive areas.

Minutes passed...or aeons. She breathed in the enticing male scent of his bare flesh, and she arched to meet his kiss. It was easy to respond, far easier than she had expected, for she had not known that she was starved. The darkness quietly shielded her from any sense of reality, even as the full bulge growing against his denim jeans warned her that she was plunging, falling downward into a tempest from which she could not rise. She was falling into the forbidden realm, a realm of pleasure, where loneliness was masked, and thirst was sated.

But then, abruptly, without a word, he pulled away from her. The only sound was the belabored rush of his breath. She knew from the heat of his flesh and the hardened feel of his body that he had not lost his desire for her. But it was over. Whatever it had been, he had ended it.

In the dim light his eyes seemed to gleam like a great cat's, sizzling and gold. He rested upon an elbow and stared curiously down at her. Wendy bit her inner lip, wondering what had driven him away.

"What's wrong?" she asked, her words a whisper.

He drew the tip of his thumb over her cheek, staring pensively at her face. He shook his head. "This—I shouldn't be doing this."

"But I came to you!"

They remained still. The only movement was that of his thumb, the callused pad stroking her flesh. She could read no emotion in his eyes; she had no idea what he was thinking or feeling.

Suddenly, her emotions crumbled, stung by the rejection. She had laid herself on the line. She hadn't been dreaming of the past; no ghosts had drifted between them. She had offered herself—and he had refused her. He'd dealt the supreme blow to her confidence.

"Oh, dear God!" she muttered. Humiliated, she shoved against him. Apparently, he hadn't expected her to touch him, at least not so vehemently. She pushed him so hard that he rolled right onto the floor.

"Wendy! Dammit, wait, listen—"

Brad's kneecap hurt where he'd slammed it onto the floor. His head had bumped against the bed frame and, all in all, he felt like an idiot.

It seemed that a guy just couldn't win. He had known he was bound for trouble, wanting her as he did. But he'd expected her to be angry with him for taking advantage of her, not for trying desperately, with a restraint that went above and beyond, to respect her. "Wendy!" Muttering to himself and wincing in pain, Brad scrambled back to his feet.

Wendy was desperately fighting the urge to burst into tears—not a little rivulet of damp tears, but a thunderous storm of wet, sloppy tears. She tore into her own room, but there was no way to lock the door against him—he had broken the lock that morning.

Wendy slammed the door anyway.

It didn't do any good. "Wendy!" Brad knocked on the door. When she didn't answer, he opened it and waited in the doorway, still breathless. She sat at the foot of her bed, her back to him, fiercely cradling her pillow. Soft light spilled in from the hall, falling over her, striking her hair with a golden glow.

"Wendy! I want to talk to you."

"I don't want to talk to you."

"Wendy, please, listen to me." He stood behind her and rested his hands on her shoulders, surprised to discover how much she was trembling.

She tried to shrug him away, but he sat down behind her. "I'd really appreciate it if you didn't touch me," she said stiffly.

He let go of her shoulders but remained behind her. "We've got to talk," he said hoarsely. "Wendy, if you would just turn around and talk to me—"

She spun around then, putting distance between them. She jerked the band out of her hair and golden locks tumbled down to her shoulders. She shook them out in absent vehemence, staring at him with shimmering silver eyes that reflected light like diamonds. "What? Talk. Say whatever it is and then go away."

He sighed. "Wendy, you're not making this easy."

"Well, I hope you'll forgive me. It isn't very easy from my side, either. I'm not good at this to begin with. I've been out of practice for some time."

"Wendy, that's just the point."

She inhaled, holding back a sob. He reached out to touch her cheek again, and he felt the warm, liquid tears there. "Wendy…"

"Stop it! For the love of God, will you stop it?"

He pulled her into his arms. She fought him, tensing and straining against him. He couldn't let her go, so he held her until she stopped fighting him, until she collapsed against his chest and let him wrap his arms around her.

"Brad, please," she murmured against his chest. She could taste the sweet salt of his flesh when she spoke; she could feel the beat of his heart, strong beneath her cheek.

He smoothed back her hair, somewhat awed by its color in the night. Angel's hair. So soft, so silky, so beautifully blond. "Wendy, I want you so badly, don't you see?"

She stiffened again. "No, quite frankly, I don't."

In the darkness, he smiled. "Wendy, it's just too quick. I want you, but I want it to be right. I don't want you to wake up in the morning and be sorry. I don't want to be a substitute for your husband, and I don't want you to regret what you did in the darkness. I want you to want me."

She kept silent for a moment, warmed by his embrace, feeling ridiculously secure, since she knew he offered her no real security. On the contrary, he offered her danger, in many different guises. "I did want you," she said at last.

"Did you? Did you really?" He kissed her forehead. Then, very gently, he kissed her lips again and smiled at her. "You're a very special lady, Wendy. And we are going to make love. Here I've been racking my head all day trying to figure out how not to drag you into bed. And to top it off, you wander into my bedroom when I've been a damned saint and shut myself up for the night. I'll never be able to leave you without knowing what we have to share. But I care too much now, Wendy. I care too much about you to not take it slowly. That's what we really want, what we both deserve. A night of passion with no regrets in the morning." He finished off his words with another kiss, a slow, languid kiss.

She felt as if her heart still beat a hundred miles an hour, as if her blood still raced through her system painfully. She pushed away from him, groaning softly as she twisted her head. "Brad, if you have any feelings for me, please! Leave me alone now."

"No."

Incensed, she tried to break free from his hold. He caught her arms and held her close. With one deft, sure movement, he pulled her back onto the bed. His shoulders and head rested against a plump pillow, and her head was tucked against his chest, her hair splayed in a lustrous array upon it.

He longed to touch that hair. He longed to do much, much more. But he was afraid to release her. He kept his arm around her, aware of the tension in her, aware that she could easily bolt.

"Wendy," he murmured, "want to know my middle name?"

"What?" He could see her bewildered frown, but he also felt some of the tension ease out of her. Daring to ease his powerful hold, he stroked the golden hair that spilled over his flesh, haunting his senses.

"Michael. Brad Michael McKenna. I'm a Scorpio."

She started to laugh, twisting around to sit in his arms. "Brad, this is my bedroom, not a singles bar."

"All right, well, that makes things a little more intimate. What was your maiden name?"

She frowned again, then a slow smile curved her lips. "Harper. Wendy Anne Harper."

"And how old are you, Wendy Anne?"

"That's damned nosy, isn't it?"

He shrugged. "You can't be that old."

"Thirty-one," she told him. "And you?"

"Thirty-five, next November. When is your birthday?"

"February fourteenth."

"Valentine's Day baby, hmm? Do you like sushi?"

"I hate it."

"Well, I love it, but I suppose that's a minor detail. You live in the Everglades, but you hate sushi?"

She laughed. "What does that have to do with it?"

"You're surrounded by fish."

"That doesn't mean that I have to eat the things raw."

She settled down, nestling her head against his chest again. Her breath fanned against him, just as her hair tantalized his naked flesh like a feather tauntingly stroking skin. He inhaled deeply, breathing in her perfume, the scent of her shampoo and the sweet female scent of her body.

She was gentle against him, soft and relaxed. She brought her hand against her mouth, stifling a yawn. He kept stroking her hair. "What's my name, Wendy?"

"What?"

"My name? What's my name?"

"What is this game? Brad. Brad McKenna. At least, I think it's your real name."

Her eyes—shimmering, liquid silver—rose to his. A painful desire jolted through him again. Gritting his teeth, he tried to ignore the clamoring demands of his masculinity.

"Yeah, it's my real name. But it isn't my whole name."

She twisted her jaw slightly, half smiling, half frowning. "Brad Michael McKenna."

He nodded, pleased. "That's right, Ms. Wendy Anne Harper Hawk, who hates sushi and lives with the gators and creatures and became thirty-one last February fourteenth. Oh—and who likes the Beatles and keeps a wonderfully neat, hospitable home." He touched her chin, drawing her eyes closer to his. "Wendy, it is nice to get to know you."

She smiled. He touched her lips with his fingers, and she eased her head down against his chest again.

He didn't remember saying anything else—nor did he think that she did. They fell asleep that way and woke up beside one another, in her bed, but fully dressed.

Awakened by a stream of early-morning sunshine, Brad mused that it was a damned unusual way for him to start the day.

But then, Wendy was a damned unusual woman. Unique.

Special.

He leaned over, kissed her forehead and rose. She looked like a sleeping angel, with a serene expression on her beautiful features and wisps of blond hair clouding around her. He kissed her again, then quietly closed the door.

An hour later, when Wendy awoke, she could smell the enticing aroma of sizzling bacon. She didn't rise right away, but remained in bed, pondering the night.

She didn't know what to think. She liked Brad more than ever; she admired him. There was a streak of honor in his character, a quality that was rare and unusual, and she appreciated it. But, then again, the hell with honor. It could have been so easy—a pair of consenting adults indulging in a quick affair inspired by circumstance.

But no. The man who cared nothing about marriage just had to get to know her first.

Who would have ever imagined…he was a lot like Leif in that sense. Leif had always had his particular sense of ethics, and nothing could ever sway him. Bright and every bit as striking a man as Eric, Leif could have traveled anywhere and accomplished anything, but his heart was pledged to his tribe and his land. Despite rich opportunities elsewhere, this had been his home.

And Leif had moved slowly with her. He would have never forced her into anything. He had just let her fall in love with him first, and then with the curious, subtle beauty of the swamp.

Yes, there was something about them that was alike, she thought, no matter how strange. Her dark, patient husband with his love of the landscape, and this tawny-haired, cosmopolitan drug agent with his total disdain for muck and mud.

A tap on the door roused her from her thoughts. Brad stood in the doorway, freshly shaved and showered, and looking as young and cheerful as a college student.

"Breakfast is almost on. You've got time for a shower if you want."

Wendy nodded. "Thanks." He returned to the kitchen, and she stole into the bathroom for a long, hot shower.

The scent of shaving cream was still fresh in the bathroom. He had wiped down the tile in the shower and cleaned the mirror and the sink. And yet, a hint of his presence lingered there. Absurdly, Wendy felt like crying again.

It was reassuring, this lingering reminder of a man in the bathroom. A second damp towel, a second mug on the counter...

A second body in bed at night.

She stepped impatiently beneath the hot spray of the shower.

Damn Brad McKenna! Things should have been left to take their course. They would have enjoyed a swift, fleeting affair of mutual passion—and nothing more. She didn't want to wonder what it would be like to live with the man longer.

By the time she came out of the shower, her mood had brewed into a volatile tempest.

Brad awaited her in the kitchen amid the aromas of coffee, fried bacon and tomato-and-pepper omelets. Two places were set at the counter. He'd done a nice job of arranging things, with place mats, napkins and even a wild orchid nestled between the plates as a peace offering.

But Wendy just didn't feel very peaceful that morning. Brad seemed too at ease, too proud of himself.

"Mrs. Hawk?" With a flourish, he pulled back one of the rattan counter stools for her. Wendy sat, watching him as she carefully unfolded her napkin. He slid into the chair beside her.

"Made yourself right at home, I see," she said sweetly, eyeing him over her juice glass as she took a sip.

He stiffened. "I guess I did. Sorry. You've led me to believe that I was welcome to anything here—anything at all."

Wendy didn't know what was simmering inside of her. She was being completely unreasonable, and she knew it. He had done her the courtesy of creating a nice breakfast. She should have thanked him. Somehow, she couldn't do it.

"I must have given you the wrong impression. I'm so sorry. I really didn't mean to."

He watched her, his jaw hard and set. "You didn't mean to give me the impression that I could fix breakfast—or that I could sleep with you? What is the point that we're making here?"

She set her juice glass down carefully, staring at her plate instead of him. Forcing her voice to remain pleasant and calm, she explained, "You're a guest here, McKenna, nothing more."

"I'm a guest here because you invited me. And I can leave. No problem."

"You really are one rude bastard, you know that? I should have left you in the muck."

"Oh, yeah! Let's bring that up again." He bolted out of the chair and stood before her. Wendy swallowed. There was a pulse ticking away at his throat, and she sensed the pulse of his heart beneath Leif's old Miami Dolphins T-shirt. She closed her eyes, trying to remember Leif in that shirt. She couldn't.

When she opened her eyes and looked up, Brad still had his jaw set in that way of his that clearly spoke of anger and hostility. His eyes were gleaming, gold as a cat's. Bracing one hand behind her on the stool and one against the counter, he leaned close to her, warm and near and threatening.

She felt his breath against her flesh, sensed the rapid pulse of his anger. "Want to leave me in the swamp, Wendy? We can go right back out there if you want. This wasn't my idea, remember? You offered. Were you that desperate to have a man in the house?"

"Oh!" She spun on the chair, ready to slap him, but he was too quick. He caught her wrist and glared down at her. Using all her strength, she wrenched free from him and slid off the stool. Ignoring him, she sped through the house to her bedroom. She found her purse and headed back down the hallway, frantic to reach the door.

"Where the hell are you going?" he called after her.

When she didn't stop, he chased her, finally catching her arm and swinging her back to face him.

"I'm going out."

"Out where, damn you?"

She freed her arm again and backed away from him. "I'm going into work."

"Work?"

"Yes, work! People do work."

"Who do you work for?"

She didn't want to answer him for various reasons: sheer perversity, perhaps, or the bubbling black cauldron of her temper, or the raw wound of hurt and rejection. "I work for Eric!"

"You work for Eric—where? Doing what?" he demanded suspiciously.

Wendy hesitated, feeling her anger sizzle and whirl inside of her again. It was the most awful feeling. She was being so unreasonable, but now she was trying to salvage something of her pride by leaving.

"I'm not one of your suspects, Mr. G-Man," she retorted, but he took another step toward her, grabbing her arms, wrenching her against him.

"I'm not a G-Man. Now tell me, *where* do you work for Eric, and *what* do you do for him?"

"My God, what does it matter to you?" She pulled back her wrist, but he wouldn't release her. At that moment she realized just how strong he was. He could be powerful and ruthless when he chose.

"I asked you a question," he hissed. "Why didn't you tell me that you worked? Why didn't you go to work yesterday?"

Wendy sighed, making a great show of exaggerated impatience. "I work for Eric, but I only go in a day or two a week. He spends some time working with the tribal council, but he also sold a book last year on Andrew Jackson's campaign against the Seminoles. This year he's doing one on the relationship between the Seminole Indians and the Miccosukees. I'm his research assistant."

"What?"

"There are two tribes down here, McKenna. Not just Seminoles. The Miccosukees have some tribal land south of here, fronting the Trail. But I'm sure you didn't know or care. This whole place is just an infested pile of wet mud to you, isn't it? Muck and savages, huh?"

Her cutting remark caused his lip to tighten. He pulled her even closer. "That's another thing. Why didn't you tell me that you had been married to an Indian?"

"What?" Wendy said blankly. Something inside of her ticked and then exploded. "Because I don't owe you any explanation! I didn't tell you that he was Norse, either. Did that matter? Does any of it matter?"

"Yes, it matters! Had I known the details, I wouldn't have gotten into a fight with your brother-in-law. I wouldn't have been frightened half out of my wits, thinking I'd enticed a criminal to your home!"

"Bigot!" Wendy snapped, trying to wrench away with all of her strength. It did her no good.

He gritted his teeth and held her even closer. "No, Wendy, I'm not a bigot, and you damn well know it. I may be ignorant about a few things that you surely know backward and forward, but that doesn't imply any lack of respect for a people. Honest to God, Wendy, I think that you do know that. Now would you mind telling me what this morning's fiasco is about?"

"I've got to go. Get your hands off me."

"Not until we straighten this out. Okay, you're mad. You're furious at me over something. You did invite me here. And I have a hard time believing that this whole temper tantrum thing is over the fact that I made breakfast! So what can it be? Oh, I know. I disappointed you last night. You thought you'd invited some stud in, and you didn't get quite what you really wanted."

"Damn you, McKenna, let go of me!" Wendy warned him. Her temper began to cool as she realized that his had risen. His eyes sparkled with a menacing sizzle, and every muscle of his body seemed to have tightened.

Wendy tossed back her head, narrowing her eyes. "I want to leave the house, all right? You're a guest. I asked you to stay. Foolish me, I thought that you might consider your life to be a valuable quantity. Now—let me go!"

He didn't let her go.

Instead his mouth bore down on hers with a startling and savage determination. His lips encompassed hers, his teeth grated against hers until she surrendered with a little whimper. His tongue plunged into the depths and crevices of her mouth so intimately that she shuddered, feeling as if her very soul had been invaded. Blind rage turned the world black to her, but then that blackness dissipated. His fingers threaded through her hair, forcing her against him.

But, despite herself, she melded to him. Despite herself, she felt her heart race, beating raggedly. Despite herself, she inhaled the scent of him, marveled at the sweet tension of his body, surrendered to the fierce and yearning power of the man.

His ankle twisted around hers; suddenly she was

off her feet, swept to the floor. He lowered his weight over her. He stared at her for a moment, then his fingers plunged into the wings of her hair, and he held her still while his mouth ravaged hers again. His body was hard against her. Rigid and hard.

Hot tears played behind her eyes. She wanted him, but she didn't want the commitment. She was afraid to get to know him, afraid that she'd enjoy the smell of shaving cream in the bathroom, or tremble at the sight of a wild orchid beside her plate. She was deathly afraid of loving him...

Wendy twisted away, breaking the kiss. "Brad! Brad, damn you, this isn't right, this isn't..." Her voice trailed off painfully.

He went dead still. For endless moments, she felt only the soft, heated whisper of his breath against her throat. Then he moved. He hunched to the balls of his feet and then stood. He offered her a hand, and when she didn't take it, he reached for her, pulling her up to stand in front of him.

Wendy couldn't face him. She lowered her head, wishing that he would free her fingers. Suddenly, he dropped them.

He crossed his arms over his chest and stared at her until she felt compelled to face him, eye to eye. "This isn't what?" he demanded bluntly.

She shook her head. "I—"

"It isn't what you wanted, right?"

"Brad, please! Can't you just leave me alone to be humiliated in peace!"

He stared at her and shook his head slowly. The tension began to ease away from him, and a rueful smile worked its way into the line of his mouth. "No.

You shouldn't be humiliated. Come here, Wendy." He reached for her, gently easing her into his arms. Tenderly, he kissed her nose and lips.

"Did I ever thank you?"

"What?"

"Did I ever really thank you? You did save my life."

"It was nothing," Wendy murmured raggedly. Her hand fell against his chest and she stared up at the gentle smile on his lips. "Still, I think I should go to work today. You are very welcome to make yourself at home. I just have to get out for a while."

He stared into her eyes and nodded. "I understand," he said softly, and she thought that he did. He grinned ruefully. "Think that the food is still edible?"

"This is the second breakfast we'll have to trash, I'm afraid," she murmured. "Well, maybe it's still edible, but I don't think that I can eat."

He nodded. "Well, worse things can happen than breakfast trashing."

"Yes."

"Wendy, seriously, where are you going?"

"Not far from here. Eric has a house on a plot of land that he owns."

"On the main road?"

She frowned, wondering at the question. "Well, the land itself fronts the main road. But the house is far back."

He stared at her, then sighed. "I should come with you."

"Not today!" she whispered.

"Wendy, Wendy!" He pulled her close, moving his fingers through her hair in a fervent massage. Then he held her away, searching out her eyes again. "Wendy,

I really shouldn't be here. I'm afraid for you, Wendy. And I'll be afraid for you until this is over."

She smiled, touched by the timbre of his voice. "Brad, no one knows who I am. If your Michaelson character happened to be looking for you, he wouldn't know me. I've never seen him, he's never seen me. And I won't be passing any public places on the way. I go near the small family village where Eric and Leif's grandparents still live, but that's all. I'll be very safe."

He stared at her a moment longer, then exhaled slowly and nodded.

"All right."

"I need you to move away from the door," she told him.

He nodded again, but it took him a minute to move. Then, when he did, he pulled her into his arms.

"Wendy," he murmured seriously.

"What?"

He gently smoothed back a wild strand of hair. "We are going to make love."

"Are we?" she queried, raising her eyebrows.

"Yes." He opened the door for her and grinned. "And don't worry. I'll be sure to let you know exactly when."

"Pompous ass!" she muttered to herself, hurrying to the airboat.

She didn't realize he was behind her until he caught up with her. He was laughing as his hands descended upon her shoulder. She swung around to face him.

"I heard that."

Wendy Shrugged. "Well, it's true. You are decidedly too sure of yourself."

"Shouldn't I be?" he demanded innocently.

"You'll tell me when," Wendy mimicked. "I just

might change my mind about this whole thing, you know."

He shook his head. There was a grave expression on his face. "You won't."

She set her hands on her hips, cocking her head at an angle as she returned his scrutiny. "Ah, yes! You think I'll fall apart and fly into your arms by darkness again."

He shook his head, that slow smile lifting his lips. "No. It will be broad daylight, lots of light—or not at all."

"Oh, really?"

"Really." He started to return to the house. At the door, he paused and called back to her in a sensual drawl. "Don't worry about it. As I said, I'll make sure to tell you when." He grinned and closed the door.

Not sure whether to laugh or refute him, Wendy merely turned away and continued down to the airboat.

7

Wendy stared down at the page she was reading and shook her head in annoyance. A history book lay open before her, and the information in it was inaccurate. She flipped back to the front of the book, looking for the copyright date. When she realized that the book had been written before World War II, she was able to take some of the misinformation more philosophically. The U.S. government hadn't recognized the two different and distinct tribes living in the Everglades back then—why would a white schoolteacher-turned-author know any better?

She set the book on the table and scratched out a note to Eric. A glance at the cypress clock on her brother-in-law's handsomely paneled study wall indicated that it was well past six. She should be heading back.

Just the thought of going home made her palms begin to sweat and her stomach churn. It was her house! she reminded herself. She had every right to go home.

She straightened all of her materials on the desk, turned off the computer, covered it—and sank back into the chair. She gnawed idly on her thumbnail. It was her house. Yes, the rights were hers. But she didn't have a right to act the way she had been acting. She had invited Brad to stay.

She'd actually invited him to a whole lot more. He was right about one thing: she needed to decide exactly what she was willing to offer.

The front door opened and closed. For a moment, Wendy sat up in panic, thinking that she'd been an absolute fool not to lock the door. But then, peeking down the long hallway that led to the front of the house, she saw that Eric was coming in.

"Wendy!" he called, spotting her from the end of the hall. She waved to him, smiling. He wore jeans and a colorful Seminole shirt, woven in various shades of red. The color contrasted with the warm bronze of his face and the startling shade of his eyes.

You need someone, too, brother-in-law, Wendy thought suddenly. He was a special man, so striking in appearance, so proud and ethical, so warm and generous to those he trusted.

Like Jennifer, his wife.

"Let me get something cool to drink," he called to her, "and I'll be right with you."

She heard the refrigerator door open, then seconds later, he appeared carrying a Sol for himself and a wine cooler for her. She smiled, thanking him. Eric knew her. Beer for fishing, wine with company dinner, ice tea or water if she was thirsty. Diet soda if she was determined on a diet, but her diets would seldom last long because she loved the taste of real sugar. She had known her brother-in-law for a decade. All those years bred real friendship, real closeness.

And Brad, who would go away very soon, wanted to know her birthday and her middle name. He should have been a dream, she thought. An imaginary lover, tan and sandy and agile and beautifully formed. A midnight visitor who would dissipate with the morning light of dawn.

"What are you doing here? I thought that you weren't going to come over while you were hosting the DEA." Eric studied her with frank curiosity.

Wendy shrugged, but she couldn't keep her eyes level with Eric's. "I—uh—I don't know. I guess I needed a little breathing space."

He took a long sip of his beer, set his booted feet comfortably upon the edge of his desk and leaned back. He surveyed her from beneath half-closed, jet lashes, then closed his eyes completely and smiled. "Sparks are flying too hot and wild for you to handle, huh?"

Wendy stared at him until he opened his eyes again. She wanted to tell him to mind his own business, but she shrugged instead. "No. I just needed some space."

"Get out of the kitchen if you can't take the heat," Eric quoted gravely.

"Eric," Wendy moaned.

He sat up, letting his feet fall to the floor. Reaching over, he tilted her chin upward. "There's something there, Wendy-bird," he teased her lightly. "I could feel it all night long. Palpable, thick." He released her, rose and stretched with the grace of a cat. His back was to her when he said, "So did you run over here because you did go to bed, or because you didn't?"

"Eric—"

"Well?"

He turned to look at her, and she felt the depth of his concern for her. She smiled. "Because I didn't. Eric, I don't know what to think. I don't know what I feel.

I mean, he's going to go away again, right? He's just here for a few days. Until they catch this Michaelson character, or until something else breaks. I like him a lot, Eric—"

"So do I, for whatever that's worth."

"I hate what he does for a living. And he doesn't intend to get married—"

"Well, if you haven't made it into bed yet, why are you worrying about marriage?"

"I'm not! I don't want to get married again."

"So?"

She shook her head, then blurted out, "So then why doesn't it just happen? Why do we have to go through twenty questions?"

Eric stared at her for a long time. At last he spoke very softly. "Because he does care, Wendy. Because he didn't meet you on a bar stool, because he thinks highly of you."

"But he said—"

"Trust me, Wendy." As he sighed, a skeptical glaze clouded the lime color of his eyes. Wendy could almost see time rolling away in the shadows of his eyes. "Trust me," he repeated hoarsely. "When a man just wants solace, none of it means anything to him. Not the day or time or date, the color of the woman's eyes or her hair. Hell, her name doesn't even matter." He sensed her staring at him. He was remembering his own wild pursuits, just after Jennifer had died. Ultimately, he'd found little peace in physical satisfaction. "He cares about you, Wendy, and I'm damned glad. I know this sounds sexist, but hell, I'm an Indian, and we always had our trouble keeping up with the times. If he weren't a decent man, I'd probably be over there trying to throw him off your property. Maybe you won't ever marry him. Maybe you'll never even fall in love, but—"

"You don't understand, Eric. I don't want to get married again. And I don't want to fall in love—especially not with a DEA agent!"

He ignored her. As if she hadn't even spoken, he continued, "But what you will have, Wendy, will be good, and it will be caring."

"You might want to try that yourself," she retorted.

He slid back into his chair and took another long swallow of his beer. "Wendy, I don't want—"

He broke off, aware that he was about to repeat her words. He laughed and shrugged. "So how did work go? Did you get anything done?"

"Yeah. I found a couple of books that you can refer to for total misinformation."

"There's a lot of that, but thanks. It's just as important to know where the bad stuff is as the good." He grinned at her. "I was over at the Miccosukee center today. Things are going full speed ahead. They're planning even more on their reservation lands. Billy was telling me that it's hard to hone in on the Seminole bingo, so they're going to try and battle the Hyatt instead."

Wendy grinned. She'd also heard the Miccosukee leader speak about his ideas, and she liked the plans as much as she liked the young man making them. It was true, the Seminoles had managed their money well. The tribe did well with bingo, and with cigarette sales. The Miccosukees were looking into those enterprises, but they were also interested in catching business from the new linkup with Interstate 75.

"So you were fooling around all day, huh?" she said.

"Yes, and no." He leaned his head back and stared at the ceiling. "We were talking the same old route. Money, education, housing. I never know quite where I stand myself. I like my house. I like owning this land. Then again, I enjoyed going to school. The years I spent in the service were traumatic—bloody and—yet, they were somehow important. Now I stand here on a crossroad. I don't want to lose the value of our customs or traditions. But I don't want to see the children of the tribe growing up without every benefit of white America. Where is the right place to be, Wendy? What is the right stand?"

She stood up and gave him a hug. "I really love you alot, Eric, you know that?"

He laughed. "I didn't mean to give a soapbox lecture."

"And you didn't. You're super, and I'm going home."

"I love you, too, Wendy." He looked into her eyes for a moment, then told her, "I think you should know, everyone seems to be commenting on all the activity going on. Along Alligator Alley, along the Trail."

"What activity?"

"Well, knowing what I know, I assume that some of the men driving around and hovering around the airboat rides and villages work for the government. There have also been a lot—I mean a lot—of cops around, and you know that the police stations are really good about letting our own forces handle our own problems." The Seminoles had a police force of their own, just as the Miccosukees did. Eric had always said that Florida was a fair state when it came to respecting the tribal laws of the Indians. The city and county police from Miami and Fort Lauderdale and the other communities seldom interfered with the Indian forces.

"Well," Wendy murmured, "I guess that it is reasonable for the government to have men trying to keep an eye out for Brad—and for Michaelson."

Eric nodded, watching her. "There's something else, Wendy."

"Yes?"

"Some of our men seem to think that something big is going to happen. They say there have been seaplane drops in the swamp, down toward the Trail."

Wendy shrugged impatiently. "Twenty miles south! Eric, think about it! Think about the size of the swamp! You have to know what you're doing to find things out there!"

"That's true. But we don't know if these are just petty crooks, smuggling in a kilo of pot—or hired assassins, hunting for Brad."

"I'm not worried."

"You should be. At least tell Brad what I've told you. I don't believe that they can just walk in and find Brad, either. Only you and I know that he's there."

"And old Mac up at the gas station."

Eric shrugged. "Mac never says a word to strangers. Never. So your secret is safe. But I'm afraid that they might stumble upon you by accident."

"They'd be idiots to molest me."

"Wendy, they're criminals." He sighed, exasperated. "You of all people should know the danger of innocence!"

Duly chastised, she lowered her head. "I'll tell Brad," she promised.

"Just warn him, that's all. He has the right to know

what's going on, the right to protect you both." He laughed suddenly. "Don't worry. I'm sure you won't have to give him up—yet."

"Very amusing, Eric," she retorted, but when she saw his grin, she smiled, too. "Want to walk me out?"

"Sure." Arm in arm, they followed the lawn to where it began to level and fall toward the canal.

"Want me to come home with you?" he teased her.

Yes! Wendy thought, but she had to fight her own battles. "I'm all right."

"You're better than all right, Wendy-bird. You're perfect."

She kissed his cheek. "Flattery is great stuff. I'll see you soon."

Distractedly, Wendy waved and started for home. The wind rushed around her and lifted her hair, gently calming her spirit.

Maybe Brad was right. He knew what she wanted, but he wouldn't give it to her, because he wanted her to have something better. And maybe someday, if she ever lay upon a psychiatrist's couch and poured out her life's story, she would be glad of it. Yes, I had a very bad time learning to step out again after my husband died. For two years I could do nothing. But then I met a man, and though he passed briefly through my life, it was something precious, and something very special.

As Wendy neared home, she made a few resolutions. She was not going to act childish as she had today. She liked Brad, and she was going to enjoy him. The teasing was fun, and it was fun to get to know him.

Of course, she'd be damned if she'd ever take another step toward him. If he really wanted her—whenever he decided to let her know when!—he'd better plan on coming to get her.

Humming softly as she cut off the motor, she wondered if he might have discovered something to cook for dinner. She walked across the lawn to the house with a jaunty step.

It wasn't until she reached the door that she began to sense something was amiss. Emptiness and silence abounded through the house. Carefully, she opened the door.

Nothing was disturbed—nothing at all. The house was neat and tidy. Rushing down the hallway, she discovered that Brad had straightened the beds. She flushed slightly, realizing that he had found the laundry hamper and the washer and dryer behind the slotted doors in the hall. He had washed the clothes that he had been borrowing—and her things. There was ample evidence of the chores he had done.

Only the man himself was missing.

Wendy let out a soft cry of fear, spun around and went tearing back out of the house. In dread she searched the yard, praying that she would not find a bloodied body. Pain glazed her heart. It was impossible. They couldn't have found him. Not here. She lived too deep in the swamp.

She kept telling herself that as she ran back into the house and found the shotgun.

Wendy loathed weapons, but she wasn't foolish. Brad was out there—perhaps in the custody of murderers. She cocked the gun and slung it over her shoulder. Fighting back the tears that stung her eyes, she set out to find him.

Nothing, absolutely nothing, should have surprised Brad about Wendy Hawk's house anymore. He had been accosted in bed by a wild panther and attacked from the roof by a green-eyed Seminole. He'd learned that the Florida panther did belong, but that only madmen kept alligators.

And yet, when he came into the living room to discover the very tall, withered old man, standing dead center in the room, Brad still didn't know what to think. There was no mistaking the fact that this man was an Indian. Half of his hair was white, the other half was blacker than midnight, long and straight. His face was near brown and weathered from constant exposure to the sun, and his features were solid and strong. His eyes were as black as onyx.

Brad thought of all the things he had learned in school. This man had the simple pride and dignity of a Chief Joseph. He had the unfaltering stare of a Cochise or a Sitting Bull.

Or an Osceola, Brad thought. This man was surely a Seminole.

I'm definitely slipping, Brad thought. He hadn't heard a single sound.

But the old man didn't seem to expect violence from him. In fact, he seemed to know that he would find him there.

"Hello," Brad said.

The Indian nodded. Brad fumed uncomfortably as he realized that he was being scrutinized, from head to toe. What if the old fellow didn't speak English? Brad raised a friendly hand, palm outward in friendship. "Hello," he repeated.

"I am old, not deaf," the Indian told him.

Brad felt like a fool. "Sorry. You didn't answer me."

"I hadn't decided what to answer."

"I didn't think it was that difficult a question."

"Where is your respect for your elders?"

"I meant no disrespect, truly," Brad returned evenly. He paused, "Uh, sir, who are you, please?"

A smile revealed a million wrinkles in the old man's face. "Hawk. Willie Hawk." He was dressed in faded dungarees, boots and a beribboned Seminole shirt. He stepped forward, offering Brad a hand.

"Mr. Hawk, my pleasure. My name is—"

"Yes, I know. You are McKenna. I have heard."

Brad frowned. He had heard? Hadn't he stressed the importance of his anonymity to Wendy? Had she told this man about him today? Or hadn't Eric realized that he was betraying Brad to give him away. Maybe Eric hadn't understood—

No. Eric was too bright not to understand the situation.

Willie Hawk seemed to have read the quick wanderings of his mind. His smile deepened and his face seemed to crinkle even more. "They have not betrayed you. Not Wendy, not Eric."

"Surely—"

Willie Hawk dismissed Brad with a wave of his gnarled hand. "You have judged them well. They have not betrayed you. I know the swamp, son. I know what happens here. I can listen to the earth. Even the alligator speaks to me."

Just what he needed, Brad decided—an Indian, and senile to boot.

Willie Hawk lowered his eyes, and Brad realized that the old man had read his mind again. "So Wendy has gone to work, and you are here alone?"

Brad nodded. "Yes, sir. Can I get you anything? This is your grandson's house. You are probably at home here."

"My grandson is dead. It is Wendy's house," Willie said, and Brad could not fathom with what emotion he spoke. If there was pain, it was well hidden. If there was love, that, too, was well hidden.

"Well, then—"

"You are alone here. There must be very little to do. The inactivity must weigh heavily upon a man who is accustomed to movement."

Brad laughed. "Yes, I guess it does get bad. The laundry is all done, and Wendy is too neat a lady to leave much else to do."

There was something intriguing about the old man's face. It suggested an ancient, enigmatic wisdom. The onyx eyes never seemed to leave his own or to cease their slow and careful assessment. He turned around suddenly. "Come with me."

"What?"

Willie paused. "Are you deaf, young man?"

"No, it's just that—"

"The Indian wars ended many, many moons ago, you know."

The old man was a bit of a dramatist, Brad decided. He saw the twinkle in Willie's eyes, and this time, the Indian laughed with him.

"What the hell," Brad said. "I'll live dangerously. But give me a minute, please. I want to leave Wendy a note. Under the circumstances, I don't want her to worry."

Willie nodded. "Yes, write a message. Tell her that you are with me, and she will not worry."

Brad scribbled out a note. He started to attach it to the refrigerator, then worried that she might get scared outside if she called him and he didn't answer. He followed Willie out the door, thinking that he'd stick his note in the mailbox. Then he realized that there was no mailbox. "How does she get her bills?" he wondered out loud.

"P.O. box," Willie advised him sagely.

"Of course," Brad murmured. He tried to shove the note beneath the door. It seemed to stick, more or less.

Willie had come by canoe. He pointed the handmade vessel out to Brad, and they started toward it. Brad offered to paddle, but Willie would have none of it.

"Sit still," he advised Brad. "There are not many times in life when you may enjoy the journey with no effort, with your eyes and ears and heart open."

"Right," Brad said. "Thank you, sir." He still worried that he should be doing the work, but knew that Willie would not appreciate his worry.

Just as they rounded out to slice westward along the canal, Brad noticed a black figure lurking around the house. On closer inspection, he relaxed. It was only Baby, prowling around the house.

"I wonder if I was supposed to have fed her something," he murmured aloud.

"She came by the village this morning. My wife gave her a chicken. Baby is fine."

Brad nodded. But Baby, he saw, wanted something. The cat was crawling up on her hindquarters to let out her savage meow. Baby wanted to go in.

Brad couldn't imagine a bag of Tender Vittles big enough for such a cat anyway. He was glad that she'd eaten elsewhere.

The canoe moved through the swamp.

Brad dismissed all thoughts of Baby, not realizing that the panther had clipped his note with one long toenail, and that, when she finally walked away, she shredded his note as she went.

Three hours later, Brad discovered himself sitting at the base of a tall pine. His hands were loosely tied behind his back, and he was smiling as a group of wild Indians danced and war-whooped around him.

As a kid he'd played cowboys and Indians. Sometimes he'd been an Indian, and sometimes he'd been a cowboy.

To the best of his knowledge, there hadn't been any cowboys in the swamps, but that was okay. He had met Marna Hawk Panther and Anthony Panther—and all the little Panthers. He had met Mary Hawk, whom Willie referred to as his raven woman because of the ink-dark tresses that still adorned her head, despite the fact that she had turned eighty on her last birthday.

Mike, Dorinda, David and Jennifer—the four little Panthers—suddenly ceased their war whoops. They raced over to hug their father, who gave them each a hug and a pat on the back. He whispered something to the children, and they all ran back to thank Brad for playing with them. Dorinda blushed and came close, giving a kiss on the cheek. "You're very, very nice, Mr. McKenna. I'm going to tell Aunt Wendy that, too."

He smiled. She was a very pretty little girl with her great-grandfather's onyx eyes, Mary Hawk's raven hair and her mother's lovely, golden skin. Brad nodded to her gravely. "Thank you," he told her. She blushed again, then ran off to join her siblings.

Tony Panther sat down beside Brad, leaning against the tree. He was a young man, dressed in a business suit that seemed somewhat ludicrous in the clearing of thatched-roof chickees. The clearing itself seemed to Brad to be a moment out of time.

Of course, there were cars nearby. Tony's Dodge was just beyond the tree. He was an accountant, who worked for the tribe. He drove in and out of Fort Lauderdale daily.

"That was nice, letting the kids play that way," Tony told Brad. "We didn't get to win very often in real life, you know."

Brad laughed, idly running the rope that had held him so loosely captive through his fingers. "I enjoyed them." He ran his fingers through his hair. "I remember playing cowboys and Indians when I was young. At the time, it was a total fantasy—pow-wows and peace pipes and scalpings."

"I'm just proud to still be here. It meant our Hawk ancestor was willing to fight and brave the swamps, rather than be sent west. But don't worry—we haven't scalped anyone in ages." Tony looked at him a long moment. "Did you really enjoy the afternoon?"

Brad mused over the question. He had. Mary had told him how the tribe had once raised pumpkins to survive. She had made him taste the old staple of their people, koontie bread, made from the koontie root. He had helped repair a chickee, and—since it was alligator season, he had also tasted the smoked meat of the creature. Tony, he had learned, was a Miccosukee, and from him, he had learned quite a bit about the two tribes who had coexisted in the Florida swampland. They shared their green corn dance and other festivals.

Then, sitting there against the tree, Brad felt the peace of the area sweep through him. The sun was setting beautifully. Out on the water, a great blue heron rose and swept into the sky. The entire horizon reflected the golden sunset.

Brad turned and nodded to Tony. "Yeah. I've enjoyed it very much."

"I wonder why Wendy hasn't shown up yet," Tony murmured, then he shrugged, seeing the worry that sprang into Brad's eyes. "She might know what Grandfather is up to. He came over to kidnap you on purpose, you know. Just to rile Wendy."

Brad laughed. "Did he really?"

He nodded. "I hope you don't find this too strange, but we are Wendy's family. Wendy and Leif met in college, when they were just kids. They married before they graduated. Her mother had died when she was a child, and her dad passed away right after they were married. She has been with us for a long time. We love her as if she were our blood."

"I'm glad," Brad said. Although he shouldn't be prying into her life, Tony Panther was willing to give him answers, so he decided to ask a few more questions. "What happened to Leif Hawk?"

Tony appeared startled. "She's never told you?"

Brad shook his head.

Tony stared off in the distance. "He was killed. In cold blood. Eric's wife was killed with him."

"What?" Brad demanded huskily.

He didn't get an answer. From the water, there was

a sudden commotion. He looked up to find that Wendy had come at last.

She seemed to fly out of the airboat. She didn't seem to see anything or anyone—until her eyes lighted on him. Her eyes were huge and sparkling and silver and—quite suddenly—sizzling with fury.

She was running toward him with all the lean energy of a pouncing tiger. Warily, Brad stood up. A moment later she catapulted herself against him, half screaming and half sobbing in fury. "You son of a bitch! You stinking—cop!"

"Wendy!" She took a swing at him and he ducked. She flew around in a circle with the force of her blow, and he caught her, pinning her arms to her sides.

"Hi, Wendy," Tony said lightly.

She ignored him, and her fierce glare bored into Brad. "You inconsiderate, careless weasel! You scared me half to death!"

"Wendy! Wendy Hawk!" She tensed and swallowed, apparently aware that Grandfather was approaching the scene. "Wendy, you calm down."

Far from calm, she struggled against Brad's hold and managed to turn. "Grandfather! You wily fox! How could you do this to me! I was so frightened."

"Wendy!" Brad swung her back around again. "I left you a note—"

"Liar!"

"Wendy!" Grandfather said sharply. Immediately, her anger softened, and Brad realized how much she loved and respected the old man. Still staring at Brad with a look that could kill, Wendy exhaled slowly.

"Wendy, he did leave the note. You do not call a man

a liar unless you know it is truth to do so. And to deny a friend, that is even worse. He is a man of his word. You must have known that, or else you would not have him at your house."

Wendy nodded, trembling in Brad's arms. "I even remembered the shotgun."

She had been truly frightened for him. Her concern was reassuring, though he hadn't meant to scare her. "Wendy, honestly. I left a note."

"I was scared to death." She tried to retain some of her anger, while regaining her dignity. Her words were still a whisper, and he longed to touch her, to kiss away her worry right then and there.

"I'm sorry, Wendy."

"Come on, Brad. Wendy, please? We're tucking the kids into bed, and they'll be heartbroken if they don't get to see you."

Wendy forced herself to tear her eyes from Brad and smile at Tony. "Of course, Tony. I'm dying to give them all great big hugs."

Brad lagged behind for a moment, wondering about the story Tony had been telling him. He needed to hear the end of it. Leif Hawk and Eric's wife had been killed—in cold blood.

The very thought of it was tragic. Wendy and Eric had shared a great deal, an ocean of sorrow, and Brad couldn't help the tug of pure sympathy that tore at his heart.

A young man, and a young woman, cruelly taken from life. What the hell had happened, and who did he ask?

"Brad, are you coming?"

They were waiting for him. "Yes, yes, I'm coming. Thanks."

As Brad caught up with them, the gold remnants of twilight left the sky and night fell, a blanket of darkness.

8

It was late when they returned to Wendy's house. They'd spent the evening huddled around the cooking fire. By its eerie light, Willie Hawk had woven tales of the past, of a people forced to run away from a white government that had betrayed the Seminoles at every turn. Brad thought it appropriate that the name Seminole meant "runaway." He'd spent most of his career running from dealers and mobsters.

His head was fuzzy from folklore and brew. Brad wasn't sure what he had been drinking all night. Tony called it a "black" drink and assured him it wouldn't do anything to him that Jack Black wouldn't. But it was potent stuff—very powerful.

In the darkness of the clearing, a blackness alleviated only by the campfire, he could almost see a mist around old Willie. And in that mist he could see the past: warriors, feathered and oiled, shaking knives and rifles in the air, clad in the colorful garb they had borrowed from the Spanish and adapted to their own use. He could see a million fires. He could hear a cry on the wind. He was entranced.

The night was black, but the wind felt refreshing

against his face as they drove back to Wendy's place. Brad reveled in the quiet of the swamp when the motor died. They were sounds that he was coming to recognize and understand.

When they stepped back into Wendy's house, he felt comfortable, as if he were home. Wendy wandered into the kitchen, and Brad went to the stereo and began to browse through her collection of tapes and discs and albums. "Okay if I turn on the stereo?"

"Whatever you want," she called back.

Whatever he wanted.

Brad found an old album by the Temptations. He carefully set the needle on the vinyl record, then collapsed upon the couch. She had an impressive music system, with dynamite speakers. He closed his eyes as the music filled the room and soothed his spirit.

When he opened his eyes, Wendy was leaning against the counter, smiling at him tolerantly. He grinned at her, then rose slowly.

Whatever he wanted. That was what she had said. He wanted to hold her in his arms.

She was a vision of loveliness. Her hair fell free about her face, and her silver eyes sparkled. She was wearing jeans and a tailored shirt. Her shirt collar angled around her smooth throat in a manner that Brad found enticing.

Her smile was the killer. Her smile revealed her essence, the sweet, elusive quality that drew him to her, that excited him, that elicited the tenderness and the yearning.

He lifted a hand to her. His head was spinning, either from the Indian drink or the devastating effect of her beauty. "Want to dance?"

"Dance?"

"Move around on the floor. Step to the music. Dance."

He caught hold of her hands. There was silver laughter in her eyes as he drew her to him, enfolding her into his arms. The Temptations were singing about "sunshine on a cloudy day" as he held her close.

"See? Dance?"

"In the living room?" She laughed.

"Anywhere."

He released her slightly, swinging her out, then back into his arms. She was still laughing as he sang off-key to the music.

"This is a classic album," he told her, pulling her close. "You've good taste in music."

"Thanks."

The music faded, then another song began. He moved with the soft, slow tempo, grateful for the lovely woman in his arms. His left hand caressed the small of her back. He could feel her flesh beneath the cotton shirt. The softness of her breasts brushing against him caused a definite reaction inside him.

The music…it seemed to be a part of them. It was so very easy to move with Wendy in his arms. But suddenly he realized that he wasn't moving at all. He was merely staring down into her eyes, her beautiful eyes, with their startling silver color and their dark, sweeping lashes. She had to know what he was feeling, everything that he was feeling.

She smiled very slowly. The little vixen, he thought.

Did she know that his pulse was pounding hopelessly out of control? Surely she could feel that he was taut and tense and that his muscles were constricted with desire. She was so close, he could feel her softness. He could feel the fullness of her breasts, the pebble hardness of her nipples through their clothing. He could feel the trembling that swept her, the supple length of her thighs, the angle of her hip, the soft and almost indiscernible swell of her femininity.

She just had to feel the evidence of his desire, straining against his borrowed jeans. She just had to...

She did. He knew by the soft, silver clouds that filled her eyes. By her slightly parted lips, by the ragged whisper of her breath.

She moistened her lips with the tip of her tongue, and they somehow became even more tempting. Glossy and sleek and still tempting. Lowering his head while the Temptations serenaded them, he kissed her.

The feeling was riveting. Their mouths fused in a passionate union, hot and electric. For a moment, they broke apart, then he held her face, searched out her eyes and kissed her again. Gently, his palms kneaded the soft flesh of her back until he reached her buttocks. Lifting her against him, he fitted her to his form while her arms clung tightly to his neck and their mouths continued to meet, exploring, melding.

She broke away, gasping for breath. He stared at her with the rage of his passion naked in his eyes.

Had she ever felt like this? she wondered. So excited that it hurt? So sensually alive and aware that his kiss seemed to reach into her body and soul, warming her through and through.

She had been married to a man she loved, and theirs had been a passionate relationship. Maybe this desire was heightened by the loss of her only love. Maybe it was due to her loneliness.

And maybe it was just Brad, the man himself.

But she had never, never felt like this. Desperate to

have more of him, she longed to latch her arms around his neck again and savor the sizzling heat that flared between them. She'd waited too long. She wanted to feel her flesh naked against his.

"Brad," she whispered against his mouth.

He paused, staring down at her.

"Brad, is this 'when'? I mean, you said you'd let me know when, so if this isn't it…" Her voice trailed away and her body grew heated and flushed. She didn't know if she was shamed by the bluntness of her query, or merely so hot with desire that fever was spreading through her limbs.

"Yes," he told her huskily. "This is 'when.' That is, if you're willing. You said I could have whatever I wanted. I want you, Wendy. God, do I want you. Now. Here. If—you're willing."

This time there was tenderness as well as fire in his gaze. She was willing, and he knew it. He didn't wait for her answer, but drew her into his embrace again, desperately moving his hands to mold her body to his. "Dear God, yes, this is when!" he murmured.

He kissed her throat and teased her earlobe. The brush of his lips grew more heated, more sensual, as he searched out the buttons of her tailored shirt. In seconds, he had cast the shirt aside. Deftly, he removed her bra.

His callused hands cupped the firm fullness of her breasts. At his touch, the pink, tawny nipples immediately hardened. Lowering his moist lips to her, he laved his tongue around a nipple, then sucked it hard into his mouth.

Wendy let out a little cry, arching against him. The staggering sensation swept like swift white lightning from her breast to her pelvis. The yearning pain between her legs intensified, so that she could barely stand. His hands splayed across her back, holding her up.

But she could not bear it. She tugged wildly upon his hair, whispering his name. Somehow she was borne to the floor. As she lay there, her heart thundering, he cast his shirt aside in such a fervent hurry that several buttons were torn away. His breathing was torn and ragged as he knelt by her side.

She couldn't stand to wait any longer. His chest was naked with its planes of muscle and tawny hair, and she had to know the feel of that nakedness against her own breasts. Whispering her wild desires, she reached for him, brushing her naked body against his. His muscles were rock hard. His hair titillated her throat and breasts, already so sensitized to his touch.

He was whispering to her, giving her hoarse little commands. His desires were burning like a flash fire, out of control. All the little things that he'd wanted to do, all the nuances of slow seduction, all were swept away amid a sudden tempest of need.

He had tried. God knew, he had tried.

Now, he couldn't wait any longer.

He pressed her to the floor and pulled off her boots and socks and jeans. Only then did he pause for the slightest moment to relish the sight of her. The spill of golden hair about her shoulders and the rise of her breasts made him wild with desire. His eyes lowered to take in the arch of her hips and the golden nest at the juncture of her thighs, visible beneath the lacy string bikinis she wore.

He looked from her supple form to her face. Her eyes

were still silver, and her lips remained parted, wet and moist. And so inviting.

He let out a groan, a guttural cry of appreciation and raw need.

Burying his face against the soft, smooth eroticism of her belly, he let his tongue trail over her flesh, and then he kissed it.

"Brad!" She arched and writhed beneath him. His fingers slipped off her panties and curled over the apex of her thighs. She was hot and sweet and damp.

"Please!" She tugged at his hair. Desperation filled him again. They wanted the same thing. "Please, please," she whispered, tossing her head. Her hands gripped his jeans, tugging at them.

A roar rose in his head. Almost blindly, he brushed his fingers against that web of gold. Desire shot through him, as hot as molten steel. The roar in his head thundered, and the pulse inside of him throbbed to a frenzied pace.

He stripped off his shoes and jeans, then stared down at her again.

He towered above her, naked and very male. His thighs were well-formed columns over his long legs. His shoulders and chest were bronze, his masculinity was shockingly brazen, yet enticing.

Wendy closed her eyes, dazed at the sight of him, stunned at the intensity of the passions that swirled inside her.

Although her eyes remained closed, she could feel his hot flesh against hers as he lowered himself over her. He had become naked, removing her husband's clothing.

Leif. She had loved him. Didn't she owe him more?

"Wendy!"

Brad spoke her name so harshly that she opened her eyes wide, startled and guilty. His gold and amber gaze, penetrated her, inciting a new panic. Could he read her mind? she wondered. If he knew what she was thinking, he would go away.

He didn't go away.

He wedged himself between her knees, stroking the sensitive skin along her inner thighs. She gasped as a wave of searing desire raged through her. She closed her eyes.

"Wendy!"

She gazed at him again. There was no tenderness about him now, but neither was there cruelty. "Lift your legs around me, Wendy. Meet my eyes. Wendy, look at me."

She moistened her lips. She couldn't have begun to disobey him.

"Now look at us, Wendy. Watch where we come together. Watch how we make love."

She cried out as her entire being seemed to rock to a new, blinding pulse. In that languid moment of ecstasy, he plunged himself within her, driving deep, deep, until he filled her, until he was completely sheathed. He stayed there for a moment, keeping his eyes fiercely locked with hers.

Then he moved.

"Watch, Wendy…"

She watched until the excitement spiraled in her so deeply that she cried out again, reaching for him. She felt him inside of her, stroking her. She cast back her head, and he trailed kisses along her throat. He tucked his hands beneath her buttocks, bringing her ever more flush. Again his lips trailed over her breasts, leaving a lingering euphoria wherever they passed.

He brought himself to the edge of her, and she writhed madly to catch him. Then he would plunge again, deep, deeper. The ache inside of her was swelling, the anguish building until she passed through the wild storm, and sunshine seemed to burst upon her. Beautiful sunshine, in golden droplets, seeping into her, sating her, filling her.

He whispered her name, he demanded that she draw her legs higher. She could scarcely obey, and yet she did, and it all began again. His movement inside of her. His touch, guiding her. His kiss, wildfire burning her flesh, raking her nipples.

Fire flared once again. Wendy gasped, caught in the whirl of a second thrill, shuddering as she felt Brad's traumatic release, rich and hot. She lay gasping, her eyes closed, savoring what had happened. She felt the weight of his body, heavy over her now, and yet she loved it. She loved the warm, rich scent of him, she loved the slick feel of his naked flesh. She loved the way that they lay, entwined.

"Wendy, look at me again."

Wendy glanced up and smiled lazily. When she reached up to touch his cheek, he caught her hand.

They both became aware that the needle on the stereo was sweeping over empty space, making a strange sound. All the lights in the house were still blazing.

Wendy stared up at Brad and her smile faded. The hardness was still there about him. She couldn't understand it. She was still feeling after-tremors, feeling so close to him, and yet he seemed so distant from her.

She had been open and honest with him. She had

wanted him; she had gladly given herself to him, trusting in him. And now, even as she lay there, naked and still filled by him, fear began to sweep into her. "Brad?" Her voice trembled slightly as she questioned him.

But then he smiled. Opening her palm, he pressed a kiss against it and lay back down beside her.

"I don't understand—" Wendy began.

"I just wanted to hear you say it. My name."

She inhaled, closing her eyes. She could have told him that she had known from the beginning that he would be no substitute for another man. Brad McKenna was in a class all his own.

"We were both afraid, a little, weren't we?" she asked.

He lifted his weight from her and stretched, resting on one elbow. His gaze remained on her, intense.

"Yeah. Afraid of Leif Hawk entering in here."

She couldn't quite meet his eyes. And when hers shifted, he abruptly straddled her, catching her cheeks between his palms. Intimacy seemed rampant between them again. She felt his thighs, his nakedness, keenly. She stared up at him, then her gaze fell away.

"You loved him very much," Brad said.

"Yes." She opened her eyes and met his at last, anger suddenly burning in her own. "But I made love with you, and you know it. So get off me, you oaf."

He caught her face in a tender hold. "That's why I made you watch me. Watch *us*. I wanted to be sure you were making love to me—not the ghost of another man." Now his kiss was slow, leisurely, yet thorough.

He rose then, a man completely at ease with his nakedness, naturally graceful in his movement. He picked up the stereo needle and set it back to the beginning of the album. Once again the room filled with music.

Wendy watched him for a moment, then started to reach for her panties.

"No, don't," he told her, noticing her movement. A smile played across his features. "Please, don't."

She hesitated. He knelt down behind her, slipping his arms around her and locking his hands beneath her breasts. "It's nice just to hold you," he whispered, resting his chin upon her shoulder.

She let her head fall back against his shoulder. "It's nice to be held," she said.

Nuzzling her neck, he added, "And we have to make love again. Tonight. Maybe a few times, maybe several times."

Wendy twisted, trying to see his face. "For a slow starter, you do get quickly into gear once the motor is running."

"Slow starter?"

"I've been willing for some time now," she teased.

"Wendy, we haven't known each other for 'some time.'"

She leaned back again, slipping her slender fingers over his rougher, callused ones. "I knew that I wanted you."

It took him a minute to answer. "Last night you wanted a body in bed. Tonight, you wanted *me*. There's a difference."

She didn't reply; maybe it was true.

He hummed to the music. "We used to have sock hops back when I was a kid. Everybody used to go. This was what we played. I never did learn to disco. Did you?"

Wendy shook her head. "No."

"Want a glass of wine?"

"That sounds good. I'll get it." She didn't know if she could be as easy as Brad about walking around her house naked with all the lights on. Of course, no one would be near, and they couldn't possibly see in if they were.

She was just out of practice.

But it wasn't bad, not really. Although she keenly felt Brad's eyes on her while she moved, it was a nice feeling. She poured two glasses of white wine and brought out a platter of cheese, salmon and crackers, too. Brad was waiting for her, leaning against the bottom of the couch. She set the tray between them.

"Salmon. Perfect. I was starving."

He picked up a piece of the pink fillet with his fingers and popped in into his mouth. Wendy started to cut cheese for the crackers, but was interrupted when she realized that Brad was dangling a piece of salmon in front of her mouth. She licked it from his fingers, her tongue sensually bathing his fingertips. He flashed her a crooked smile. Blushing, she turned back to the cheese again.

"Oh, Wendy," he murmured. His eyes studied her intently. She had never imagined she could feel such a rush of warmth, just from the way a man looked at her.

When she handed him a cracker with cheese, her fingers were trembling.

He slipped an arm around her while they ate and sipped wine. Although their conversation was casual, Brad never passed the opportunity to add a few sexual innuendos. Every time he sipped his wine or nibbled on a morsel of food, he somehow intimated how the mouth could be used effectively on flesh. He promised to demonstrate.

"Brad!" Wendy protested at last. She was laughing, amazed at what words and looks could imply. But then again, he was touching her, too. His arm was around her shoulder and his hand dangled idly over her breast, his fingertips teasing her nipple. His whisper fell against her hair, her throat, her ear.

"What?" he asked innocently.

"You're making me crazy!"

His gaze was lazy, his tone sultry. His tawny lashes lay half-closed as he looked at her. "Why? I'm not going anywhere, you're not going anywhere." He paused for a moment, suddenly becoming serious. "I didn't mean to be so selfish. I just—I just couldn't wait anymore."

"Selfish?" Wendy echoed blankly.

He kissed her forehead. "Yes."

"But you weren't—"

"I intend to make up for it."

"Brad—"

"Cracker?" He slipped one in her mouth.

Wendy chewed it, watching him gravely. "Brad, I know that you're not married. But what you said about Leif…well, you were right. It wouldn't be fair to anyone if I tried to find a substitute for him. And maybe I did want to do that at first. But you'd never stand for that." For a moment her voice trailed. "I know you don't have a wife, but I really don't want to be a stand-in, either. Your lover, just because of this 'convenient situation.'"

He lifted her chin and kissed her lips lightly. "There's no one special in my life, Wendy. Honestly. Just you." He didn't release her but kept studying her eyes. "Wendy, what happened? To your husband—to Eric's wife?"

Wendy inhaled sharply. She wanted to wrench

away from him and crawl into the darkness. His words brought the past rushing in on her and despite the healing effect of time, the wounds of the past still hurt.

"They were killed."

"I know that. How did it happen?"

She shrugged. "We—we were having a party at Eric's. It was his and Jennifer's third wedding anniversary. Jennifer was partial to a certain burgundy, so as a surprise, Eric and I had ordered some from a friend who owns a liquor store."

She paused, swallowing. She hated remembering that night. Hated it. The last time she had seen her husband and her sister-in-law, they had both been laughing. The four of them had been so close, she and Jennifer, Leif and Eric.

She told Brad about how stunning Jennifer had looked in her white dress. Her honeyed skin had posed a striking contrast, as had her waist-length, jet black hair. She'd been so happy, and so in love. Leif had also been clad in white, a white dinner jacket. The shirt he wore beneath it had almost matched the unusual shade of his eyes.

At the last minute, the friend who owned the liquor store in Fort Lauderdale had been detained at the shop. Wendy had been cooking, since she had ordered Jennifer not to do a thing for the party. Eric had been trying to help Wendy with the outside grill.

And so Leif and Jennifer had gone together to pick up her present. Jen had been so pleased with the gift, the picture of giddy innocence in white. The two of them had left, arm in arm.

"They walked right into an armed holdup," Wendy explained. "The owner of the store was already dead.

When one of the robbers slapped Jennifer to the ground and aimed the gun her way, Leif sprang upon him. He strangled the assailant with his bare hands, trying to buy Jennifer some time. But there were four robbers, and Leif was unarmed. As she turned to flee, Jennifer was caught."

Later the police told Wendy that the first shot had killed Leif instantly, piercing his heart.

They'd shot Jennifer three times. She had suffered slowly, bleeding to death.

I shouldn't have asked, Brad thought. He shouldn't have done this to her. And yet the story went on as Wendy continued in a strange monotone.

She and Eric had had to visit the morgue to identify the bodies—the hollow shells of Jennifer and Leif.

"And all I could remember was the blood. So much blood, staining the beautiful innocence of their white clothing. So very, very much blood." Wendy swallowed down her wine in a gulp.

Brad saw that her eyes were wide and unseeing. He understood why she had hidden herself here in the swamp for so long. And this certainly explained the closeness between Wendy and Eric.

But she had reached out, leaving the past behind. She had wanted him.

And now, he saw, they'd lost that special warmth. Wendy was shivering now, reaching for her clothes, ashamed of the way that she sat with him. She set her glass down. "I'm going to take a shower." She stood up. Brad reached for her, trying to catch her fingers.

"Wendy, wait—"

"Damn you, Brad! Leave me alone!" She ran down the hallway.

He sat back, brooding in defeat. He couldn't let her retreat to the past she had begun to leave behind.

Brad picked up the remnants of their meal and brought them to the kitchen. Deep in thought, he stared down the long hallway. Despite her denials, he knew that Wendy was trapped in the past, haunted by the memory of her husband. He couldn't let her wallow in that misery.

The shower was still spraying loudly when Brad strode into the bathroom and ripped open the shower curtain. With a bar of soap in her hand and her hair plastered over her face, Wendy turned to him. "Brad, damn you, leave me alone! Don't you understand—"

She gasped as he stepped into the shower. The water hit his hair and his back but he seemed not to feel it as he stared down at her.

"Brad, get out of here!"

"No, I don't think so, Wendy." Her skin was wet and slick and fragrant with the clean scent of soap. The shower water slid over them as he slipped his arms around her waist.

She twisted away from him. Tears stung her silver eyes. "You made me remember! Can't you understand—"

"I'm sorry. Yes, I made you remember the past. But now I'm going to help you forget." He planted a kiss on her neck. "Come on, Wendy. Let's wipe the slate clean."

Her eyes narrowed in amazement and fury. "Well, now, McKenna," she spat out, "you can damn well guarantee that I'll be thinking of him."

"Oh, no, Wendy," Brad assured her with confidence. "I can damn well guarantee that you won't."

Holding her squirming form in his arms, he kissed

her with his mouth and his teeth and his tongue. He clung to her naked, dripping body with his left hand, while using his right to explore and caress her. He followed the pattern of her spine, kneading her buttocks. Tracing the curve of her hips, he found the soft apex of her legs and gently explored the feminine flesh there, seeking and finding the soft button of greatest pleasure.

Overcome by sensation, she went limp against him.

Then her body tautened. Her lips parted willingly to his, her tongue met and mated with his. Rising up on her toes, she buried her head against his shoulder. He leaned to whisper against her ear. "Everywhere I touch you, I will love you."

The water was hot as it pelted their skin. With the drive of the water against his back, Brad tasted her lips again. Then he cast her into a sea of trembling as he slowly, determinedly, kissed her breasts, taking his sweet time, his sweet pleasure. Bracing herself against his shoulder, she whispered his name, and then moaned in ecstasy.

As he lowered himself against her, she could feel the texture of his wet body against hers. Beneath the cascade of the shower, he knelt, gripped her buttocks firmly and buried himself against her.

Fire swept through her loins as she trembled fiercely and fought to hold on to his shoulders. The sensations were so overpowering that she could barely think. All she could do was feel and arch and undulate and burn.

"Brad!" She tore at his hair. He knew no mercy. "Please, really, I'm collapsing."

Her words had no impact. Breathlessly, barely able to form a coherent sentence, she continued. "Please! I'll fall against the tile. I'll die of a concussion."

Finally her words reached him. He rose, wet and gloriously handsome.

He did turn off the water.

But that was the only concession he gave the shower, or their drenched state. He swept her off her feet, dripping and naked, and carried her into the bedroom.

When she was safely nestlcd upon the bed, he continued his assault. She tossed her head and cried out his name. And he reminded her that she could not fall, for she already lay before him.

In seconds she soared to a volatile climax, and then he climbed atop her, parting her thighs to slide inside her. Exhausted and spent, she whispered that she could not go any further.

But he provcd that she could. He touched her, inside and outside, and she felt the heat kindle inside of her again. He was the match to set her aflame. She ached again, she wanted again.

And she burst with the sweetness of it, once again.

She fell asleep in his arms, exhausted.

Brad lay awake for a long while, stroking her hair. Listening to the velvety sounds of the night, he felt the peace of the swamp surround him.

9

Brad woke late. The sun was high in the sky when he opened his eyes. But then, it had been very late when they'd gone to sleep. Wendy was still sleeping.

She was curled halfway upon his chest, her hair a teasing cloud fanned over his shoulders. He carefully shifted her head to the pillow, then he watched her as she lay there. Her skin was as smooth as honey and cream against the sheets, and he was tempted to touch her all over again. She looked somewhat like an angel, he thought, a tender smile curving his lips. It was the color of her hair, he knew, and the classic lines of her face that reminded him of a heavenly spirit. And also, perhaps, her inner purity, her essence, that had warned him that Wendy was someone special, someone unique. A woman not to be taken lightly.

A woman to whom a man could lose his heart.

Warmth invaded his system again. No angel last night, he mused, but a siren, a tempest, stirring him up, beguiling him. Of course, he had wanted her. He had wanted her from the start. They'd been destined to come together. But it was wrong. He didn't belong here. He would have to leave, return to his own life in a world miles away from this marshy refuge. He swallowed fiercely, remembering his partner who now lay dead. Wendy did not belong in his life. He did not belong in hers.

She opened her eyes slowly, her dark lashes blinking over soft silver-and-gray eyes. At first she studied him with a misted confusion, then she smiled with a soft, almost shy welcome.

She yawned and shifted, and the dusky crest of her nipple became visible to him. He groaned inwardly. It was his fault. She had just wanted to be held; she had wanted a figure in the darkness, a man to hold. He had insisted on knowing her. He had wanted her to know him, to make love with him, and not with some forgotten dream.

Yes, he had wanted to know her. He had wanted it to be slow and careful, a union that mattered. But now the mere sight of her smile sent him plummeting into a downward swirl that gripped his loins and his heart in a painful vise. He should be running for his sanity.

Yet he could not leave her. He didn't know how much time they had in this strange Eden, but while it lasted, they were entwined, and he could not give that up.

She reached out and stroked his cheek, running her fingers slowly down his torso. She paused at his waist, drawing circles idly with her fingers, then her hand curved seductively and plunged lower as her fingers locked around him. She edged toward him. The tip of her tongue played over his chest.

Spasms of desire stabbed him like a white-hot lead. He leaned over and kissed her.

This was no angel, he thought as he lifted her above him. Her hair fell in golden sheets over her rosy breasts.

She was as beautiful as an angel, but she moved with an ancient, earthy wisdom. And she gave herself to him, completely.

"Wendy..."

He pulled her down. Hers was the kiss of a total temptress, a seductress who made love with her body, her soul and her heart. Soon, Brad forgot that there was a world beyond them. All that mattered was the steaming crest they rode, in a writhing glory of kisses and whispers and slick, entangled limbs.

When it was over, she smiled at him. So sweetly. An angel again. She curled up just like a kitten and fell asleep against his chest.

Later, Wendy reflected that it was one of the best days of her life. She'd never known what it was like to have so much fun doing so very little.

She was more of a sleeper than Brad. She woke again to the scent of sausage. He was lingering in the doorway, naked, a tray of food in his hands, a wild orchid held in his teeth. When she laughed, he nearly dropped the tray. Instead, he deposited it on the floor to leap on top of her, mercilessly tickling her and demanding that she show more respect.

She laughed all through the meal.

When breakfast was over Brad turned on the news, but there was nothing reported about the case. Then an old-time mystery came on, and they watched the show, lazily entwined. An hour or so later, Wendy decided she wanted a shower. Brad decided to shower with her, and they made love once again, with Brad promising Wendy that he could do so in the shower without killing her or causing a serious concussion. She laughed until she cried out with the ecstasy of it, until she was breathless and spent, until his gold-and-amber eyes locked with hers and the world went still.

They sat in the living room and pored through her music collection. He told her grimly that his home had been destroyed, and Wendy was painfully reminded that Brad was a stranger here, that he belonged elsewhere. She told him that he was welcome to begin a new collection with some of her old albums. He shook his head with a rueful smile, then reached out and stroked her golden hair. He whispered that she was incredible, and then he kissed her and made love to her again.

Wendy prepared stuffed Cornish game hens for dinner, and despite the fact that Brad kept pulling her out to the living room to dance to some old treasure that he had found, she managed to put the meal together rather well. Baby made an appearance at the door soon after. After consuming a hefty slab of raw beef, the panther settled down at the foot of the couch.

Later on, Brad led Baby back outside. He didn't want that much company tonight.

When Wendy locked up for the night, Brad was waiting for her in the darkened hallway. He kissed her there, lifted her into his arms and carried her off to bed. They made love again, before drifting into a deep and peaceful sleep.

The next morning, when Wendy awoke, Brad was no longer with her. Worriedly, she jumped out of bed, wrapped the sheets around herself and hurried down the hallway. Finding the house empty, she opened the front door and breathed a sigh of relief. He was there. Baby had come prowling home. Brad was petting the panther's head as he stared out over the swampland, watching as morning burst upon it.

The sun was radiant, glittering in diamonds upon the water. The sound of silence was awesome, until some distant gator let out a grunt—very much like that of a pig, Wendy had always thought—and a mockingbird let out a screeching call.

He was wearing a pair of Leif's faded jeans, along with a Seminole cotton shirt, richly colored in deep blues and crimsons. Mary Hawk had made it for her grandson, as a Christmas present one year. Wendy bit her lower lip, remembering how tenderly Leif had thanked his grandmother. Leif had always shown Willie and Mary deep devotion and respect. That was one of the things that had always made her love her life here, despite the fact that her in-laws were so near. The members of the Hawk family cared for one another. They knew an ancient courtesy and a tender wisdom.

But Brad shared some of those qualities. She had been in a flying fury the other night when she had found him—she had been so worried by then. And it had taken her a while to realize that Willie—that sly old fox!—had been determined to find Brad, introduce himself in his unique way and make his own assessment.

And it seemed that Willie had judged Brad well. Brad had been a natural in Willie's small village. Willie was an old man who liked the old way of life, and many of the younger people, too, were now trying to maintain tribal traditions. Brad hadn't made judgments. He had fitted right in.

A sledgehammer suddenly seemed to slam against her heart as she watched him. She truly admired Brad McKenna. It was difficult to believe that it had not quite been a week since she had met him. And yet it was all too easy to remember that first night, to remember removing his muddy clothing and thinking with inner tremors that he was really beautifully built, powerfully male. She had admired him then; there was no denying the way she'd been drawn to him. Perhaps her loneliness had contributed to the attraction. But since then she had discovered so much more to respect, so very much to like.

And he was going to leave. He'd warned her not to care too deeply; he'd warned her that he would never marry.

And she had assured him, and herself, that it didn't matter.

But it did, now. It mattered so much.

It was easy to live with him, easy to adjust to the extra damp towel in the bathroom, his coffee cup in the sink. It was easy to share things with him—meals and laughter and conversation—and most of all, it was easy to sleep beside him, held tight in his arms.

Don't fall in love...

I'm not in love, Wendy assured herself. As an independent woman, she had opted for this. When he walked away, she'd hold her head high.

And it would be all for the best, wouldn't it? she demanded silently to herself. If she had ever thought that he could stay, she had been living in a fantasy.

Suddenly she found it difficult to breathe. Horrid images flooded her mind as she remembered the violence that had made her a widow. Leif had stumbled upon that violence. Brad made a living at it.

If she and Brad were to fall helplessly in love, it would still be a dead-end relationship. She wouldn't be able to bear it. Every morning when he left for work, her palms would sweat and then she'd begin to tremble...

Brad turned around suddenly, as if he sensed her thoughts. She wanted to raise a hand in cheery greeting; she wanted to smile. She couldn't. Something in his somber gaze warned her that he had been having similar thoughts. Those thoughts were causing harsh lines to become ingrained upon his features. In silence, she merely held the sheet closer to her as a soft breeze whispered against her flesh. Then she returned to the house.

When she had showered and dressed, Brad was in the kitchen. He had made coffee, scrambled eggs and toast. Solemnly, he sipped his coffee.

"Thank you, that looks delicious," Wendy said. She slid onto a stool and tried to take a bite of the eggs. Unfortunately they stuck in her throat. She set her fork down and swallowed some orange juice.

"I need to go back to the gas station and make a phone call," he said.

She put her fork down. "I'll take you in. I need my car anyway. I want to drive into the city and buy some groceries and things." She stood and picked up her plate to take into the kitchen. She couldn't even pretend to eat.

Brad leaned across the table and caught her wrist. She paused, looking down at him. "Wendy, I don't think I should stay any longer."

She forced herself to shrug, pulling at her wrist. "Whatever you think."

"Wendy—"

"Brad, do whatever you think is best."

He stood in annoyance, taking the plate from her hands and setting it on the counter. His eyes burned a passionate gold, and his face was strained and tense. "Don't. Don't do that to you, or to me."

"Don't do what?" she demanded, trying to retain the coolness of her first words. She wanted to remain aloof and above it all.

"Don't pretend that it doesn't matter!" He was nearly shouting. She couldn't quite meet his gaze, but she managed to speak with extreme impatience. "Pretend what, McKenna? You're the one who made the big deal out of this. 'Let's get to know one another.' You're the one—"

"Wendy, I care about you, you little idiot. You just weren't made for one-night stands—"

"Why not, if I so chose? Damn you, I made a decision." Both their tempers were rising. Although Wendy was trying to hide her emotions, they spilled from her. Anger seemed the only way to combat them. She so desperately wanted to hold on to her pretense of sophisticated distance. But sarcasm entered her voice, a sharp, sharp edge that rang out like a call of battle.

"I made a decision, Brad!" she repeated. "That first night. Yeah, it's been a while. I took one look and decided, an attractive guy. Just what I need—a little uncomplicated sex. When you warned me not to care too much, it seemed so perfect. A mature, adult relationship…a consenting man, a consenting woman—"

"Wendy, stop it! We both know—"

"We don't know anything! What is your problem? If you want to leave—leave! There's nothing keeping you here! You are the last person I want as a permanent fixture in my life. My God, you kill people for a living—"

"That's not true!"

"Your partner was just killed, for God's sake!"

"Yes! And planes crash, and trucks kill people crossing the road."

"But you ask for it!"

"Wendy, other than target practice, I think I've actually fired my gun three times in almost ten years."

She backed away from him, her hands on her hips. "Why are you trying to convince me—"

"You're making it sound like I'm some kind of contract killer!" Two steps brought him back to her. He gripped her shoulders, staring furiously down at her. "I try to keep crack off the streets, Wendy, that's what I do. I try to keep drugs from high-school kids. And I try even harder to keep them out of the grade schools. Ever see a twenty-year-old dead on a cocaine mix? Or a kid in junior high with needle tracks on his arm? It doesn't do any good to arrest that poor kid—you can only pray that he kicks the habit. You have to get guys like Michaelson. The guys who orchestrate the big deals—and make big bucks on the drugs."

The heat that emanated between them seemed to crackle like dry lightning. "Fine, Brad. You go after the Michaelsons in the world, and quit worrying about me! I've gotten what I wanted from you—"

"What?"

His tone was so sharp that she paused for the fraction of a moment. She was trembling, rocked by fury and fear. The truth had descended upon her like a falling weight. She was falling in love; she *had* fallen in love. But she could never use that to hold on to Brad.

"I said, I've gotten what I wanted—"

"Sex?"

"That's right."

He stared at her incredulously. "Just sex?" His temper was roiling and boiling, but it didn't change the way he felt about her. He still wanted her. He had desired her when she laughed, and when she stared at him with tender, sultry eyes. And now, despite the way she lifted her chin and scowled at him with cool, complete disdain, he still wanted her.

Her cool facade was a hoax. He could swear that it was all a lie. Brad wanted to rant and rave; she could evoke such extreme reactions in him! But he didn't. Even while a hot, soaring pulse took hold of him, he forced himself to smile lazily. He wanted so much from her, and he was desperately afraid that this fantasy would end. Couldn't he touch her soul? Couldn't he reach her heart? He had to find out.

"Just sex, huh? Is that it, Wendy? You took one look at me and decided that I'd do for a fling?"

Something in his tone warned her. "Brad—"

Fiercely, he pulled her into his arms. His kiss was sweet and savage; his hands moved in torment.

Although she wanted to lash out at him, she was losing the desire to fight. His lips nearly bruised hers; his tongue ravaged her mouth. His body was white hot, fevered. The anger, the tempest, the sudden blinding need exploded from him and filled her. A surge of urgent longing seized her, spiraling into her loins. She knew she should twist away from his kiss, but she could not. Instead, she pressed more closely to him. And with the desperate, lingering assault of each kiss, the idea of protest faded from her mind. Instinctively, her fingers curled into his hair. They played over his neck and raked his back. She felt his hands beneath her shirt, freeing her breasts from her bra, stroking them.

He unsnapped her jeans, then slid his fingers beneath the waistband, searching for her most sensitive area. She wrenched his shirt from his pants, touching his bare back, moaning softly.

Somehow, together, they lowered themselves to the floor. For a moment she was a tangle of clothing, and then she was naked. She prayed that he would come to her swiftly, that he would assuage the yearning, the desperate longing.

He did not. With a feverish pitch, Brad made love to her more thoroughly than he ever had before. She whispered to him, pleading and crying out…begging him. But still he explored her, finding new erogenous zones, leaving no sweet inch of bare and vulnerable flesh unaware of his touch, of his kiss.

When he came to her at last, it was instantly explosive, but he did not let it lie at that. He moved while she lay limp, until he roused her again. Then her cry mingled upon the air with his, as they soared above the earth.

Their descent was slow and leisurely. Time had no meaning for Wendy when she was locked in Brad's warm embrace.

"Wendy, I know it's—"

He broke off, and they both jumped at the sound of a tapping against the door.

"Dammit!" Brad swore, casting her a quick, angry glance as he moved to the window. "I am slipping to hell since I've met you!"

"Wendy? Brad? Anyone home?"

Although Brad relaxed at the sound of Eric's voice, Wendy was overcome by a sudden panic. She knew that Eric liked Brad. But still, a terrible feeling of guilt swept over her, dark and poignant. Like a high-school girl caught necking in the car, she scrambled for her clothing.

Brad watched as she stumbled quickly into her clothes.

She was such an enigma to him, this sultry, silver-eyed angel. After all, she had claimed that she wanted sex only. She had hurt him with her callous words. But what else could she have said to him? *I understand, please do go, we are getting too involved. Yes, you're right, please do get out of my life before I fall irrevocably in love with you.*

"Would you please get dressed!" Wendy whispered hoarsely.

He looked at her as if he were weighing her words for a moment, then he shook his head and pulled on his jeans. Wendy had barely tucked her blouse into her jeans before he smiled with sarcastic sweetness and strode over to open the door. His shirt hung open, and his feet were bare.

"Hi, Eric," he said, opening the door.

Eric hesitated in the doorway, looking from Brad to Wendy. Eric's emotions were always almost impossible to read. Wendy unwittingly put a hand to her hair, trying to smooth back the wild disarray. Eric glanced at Brad. "Bad timing. I'm sorry."

"Don't be ridiculous—" Wendy began.

"The timing is just fine," Brad interrupted her. "In fact, it's good to see you. We were heading off to the garage to use the phone in a few minutes. Come on in."

Sensing the tension, Eric offered Wendy a curious frown. She smiled at him as innocently as she could. "Want some coffee, Eric? Ice tea, a beer?"

"I'll have some coffee, thanks."

Eric noticed their breakfast plates, barely touched.

Wendy was relieved that he made no comment, but accepted a cup of coffee and turned to Brad. "Willie enjoyed taking off with you, you know. He did give Wendy quite a scare, but he enjoyed having you so much that it was worth it, I think."

Brad told Eric that he had enjoyed meeting his family. When the two men moved into the living room Wendy exhaled, relieved. She picked up the breakfast plates and mournfully realized that they seemed to have a serious problem with breakfast. No matter who made it for whom, the meal had a tendency of winding up in the garbage.

What are we going to do? she wondered in a fleeting panic. Then she realized that she had no choice. Their future was in Brad's hands. Whenever he left, it was over.

A glance over the counter told her that the men were still engrossed in a discussion. Retreating to the bathroom, she brushed out her hair and splashed cool water over her face. As she stared at the reflection of her own wide, silver-gray eyes, she was certain that they wore a telltale glaze, the glow of a woman in love.

"Wendy!"

Brad's voice came to her like a roar. She was sure Baby had never sounded more menacing. The sound of it irritated her, and she gritted her teeth.

When she squared her shoulders and strode out to the living room, her hands on her hips and her brows arched in an irate query, she discovered that Eric was staring at her the same way Brad was—as if she were a child.

"What?" she snapped. They exchanged glances with one another.

"Eric said that he gave you a message for me. About strangers in the swamp—possibly here to hunt me down."

She hesitated, feeling mortified that she could have

forgotten such an important warning. But first, she had come home to find him missing. Then they had spent the evening in the village with Willie and Mary and the family, and then when they had come back...

She shook her head. "I—I forgot."

"You what?" Brad said, his eyes narrowing.

"Wendy, it was important," Eric said mildly.

"I'm sorry."

"Sorry!" Brad looked as if he were about to go through the roof. He spun around, hands on his hips, his head lowered, as he fought to control his temper.

But she didn't think that he was so angry about the omission. Even a minor problem would test the limits of his temper right now. Because nothing had been settled between them, nothing at all.

He turned around again, looking at Eric. "You think they've got seaplanes coming in to the swamp? Near here?"

Eric nodded.

Brad shook his head. "That's why we were here, trying to infiltrate his organization. We knew he was securing his stuff out of Colombia, but we could never get a fix on the checkpoints. I knew that he was up to something out here. We were trying to trap him...that's when I wound up out here." He glanced Wendy's way. His eyes were dark, unreadable. His gaze lingered upon her, then he returned his attention to Eric. "But I don't understand how our agents haven't caught him if he's still operating here."

Eric interrupted him with a soft laugh. "Brad, you're not considering the size of the swamp. The grasslands go on forever. There are endless miles of marshes, deep canals and high, dry hammocks with pine trees. There are also lakes, large lakes, with plenty of room for a small seaplane bearing millions of dollars worth of white gold to land."

"So Michaelson's got a drop spot near here," Brad said, calculating. "I've got to find it." Tension constricted his muscles as he studied Eric appraisingly.

"Oh, no!" Wendy swore suddenly. "McKenna, you royal son of a bitch! You haven't the sense to hide out from a man who has one purpose in life besides the pursuit of money—killing you! And if you think that you're going to take my brother-in-law—"

"Wendy!" Eric stopped her furiously.

"No!" Tears stung her eyes. "You idiots! Eric, it would kill your grandfather if something were to happen to you! And, Brad, damn you, I know your boss didn't hire you to act stupid! To foolishly get yourself killed—"

"Wendy, stop it!" Eric insisted. He reached for her, but she twisted away. "Wendy, I prowled the jungles of Asia. If I'd been killed, Grandfather would have understood."

"We're not going anywhere or doing anything," Brad murmured. He paused. "But I told you this morning, Wendy. I don't think that this is safe for you anymore."

She didn't believe them. She was convinced that Eric intended to take Brad deep into the swamps, deep into all the villages to meet with his friends, Seminoles, Miccosukees and the whites who made their homes out there. Michaelson was hunting him, and Wendy realized that Brad was growing tired of it. He was ready to hunt Michaelson instead.

"Well, maybe leaving here is the best thing for you," Wendy said softly. Then she went back to her bedroom and snatched her purse and the airboat keys that sat on her dresser.

Brad was in the hallway when she emerged. He still looked angry, but not as angry as she was becoming.

"Get out of my way."

"Wendy, you have to understand. We have to talk."

"Talk? No, I don't think so. I don't want to talk, Brad. I want to get out of here. I want to go talk to some store clerks and salespeople—maybe a bartender or two. Someone who doesn't make a living at violence!"

"Wendy, I told you—"

"Yeah, yeah, yeah, you never draw your gun. I found you with a bullet hole in your forehead. That's what it was, right, Brad? A bullet hole. And you're ready to leave, right?" Tears were as hot as molten lead behind her eyelids, and she was afraid that she would shortly grow hysterical and throw her arms around his legs and tell him that she couldn't bear it, she couldn't let him go anywhere, she couldn't let him go away and get himself killed. She was in love with him.

But she was the fool; she was the one losing control. Brad could handle this. He had warned her that he couldn't love her. He had warned that he had to leave.

"Wendy—"

"No!" She shoved past him. "Eric will take you to the gas station. I'm sure that he and Mac will see that you make your phone call—and that you're able to get wherever you want to go."

The tears were about to spill over. Blindly, she spun around. "Goodbye, Brad."

Not wanting to break down in front of him, Wendy ran out of the house to her airboat. Eric would understand, she thought. Eric would see that Brad got wherever he wanted to go.

She doubled over, listening to the drone of the motor, barely seeing the grasses that dipped and swayed as she passed them, barely aware of the wind that dried her tears.

He had been safe. He had been safe at her house—surely, no one would have found him there. But he couldn't stay put, he just didn't have the patience to keep hiding out.

He was gone. He was out of her life. She had claimed that she had gotten all that she wanted, and he was gone now.

No, he wasn't gone—not when she could close her eyes and feel him with her still. The subtle scent of him lingered against her skin. She could imagine his touch in each lilting breeze. She could remember his laughter, his tenderness, his raging passions.

She would never forget his golden eyes and his soft words. There had been so very much between them.

But no amount of passion could deny the disparity between their chosen lives. He wasn't a killer. She knew that. She understood his job. And she understood that he could have no room for her in his life, while she couldn't bear to live with a man in his profession.

She scarcely knew him, she tried to tell herself.

But it didn't matter. Imagining a future without him now seemed as cold and austere as an arctic plain.

10

L. Davis Purdy had been silent on his end of the phone for so long that Brad began to think that they had been disconnected. When he answered at last, he chose his words carefully.

"What do you know?" he asked Brad.

"What do I know—for fact? Very little. Except that I have a—a friend—" He paused, looking out the window. Eric Hawk was leaning against the building, listening to old Mac go on while he waited for Brad to finish the call. Eric wore a low-brimmed hat, jeans, a denim shirt and cowboy boots. His jet hair fell over the collar of the shirt, but even with the brim of the hat covering his eyes, there was an air of quiet confidence about the man. Yeah, Brad decided. If Eric Hawk had said that something was going on, then it was going on. Hawk would make a good partner. More so than many men Brad had worked with, he felt as if he could trust the Indian with his life.

He cleared his throat and continued. "I have a friend who knows this place like the back of his hand. He says that the deal is going down in the swamp, and I believe him. Michaelson is out here. He's waiting for the next drop, and it's going to happen here. I'm sure he's still looking for me, too, but money means more to him than revenge."

Brad vaguely heard Purdy warn him to investigate, but not to make any moves without checking in. Somberly reminding Brad of his partner's death, Purdy admonished him to be careful. Brad clenched his teeth in anguish, reliving that moment. But then as Purdy's voice went on about procedure, Brad's mind wandered.

He had meant to leave today, to go back to the city, to do it by the book, live under constant guard until they could do something about Michaelson. He'd meant to leave Wendy, to get out of her life. To leave her safe and alone. To leave her, before…

Before they fell in love.

She had told him to go ahead and leave. When she'd stormed out of the house, she hadn't even looked back. She wouldn't expect him to be there. Maybe he shouldn't be there, maybe he should stay with Eric. But he wasn't leaving. Purdy had agreed that Brad was better off staying in the swamp—especially since his agents were getting closer to Michaelson.

Brad had to talk to Wendy; he had to see her again. They couldn't just leave things the way they had.

He realized that Purdy had finished his lecture, and that he was hanging up. Just in time, Brad made the proper response. Promising to stay in touch, he hung up the phone.

He left the office and came upon Mac and Eric still involved in conversation. "Can't tell me these guys are all here for gator season," Mac insisted. He spat on the ground. "No sirree, I know the hunters when they come. I know the office boys who dress up in khaki and shoot up beer cans and sit around in their skivvies, and I know when I see a horde of people comin' through here that don't belong. They just don't look right. They look like they're still wearing suits, no matter how they try to dress like hunters."

Brad winced. He was sure that half the guys who looked so ridiculous in khaki or denim were either FBI or his own associates from the DEA office. But all the telltale signs were evident. The swamp was crawling with men—bad guys and good guys. Brad hoped to God he would know the difference when he came across someone.

"Well, if anyone asks, remember—you've never seen this man," Eric instructed Mac.

The old man grinned at Brad. "I've seen the news, Eric. I know when to keep quiet."

"Thanks a lot, Mac."

"Nothing to thank me for." He looked at Eric again. "You going to be out on the swamp today?"

"Yeah, I thought maybe we should check out a few of the canals."

"You want me to fill up the cooler?"

Eric laughed. "Sure. Fill her up with some cool brews, and some mullet, if you've got any. And throw in some snacks—cheese balls, corn chips—whatever you've got handy."

Mac loaded the airboat with supplies from his limited stock of grocery items. When they stepped back into the airboat, Eric suggested that Brad pilot the vehicle. Within a few minutes, Brad had more or less mastered the craft, and he loved it. Eric grinned tolerantly as Brad let out a whoop and raced pell-mell across the open water.

When Eric warned him that they were coming into a narrower channel, Brad cut the speed and Eric took over.

They spent the morning traversing a myriad of hammocks. They came upon a few isolated Indian villages and a few deserted shacks that weekend hunters had built but didn't really own because the state had taken over the land. Although they didn't run into any hunters, they did discover one shack that had been recently inhabited by someone who smoked expensive cigars and drank high-grade brandy.

Setting an empty bottle back on the rough table, Eric arched a brow. "Michaelson?"

Brad nodded slowly. "Maybe. Though I can't see Michaelson coming this deep into the swamp. He's a city boy all the way. He likes his conveniences—brushes his teeth with mineral water. But it might be a couple of his boys, copying his habits."

"We'll wait it out a while, see if they come back," Eric said.

They waited on the airboat, hidden behind a pine hammock a few yards from the rustic cabin. Eric broke out the beer and a bag of potato chips. After casting fishing lines into the water, they both leaned back.

Brad took a long look at Eric. "Thanks. I realize I'm taking up a lot of your time."

Eric shrugged. "I don't live a nine-to-five life. I use my time when and where I think it's important."

It was hot and humid as a summer day in Hades. Brad swallowed down half a can of beer, then shook his head. "Still, I appreciate what you're doing."

"Sure thing."

As the strange silence of the swamp surrounded

them, Brad realized that it wasn't silent at all. He could hear the buzz of insects, the chirp of birds and the rustling sound of the breeze. When he heard a grunting noise, he knew it was the sound of a distant gator.

"She's right, you know," he said.

"Wendy?" Eric grinned.

"Yeah. I have no right dragging you into this."

Eric swore. "Look, I'm here because I want to be, all right? This is my land those bastards are screwing up. My territory. I'll deal with Wendy."

Brad nodded, enthralled by the sight of a long-legged crane that stepped delicately over a patch of marshland. He finished his beer, and Eric tossed him another.

Brad nodded at Eric. "Wendy told me what happened. To her husband—and your wife. I'm sorry."

Eric's muscles tightened as he swallowed. "Thanks. It was a long time ago. I guess we've dealt with it differently, Wendy and I. I spent months alone, then I went wild. Eventually, I settled down, finding peace in this land, getting support from my family. Wendy has just stayed home—alone." He hesitated. "I wanted to find those guys myself. I wanted to bring them out here and kill them my way." He looked across the water. "I did find the one guy in the end. I managed to turn him over to the cops. Then I knew that I could go on. Wendy, well, Wendy never had the same satisfaction, but she goes on. I think you've been good for her. Damned good for her." He shrugged, managing to smile again. "So, I may have a bit of an argument on my hands. But, come to think of it, you're going to have more to explain to Wendy than I will."

Brad looked back at Eric. "I—I don't know if I should even go back there."

Eric appeared amused. "She doesn't bite. Or does she? Whoops, wait a minute, none of my business."

"You sure about that?" Brad grinned.

"About what?"

"It being none of your business."

"All right. It is my business. But only in the sense that I care about her happiness."

"So what do you think I should do?"

Eric shrugged. "What do you want to do?"

"You heard her this morning," Brad said huskily. "I don't think that she wants me around."

"I'm willing to bet that she'll open that door for you if you go back to her."

"She thinks I'm a killer."

"She knows you aren't a killer. She's scared, and in defense she's lashing out with accusations. She has a right to be scared. She's been hurt before. She's had her heart and soul severed. Tolerate her."

Brad laughed. It was so much more than a matter of tolerating a nervous streak! "I don't know, I have no promises for her."

"No one really has promises these days. I think you owe each other more of your time. While you've got it, you owe it to one another."

"Maybe."

Eric grinned suddenly. "Grandfather has a great saying for any dilemma. He says that life is a river, and we chart out that river with our hearts, our minds and our souls. When it matters most, he says, the heart should be the guide. The mind is made of logic, the soul is saddled with pride. Only the heart has no logic, and only the heart can bypass pride. You're welcome to come back home with me tonight. Or else I'll take you back to Wendy's. You decide. Just let me know."

"Yeah, I will," Brad answered, though it was only a pretense that he needed to make a decision. They both knew where Brad was going for the night.

"Hey!" Eric cried suddenly.

"What?" Brad set down his beer can.

"I've got a bite on my line!"

"Oh," Brad said in relief. Then he laughed. "Oh."

Eric looked up at him, realizing that Brad had thought someone was near them, stalking them. He grimaced. "Sorry." Then his line plunged, and he rose to battle it out with the fish. But it was too late. The fish had cleverly slipped off the hook.

"You made me lose him," Eric complained.

"I made you lose him?" Brad protested.

Amid an easy chorus of laughter Brad took out two new cans of beer, and they settled down to wait again.

Dusk came, illuminating the canals in shades of gold and red and mauve. The white cranes on the water seemed to be bathed in pink. Then darkness fell, nearly complete.

"I don't think that anyone is coming back here today," Eric said.

Brad shook his head. He could barely see Eric in the darkness, but his eyes were starting to adjust to it. "They've got something going here, though, I'm sure. Maybe every third day or so. How the hell did they ever find this place?"

"Airboat. There are shacks all over the Glades. Somebody found it to be a convenient spot. Maybe they're gone for good, maybe they'll come back. We can check it out again tomorrow."

Brad nodded. "Thanks."

"Quit that, will you?" Eric charged him. "I told you—this is my territory your man Michaelson is messing with." Eric started the boat motor, and they began to sluice through the canals, the headlight on the airboat their only illumination except for the stars above. There was barely a sliver of a moon that night.

Although he still hadn't said anything to Eric, Brad realized that they were heading for Wendy's house.

But as they came upon Wendy's, Eric quickly cut the motor. The house was too empty; it was too dark.

"We'll go around to the marshy side where there's more saw grass to hide us," Eric whispered.

As Eric secured the airboat, Brad stepped off into deep muck that pulled at his borrowed shoes. He hurried through the marsh until he reached dry land. Eric joined him shortly, moving more easily in his high boots.

"She isn't here!" Brad said tensely.

"Well, maybe—"

"It doesn't take that long to go shopping!" Brad insisted. Fear clawed at his throat and ravaged his gut. What if Wendy's cabin wasn't hidden deep enough in the swamp? If someone had been biding time in an old wooden shack, couldn't they have also discovered Wendy's handsome home with all the modern conveniences?

He tried to swallow down his fear for her; he tried to think professionally and rationally.

"I'm sure," Eric said very quietly, "that she just hasn't come home yet. She might have gone out to the village. And she might have visited some friends in town. There are any number of things that she could be doing."

Sure, Brad thought. Any number of things. All he knew was that she wasn't nearby, where he could touch her and see her and know that she was safe. "Let's check it out," he said softly.

By instinct, they nodded at one another and stealthily crept around the house in opposite directions, Brad going left, and Eric moving to the right.

Although Brad's instincts told him that there was no one there, he couldn't control the pounding of his heart, the naked fear that Michaelson might have snatched Wendy.

At last he reached the back of the house. He sensed movement, then heard a birdcall. Despite his tension, he smiled. It was Eric. It was a damned good birdcall; a week ago he would have thought that it was real. One week in the swamp had sharpened his senses.

He stepped out around the back. Eric joined him.

"Nothing?" Brad asked him.

Eric shook his head. "Nothing. I don't think anyone has been here since we left earlier today. But come on, we'll check the house."

"Think we really ought to break in?"

"No." Eric grinned. "I have a key."

When they surveyed the house, Brad quickly saw that nothing had been touched since they had left that morning. He expelled a long sigh and sank onto the sofa.

"What if Michaelson grabbed her?" he said out loud. "What if he somehow figured out that she was sheltering me, and he grabbed her out in the swamp?"

"Come on, Brad, she's a big girl. She was upset. Probably wanted to talk to Grandfather, or maybe a friend, as I said." He grinned. "Ordinarily, she would have talked to me, but hell, it looks like I've joined the enemy. That meant she had to find someone else. She's all right. I'm sure of it."

Was he so sure? Brad wondered. Despite his words, Eric was pacing, too.

Then they both froze.

There had been no sound of a motor, no sudden flash of headlights.

But someone was outside now, moving around the house in secrecy and stealth.

They looked at one another and rose quickly. Silently, they headed for the front door. Brad opened it cautiously, then both men paused to look out. There was nothing there. The lawn was covered in a soft glow of light from the house, but the edge of the yard was surrounded by shadow. The high pines to the right seemed like a dark forest where a million demons could dwell— a million Michaelsons.

Eric motioned to Brad, who nodded. They started to retrace their earlier steps, silently circling the house.

When Brad came around the back, he saw the form, dark and huddled low, trying to look in one of the windows. Quickly, silently, Brad began his approach. The figure started to turn, to rise, but he was already upon it.

With impetus in his last step, Brad hurtled himself against the form. A low growl issued from his lips. Then he heard a whoosh of air and a soft scream.

He was on the ground, straddled atop her, before he realized that the figure in the darkness was Wendy. With her wrists pinned to the ground, she looked so frightened and helpless.

"Wendy!"

"Brad!" Her eyes opened wide, and then narrowed. "Brad! You slimy son of a bitch—"

"Well, what a nice reunion!" Eric interrupted brightly. He was leaning comfortably against the wall.

Wendy cast him an evil glare, then turned her furious stare upon Brad once again. "What the hell—"

"Where were you?" he demanded hotly.

"What?" she returned.

"Where were you? Where the hell were you?"

"That isn't any of your—"

"You scared me to death!" Brad shouted.

"*I* scared *you*! You muscle-bound Kong—you attacked me! You're sitting on me. You—" She paused. "Eric! Tell him to get off me."

Eric smiled as he hunkered down on his toes near her head, chewing on a blade of grass. "I'll bet if you just ask him real nice, he'll get up on his own."

The grate of her teeth was audible.

"Dammit, Wendy, where did you go?" Brad insisted.

She exhaled. "This is ridiculous!" Despite her anger, there was a glaze to her eyes, as if she had been crying. Dimly, through the maze of fear and relief and anger, Brad wondered if she had been crying because of him.

Then he wondered what the hell he was doing here, making the situation worse. But wasn't this better? If someone had stumbled onto his trail, they would find Wendy—whether they found him or not. Now she was better off with him than without him. Now they would both be better off not to take any chances at all.

"Wendy!" Nervous energy racked his body. She meant so damned much to him.

"You…" Her teeth grated again as she struggled against his hold. Her eyes grew brighter, as if she were on the verge of tears.

"Not that my whereabouts are any of your business!" she hissed, twisting her head to stare at Eric. "Or yours!"

"I'm just an innocent bystander."

"Could you go stand somewhere else?"

Eric laughed, but he didn't move. Wendy stared from one man to the other—Eric, who seemed to be having the time of his life, and Brad, who still seemed deathly pale in the darkness.

"I went to the damned store!" she spat out.

"All day?" Eric queried politely.

"Where's the airboat?" Brad demanded.

"I have my car!" Wendy snapped. "The boat's across the water. I went into the garage, I talked to Mac. I got my car. I drove into Fort Lauderdale. I went to the drugstore, and I went to the grocery store. You want to know what aisles I perused? I bought a can of Pepsi from a vending machine. I stopped for a copy of the newspaper."

"That still doesn't take all day! Dammit, Wendy, you scared me half to death."

"Well, dammit, Brad, you did the same to me! How the hell do you think it felt to know that someone was in the house?"

"You knew that Eric has a key."

"But neither Eric's car nor his airboat were visible. Why the hell am I explaining this to you?" Wendy exploded. She swallowed, wondering whether to laugh or cry or keep screaming. She was shaking, trembling inside and out because he had come back, because he was still with her.

Grandfather had told her that he would be there. He had smiled and told her to be patient. He had told her to go home and wait, to trust in her heart.

Although she had told Brad to go away, she had prayed that he wouldn't. She had bought groceries for two. In the drugstore she had tried not to indulge in fantasy, but she had bought extra shaving cream and toothpaste and soap…

For two.

Which had been foolish. Eventually, he had to go away.

Eventually, but please, God! Wendy silently prayed, not now. Let us have some time. I need that second damp towel in the bathroom just a little longer.

"You're explaining it to me because you worried me to death!" Brad yelled back at her.

"You're not even supposed to be here!" she reminded him.

Eric cleared his throat. "Maybe we should hassle over the finer points inside." He cleared his throat again. "Brad, er, I think you're about to cut off her circulation at the wrists."

Brad instantly released Wendy's wrists. Then he took her right hand in his own and began to rub it. "Did I hurt you?"

"No," she replied. "Just move, will you please?"

Slowly, he came to his feet, then reached a hand down to her. She took it, eyeing him warily as she stood.

"Did you leave packages in the car?" Eric asked.

She nodded, then smiled sweetly. "Except for the bag that I was carrying. I dropped it in the bushes there when the G-man jumped me."

"Oh, well, no harm done," Eric said, shaking out the tattered brown grocery bag and collecting the canned goods and cereal boxes that had fallen out.

Brad and Wendy were still staring at one another heatedly. Eric shoved the bag into Brad's arms. "Why don't you take this into the house," he suggested. "I'll go for the rest."

"Yeah, thanks," Wendy said. Brad was still staring at her. Rumpled and handsome, his tawny hair was all askew. She brushed by him and headed for the front.

He set the bag down on the kitchen floor. By then, Eric had returned with two more sacks. "On the counter, Wendy?"

"Yes, thank you."

Brad stood by the counter. "Wendy, where were you?"

"I wasn't out making a million-dollar coke deal, if that's what you're asking," she said flippantly.

"Oh, jeez," Eric groaned.

Brad grabbed her arm. "Wendy, I'm asking you a civil question! I want a civil answer!"

"Civil!"

"Wendy—"

"I told you, I went to the stinking store! Then I came back and I went out to see my family. I went to the village. I had dinner with Willie and Mary and the kids. That's it, that's all! And it's none of your business, anyway! You told me that you were leaving!"

He swung around on his heel. Wendy glared at Eric, who merely shrugged and followed Brad outside.

Brad was on the lawn, still tense and angry—but deflated. He looked at Eric. "Where the hell is her car?" he demanded.

Eric laughed. "Come on. I'll show you."

He led Brad to what looked like dark water, but there were stones beneath the water, which was barely an inch deep. It seemed that they walked across water, but of course they didn't. There was even a trail hacked through the tall grass on the other side, and there, high on a dry clearing near the end of a dirt road, was Wendy's small station wagon.

Together, the men collected the rest of the groceries, then returned to the house.

Wendy was putting things away, slamming every door she touched.

Eric set the last of the grocery bags down. "Want some help, Wendy?"

"No," she said curtly.

"Suit yourself. You want a beer, Brad?"

"Sure," Brad said.

Eric sauntered casually past Wendy and reached into the refrigerator, helping himself to two cans of beer. He tossed one over to Brad.

Wendy stood at the sink, separating a pack of steaks into individual freezer bags. She sniffed. "The two of you already smell like a brewery."

"What?" Eric protested. "I'm crushed."

Wendy swung around to face him. "All right, where the hell have the two of *you* been all day?"

"Fishing."

"Fishing." She paused in her efforts and stared at him. "Fishing. All day. *All* day?"

"Fishing. Shooting the breeze. Swilling beer. You know. Having a good old time."

Wendy turned back to her steaks. "Liar," she said softly.

"Ask Brad. I had a catfish on the line that you wouldn't believe. He made me lose it. City slicker."

She looked up at Eric. He smiled blandly. "You going to let him stay on here?" he asked her bluntly.

"What?" She flushed.

"Well, I'm going home. I was wondering if I should take him with me?"

Brad's eyes opened wide in amazement. "Eric, I can sink my own ship!"

"Stop it!" Wendy snapped. "Brad can stay."

"Stop shouting. I just asked a question," Eric said defensively.

Brad swallowed a sip of beer. Wendy was alive and well, and they were together. Heat filled him at the idea that their time together wasn't over yet.

"Good night." On his way out of the kitchen, Eric offered Brad a wink. "Just watch out! She's dangerous."

Wendy swung around. "Watch out? *He* tackled *me* out there, and I'm supposed to be the dangerous one."

"I think I can handle her," Brad said.

Wendy glared at him. A curious golden light was in his eyes as they swept over her. It made her feel warm. No, it made her feel hot, as if she would melt to the ground. Just seeing him there, tall, ruffled sandy hair, bronze and sinewed, made her remember the morning. She remembered what it felt like to run her fingers over his shoulders, over his back. She remembered watching the play of his muscles as he held her, remembered seeing the taut flicker of passion in his face as he gazed down at her...

"Yes," he said softly, "I think that I can handle her."

"Maybe," Eric said. "Maybe not. You know, friend, she could be trying to trap you."

"What?" Wendy and Brad said simultaneously. They both stared at Eric, who maintained his facade of a friendly calm.

"Trap you, Brad. She's always wanted a baby. Did you know that? Did you ever tell you? She was trying to get pregnant before Leif died. Maybe she's using you. Maybe she intends to trap you into marriage."

"And on the other hand, don't you think you're misleading her? You're not the kind of guy to settle down. You've got important work. A hell of a job. And heck, any damn day of your life could be your last. Do you use that as a ploy to take advantage of lonely women?"

"Eric!" Wendy snapped in disbelief and horror. No. Eric was her friend, he loved her. Why would he ever say such things? "Eric!" Her voice was small but strong, and it was laced with anguish. "Get out of my house! Get out! How could you—just get out!"

She was as white as chalk.

Eric nodded. "I was just leaving."

He walked out the front door. She heard it close. In absolute dismay, she let her eyes meet Brad's at last.

He was staring at her, staring at her hard. He started walking toward her.

"Wendy..."

"No!" Knowing that she was going to burst into tears, Wendy turned to run down the hallway. She just couldn't stand any more, not today.

Brad caught her by the shoulders, then swung her around into his arms.

"No!" She struggled against his hold.

"Use me, Wendy, if you would," he whispered softly. Then his lips caught hold of hers, hot and searing, and she gasped at the power of his hands moving over her. He was lifting her, lifting her high into his arms, she couldn't help but respond to the feverish heat of his body.

11

It was so good to touch her, so good to kiss her, to hold her soft and pliant in his arms. Her lips fused to his, seemingly as hungry as his own. He could have held her all night, drinking in a kiss such as this...

At first he ignored the sound that came to him from the swamp outside.

But then it came again, that sound in the darkness of night, and it penetrated Brad's mind. It was a birdcall, soft but clear, cutting through the night, cutting through Brad's desire and causing a prickle of danger to streak along his spine.

Brad slowly lowered Wendy until her feet touched the floor. Her arms were still around his neck, but her eyes met his. She, too, had sensed the danger.

"Eric?" he asked.

She nodded. "Yes, it's Eric."

"You said you had a pistol. What about ammunition?"

She nodded and quietly slipped away from him. He stayed in the hallway, listening. Concentrating, he tried to clear away all other sounds. Then he heard the footsteps outside.

He knew that Eric was out there…somewhere. But Eric had called to him, warned him, because someone else was out there, too.

Wendy returned with a Smith & Wesson .38. He took the weapon from her and cocked it. "Stay here," he whispered. "I want you to find a sheltered corner and stay low. Hold on to the shotgun. All right?"

At last she nodded. He turned away from her and hurried down the hall to the front door. The lights were on in the kitchen and the living room. He turned them off and went to the window, where he stared out across the lawn. Nothing moved. He went to the front door and slipped out.

Perched on his haunches by the corner of the house, Brad hesitated, then sprang around. His weapon was aimed straight ahead, at the ready. There was no one there.

He moved silently along the side of the house. The night was dark, so damned dark.

The birdcall sounded again. Someday, Brad decided, he was going to have to ask Eric what kind of bird it was supposed to be. An owl?

It didn't matter now. What was important was that he knew that Eric was moving almost opposite him, on the other side of the house. Within a few minutes, they'd both be at the rear, and their prey would be caught between them then.

Their prey…

He knew that someone else was there. He could feel it, smell it, sense it. All he had to do was turn the corner.

At the edge of the wall, Brad paused, his heart thudding against his chest. He held the gun steady with both hands, and then he sprang smoothly around, prepared to shoot.

A man was there, in back of the house. He hadn't heard or sensed Brad or Eric yet—he was busy at work on Wendy's bedroom window.

"Hold it right there. Get your hands up—up high, clear in the air!" Brad demanded.

The man dropped low. Brad saw a glint of the pale moonlight gleaming upon something in the man's hands. He had a gun, too, and he was getting ready to shoot.

Brad shot first. Carefully, very carefully, he squeezed the trigger. The gun went flying and the man screamed, clutching his hand.

Eric flew around the corner, stooping silently to retrieve the thrown gun even as the fallen intruder tried to reach for it. Brad came forward, keeping the .38 aimed at the man.

"Three fifty-seven Magnum," Eric observed. "He meant to plug a few holes in you for keeps."

"Yeah," Brad said softly. "Michaelson's men do play for keeps."

"Cripes! I'm bleeding to death down here! You're supposed to be the cop, McKenna. You'd better get me to a hospital quick, or I'll be screaming my head off about police brutality."

Brad squatted down by the man, seeing a swarthy, pockmarked face. He'd thought he recognized the voice.

"I'm not a cop. I'm worse than that, Suarez, and you know it. I'm DEA. A fed. And you know what? We've been losing some good guys to scum like you lately. We don't take the same heat as the poor local cops. I don't care if you rot away of gangrene, Suarez."

"You know him?" Eric asked.

Brad nodded, careful to keep the gun aimed at the slender but dangerous man on the ground. "Tommy Suarez. He's so high up with Michaelson that he rarely has to take on the dirty jobs these days. We think that he killed a lot of people to get to his position. He used to give me my 'order'—where to pick up cash, where to drive, that kind of stuff." He hesitated. "This bastard killed my partner." He pulled back the trigger so that it clicked.

In a timeless moment he gritted his teeth, realizing he had to stop. He was emotionally involved here. But this guy had been the triggerman who killed his partner. Suarez had also been working away at the window to a bedroom where Wendy might have been sleeping.

Sleeping, all alone. If Brad had left, Wendy would have been there—alone, innocent, vulnerable. And God alone knew what Suarez might have done with her to extract information about Brad—or just for the hell of it, because she was a beautiful woman.

He aimed the gun straight at Suarez's temple.

"Hey!" Suarez whined. "You can't do that! You're—"

"Who else is hanging around here, Suarez?" Brad demanded.

"No one," he said sullenly. "Hey, my hand is bleeding. You've busted it all to hell, you ass—"

"Hey!" Eric grinned. His teeth were a bright white slash against his bronze skin in the pale moonlight. "My turn, Brad. I'm not with the government. I don't have a scruple in the world, dealing with this swine. You hear that, Suarez? I'm not a cop, and I'm not an agent. I'm an Indian. And you know what, buddy? I've had enough of you guys slipping that rotten crack to our teens. They're not starting out with a real fair deal to begin with. You know how many overdoses we've had out here in the last year? Since your friend Michaelson decided to make a septic tank out of our swamp?"

Suarez licked his dry lips. Eric held him by the lapels of his shirt. His eyes darted nervously from Brad to Eric and back to Brad again. "Tell him to let me go. Tell Mr. Rain Dance there to get his hands off me!"

Eric's laugh was harsh and bitter. "Rain Dance, Sitting Bull, yeah, you got the message, Suarez!" Brad hadn't known that Eric carried a knife until he saw the flash of the steel blade pressed against Suarez's throat. "Mr. McKenna asked you a question."

"Please!" Suarez whined. He seemed afraid to even swallow. "Please, tell him to get the knife away. He's going to kill me."

Brad nodded to Eric. Eric sheathed the knife beneath the edge of his boot. "Hell," he moaned. "And I thought I was going to get to see if a rat could live after it had been scalped."

"Who knows you're here? How did you find this place?" Brad asked. Suarez remained silent, his eyes wide with panic. Brad swore softly. "So help me, Suarez, start talking or I'll just turn my back and let Rain Dance experiment on you."

Suarez kept stalling, until Eric brandished the shiny blade of his knife once more. Ultimately, Suarez believed the threat. He started talking. No one knew where he was; he'd come out on his own. He'd been holed up in a hunter's shack, but some hillbillies in an airboat had been hanging around all day, guzzling beers and trying to catch fish. He hadn't dared go in anywhere close, so he'd done a little exploring on his own.

"Come on, Suarez, you weren't out here alone."

"Charlie Jenkins is supposed to be with me. He had to take a ride this morning. I'm alone, I swear it."

"Okay, okay. You and Jenkins have been hanging out in a shack in the Everglades." That rang more true. Charlie Jenkins had grown up in southern Georgia, in the Okefenokee swamp. He would know how to get around down here.

"Why are you guys staked out here?"

"We're looking for you," Suarez said.

"There's more," Brad told him.

"Yeah, all right, yeah. Michaelson has been using the Everglades. You knew that—hell, half the law enforcement in the state knows that." He sneered, revealing tobacco-stained teeth. "Everyone knows that. But Michaelson is slick, real slick. He can't be caught. Just like the water moccasin, he slinks away when he doesn't want to be found."

"When is the next shipment coming in?" Brad demanded.

"I don't know—"

Quick as lightning, Eric pulled his knife out and pressed it against the man's throat. The blade glinted even in the dim moonlight. "I swear it! I swear it!" Suarez screamed, looking apprehensively at the blade so near his jugular vein. "Charlie Jenkins is supposed to know, when he comes back."

Convinced that Suarez was telling the truth, Brad nodded to Eric. Eric backed off, silent as the night.

"I've got to take him in," Brad said.

"You mean we don't get to kill him?" Eric sighed deeply in mock disappointment. When Suarez shivered, Brad was barely able to suppress a grin. "Not this time, Tonto. Sorry."

Eric grinned. Suarez started blubbering again. "I swear, I'd tell you anything. I don't know nothing else, honest."

"Let's go tell Wendy—" Eric began, but just then an explosion rent the darkness of the night.

"Hands up, everyone. All the way up."

Apparently, Wendy had waited long enough. She had silently crept around the house, but the kick of the shotgun had announced her arrival and sent her stumbling backward. Fortunately she hadn't lost her grip on the weapon; she still held it cocked and aimed.

"Wendy!" Brad snapped. "Dammit, I told you to stay in the house!"

"I told you she had definite problems," Eric warned.

"I was worried when you didn't come back."

"But I told you to stay inside—"

"Like a sitting duck. You might have needed me."

"Well, we didn't! Everything is well in hand." Or it had been, Brad thought. Now he was trembling again. Maybe it was a damned good thing that he had come here. Suarez had just been exploring in the night. He would have stumbled upon Wendy, and she would have been completely unaware. He would have attacked her in the night, and she could have screamed forever, and no one would have heard her....

Wendy. His angel. She held the shotgun with poise and regal grace. Her hair gleamed in the dim moonlight with a splendor all its own. She seemed so small and slender, and yet so feminine. It was strange how something like denim work jeans could hug a woman's figure, making her appear so sexy. And it was strange, too, how a simple cotton shirt could hang so evocatively upon a body.

Suarez inhaled sharply. Brad looked down at the man. He was watching Wendy with a sizzle in his eyes.

"Wendy, get back into the house, now!" Brad ordered.

"I am not your personal lackey!" she protested. "Damn you—"

"Break it up, break it up," Eric interrupted. "We've got to deal with this guy. Brad, his hand is shot up badly."

"You shot him?" Wendy accused Brad.

"Well, excuse the hell out of me!" Brad returned. "I shot him before he could shoot me, do you mind?"

When she rushed over to examine Suarez, Brad stopped her. "It's not a pretty sight."

She stared at him, then pushed his hand away. "I told you, I was a nurse. Trust me, I've seen worse."

She hunched down on the balls of her feet and examined the man's hand. Suarez stared at her in that same way that made Brad so uncomfortable, and yet he blessed her in Spanish and in English and told her that she was an angel of mercy.

She scowled at Brad. "This wound is serious. He needs to be in a hospital. You shouldn't have kept him here so long."

"So long!"

"I heard that shot a long time ago," Wendy said.

He wanted to grab her and shake her. She didn't realize that this sleaze might have friends, nor did she even seem to realize that he meant to break in through her window and...

"Don't pull a Florence Nightingale act on me. This

man meant to come through that window, and rape you. And hell, he might have even killed you."

"C'mon, break it up for the moment, huh?" Eric suggested lightly. "Wendy, this guy isn't exactly Mr. Rogers, you know, dropping in on the neighborhood. Let's get him in—"

"I'll take him—alone," Brad said. He didn't want Wendy along, and he wanted Eric to stay with her.

"That's well and fine, but I'm not sure you can find your way around at night," Eric reminded him.

That was true, Brad thought dismally. Although he'd become familiar with the swamp, he couldn't safely navigate at night.

"What about the car?" he asked Eric.

Eric shrugged. "You still shouldn't be venturing out alone. Why don't you call your boss. I'll turn this thug over to the tribal police. From there he can be transferred over to your people."

Brad nodded. Eric's plan made sense.

Wendy turned around. "I'm going to get some bandages."

"I don't want her left alone," Brad said to Eric.

"Want me to take him in?"

Brad shook his head. "I'll have to call Purdy and see what he wants to do with this scum."

"That's some *chica*," Suarez said nastily.

"Shut up." Brad kicked him, then turned away. "I don't want her left alone, Eric."

"Then we'll all go. I'll drive. Wendy can ride up front with me, and you can ride in the back with our friend here."

Brad thought about it for a minute. He didn't want Wendy anywhere within reach of Suarez, but Eric's plan seemed like the best solution. Brad didn't want her left alone, either. He definitely didn't want her alone. Jenkins was coming back somewhere along the line— according to Suarez—and Brad wasn't going to take any chances.

"All right," he told Eric.

Wendy returned with a bottle of antiseptic and white gauze bandages. A true professional, she knelt down by Suarez. In a no-nonsense tone, she warned him that it was going to sting like hell, then she poured the contents of the bottle over his hand. He screamed in pain, trying to clutch his hand away, but Wendy didn't let him. Deftly, she wrapped the injured hand in clean gauze. She handed him a little white pill and told him to swallow it. "Percodan. It will help the pain."

"Let's get him a suite at the Biltmore," Brad murmured sarcastically.

"Brad, you did put the man in pain," Wendy said.

"Yeah. And he meant to put me six feet under."

"Are you two going to take him into town?" Wendy asked, smoothing back a loose strand of her hair.

"No, *we three* are going to take him," Brad said.

Her eyes widened. "I don't want to go."

"You're going."

"The hell—"

"You're going." His teeth were grating and his muscles were tightening. It had been such a damned explosive evening that he was ready to throw her over his shoulder and carry her into the car. Of all the damned times for the woman to be so stubborn!

"Okay, okay!" Eric stepped between them. "Wendy, give the guy a break, will you? He's worried about you. Brad, I'm glad that you're in law enforcement and not the diplomatic corp. Now, for God's sake, let's get this show on the road!"

"I'm all for that, Rain Dance," Suarez agreed. The Percodan was working fast, Brad thought. The guy's eyes were already glazing over. Suarez almost looked agreeable.

"Rain Dance?" Wendy's eyes widened. Brad almost smiled. He could see her fury growing. She'd fight anytime for someone she loved, and she loved her brother-in-law. "Why, you slime mold!" She hissed to Suarez.

Her love was so fierce, so loyal. *I want you to love me with that fury, that passion,* Brad thought. *But like a lover.*

Eric groaned. "Wendy, I've got it under control, okay? Can we please go?"

"Let's do it. Suarez, up," Brad said.

Brad was holding the gun, so Eric gave the man a hand. He struggled to his feet. Brad stared at Wendy fiercely.

She returned his stare, then her rich lashes fell over her cheeks. "I'll be just a moment," she said, hurrying back into the house. When she returned, she was still carrying the shotgun. Brad was sure that she had more shells for it, too, probably packed away in her brown leather purse.

Suarez was convinced that they were trying to drown him when they told him to walk over the stones. Then, when Eric showed him how it was done, Suarez was convinced that Eric was an Indian god.

"What the hell did you give him?" Brad demanded of Wendy.

"I told you—Percodan!" She proceeded over the

stones herself. "See? I swear, you'll barely get your feet wet."

Suarez followed her at last. He looked back longingly at the canoe, drawn up on the shore, that had brought him to the house in the woods. "I shouldn't have come here. I should have shot those hillbillies in the airboat and drank up their beer."

"Nothing like hindsight, is there, Suarez?" Brad said, prodding his prisoner with the barrel of the gun. "Let's move."

At last, Suarez gingerly walked over the stones. When they reached the car, Brad helped Wendy into the front seat, then pressed Suarez into the back. Eric asked Wendy for the keys, and she tossed them to him.

The car was eerily silent as they started out. Eric flicked on the car radio. A latino tune came on, and Suarez decided to sing along.

Brad was getting a horrible headache. He tried to watch the terrain as Eric drove, but the headlights of the small car didn't alight upon any recognizable landmarks.

By car, it was a long trip. Brad understood Wendy's affection for her airboat. It took less than forty-five minutes to reach Mac's garage by way of the airboat. Now time seemed to drag horribly. They drove for more than an hour before they pulled up beside the garage.

"We're going to have to wake up Mac," Wendy said. Eric turned the car off, and she hopped out.

"I have to go," Suarez said.

Eric and Brad exchanged looks of annoyance. Eric came out of the driver's seat and opened the door. Brad followed Suarez out, keeping the gun trained on him at all times. He knew these people too well to trust even a simple call of nature.

Between them, they led Suarez over to a clump of bushes. Brad looked toward the station and saw that the office door was opening. Wendy had managed to rouse Mac from his bed in the back room of the office.

He handed the gun to Eric. "Don't trust him."

"He won't pull anything," Eric said, "if he values his life."

Hurrying toward the station, Brad smiled, shaking his head slightly. Suarez was thoroughly convinced that Eric was probably worse than the entire Indian contingent at the battle of the Little Bighorn.

"Come on in, Mr. McKenna. Come in and make whatever calls you want," Mac said, opening the glass door.

"Thanks, Mac," Brad said.

"Wendy, you want some tea or something?"

"Sure, I'd love some tea," Wendy murmured. It would give her something to do while Brad started dialing numbers.

Brad phoned Purdy, who agreed that it was a good idea to bring in the tribal police. His people would meet them at the entrance to the swamp and extradite Suarez. Purdy planned to interrogate Suarez as soon as he had received medical attention.

Brad glanced over at Wendy. "I—I can't come in now."

Purdy was quick, Brad gave him that. He hadn't gotten where he was by being stupid.

"You don't want to talk? You're worried about your friend? The girl you're staying with?"

"Yes. Exactly."

"Fine. Hand Suarez over to the tribal police and go back with her. Call me tomorrow at noon. Maybe it's time to get some backup out there."

"Yeah. I think it might be."

"But play it smooth, huh? You've got a nice trap sitting out there. Maybe we can bag something else."

"Carefully."

"Carefully, beyond a doubt. We won't let the woman get hurt, Brad."

"Thanks." He dared another glance at Wendy. She was talking to Mac, but he was sure that she had heard everything he had said. He was glad that he had kept it simple, glad that Purdy was perceptive.

He hung up. Purdy was going to contact the tribal police.

"Everything taken care of?" Mac asked.

"Yes, thanks. Thanks a lot," Brad told the old man. Mac smiled. "Tea?"

"No, thanks just the same." He shook Mac's hand. He wondered if there was any way that he could repay the old guy, if there was anything that Mac wanted. In many ways, Mac had helped keep Brad—and Wendy safe.

When Brad left the office, Wendy started to follow him.

"Stay inside with Mac," he told her.

"Don't you—"

"Please! Stay with Mac."

Wendy looked into his eyes, so fiercely gold, so powerful. Her rebellious nature balked at the order, but she swallowed her pride and went back inside to wait with Mac. It had been such a rough day! She'd been trying so hard to pretend that her life was entirely normal.

But life wasn't normal anymore. Brad had entered

into her world, and she had fallen in love with him. She had cried as she'd strolled down the aisle in the grocery store, and despite herself, she'd bought enough food for two. She'd burst into tears in the drugstore, and again, she'd bought supplies for two.

And at first she hadn't been able to go home to her empty house. She'd gone to see the family, because she had needed them so badly. She'd needed Grandfather's wisdom, and Grandmother's support. Willie had held her when she cried, and she'd known with an even greater strength than ever before just how much they loved her. Leif was dead, but the Hawks still loved her. They were such good people. Blood was a strong tie to them, but love was even stronger. She was Willie's granddaughter, blood or no, for he claimed her as so. He knew that she had loved Leif.

And he knew that she loved Brad now.

"He is a good man," Grandfather had told her.

"He is gone."

"Go home. Wait for him. He will come back."

"What if he doesn't?"

"Then you will cry, but life will go on. And you will be richer for the time that you have shared."

And now, looking out the window at Brad, she didn't know whether to laugh or cry. He had returned to her house, he had returned to her arms. But danger had come between them.

She was a fool. Brad McKenna lived with danger—it was an occupational hazard.

And yet she loved him anyway.

A while later, Wendy saw the flash of headlights. When the car parked outside, she recognized the emblem of the tribal police. After a very brief conversation with Brad and Eric, the tribal police took Suarez away.

Then Brad opened the door and stretched out a hand to her. "Wendy, it's time to go back home."

Back home. Yes, it was time to return to her home—with him.

Eric drove again. Wendy sat in front with him; Brad sat silently in the back. The only sound was the music from the radio, though Eric switched the station a dozen times.

At last, they were home. Still in silence, they parked and locked the car, then traveled over the stones to reach the house.

"You need to give Brad a decent pair of boots," Eric commented. "He's soaking his shoes on those things."

"They're your brother's shoes," Brad said.

"Yeah, well, my brother had boots, too. And he can't use any of them now. Boots are a necessity in swampland. Leif's old leather pair were strong enough to break the grasp of a rattler or a cottonmouth."

Ahead of the two men, Wendy was unlocking the door. "Leif's boots are in the closet. Take them."

It had been a long, long night, and it was nearly three in the morning. Too tense to be tired, Brad glanced at Eric, wondering when they were going to tell Wendy what they had decided while waiting for the tribal police.

Wendy went in and set her purse on the counter. She looked at the two men invading her life, her brother-in-law and the lover she was so afraid of losing.

"Do you two want anything?" They were staring at her so expectantly, like two big dogs.

"Yes!" Brad said, suddenly realizing that he hadn't eaten a decent meal all day.

"Yes, please!" Eric echoed.

She opened the refrigerator. "Like what?"

Brad requested two of the steaks she had just brought home. Eric agreed with that, and he also wanted broccoli in cheese sauce. Brad thought a salad would be great. Eric said they should add some microwave baked potatoes to the menu, too.

So at 3:00 a.m., they started cooking.

The conversation remained casual and polite. Wendy kept her distance from Brad, who seemed careful to do the same.

When they had eaten and cleaned up the dishes, Eric still remained. Wendy looked at him curiously.

Brad cleared his throat at last. "Uh, Eric is taking the first watch."

"First watch!" Wendy looked from Brad to Eric and back to Brad again.

"First watch, Wendy." Eric reached over and squeezed her fingers. "I'm going to stay awake, while Brad sleeps. Then we'll switch. It's safer that way."

"I see." Wendy set her dish towel on the counter and turned away from them both. "Well, then, good night."

She walked down the hallway. Maybe she was just so tired that she felt like a zombie. Maybe she was so desperately in love she was losing her spirit. She showered and dressed for bed in a long cotton gown. She was so overtired that she was afraid she would throw some ridiculous, childish fit if she encountered either of the men, so she hurried into her bedroom and closed the door.

Sleep eluded her. She heard someone go into the

shower—Brad, she assumed. The water roared on, then there was silence.

A few moments later she heard a soft knock at her door.

Brad leaned in, his hair still damp and glistening from the shower. "Good night," he told Wendy softly, then closed the door.

"Good night," she called after him.

She sank back against the pillows for a moment, then threw back the covers and raced to the door. She opened it and saw Brad standing in the threshold. Her heart skittering away, Wendy ran to him. She leaped off the floor, hurtling herself into his arms, locking her legs around him.

He held her to him, kissing her hungrily. Holding her so, he walked straight to her bed. Together they fell backward onto the billowing sheets.

Wendy broke from his kiss. "The door. We're not alone."

Brad got up and closed the door. When he reached for her again in the darkness, she was naked.

And she was waiting for him.

Forgetting the turmoil of the day, he buried his heart, his soul and his body into her never-ending sweetness.

12

Brad was beside her, sound asleep, when Wendy woke, late in the morning. She assumed that he had spelled Eric, staying awake for the second part of the night, and that he'd come to bed after that, to sleep for the first time.

She showered and dressed. Eric wasn't in the living room when she came out. Looking out the window, she saw that he was sitting on the lawn, sipping a mug of coffee. Apparently, he had just fed Baby; the big cat was curled up next to him just as sweetly as a Persian kitten. She watched Eric for a moment, remembering what he had said before all the commotion had begun last night. He'd made some lousy accusations! She went into the kitchen, poured a glass of ice water and went outside.

She couldn't sneak up on him; she knew that. When he looked up and flashed her a smile of greeting, she smiled back. She came up behind him, then squatted down to pat Baby.

"Sleep well?" he asked her innocently.

"Fine," Wendy said sweetly. Then she poured the water directly over his head.

He sputtered, swearing and jumping to his feet. "What the hell was that for?" he demanded in outrage.

"You know damned well what that was for! Your wonderful little performance last night!"

Annoyed by the whole thing, Baby stretched and walked away in search of peace and quiet. Dripping, Eric stared at Wendy, then started to laugh.

"Well, apparently it didn't do any harm."

"Eric! How could you say those terrible things about me? You're supposed to be on my side!"

"Wendy, Wendy..." He opened his arms to give her a big hug.

Wendy quickly realized that he only wanted to drench her, too. "Eric!" She eluded him, but sat down on the lawn a safe distance from him. He sat down beside her. The sun was high in the sky; he would dry quickly.

"I *am* on your side," he told her.

"Then what was that all about? Brad's going to leave. We all know that."

"Do we?" Eric arched a brow to her and she flushed. "Oh, yeah, that's right. You don't want anything to do with a fed agent, do you?"

"Eric—"

"Well, whatever I said, it didn't seem to do any harm to either of you. Seemed to me that things went well enough."

"Eric—"

"You know, Wendy, your life is your business. And Brad's life is his business. Your decisions have to be your own."

"Then—"

"I just wanted to make sure that you were both playing with a full deck, that's all."

Wendy groaned. "You're making me crazy!"

He grinned, glancing over his shoulder. "Well, morning has broken. Here comes the fed. Excuse me. I think I'll make more coffee."

Wendy twisted slightly. Brad was coming out the front door, shirtless, shoeless and clad only in a pair of jeans. His hair was still tousled, and though she could see that he had shaven, he still looked somewhat bleary-eyed and disoriented. He was carrying a coffee cup. Eric, heading back into the house, paused. The two men exchanged a few words, then Brad joined Wendy outside. He cradled his coffee cup in his hand and smiled at her. "Good morning."

"Good morning."

They didn't say anything else for several long moments. He took a sip of the steaming coffee and stared out over the terrain. Baby reappeared and curled up beside Wendy.

Brad slipped an arm around her. She watched his profile, setting a hand lightly on his knee.

"None of that was true, you know."

He looked her way again, a small smile playing against his lips.

"What Eric said."

He paused. "You didn't want a baby?"

She looked down at the ground. "Well, yes, I did. That was true, but the rest—was absurd. I would never try to trap you."

He set his coffee cup down and threaded his fingers gently through her hair, kissing her tenderly. "Would you want to trap me?" he asked softly.

She shook her head. "No one should ever be forced into anything. I wouldn't, I just wouldn't, and I hope you believe that." She spoke flatly, trying to escape his hold. He laughed and pulled her tightly against him. His hand lay beneath her breast, and they could both feel the pulse of her heart.

"I know that you would never force anyone to do anything. Sometimes it's difficult to get even an opinion from you."

"What do you mean by that?"

"You don't want to admit how you feel."

Wendy scratched Baby's ears and looked out over the water. "I let you know how I feel," she said softly. "You know that I care." She turned and stared searchingly into his eyes. "You know that I'm afraid of your work. You're afraid of what it can do to two lives—you've warned me not to care too deeply. Nothing has changed. This—" She hesitated. "This will end. But I want you here with me, for as long as possible. I'll never regret this time. I—"

She wanted to be open and honest. But she couldn't tell him that she had fallen in love with him. She knew that he cared about her, but love was another story altogether. And because she loved him, she would let him go. What she had said was true. She was afraid of losing him...but he had set his priorities long ago.

His fingers curled tensely around hers. "What were you going to say?"

She shook her head, looking down at Baby again. Fortunately, she was spared when the door opened loudly.

Eric had come out. "Hey, Brad, aren't you supposed to call in at noon? We've just got time to make it in to the garage."

Brad was still studying Wendy. "Yeah," he said with a soft sigh. "I guess we'd better go."

Before he could slip into the house for a shirt and shoes, Wendy caught his hand. "Brad?"

"What?"

"I take it that you and Eric were the 'hillbillies' sitting out there fishing and watching that shack that Suarez was talking about last night?"

He hesitated. "Yes."

"Is that what you're planning to do today?"

"Wendy, it's my job. Charlie Jenkins will probably come back to the shack. He's my link to Michaelson." He ruffled her hair, then reached down to take her hands. "Come on."

"Come on?" She raised her eyes to his.

He exhaled again in a soft sigh. "Wendy, I can't leave you here alone."

"It's broad daylight. I know how to use a shotgun. And Baby is with me. People don't argue with her."

"Baby is a big cat, but Michaelson moves around with big guns. He's been known to carry M-16s. I want you to come with us."

She opened her mouth to protest.

"Please!" Brad said before she could say anything more.

"All right." Wearily, she rose with him. The sun cast a golden sheen along the ripples of his shoulders. She didn't want to argue with him, and she didn't want to dread the future. She wanted to run her fingers and her tongue over that sleek bronze flesh and feel him come alive to her touch.

She couldn't do that. Not now—not ever.

She was losing him. She felt it. Some force beyond their control was tightening its grasp around them, surrounding them like a writhing python. They had discovered something, and now they were losing it, before they could ever hold it tightly and give it a name.

"Brad?"

He paused.

Placing her palms against his chest, she rose onto her toes. She kissed his lips softly, then slid to her feet against him.

"What was that for?"

"I just needed it," she told him.

He gave her a quick hug. "I needed it, too. I needed it, too."

They headed for the house together. As Brad went into the bedroom to dress, Wendy called to him that he really should be wearing boots.

"Where are they?"

"In the closet."

Five minutes later, he still hadn't found the boots. Wendy came into the bedroom and began searching through the cluttered closet. When she glanced up at Brad, he was sifting through the collection of Leif's clothing that still hung in the closet.

He shook his head, looking down at her. "Wendy, you've got to get rid of these things, really."

She nodded, finally locating the box with the boots in them. "You should be glad that I kept this stuff," she said, handing him the boots. "I don't think that my jeans would have fit you."

He smiled at her, leaned down and brushed her cheek with his knuckles. "Very cute, smarty-pants. But seriously, I hope you don't plan on stripping every stranger who crash-lands on your doorstep."

"What an interesting possibility to explore," she said sweetly.

He pulled her to her feet and kissed her. She let out a surprised cry as his palm circled around her rump. "Not amusing, Wendy," he told her. "Now, behave."

"I was behaving!"

He sat at the foot of the bed and pulled on the boots. They were a little tight, but the rugged leather would provide necessary protection in the swamp. Brad gazed at her curiously. "Want to suggest a shirt?"

She turned around without a flicker of emotion and pulled out a red plaid. It still hurt, she thought. Even discovering that she was in love again could not completely release the past. She'd never been able to get rid of Leif's things; it had seemed so cold, so final. She couldn't throw away Leif's clothes any more than she could throw away his memory.

But Brad was right, she knew. She shouldn't throw things away, she should give them away to someone who needed them. That would be the best way to remember her husband.

Brad took the shirt from her and slipped it over his shoulders. "Thank you." She nodded while he buttoned up and slipped the shirttails into his jeans.

She lowered her eyes, trying to ignore the tight knot of fear in her throat. It was as if a noose were tightening around them. Something was going to happen. She was going to lose Brad—she could feel it in her blood. Then her life would be empty again, and it would be just as if this had never happened between them. No, Grandfather had told her that she would be richer for it.

She hoped that she could feel that way when he was actually gone.

Impetuously, she went up on her toes, and she kissed him again, tasting him, inhaling him. She did want to hang on to him, she didn't want to let him return to his real world.

It was wrong.

She broke away, turning around, reaching for the door. "You've got to call your boss, remember?"

"Yeah, I remember."

Half an hour later, they were back at the garage.

Brad went inside to call Purdy. Eric lingered beside the gas pumps, talking to Mac. Wendy hovered near the airboat, afraid that she wouldn't make much of a conversationalist that day.

The air was hot and sticky. Listening to the endless drone of a horde of mosquitoes, she absently lifted her hair from the back of her neck. She could see Brad through the glass enclosure. He looked so serious, almost like a stranger. She bit her lower lip. He was serious—very serious about his work. Unlike the man she loved, this Brad frightened her. He meant business.

She turned away, clenching and unclenching her fingers as she idly walked along the canal. She was so nervous that she didn't realize how far she had wandered. Nor did she notice the car that crept along the road, or the canoe that moved silently behind her, coming closer and closer.

She was so involved with her thoughts that she didn't begin to sense danger until it was almost upon her. And then, it was too late.

Behind her, a shadow loomed against the sun. Absently noticing the darkness, Wendy turned, frowning.

Two men stood before her. The first was tall and lean, with watery blue eyes and steel-gray hair. The second man was younger. He was huskily built, brawny.

His eyes were brown, but they had the same chill glaze of ruthlessness.

Every nerve tensed as she sensed danger, cold, sharp, lethal. She opened her mouth to scream, but she was never able to issue a useful sound.

The brown-eyed man caught her by the neck and stuffed a cloth into her mouth. She thought she would choke to death, but she couldn't even cough properly, he held his hand so tightly against her. Desperate, she tried to lash out, but the smell of the cloth, sickeningly sweet, assailed her. She started to grow dizzy. The sun, the man, the sky, the world…everything swirled before her.

Dimly, she realized how foolish she had been. She had followed the canal around a curve. Eric wasn't really so far away, but he was talking to Mac beyond the rise of the grass. He couldn't see her, and she couldn't scream, so he couldn't hear her.

Her world was dimming so rapidly. She tried to struggle. She tried to free herself from that restricting hand, but it was like a steel band. The man's fingers bit into her flesh as he held her tighter and tighter. Barely, just barely, she managed to free her right arm and drag her curving fingers against his cheek.

He swore softly as her nails caught his face, drawing blood. He secured her hand again and hissed out a warning to her.

But he didn't lift the soaked rag from her face. The sticky sweetness created a buzz around her. Wendy never felt the cuff he gave her across the cheek. By the time he struck her, she was already falling. The world was spinning to blackness.

She was unconscious when he hoisted her into

his arms and silently turned to follow the other man through the tall grasses to the waiting airboat.

Brad thoughtfully hung up the phone. It was basically over—if not the case, then at least his strange idyll out here. He was going to spend the day prowling through the swamp keeping an eye out for Jenkins or Michaelson. By tonight, he'd have a number of reinforcements out here: a few men to keep an eye on the shack, and more men to spread out, to wait for the drop that was scheduled. They didn't have Michaelson yet, but he wouldn't be looking for the man alone anymore. The noose was being tightened—and all they had to do was hope that they didn't scare their quarry away.

Purdy was determined to see Michaelson locked up. He was banking on Brad's eyewitness testimony against the man. And if they played it right, they could catch him red-handed with the drugs coming in from South America. The big machinery was moving. Brad realized that he was just a small part of it now, and he didn't know whether to feel relieved or deeply bereft.

Things wouldn't be the same. He wouldn't have a chance to be alone with Wendy again. Not as a pair of castaways in a strange paradise, isolated from the world. Today he would have to accept Eric's help, and he didn't want Wendy along with them: It was too dangerous. He had never known that Suarez had been watching him and Eric in the airboat the other day. Even if Suarez hadn't been able to come close enough to recognize him, he had seen Brad and Eric. To Brad, that was unnerving. He decided that Wendy should spend the day in the village with Willie and Mary. She should be safe with the family. Brad was certain that Willie knew how to protect his loved ones.

It was almost over. The realization hurt so much that he could hardly stand it. Hell, he'd known he had no right touching a woman like Wendy. They'd both said that they could take what came. They had both claimed to be adult, mature—willing to accept an affair for the time that they had together.

She had warned him not to care too deeply, just as he had warned her. And now here they were, at the end of it all....

And he felt like doubling over with pain, it hurt so damned much. Pain chewed at the walls of his stomach—and his heart.

She cared for him. He knew that. But he also knew that she didn't want a life with a man who lived in danger. She definitely didn't want a life with him. So that was that. There was a real world, and he had to return to it. He had a job, and he'd always known that it wasn't a job that was conducive to...

Marriage.

He wanted to marry her. He wanted her beside him when he woke up in the morning. She was a radiant angel, and he knew that she would be every bit as beautiful to him in fifty years. He wanted her all to himself for a while, and then he wanted to have that baby with her that she had once wanted and could surely want again.

But he had no right. His job was a necessary one, and he was good at it. He had no right to want her to suffer for him.

Maybe he owed them both the honesty of the depths of his feelings. She had told him this morning that nothing had changed in their lifestyles. But the feelings between them had grown. She might have denied them a future with her words, but her kiss had said otherwise.

When he saw Eric smiling at him through the glass, Brad realized that he had been standing at the door for several long minutes.

This was idiotic. The idyll might be over, but Michaelson was still out there. And he had to be caught.

Swallowing hard, Brad impatiently turned to leave the office. Eric excused himself to Mac and came over to Brad, looking at him expectantly.

"There'll be some backup here tonight. We're still going to lie low, because we want to catch Michaelson with the goods. I want to keep my eyes open for Charlie Jenkins today—then I need to meet some men here tonight. They're sending a few to keep an eye on the shack, and—" He paused. "And a few to keep an eye on Wendy's place. Purdy agreed that we've put her into the path of danger. She needs some solid protection until this is really over." Brad didn't have to admit that he was too emotionally involved to be effective himself. Though he and Eric were a good pair, they'd be better off with some objective help around. "Would you mind taking a ride back out by the shack?"

Eric shook his head. "Not at all. What about Wendy? I take it you don't want her home alone, and I don't think she should be along with us."

"I thought we'd take her to Willie's." He grimaced. "She's not going to like it, but..." His voice trailed away and he shrugged. "We might as well get going."

Eric nodded, turning to look toward the canal. Suddenly, a frown compressed his features in hard lines. "I don't see her."

Brad's entire body seemed to constrict as he stared across the gas pumps toward the road. A car whooshed by, moving fast. He turned toward the canal. He had just seen her. He had been looking out the window while he had been talking to Purdy, and he had seen her standing there. Her hair had been loose on her shoulders, catching the sunshine. Her hands had been jammed into her pockets, her boot heels dug impatiently into the ground as she waited. She had been there, just moments ago.

He and Eric started to run at the same time. They reached the canal and the high grass together, sloshing their way into the water. His heart in his throat, Brad prayed that he would not find her. There'd be a bullet in her heart if Michaelson had found her. She'd be face-down in the swamp if she'd met with a cottonmouth or a diamondback. No, no, Wendy was too smart and too savvy to panic at a snakebite. She would have called for help. She would have known what she was doing. It had to have been Michaelson....

They didn't find her in the water. Brad tried to breathe, he told himself that he had to breathe. As Eric stared at him with his curious lime-green eyes, Brad noticed that behind the stonelike mask of the bronzed warrior, Eric was fighting a raw, clawing fear himself.

"Look at the road."

Brad did so. He saw where her boots had been dragged against the earth; he saw the scuffle of foot-prints.

"Michaelson," he swore in anguish.

"I don't think that he's killed her," Eric said tone-lessly.

Brad shook his head, trying to clear it. "No, he wants her for something. Or else he would have—he would have killed her, quiet and quick, right here." He stared at Eric for a moment, then plunged through the shallow rim of grass and muck to the airboat. He looked about hastily, until he saw what he wanted. A stone held a note to the flooring by the motor. Brad tried to read the words, blinked furiously and made sense of the letters at last. He nodded at Eric.

"He's taken her to the shack."

"And he wants you to come?"

Brad nodded. "Both of us. Precisely—'bring the Indian along.' No one else, or he'll slit her throat."

"Why me?" Eric murmured.

Brad thought he understood. "I just got word that his plane came in—crashed in the swamp. Purdy thinks that it's out there buried in the muck somewhere, and Charlie Jenkins, the boy from the Okefenokee in Georgia, just isn't good enough in this maze. I'll wager that Michaelson wants you to find his stuff."

"And you?"

"He wants to kill me. I'm just a case of revenge."

Eric frowned. "And Wendy?"

"He'll keep her alive long enough to make you do what he wants." He paused, breathing deeply. "Hell, who knows. He—he might want more." He swore softly again.

Eric lowered his head, his fingers winding into impotent fists at his sides.

Brad realized that he was praying when he needed to be thinking—or maybe he needed to be doing both things. He braced himself and got a grip on his emotions.

"I'm calling Purdy back. He should know that Michaelson has Wendy. Maybe there's something he can do to help. Then we've got to get out to the shack. Is there any way to come around on that cabin from a different direction?"

"Go call. Let me try to see the terrain in my mind."

Brad hurried in to call Purdy. The boss was going to put his machinery into action sooner.

After he'd hung up, Brad gritted his teeth and explained the situation to Mac. Then he hurried down to the airboat to join Eric. The plan was risky, but it was their only chance. Otherwise, they were surely dead.

This way they had a chance. The odds were bad. Very bad.

But then, they were the only odds they had.

Brad leaped onto the airboat. Eric was already starting up the motor.

"I think we can approach from the back," he said. "I'll cut the motor and we'll paddle around the rear of the hammock. We'll have to wade through muck, and there might be quicksand. But we can come up around the back of the shack."

Brad closed his eyes and breathed a prayer of thanks. The odds were beginning to look a little bit better.

"Let's try it," he said. Eric nodded. They were tense and silent then as they wound their way back into the primitive depths of the swamp.

Wendy woke with a foul taste in her mouth, a taste similar to the sickening smell that had brought her to unconsciousness. She had a horrible headache and the world was still spinning so rapidly that she didn't know if she was sitting, standing or lying flat. Her arms ached, but not as badly as her head. For several long minutes, she was aware only of pain.

She opened her eyes and closed them again. She fought a wave of nausea and swallowed hard. Then she tried to open her eyes again.

She was able to focus this time. Above her were the boards of a bare and rotting roof. She was lying flat. Her arms hurt because her wrists were tied tightly together with rough rope. Her flesh was chapping and her shoulders were being wrenched by the miserable position.

"He's taking his sweet time."

At the sound of the voice, Wendy closed her eyes again. As heavy footsteps moved by her head, she slit her eyes open, feigning unconsciousness.

It was the man with the brutal hold, walking by her. The man with the brown eyes who had nabbed her and shoved the chloroform over her face.

"He'll come, Jenkins. Trust me. He'll come."

Another voice, very soft and somehow more menacing for it, answered. Wendy tried to let her head fall naturally to the side so that she could see the man.

It was the gray-haired man with the ice eyes. She didn't need to be told that this was Michaelson. Sitting at a crude table in the center of the small shack, he seemed entirely out of place. She could see that his shoes were expensive leather loafers. His suit looked to be fashionable linen. In the midst of the swamp, he was wearing a tie. He had spoken calmly, but he obviously didn't feel comfortable here.

"He'll come, yeah, but what about the Indian? What's the connection there?"

A third man spoke, a man with a definite accent. Wendy tried to survey the small cabin. She didn't dare open her eyes fully, and even the slightest movement was painful and difficult. It was the typical cabin of the weekend hunter, hastily built by non-professional labor. There were two windows, a bunk in one corner of the room, and a table in the center. A dark man, cradling some type of huge firearm, sat on one of the window-sills, dangling his legs. The brown-eyed man, Jenkins, kept pacing by Wendy's head. At least he was better dressed for the occasion, wearing military khakis. A rifle was slung over his shoulder.

She clenched her teeth, afraid that she was going to start shivering. These men meant to kill her, to kill them all. For a moment the horror of it was so great that a wave of icy fear washed over her, paralyzing her. She nearly screamed in sheer panic.

She fought it, clenching her teeth more tightly. She was a victim, just as Leif had been. But Leif had fought to the bitter end, and, dear God, she would fight, too. They were trying to trap Brad, but she was sure that he would realize that. And they were talking about Eric, too....

"We need the Indian," Jenkins said.

Michaelson let out a snort of derision. "Yes, we need the Indian. Because you have proved yourself worth-less!"

Jenkins lunged over the table and slammed his fist against it. "You fool! Don't you understand! I'm good at tracking, damned good. You wouldn't have the girl if it wasn't for me. I'm the one who followed Suarez's trail to her house. I'm the one who knew about the girl, about McKenna's involvement with her—and even the damned Indian you want so badly now. But listen to me, and listen good. This mire out here is deadly, can't you comprehend that? Your plane went down in the mid-dle of an area that's infested with snakes, and riddled with quicksand pits. Only a man who really knows this swamp can salvage the damned thing."

Michaelson rose, his face rigid. He continued to speak softly. "Don't ever address me in that tone of voice, Jenkins. Ever." He strode over to the window and looked out. "If the Indian doesn't come, we'll have to rely on the girl." Wendy felt his gaze fall her way. "She lives out here. She'll know what she is doing."

The dark-haired man with the accent let out a snickering sound. "I'm sure she knows what she is doing. I'm sure she does it very well."

"Shut up, Pedro," Michaelson said. "Keep your mind on business and off the girl. When the plane is found, you can have her. Hell, you can have her any way you want her. But not until then, do you understand?"

"*¡Sí!*" Pedro agreed sullenly.

Wendy felt the bile rise in her stomach again. She swallowed, fighting off another rise of panic.

"Hey!" Jenkins said suddenly. The sound of his footsteps seemed to slam against Wendy's head, and then she did scream because he wrenched at her shoulders, dragging her up. "She's awake. The little bitch is awake. She's been listening to us."

He jerked her to a sitting position and she nearly screamed again from the pain in her arms. Her eyes flew open, meeting his stare with a gaze of silvery fury. He laughed, watching her. "Pedro must be right. I'll bet she's a lot of fun."

"Leave her alone," Michaelson said. "There's work to do."

"Hell, we've got to sit here and wait..." Jenkins said. He smiled. His face was so close to Wendy's that she could feel the foulness of his breath.

She spat at him and he howled in outrage, slapping her.

"I told you, leave the girl alone!" Michaelson's voice rose at last. He indicated the window. "You think that McKenna is a fool? I don't. I don't want him attacking us while you lie there with your pants down, you fool! Now, get away from her."

Jenkins shoved Wendy back down to the floor and wiped the spittle from his face. "Later, baby. I'll make it good. I promise."

"What's that?" the Latin man said suddenly.

Michaelson and Jenkins both moved toward the window.

Wendy heard a birdcall—soft and low, but clear and beautiful, slicing cleanly through the air.

"It's McKenna!" Jenkins said, startled. "It's McKenna, walking straight toward us."

Wendy tried to rise. She sat up, wincing against the hold of the rope on her wrists. Her heart began to leap and slam—and sink. What was he doing? Tears stung her eyes. He was coming for her! Well, of course he would. It was his job. Even if he had barely known her, he would have come for her. It was what he did for a living.

But he shouldn't have. Not that way. He shouldn't have just come to give up his life for hers. Didn't he know…?

"He's alone," Jenkins said harshly. "He took the damned airboat and came out here alone. We don't need him! We need the damned Indian."

Michaelson looked pensively at Wendy.

"We've still got the girl."

She forced herself to stare straight at him, trying to look calm. She had to stop panicking.

Brad was no fool. Nor was he alone. She had to proceed carefully.

Michaelson turned back to the window.

"When he comes close enough, shoot him," he told Jenkins.

"No!" Wendy screamed.

"Shoot him in the kneecap. Make it painful, make it slow. Make him see what happens to spies in my camp."

"No!" Wendy staggered to her feet. "No! So help me, you touch him, and I'll never help you find a thing. Your dope can rot out there with your pilot—"

"I can make her docile," Pedro interrupted. He glanced out the window, then sauntered toward Wendy and picked up a handful of her hair. "I can make her scream and cry and take you any damned place you want to go, boss."

Wendy jerked her head back, staring at the man defiantly. "Can you? You'll have to kill me first, and you won't get anywhere at all if I'm dead, too, will you?"

"Get away from the girl!" Michaelson ordered. "Leave her the hell alone until I say! Jenkins, you, too, ass!" Jenkins had turned to watch the Latin man. Michaelson scowled at them both, then turned to look out the window again. "Where is he?"

"What?" Jenkins demanded.

Michaelson seemed to explode. "He isn't there any more! McKenna has disappeared. Where the hell is he? I can't see him anymore!"

"He has to be out there!" Jenkins insisted.

"Yes, he's out there," Michaelson said. "He's out there, but it's a trick! It's some kind of a trick!"

There was silence as they all stared out the window. Then Michaelson cursed them all. Swerving around, he pulled an automatic from his breast pocket. Long strides brought him to Wendy.

He wrenched her in front of him, shoving the smooth steel of the gun against her cheek. "Let's go, sweetheart. I want McKenna dead almost as much as those jerks want you alive. The same kind of pleasure, you know, the same kind of high."

She tasted the steel. A small cry of pain escaped her as he prodded her with the gun. He threw open the door and pushed her out into the sunlight.

"McKenna! Show yourself." The nose of the gun pressed against Wendy's jaw. "Show yourself. Or else your girlfriend loses her face. You've got ten seconds. I'm counting. Do you hear me, McKenna? I'm counting."

Wendy winced, afraid to swallow. She heard the gun cock. She felt it, icy cold and hard against her skin. She closed her eyes, afraid to imagine the explosion of the flesh.

"I'm counting, McKenna. I'm counting!" Michaelson repeated in fury. "You've got until ten. One, McKenna. Two. Three, McKenna. Four. Five. Six…"

13

"Stop!"

The metallic nose of the gun relaxed against Wendy's face at the cry. But it wasn't Brad who appeared this time; it was Eric.

He eased out from the tangle of foliage on the hammock and started walking toward them with long strides.

"I want McKenna, boy!" Michaelson called out. "You and your little girlfriend here can give us a few directions, and then go on your way. But I want McKenna. I have a score to settle with him."

Wendy thought that she would lose her mind with fear. Michaelson was still holding a gun on her, Eric could be shot and killed any second, and Brad had disappeared somewhere.

"McKenna took off on me, the stinking coward." Eric spit into the grass. "He's hiding here somewhere. Give me a chance—I can catch him."

Wendy winced as Michaelson raised the nose of the gun to her temple. "You'd better not be bluffing, boy."

"He's got to be back here. Help me. We'll get him."

Wendy sensed Michaelson's hesitation. Then he lowered the gun and aimed it against her spine. "Walk, girl. Walk straight toward your Indian friend." He turned back to the house. "Jenkins! Pedro! Come on—now!"

He pushed Wendy forward. She started walking. As she moved ahead the grass was growing thicker and the ground was beginning to give way. The shack stood on the high part of the hammock. This was treacherous ground below. Her boots sank in the mud.

As she came closer and closer to Eric, she stared into his eyes. Green and steady, they gave nothing away.

Where the hell was Brad? she wondered.

Michaelson was wondering the same thing. "This better not be a trap, Injun boy. If you make one false move, she's dead. I'll kill her slow. I'll crack her spine and shatter her tailbone."

Wendy shivered. She could still feel the cold steel barrel of the gun.

"No trap, I swear it," Eric reassured. "That slime just lit out of here. He was willing to let Wendy get killed in his place. If I find him, I want him. I know how to make people die slowly, too."

Michaelson grunted. Wendy stared at Eric, praying for courage.

The muck was growing deeper. Leif had taught her to avoid terrain like this. Too easily, the muck became quicksand. They shouldn't be walking here. Any step could be a false step.

"Come on, Wendy!" Eric called to her. "We've got to find that bastard! He split and ran out on us!"

"Eric…?"

She looked at him, begging for an answer. Ignoring her fear, he led her farther away.

Michaelson shoved her in the back with the gun. "You heard him! Move. I want that G-man dead."

"Move, Wendy!" Eric persisted. She kept coming.

Then she realized that there were no sounds coming from behind them. Michaelson had ordered Jenkins and Pedro to come along behind him. They hadn't done so.

Michaelson muttered something. As Wendy felt the suck and pull against her boots, she remembered that Michaelson was wearing fancy leather loafers.

Struggling to lift her foot, she took another step. She stumbled, barely recovering before falling forward. She tried to pull her foot up again, but the suction was too strong. She sank deeper.

Michaelson crashed into her and his gun slipped from his fingers. Beneath them, the ground gurgled. Wendy looked down, watching as Michaelson's weapon was swallowed into the muck.

He began to swear again. Even as the words came out of his mouth, the muck rose around them.

It wasn't rising, Wendy thought hysterically. They were sinking together.

"Bastard!" Michaelson screamed out. Wendy realized that he was screaming at Eric, who continued to stare at him.

The ground held on to them, tightly. Wendy realized that she'd sunk up to her thighs in the grasping muck. A scream rose in her throat.

Just as she cried out, a terrible sound of agony exploded on the air. Michaelson twisted. Wendy realized that the bellow came from behind them, from the cabin.

Michaelson wrapped his arms around her tightly. "She goes down with me! Bastards! She goes down with me!"

Wendy cried out in pain and panic. His arms were choking her. He was bearing her down, down deeper and deeper into the relentless hold of the earth. He no longer held the gun, but he held her. And there was no escape.

She cast back her head and screamed.

Inside the cabin, Brad heard Wendy's scream.

So far, things had gone like clockwork, smooth as ice. He and Eric had carefully pondered the plan, and though it hadn't been foolproof, it had been the best they could do.

But it had gone well. He had managed to walk straight toward the cabin, then disappear flat against a side wall. If Michaelson, Jenkins or Pedro had looked around, he would have been finished before he had ever begun.

But they hadn't.

And Michaelson's temper had snapped, just as Brad had gambled that it would. Michaelson had dragged Wendy out. Then it had been hard to concentrate. Brad had reminded himself that their lives depended on his action during the next few minutes. Pressed flat against the cabin, he told himself that he was trained for this, that he needed to be cool and calculating.

It was probably the hardest thing he would ever do.

Watching Michaelson slam the gun against Wendy's cheek, he'd turned and darted around the building, entering the cabin the very way that Michaelson had just exited it.

Pedro and Jenkins had been standing at the window, staring out.

Jenkins hadn't realized that Brad was in the cabin until he'd already knocked Pedro out with the rifle butt.

Jenkins was good with terrain, but he was too heavy to be a good fighter. He couldn't move quickly enough. Brad grimly took him with a knee jab to his gut and a swing of the rifle butt against his chin.

Pedro would be out for a long, long time. Although Brad was pretty sure that Jenkins had a broken jaw, he used his belt to tie up the man's arms. Jenkins was dangerous, more dangerous when he was wounded. Just like an animal. Hell, they were animals.

Brad was just finishing with Jenkins when he heard Wendy's scream.

His heart soaring to his throat, he burst out of the cabin and raced around the side.

He could see Eric running. He was a burst of speed, racing toward the quicksand pool.

And Brad saw why.

Wendy had played it like a trouper. Eric had worried that she would sense the quicksand and panic. But she had played the stoic and kept walking. Michaelson had become disarmed, which was even better than they had hoped. They had figured they would have to bargain for the gun.

But now they were going to have to bargain for Wendy's life.

Michaelson had her in as tight a grasp as the sucking earth. He was moving frantically, and with each movement, the two of them were sinking deeper.

"Let her go!" Brad hardly recognized his own voice, nor could he feel his feet against the ground. "Let her go!" he screamed again. He needed to be logical; he needed to talk, to tell Michaelson to calm down, to stay still. "Let her go!" he thundered out the command again.

Eric had already reached the black pool. He laid his body flat, reaching for Wendy's hands.

Brad thrashed into the mud. Instantly, he felt the pull of the muck, slithering over him, grabbing on to him. It was like an evil, living creature.

He ignored it. Wendy was before him, but Michaelson's arms were around her neck. The muck was up to her breasts.

"Brad!" she whispered his name. She was white as ash, filthy and trembling. Michaelson's hands were around her throat, bearing down on her. And still her eyes were beautifully silver. She was slipping away from the world, and still, her eyes were telling Brad that she loved him.

He let out a yell, a sound that he'd never heard before. It was a cry of the wild, as harsh and merciless as the land.

He caught on to Michaelson's hands, wrenching them from their choking hold on Wendy.

Michaelson wasn't beat. "Bastard!" he hissed at Brad. "Fed bastard, you'll go down with me."

Brad got off one good punch. Michaelson staggered in the muck, trying to aim back at him. Brad turned to shove Wendy toward Eric. She was slipping farther and farther. The pool of black mud was rising to her chin. "Give me your hand!" he called to her, reaching into the endless blackness. His fingers curled around hers. He screamed out a curse and a prayer. With a horrible sound, the muck relinquished Wendy's hand.

Eric reached her; Brad was afraid that he would not be able to hold her, that the muck would be too slick and slippery.

Eric's fingers were a vise around Wendy's wrists. He had her.

Just in time. With peripheral vision, Brad saw Michaelson locking his fists to pound them down on him. He leaned to the side and Michaelson's blow just grazed him. Brad was sinking deeper, he realized. The muck really did seem to be alive. Like a breathing, black demon, it swarmed over his body, caressing his flesh with a sure promise of death.

"You're going with me, cop," Michaelson said. He started to laugh. Brad decided that the man was insane, but then, anyone who had ice in his veins instead of blood, the way Michaelson did, could not be completely sane.

"I'm not a cop," Brad said. "I'm DEA." Unfortunately, Brad realized, it was a moot point under these circumstances.

"Brad!" Wendy screamed his name. Twisting around, he could see that Eric had pulled her free. She was covered in the black muck, but she was free.

And he was nearly up to his throat.

"Brad! Take my hand!" Wendy cried. Those beautiful silver eyes of hers were on him. Her hair was covered in muck, but her eyes were pure.

"No, Wendy—"

"Take her hand!" Eric yelled. Brad realized the grip that Eric had around Wendy's legs. His heart pounded. *No,* he thought. *Wendy, go. Wendy, you're safe. Run out of here, I dragged you into this.*

"Brad!" she screeched.

"Dammit! I know what I'm doing!" Eric said.

Brad realized that he was suddenly exhausted. He

could barely lift his arms. It required a supreme effort to move.

"Brad!"

Her cry gave him strength. He reached out, and her fingers curled around him. He could feel the tremendous effort that she and Eric put forth. He closed his eyes. He was the rope in a tug-of-war. The earth wanted him.

Then it began to give. Staring at Wendy's mud-covered fingers on his arms, he realized slowly that they were overcoming the pull of the muck. He was easing out of it.

There was a long, mournful sound. The muck seemed to cry out.

Then it bubbled and gurgled, and suddenly, he was free.

He landed on top of Wendy and Eric. Although they were all covered in mud, they began to laugh.

"Bastard! You lousy bas—"

Michaelson never finished the last word. His head disappeared with a sickening whoosh of suction.

It was almost me, Brad thought. It had almost been Wendy.

"Oh, God!" Wendy whispered.

He kissed her. She tasted like mud. When he released her, she was still laughing.

Then his spine tingled with awareness. A strange shadow had fallen over them.

Wendy's eyes widened as she felt the sudden constriction in Brad's muscles. She looked up and saw a stranger staring down at the three of them. Tall and lean with silver hair, he was a striking man. His eyes were blue, and they looked as if they could be hard. But there was warmth in them now—warmth and amusement.

"Purdy!" Brad said, astonished. "Sir!"

L. Davis Purdy stared down at the three of them, his hands on his hips. "McKenna, I run my ass ragged, I drag that distinguished older gentleman—" he paused, backing away slightly. Wendy saw that Willie was just behind him "—around the swamp, and what do I find? You—mud wrestling with his granddaughter."

"McKenna, you do get the hard assignments." A younger man stood at Purdy's side. He was shorter than Purdy, but lean and rip-cord hard. He had red hair and freckles, and he grinned at Brad and winked at Wendy.

"Gary," Brad said.

"What is this?" Eric demanded.

"Eric, Wendy—meet Mr. L. Davis Purdy. And Gary Henshaw."

Wendy automatically reached out a hand, then realized that she was covered in mud and still lying on the ground.

Purdy laughed, clutched her hand and helped her to her feet. "Mrs. Hawk, it's a pleasure to meet you. And Eric." Eric jumped to his feet by his own power then. Wendy offered Purdy a wavery smile, then she turned and ran to Willie, who hugged her fiercely.

"How did you get here?" Brad began, then he gazed at Willie, and the old Indian nodded to him gravely.

"Your friend from the garage, Mac, got us out to Mrs. Hawk's home, where we found the senior Mr. Hawk. He brought us out here." Purdy's pleasant smile faded for a moment. He inclined his head toward the quicksand pool. "Michaelson?"

Brad nodded to his boss.

"Maybe it's just as well," Purdy murmured. Then a smile curved the corners of his mouth. "You are a mess."

"Yeah? Well, where were you when we were becoming a mess?"

Gary laughed. "We checked out the shack. It looks like Pedro is waking up, but I don't think he's going anywhere."

"Oh?" Brad said.

"There was this great big cat standing over him. I was ready to shoot the thing, but Mr. Hawk assured me that the panther was a trusted and loyal pet."

"Baby!" Brad said.

"Honestly." Purdy looked at Gary and shook his head. "Leave the boy alone in the woods for a week, and he goes right to hell. Mud wrestling. And he thinks a hundred-and-fifty-pound panther is a pussycat. Hell. What's this man coming to?"

Brad glanced at Eric, and both men laughed. Purdy started walking back toward the shack. "We've got a few things to pick up at the shack. McKenna, you need a bath. Let's get moving here, shall we?"

He wasn't going to get any time alone with Wendy, Brad saw that quickly. From that moment on, they weren't even together.

Purdy ordered Gary to stay with the Hawks and help them in any way possible. He wanted Wendy and Eric to come back with them for statements, but he intended to let them go home first to bathe and change.

He wanted Brad to come with him immediately. It seemed there would be an informal interrogation with Charlie Jenkins and Pedro.

Before they parted, Brad noticed Wendy watching him. He saw the silver light in her eyes, glistening like tears, a shadow of sadness.

His heart plummeted and hammered. She considered it over, he realized. Right then and there, it was over.

He wanted to scream out her name, to push everyone aside and race to her. If he could hold her tightly enough, he could tell her that they were stronger than life's obstacles, that they could make it together.

He never had the chance to say a word. She stared at him a final second, and then she turned away.

"Brad, let's go," Purdy admonished him impatiently.

From then on, the day became a blur of rapid-fire activity. Purdy conducted questioning in the shack. Neither Pedro nor Jenkins put up much of a fight. Purdy wanted to know about the plane, and they were willing to answer questions, not that they could provide much help. Michaelson knew that the small cargo plane carrying his shipment had crashed somewhere in the vast swampland almost two days ago. They assumed the pilot was dead—there'd been no radio contact. Jenkins drew pictures on the ground, showing them where he thought the plane was. Then he begged for a doctor to set his jaw.

Purdy nodded to one of his men, a medic. The young man came over to Jenkins, gave him a pain pill and wrapped his jaw tightly. "There will be a chopper out here soon to rush you down to Jackson," Purdy assured Jenkins.

Purdy had barely spoken before the helicopter could be heard hovering above them. Since it couldn't land in the swamp, Jenkins was sent up first in a basket rigging, then Pedro followed. Brad stood on the ground and watched them go, rising into the sky. They would both heal. They would probably get stiff prison terms. Along with whatever else the D.A.'s office charged them with, kidnapping was sure to be a part of the prosecution.

Purdy set up a task force to search the swamp for the plane. He radioed in for air assistance, then he surveyed Brad from head to toe. Taking in the drying muck, he smiled.

"Well, it's over for you, McKenna."

Over, God, he hated that word. It couldn't be over. Even if she had turned away from him, it couldn't be over.

"Let's go back in," Purdy said. "I told you, you need a bath. Badly."

"Sir, I've come to know something about this place. I might be helpful in searching for the downed plane."

"Brad! It's over. You've done your job. And I need you back at the office to file reports and give your statements to the D.A. Let's move."

Brad exhaled and started walking. "I don't even have a lousy home to go to for a bath! My clothes are gone... my record collection is gone. I'm just damned grateful that I didn't have a German shepherd!"

Purdy slapped him on the back. "I rented an apartment for you—right on the water. The boys and I put together for a few outfits, and if I'm not mistaken, your insurance check is on the kitchen counter. But I need those statements and paperwork from you this week, so come on."

There wasn't anything wrong with the apartment Purdy had rented for him. And Purdy and Gary and some of the others had gone out and bought him some things, so he was able to take a shower and dress in a clean suit. There was even some stoneware in the cabinets, a few groceries and a kettle, so he was able to brew himself some instant coffee before heading into the office to start the endless paperwork.

There was nothing wrong with any of it. He had to admit that the apartment was even nicer than the one that Michaelson had blasted. The guys knew his taste fairly well, so the clothes were fine.

But the apartment seemed empty—empty as hell.

It wasn't his apartment that was lacking, it was his life.

He sat back on the sofa and closed his eyes. What would he be doing now, he wondered, if he had come back to his life exactly as it had been?

He'd have played one of his discs while he showered and dressed, for one. And what else? Well, he'd have gone back into the office, and when he was done, he'd have gone out with the guys to celebrate the fact that the job was done. It was over. They'd have gone to a nightclub on the beach for a few drinks.

And there might have been a woman. Someone career-minded, pretty, flashy. Someone out to have a good time, with no strings. They'd have liked each other, sure. They'd have had a good time. They might have made breakfast in the morning. They might even have remembered each other's names.

But Brad wasn't going out that night—not even for a few beers with the guys. He was going to file his paperwork, and he was going to try to see Wendy.

Unfortunately, his plan was thwarted. When Brad reached his office, he discovered that Wendy was being questioned by the district attorney. When he reached the D.A.'s office, he found out that Wendy had already gone.

Amazed, Brad asked Gary, "That's it? She's gone?"

"Oh, well, they may need to call her in again before the trial. The attorneys will want to talk to her again, I'm sure—"

"No, no. I mean, she left? Just like that? Did she—" He hesitated, his pride tripping him up. "Did she leave me a message?"

Gary shook his head. Brad stared at him a long moment.

When Brad was interviewed by the D.A., he answered every question in a tired monotone. When he was done, he headed back to his office, initiated the extensive paperwork, and later returned to his empty apartment.

He drank a beer, then drank another beer. He picked up the phone, and then he remembered that Wendy didn't have a phone.

She hadn't left him a message. She hadn't even said goodbye. Hell, they were worth more than that.

He had another beer. And another. Around 3:00 a.m. he finally fell asleep whispering her name. He didn't know if it was a curse or an anguished plea.

There was one nice thing about living alone, Wendy thought: privacy.

For two days, she'd been able to mope around the house. She'd been able to indulge in ridiculous crying sprees and talk out loud, cursing Brad and railing against him. She'd spent long, pensive hours staring at the blank television screen, reminding herself that she did not want him anyway.

She couldn't live with his job, and she knew that it would be wrong to ask him to change it. Even if she did, he would eventually resent her for it. It just couldn't work.

And the wretched man hadn't even come to see her when she had spent all those miserable hours with the D.A.! She'd answered a million questions then they'd somberly reminded her how much they would need her testimony to put away Jenkins and Pedro. The district attorney had seemed concerned over her volatile emotional state. She couldn't explain that her unbidden tears had nothing to do with the case—but with the DEA investigator. Fortunately, Eric had accompanied her. He had assured them all that Wendy was far stronger than she appeared.

And so she waited. For the first few days, she waited. She was convinced that he would come to her. She dreamed that she would wake up to find him there, standing in the doorway, dressed in old jeans. He would walk across the room, bend down to her and take her in his arms. In her dreams, their clothing would miraculously disappear, and she would feel the hot fire of his flesh next to hers.

But then she would wake up—alone. Or else it would be worse—Baby would be sprawled out on the bed, and she would growl and hiss in annoyance when Wendy threw her out.

Wendy returned to work at Eric's, but she couldn't concentrate on her work. She didn't know that she was absolutely worthless until Eric came in one afternoon, pulled the book she was reading out of her hand and turned it right side up.

Eric sat across from her, folding his fingers in contemplative fashion, studying her for several moments.

"Why don't you go in to Lauderdale and see him?" he suggested at last.

She shook her head. "If he wanted to see me, he would come here."

"That seems logical to you. What if he's thinking the same thing? That you'd come see him if you wanted to?"

"I was there and he wasn't!"

"He probably had a million things to do, Wendy. Be reasonable. I'll tell you what. I've got a dinner date with some old friends on Las Olas next Friday night. I'll drop you by Brad's, and if you're unhappy there, you can just come and join me."

"No."

"Why not?"

"It's not right. I mean, what for, anyway? He likes his life the way that it is. I can't really be a part of it."

He grinned at her and leaned forward, taking her hands. "Wendy, people change. They fall in love, and their priorities change."

"Who says he's in love?" she whispered.

Eric shrugged. "I do. As Willie says, life is a river. To live it, you must follow your heart."

"I'll let you know," she told him softly.

By the time Friday rolled around, she had summoned up some courage. She had spent the day in a tub of bubble bath, washed her hair, given herself a manicure and a pedicure and laid out a silk cocktail dress.

At four in the afternoon, she was practically whitewashed. But her hair was still soaking wet and she was pacing around in a worn, floor-length terry robe, trying not to chew her nails while she thought it over.

She was confused about her purpose. What was she going to say? Can we hop into bed one more time, Brad, for old time's sake? Hi, Brad, I was in the neighborhood, so I just stopped over?

What if he had a woman there?

Her courage was beginning to fade when she heard the sound of a motor. She was surprised to see that it was Eric. They weren't due to leave for the evening until about seven, and he was supposed to be driving over. She opened the front door and saw her brother-in-law walking toward her with a packet of mail. "I picked this up at the post office," he said, handing her the mail. "And I just wanted to check on tonight. We still on?"

"I don't know, Eric—" Wendy began.

"I'll be back in a couple of hours." He waved to her and hurried away. She thought about calling him back to tell him that it was definitely off.

She didn't. Maybe she would just go to dinner with Eric and his friends. It might be good to get out.

Wandering into the bathroom, she examined her pale face and wet hair and decided that for a woman who had spent the entire day trying to look and smell delicious, she'd failed miserably.

Then she wandered back into the kitchen, idly leafing through the mail. She found the usual assortment of bills and junk mail, then her heart began to pound when she saw that one of the letters addressed to her was from Brad's office.

The bills fell to the floor as she ripped open the official-looking letter.

After she had opened it, she read it over and over. Then she felt as if she were a kettle, that heat was rising inside of her and she was fast approaching a boiling point.

It was a thank-you from the department. An official thank-you for her part in accommodating the agent.

It was meant from the heart, she was sure. But it was all so formal, so final.

"There are definite advantages to living alone!" she screamed in fury, throwing the letter down and stamping on it. Still, she didn't feel any better.

"That son of a bitch!" she swore, pacing up and down the hallway. She stormed into her bedroom, threw herself on her bed and slammed her fist against her pillow.

Then she realized, very slowly, that she wasn't alone. She swung around.

He was there, just as he had been in her dreams. Well, he was dressed in a blue business suit, but he was standing in the doorway, staring at her.

He looked good—damned good. He was handsome in navy. His white shirt was tailored and crisp, and he even had good taste in ties. His hair was combed back. His eyes appeared a little more haggard, his face a bit leaner.

But he was standing in front of her.

Automatically, her fingers moved to her wet hair. She'd planned this out so well! She'd meant to come to him in complete control, svelte and sophisticated, armed and armored against any vulnerability.

But he had come to her when she looked about as sophisticated as Tinkerbell. Her temper soared again. Wendy sprang to her knees, and then to her feet.

"You bastard!" she hissed.

"I—uh—I did knock. You didn't hear me."

"I didn't hear you?" She began to advance on him. "I let you in, I turn my home, my life, inside out. I get kidnapped by dope dealers. And do I get anything from you? Like maybe, goodbye, Wendy, thanks, it's been sweet? No!" She slammed both her fists against his chest. "No! I get a thank-you from the department for accommodating you!"

"Wendy—"

"I hate you! I absolutely despise you. You're a ruthless ingrate!" She took a swing at him. He ducked and caught her arms, imprisoning her against his body.

"Wendy—"

She struggled against him in a frenzy. "You weren't even there! I came into that office and I was a wonderful, model citizen, and you weren't even there!"

"Wendy—"

"You can go and rot in hell, Brad McKenna!"

He scooped her off the floor. Automatically, she looped her arms around his neck and stared into his eyes.

He started walking toward the bed. "I tried to see you," Brad said.

Her heart seemed aflame, her flesh seemed aflame. He was touching her, holding her again. He was walking straight toward the bed.

He laid her down. Gently tugging on the cord to her robe, he watched as it fell open. He caught his breath at the naked length of her. She saw the pulse start up against the bronze flesh at his throat. He laid his face against her and kissed her belly. She slipped her fingers into his hair.

"I was coming to see you tonight. I had it all planned out. I was going to wear silk. I was going to be beautiful."

"You are beautiful," he whispered huskily against her flesh. "Beautiful."

"You are a horrible, inconsiderate bastard, and I hate you," Wendy breathed. She could feel his lips, just grazing her skin.

He straightened and looked into her eyes. "Will you marry me, Wendy?"

Her eyes widened. "What?"

He loosened his tie. "I've thought about it. I know the way that you feel, but I think that we can come to some compromises. Life means much more to me now. I never knew how much it could mean until I found out what it was like to share. I love you, Wendy. I can't change what I am, my convictions, or the way that I feel, but I love you. I think that you love me, too. I've sat home these weeks staring at empty walls. I wanted you so badly. I thought that maybe you could forgive me for what I was. I thought that you would call me—"

"You didn't call me!" Wendy protested.

"You don't have a phone," Brad reminded her. "That's one thing that we're going to fix."

"What?" she said carefully. "We're going to live— here?"

"Well, it will take me at least an hour to get to work in the morning. But I figured that when I was working in Manhattan, my commute on the trains took me an hour, too. I'll still be with the DEA, but I'm through with the fieldwork. I want to come home at night—to come home here, to spend every night with you. We'll live here. With a phone."

"With a phone," Wendy repeated.

Brad's tie fell to the floor. His jacket, vest and shirt followed, but Wendy was still just staring at him, dumbfounded.

When he kicked off his shoes and trousers, she trembled and shuddered, alive with anticipation from head to toe. He stretched out over her and took her lips, kissing her slowly, savoring her lower lip, playing with her tongue. His left hand caressed the fullness of her curves, dallying over her breasts and between her legs. She was breathless when he pulled away from her, seeking her eyes. "Well?" he whispered.

"What?" Her mind wandered. What was he talking about? She returned his kiss so ardently and touched him with such fervor. He couldn't begin to think that she would deny him—not at this point.

Slow down, she warned herself. She smiled sweetly, trying to ignore the spiraling need inside of her. She drew her fingers down his chest and tightened them evocatively about the aroused shaft of his desire.

"Well? What's the verdict?" He kissed her lips, nuzzling his clean-shaven cheek against her throat. Then he met her eyes again. "Will you marry me?"

"Yes! Yes, I will!"

"Good." Brad smiled complacently. Then he lowered his weight upon her and thrust deeply inside of her. Deeper, and deeper, and then he held still. "I missed you so much," he whispered. "I can't leave you again. I really can't."

Wendy wound her arms around him. "I love you." She swallowed, savoring the feel of him. "I love you, and I don't think that I could ever let you go again."

Brad murmured something else, but she couldn't decipher his words. As he began to stroke her, hard and fast, the words just didn't matter anymore....

They were still lying there, drowsy and half-asleep—having made love several times to make up for lost time—when Wendy heard the motor of the airboat.

"Oh, dear!" She tried to leap up; some weight stopped her. Baby! The cat had come in when they had drifted off and made herself very comfortable, despite the two humans in the bed. "Baby, get off!"

"Out!" Brad commanded. Baby growled at him. He gave her a shove. "Off, I said!"

Baby obeyed. Wendy laughed, struggling back into her robe. "That's Eric," she told Brad. He arched a curious brow, lacing his fingers behind his head and stretching out comfortably. "Hey!" She shoved him. "You get up, too!"

He laughed and stepped into his trousers. "He's going to know exactly what we've been doing," Wendy wailed.

Brad laughed. "And what did he think he was bringing you into the city to do?"

"To go respectably out to dinner!" Wendy lied indignantly. Brad just laughed and walked into the living room. By the time Wendy belted her robe, she could hear the two men talking to one another. Guiltily straightening her tousled hair, she joined them. Brad swept her into the circle of his arm.

"He says that he'd be honored to be an usher at our wedding. He's sure that Willie will be delighted to give you away, and that maybe he'll break down and get a phone when we do, too."

Wendy burst out laughing. Eric laughed and kissed her.

"I told you, Wendy," he whispered, "we are all fated to follow our hearts." He gave her a squeeze. "Hey, have you got any champagne in here?"

Wendy did. It was warm, but they plopped a few ice cubes into it, and Eric toasted them.

* * *

Two months later, in the Church of the Little Flower, Willie did give her away. She wore a dress of soft gray, which highlighted the silver in her eyes.

Later, Brad told her that she was the most beautiful bride he had ever seen.

"Really?" she asked him. He had just been telling her how much he loved her gown, but that didn't seem to stop him from being overly anxious to remove it.

"Really."

"I'm so glad we were married."

"So am I," Brad said absently. There were a million little tiny hooks on the gown, and she wasn't helping him one bit.

"'Cause I think we're going to have a beautiful little newcomer," Wendy said demurely.

"That's nice," Brad murmured, annoyed by the maze of hooks on the damned dress.

Suddenly his fingers went still as he turned her toward him. "What?"

"Well, it could be a tawny-haired little visitor with golden eyes." Her voice trembled suddenly. "Do you mind?"

"Do I mind?" He could barely whisper. "I—I—no!"

He couldn't seem to find the proper words to tell her that he loved her, and that he was thrilled and awed by the prospect of a child—their child.

So he leaned over and kissed her, and showed her instead.

* * * * *

Also available from Delores Fossen

HQN Books

To see the complete list of titles available from
Delores Fossen, please visit www.deloresfossen.com.

STANDOFF
AT MUSTANG RIDGE

Delores Fossen

1

Deputy Sheriff Royce McCall drew his Colt .45 and stepped behind the ice-crusted cottonwood tree.

Mercy.

He didn't need this. It was too cold for a gunfight or even an arrest, but he might have to deal with both.

He glanced out at the hunting cabin and especially at the sole window that was facing his direction. He didn't see any movement, but he'd seen footprints in the snow that someone had tried to cover up. Those footprints came from the woods and led straight to the cabin.

Hiding footprints usually wasn't a good sign.

Of course, anyone inside was trespassing since the cabin was on McCall land, but he'd sure take a trespasser over an armed robber.

Normally, Royce wouldn't have been concerned with suspected felons this far out since the cabin wasn't near any main roads and a good twenty miles from the town of Mustang Ridge. But a cop from Amarillo P.D. had called earlier to warn him of a bank-robbery suspect who might be in the area. The guy could have found his way here with plans to use it as a hideout.

Without taking his attention off the cabin, Royce

eased his phone from his coat pocket. There wasn't enough signal strength to make a call in this remote location, but he fired off a text to his brother, Sheriff Jake McCall, to let him know about the possible situation.

A situation Royce would likely end up handling alone.

It would take at least a half hour for his brother to respond to the text and get Royce some backup all the way out here. With the temperature already below freezing and with the wind and snow spitting at him, he didn't want to wait another minute much less an hour—even if it meant he'd get a tongue-lashing from Jake.

Royce hoped that was all he got.

The Amarillo police had warned the fugitive was armed and dangerous.

Royce took that warning into account, pulled off the thick leather glove on his right hand so he'd have a better grip on the Colt, and he inched out from the cottonwood. Thankfully, there were other trees dotting the grounds, and he used them to make his way toward the cabin. He was nearly at the front when he heard something.

Movement inside.

So the person who'd tried to hide those footprints was definitely still around.

Royce used one of the porch posts for cover, but he knew there was a lot more of him exposed than there was hidden. He waited and listened, but the only sounds were the ragged wind and his own heartbeat crashing in his ears.

He'd been a deputy of Mustang Ridge for eleven years and had faced down an armed man or two, but it never got easier. If it ever did, Royce figured that'd be the time to quit and devote all his time to running his portion of the family ranch. Danger should never feel normal.

With his bare hand going numb, it was now or never. Steering clear of the window, he reached over and tested the knob.

It was locked.

Royce didn't issue any warnings. He turned and gave the door a swift kick, and even though it stayed on the hinges, the lock gave way, and it flew open. Before it even hit the wall, he had his gun ready and aimed.

He took in the place with a sweeping glance. Not much to take in, though. There was a set of bunk beds on one side, a small kitchen on the other and an equally small bathroom in the center back. Since the privacy curtain in the bathroom was wide-open, he could see straight inside. No one was there unless the person was in the shower.

Keeping a firm grip on his gun, Royce inched closer, and he heard some movement again.

Yeah, it was definitely coming from the shower stall.

He took a deep breath and made his way into the cabin so he could get a look inside the bathroom.

"I'll shoot," someone called out.

Royce froze. It was a woman—not the male robbery suspect he'd braced himself to face. However, it was hard to tell who the woman was with that quivery voice. Plus, he couldn't see much of her because the overhead lights weren't on, and the shower stall was hidden in the shadows.

Usually if threatened with violence, Royce would threaten right back. However, after one glance at her hand, the only part of her he could actually see, he realized a threat might not be the way to go.

Yeah, she was armed all right. She was holding a little Smith & Wesson, and it was possible she was even trying to aim the gun at him. But she was huddled in the tiny tiled shower, and her hand was shaking so hard she would have been lucky to hit him or anything else within ten feet of where she was trying to aim.

As his eyes adjusted to the darkness, he saw the woman was wearing an unbuttoned coat over what appeared to be a nightgown. No hat, no gloves, and those flat house shoes definitely weren't cold-weather gear. She had to be freezing.

"You need to put down that gun." Royce tried to keep his voice level and calm. Hard to do with the adrenaline pumping through him and the cold blasting at his back. She didn't look like much of a threat, but she was armed.

"I won't let you kill me," she said in a broken whisper.

"Kill you?" Jeez, what was going on here? "No one's going to kill you, lady. I'm hoping you've got the same idea when it comes to me and that Smith & Wesson you got wobbling around there."

She looked up at him as if confused by that remark, and when she took a single step out of the shower, her eyes met his.

Oh, man.

"Sophie?" And he cursed some more when he got a better look at her face. Yep, it was Sophie Conway, all right. A neighbor of sorts since her daddy, Eldon, owned the sprawling ranch next to his own family's land.

Sophie and Royce weren't exactly friends. All right,

they were pretty much on each other's bad side, but
Royce still didn't think she'd shoot him.

He hoped he was right about that.

"It's me, Royce," he said in case by some miracle
Sophie didn't recognize him. He leaned in a little so
she could have a better look at him, and he maneuvered
himself into a position so he could disarm her.

"I know who you are," Sophie said a split second before she tried to scramble away from him.

He blocked her path, which wasn't hard to do since
the rest of her was as wobbly as her aim. "Look, I'm
not too happy about seeing you, either," Royce let her
know, "but there's no reason for you to hold a grudge
and point a gun at me."

Well, maybe there was a reason for the grudge part,
but Royce wasn't getting into what'd happened between
them four weeks ago.

"Are you drunk or something?" he asked.

She frowned, obviously not happy with that little
conclusion. "What are you doing here?" She kept the
gun pointed at him. "Did you come to kill me?"

Royce huffed. "No." He drew that out a few syllables.
"I'm here because my family owns the cabin."

Sophie glanced around as if really seeing it for the
first time. "This is your place?"

"Yeah." Again, Royce gave her a good dose of his
smart-mouth tone, something his brother, Jake, had told
him he was pretty good at doing. "I was out here looking for a couple of horses that broke fence, and maybe
even an armed robber, so I decided to stop by and check
on things. Now, care to tell me why you're here?"

Again, she looked around before her gaze came back
to him, and while she was semi-distracted, Royce did

something about that Smith & Wesson. He lunged at her and clamped his hands around her right wrist.

"No!" she shouted, and despite her shaky hands, she started fighting. "I need the gun."

Sophie kicked at him and tried to slug him with her left hand. She connected, sort of, her open hand slamming into his jaw.

And that's when Royce knew he'd had enough.

He knocked her hand against the sink, and her gun went flying into the sleeping part of the cabin at the same moment that she went flying at him. Even though he'd managed to disarm her, that didn't stop her from continuing the fight. She pushed and clawed at him, and he tossed his gun aside to stop it from being accidentally discharged in the fray.

Royce tried to subdue her without actually inflicting any bodily harm, but it was hard with Sophie fighting like a wildcat.

"Sophie, stop this now," he growled.

When she tried to knee him in the groin, Royce caught her, dragged her to the floor and flipped her onto her back. He pinned her body down with his.

Still, she didn't stop struggling.

She made one last attempt to toss him off her, and it was as if that attempt took all the fight from her. She went limp, and because he was so close to her face, just inches away, he saw the tears spring to her blue eyes.

Her eyes were still wide, and her chest was pumping for air, but at least she looked directly at him. "I won't let you kill me," she whispered.

Man, they were back to the crazy talk. "I'm guessing you've got a bad hangover from a New Year's party, because you're not making any sense."

The new year was already two days past. Still, maybe she'd been on a bender. After all, she'd been pretty darn drunk the last time he'd seen her a month ago.

Blowing out a long breath, Royce caught onto her face so he could examine her eyes and the rest of her. Too bad *the rest of her* was what really caught his attention.

The struggle had done a number on her long dark brown hair, and strands of it were now on her damp cheek and neck. On him, too. Royce didn't want to feel anything other than anger and maybe some confusion when he looked at Sophie. But he failed at that, too.

He felt that kick of attraction.

The same stupid attraction that had gotten the better part of him four weeks ago when he'd had way too much to drink and run into her at a party. Royce had been nursing a bad attitude because his three-year-old niece had been so sick. Heaven knows what Sophie had been nursing, but she'd been as drunk as he was.

He should have remembered that huge amounts of liquor, a surly attitude and an attractive woman just didn't mix.

Especially this woman.

Sophie was too rich for his blood. Not that he was poor. Nope, his family had money, too, but they were basically ranchers. Sophie had been city-raised, and ever since she'd moved back to Mustang Ridge about a year ago, she had always seemed to turn up her nose at anything and anyone in the small ranching town that he called home.

Well, until that party at the Outlaw Bar.

She was the last person he'd expected to find stinkin' drunk, and that was the only explanation for why he'd ended up at the Lone Star Motel with her. Though his memories were a little blurry when it came to the details. The only thing that was clear was there'd been some clothing removed and a little intimate touching before they'd passed out.

"Wait a minute," Royce said, thinking back to that fiasco at the Outlaw Bar and the Lone Star Motel. "Do you think I came here to kill you because you told me to take a hike after you woke up that morning?" He didn't wait for an answer to that asinine question. "Because, Sophie, I got over that *fast*."

Besides, they hadn't been in a relationship or anything. They'd only been together that once, and when Sophie woke up that morning, she'd pitched a hissy fit.

"I told you to take a hike," she repeated. Sophie's forehead bunched up as if she was trying to recall that or something.

"You said you were about to get engaged, and if I came near you again, you'd file charges against me," he reminded her. His jaw tightened, and that cleared his head and body of any shred of lingering attraction. "Trust me, I got the message. I've got no time for a high-maintenance daddy's girl who won't own up to the fact that she got drunk and nearly had a dirty one-night stand with a cowboy cop."

She swallowed hard, stared at him.

Maybe he'd hurt her feelings. Well, he didn't give a rat's behind about that, but Royce did move away from her so he could stand up and get his body off hers. He needed some answers, and then he could get her the heck out of his cabin and off his land.

He had enough memories of Sophie without making more.

"Why are you here?" he demanded. "And this time, don't give me a stupid answer about someone else or me trying to kill you." He tapped the badge clipped to his rawhide belt. "In case you've forgotten, I'm a deputy sheriff. I try to make a habit of not killing people—even ones who trespass on my land and point guns at me."

"I haven't forgotten who you are," Sophie murmured. She didn't say it with as much disdain as he'd expected, but there was a lot of unexpected stuff going on here today.

"Why. Are. You. Here?" he repeated.

Struggling and mumbling, she pushed herself to a sitting position. "Swear you aren't going to kill me."

"I swear," he snapped. He was about to chew her out for daring to ask him that, but Royce held back and just waited for her to continue.

"After I got the phone call… I started running." Sophie pulled in a hard breath, and by hanging on to the wall, she managed to get to her feet. "And this cabin was the first place I reached. I thought maybe I could hide until my father answered my text message." She paused, rubbed her forehead. "My phone doesn't work up here on the ridge."

That last part was the first thing she'd said that made a lick of sense. Cell service here was spotty at best. But it didn't explain why she'd run to the cabin in the first place. "What happened?"

Her gaze came to his, and her eyes widened. "Oh, God. We have to get out of here," she said, her voice trembling again. Heck, Sophie started trembling again, too. Shaking from head to toe.

Royce stepped in front of her when she tried to go toward the door.

"We can't stay," she insisted. "If they find us together, they'll try to kill him."

Great. Now they were back to her talking out of her head. Royce leaned in and took a whiff of her breath. No smell of booze, so maybe she had been drugged. Something was certainly off here.

"Okay, I'll bite," he snarled. "Who's the *him* that they'll try to kill?"

She pushed him aside and tried to get to her feet again. "The baby they believe I'm having," she mumbled.

Royce stared at her. "Wait a minute." He shook his head. "Are you pregnant?"

Sophie didn't answer right away. "No. But I told them I was."

Royce would get to the *them* part later, but for now he wanted more on the fake pregnancy claim. "Why the heck would you tell someone you're pregnant when you're not?"

Sophie groaned, a sound that came from deep within her throat. "I didn't have a choice. I thought it'd keep us alive."

Royce was sure that he blinked. "Us?"

The tears came to her eyes again. *"Us,"* she verified. "I told them the baby was…yours."

He felt as if someone had slugged him—twice. "You what?" And that was the best he could manage. Royce just kept staring at her and probably would have continued if she hadn't latched on to him.

"I'm sorry, Royce. So sorry." Her breath caught in her throat. "But I just signed your death warrant."

2

Sophie wished her teeth would stop chattering so she could hear herself think. Clearly, she'd been wrong about Royce wanting to kill her because he'd had more than ample opportunity to do that and hadn't. Of course, he might change his mind when he learned what she had done.

"My death warrant?" Royce snarled. He grabbed his dark brown Stetson that had fallen off during the scuffle and shoved it back on his head.

His jaw muscles were so tight that she didn't know how he managed to speak, but even without the words, Sophie could see his narrowed eyes. That, and every muscle in his body seemed primed for a fight. For answers, too.

Answers that Royce expected her to give him.

"We have to leave," she reminded him.

Even though her feet felt frozen to the floor, Sophie pushed her way past Royce and went to the front window so she could look out and keep watch. The bitter wind howling through the open door cut her bone-deep, but that was minor compared to everything else she was feeling.

"How did you get here?" she asked.

"My truck. It's parked over the ridge because the trail

here isn't passable in winter." And that's all he said for several seconds. However, he did shut the door. "What did you mean about signing my death warrant?"

"Please, can we just go now and you can ask your questions once we're out of here?" But she stopped and realized if their positions were reversed, she would have dug in her heels. Just as Royce was doing now.

Maybe the partial truth wouldn't get them both killed. "I didn't want you involved in this, but I couldn't stop them—"

"Who are *them* and what is *this?*" he interrupted.

Sophie opened her mouth. Closed it. And she shook her head. Where was she to start? The beginning, maybe, but she wasn't even sure where the beginning was.

"About a month ago, my father arranged my marriage to his business partner, Travis Bullock—"

He cursed. "Sophie, how the heck is that related to my so-called death warrant?"

"It's related," she insisted. "I didn't love Travis, but my father said the marriage would ease some of his financial burdens. He had some investments that didn't pan out." She checked out the window again. "My late mother left me the entire estate. Long story," Sophie added in a mumble. "But I couldn't give or loan my father any money because the terms of my mother's will forbid it."

"I'd heard rumors of that." Royce paused a moment, waiting, and made an impatient circling motion with his fingers. He stooped, retrieved his Colt and slipped it back into the leather shoulder holster beneath his coat. He also put her gun in his pocket.

"Travis said that he'd cover my father's debts if I married him." Now it was Sophie's turn to pause. "He said he was in love with me and that he was willing to pay that price to have me."

Royce stared at her, and Sophie wished this meeting had been under different circumstances. She owed him a huge apology. Several of them, in fact.

"Royce," she muttered, her voice a whisper now. "I'm sorry."

"So you've said. It's not helping with this explanation. I still don't know what the heck is going on."

He gave her a scowl, the muscles stirring in a face that was far more handsome than she wanted it to be. Not that this would have been easier with a less attractive man, but those good looks—the coffee-brown hair and sizzling green eyes—had always unnerved her.

Attracted her, too.

Easy to attract in those cowboy-fit jeans, boots and Stetson. And it'd been that stupid attraction that had made her involve him in this equally stupid mess. Talk about a dangerous tangled web, and now she might have trapped Royce and her both in it.

Royce made another of those impatient sounds, and Sophie continued with what she hoped would be good enough answers to get them moving. "I started to have second thoughts about marrying Travis," she added. "He definitely wasn't the decent, honest man my father said he was."

"So, to get out of a loveless marriage," Royce concluded, his voice flat, "you told Travis we'd had sex and that you're pregnant with my baby?"

She nodded. It was more than that. Much more. But she instinctively knew that telling Royce all the details wasn't a good idea, especially since it didn't appear he was so furious with her that he was out to kill her.

"We didn't really have sex, did we?" he asked.

Sophie took a deep breath, shook her head.

Relief went through his eyes, and it wasn't a small amount of it, either. "Good. Because I was drunker than I'd ever been in my life, and I shouldn't have let things get that far."

"We didn't have sex," she snapped. "Now, just leave it at that, all right?"

"All right," he growled. "But Travis believes otherwise and he also believes we made a baby that night. Now he wants to kill us."

"Maybe," she mumbled. But again, that was just a small piece of the story. She turned back to the window and tried to assure herself that she hadn't been followed. "The reason I was trying to get out of the marriage was because I found out some things."

And here's where her explanation would have to veer off. She couldn't implicate her father in this.

Sophie chose her words carefully. "I believe Travis was into some illegal activity, and I was in the process of working with an FBI agent to uncover that activity. I was copying files and sending them to him."

Selective files, but that was yet something else Sophie wasn't about to tell a lawman who could, and would, arrest her father.

"Last night Travis confronted me and said he thought I was betraying him because I'd been acting suspicious." She glanced at Royce, ready to ask again if they could get moving, but he just motioned for her to continue. "I thought I'd settled his mind, but then after dinner, he confronted me again. He kept pushing for the truth, and the image of you flashed through my head."

Specifically, the image of them half-naked at the motel.

But she kept that to herself.

Best not to let Royce know that it was a particular image she couldn't get out of her mind. Or her dreams.

"And that's when you lied?" he asked.

She nodded, checked the window again. "More or less. I said I was pregnant with another man's child, and Travis told me he'd seen pictures of you and me together."

"Pictures?" Royce flatly repeated.

"I don't know if Travis had them or not, and he didn't show them to me. Maybe someone at the party at the Outlaw Bar took them." Or maybe they'd been a bluff.

"But these pictures convinced him that I'd gotten you pregnant." He paused. "Hell, I'm guessing Travis didn't take that news too well?"

"He didn't. He slapped me and stormed out."

Royce's jaw muscles jerked, tightening even more. "You should have had his sorry butt arrested for hitting you."

She'd wanted to. Heck, she'd wanted to slap Travis right back, but Sophie hadn't. Besides in Travis's state of mind, he might have done a lot more than slap her.

"I thought it was over, that Travis was out of my life," Sophie continued. "Until this morning, that is. I got the call from the FBI agent." Just saying it required a deep breath. "He said he'd gotten word from a criminal informant that someone had hired a hit man to go after you and that someone else had been hired to kidnap me."

Royce stood there, staring, with his forehead bunched up. It was a lot to take in. She'd had several hours and still hadn't managed it.

"I told the agent I was going to call you," she continued when Royce didn't say anything. "I wanted to warn you, but the agent said I shouldn't."

"Really?" No more bunched-up forehead. Instead, Royce rolled his eyes and cursed. "And why is that? Why wouldn't I need to know something like that?"

"Because he thought you might be trying to kill me, too."

Royce's cursing got worse. "Why the hell would you believe I'd want to kill you?"

"Because the agent said Travis might have convinced you to do it."

In hindsight, it wasn't a good reason, but it had made some sense at the time. In her terrified mind, Sophie had figured that Travis was angry enough to convince Royce that she'd trapped him into this pregnancy. Her fears hadn't calmed a bit when Royce had shown up at the cabin with his gun aimed at her.

"Why didn't the FBI send someone to the ranch to protect you?" Royce asked. "And why the hell didn't they call me or my brother to tell us what was going on?"

"I don't know. I wasn't thinking straight, and maybe the FBI had someone on the way. I'm not sure. Right after the phone call, I looked out the window and saw two men dressed all in black. They both had rifles."

After several more moments of his intense stare, some of the skepticism left Royce's eyes. "You should have called me then and there."

"Maybe. But remember, I was still of the mind-set that you might want to do me in for ruining your life and getting you in hot water with Travis."

"I can handle Travis," he snarled. "And later I'll want to know why this FBI agent put such crazy ideas in your head."

Sophie wanted to know the same thing. Of course, she could have misinterpreted what the agent had said since she'd never been that scared in her life.

"Why didn't you just hide or yell for your father when you saw those two armed gunmen?" Royce asked. "Certainly, he's got a ton of men around the ranch?"

"Normally. But most are still on holiday break. Plus, he let some hands go because, well, to save money. I don't know where my father and brother are, but I realized I was in the house alone. I got dressed, grabbed the Smith & Wesson and left."

He glanced at her gown, silently challenging that getting dressed part.

"I *partially* dressed," Sophie amended with a huff. "And I hurried out from the other side of the house so the men wouldn't see me. I started running and ended up here." She'd more or less stumbled her way to the cabin.

Royce opened his mouth to say something, but then he cursed again when his phone buzzed. He jerked it from his coat pocket as if he'd declared war on it and looked at the screen.

"Trouble?" she asked, holding her breath.

"My brother. He's just checking on me." He replied to the text, and he shoved the phone back in his pocket. "I told him I was on my way back to town and that he was to send a deputy to your father's ranch." Royce looked at her. "You need to come with me to the sheriff's office so I can take your statement."

A statement with more questions than answers. Had Travis really sent two gunmen to kidnap her because she'd told him she was pregnant with Royce's child?

Or was this about something else?

"I'll have Travis brought in for questioning, too,"

Royce added. He went to the porch, motioning for her to stay back, and he looked around the area. Not an ordinary look. The thorough kind a cop would do.

Finally, he motioned for her to follow him. "I'll need to speak to this FBI agent, too. What's his name?"

"Keith Lott."

Royce repeated it as if trying to figure out if he'd heard it before. "How'd you meet him?"

"He contacted me. Lott asked me to help him look into Travis's business files, and since I was suspicious, I agreed to help him."

Plus, she wanted a way out of the marriage.

"I'll also need to talk to your father," Royce insisted.

Sophie went stiff. "He didn't have anything to do with this."

"There had to be a reason he wasn't at the ranch this morning."

"But that reason has nothing to do with those two gunmen," she countered.

Royce made a skeptical sound. "I'll still be questioning him. Can you walk down the ridge?" he asked before she could respond to that.

"I'd crawl if it means getting out of here."

"Crawling's not necessary, but I don't want you falling. Those shoes aren't exactly meant for trekking through snow and ice."

She nodded, knowing he was right, but she'd grabbed the first pair she could find. Sophie caught onto the back of Royce's jacket as he led them out of the cabin. They both continued to keep watch.

"Why aren't you chewing me out because of the lie I told?" she whispered.

He lifted his shoulder. "Desperate people do desperate things."

Yes, she had indeed been desperate. "I honestly didn't think it would make Travis come after you. And me."

Royce didn't respond to that. He kept trudging through the ice and snow that blanketed the trail, but she figured he was chewing her out in his mind.

She certainly was.

Mercy, she'd been so stupid to blurt that out and even more stupid to have agreed to the marriage in the first place. Of course, her father hadn't given her much of a choice about the marriage.

Soon, she'd have to figure out how to handle her father's situation, too.

Royce stopped so quickly that Sophie plowed right into him, and he turned, caught onto her to stop her from falling. She was about to ask him why he'd stopped, but he put his finger to his mouth in a "stay quiet" gesture.

And he reached into his jacket and drew his gun.

That robbed her of her breath, and her gaze darted around so she could see what had alarmed him. But Sophie didn't see anything other than the winter landscape. Didn't hear anything, either, but that wasn't surprising since the wind was starting to howl now.

Royce lifted his head just a fraction, and without warning, he latched on to her arm and threw her to the ground. The impact nearly knocked the breath right out of her.

Sophie didn't have time to ask why he'd done that, because she heard something. Someone was moving in the trees behind them. And that sound barely had time to register when the shot blasted through the air.

3

A dozen things went through Royce's mind, but first and foremost was to get Sophie out of the line of fire. He dragged her behind the nearest tree. When he looked out, ready to return fire, he saw nothing.

But someone was definitely out there.

The shot was proof of that.

Royce figured it was too much to hope that it was a hunter who'd fired a stray shot. No, he wasn't that lucky. However, he wasn't sure he believed all of Sophie's story about hit men and kidnappers.

That left her ex, Travis.

Royce hardly knew the man since Travis had only moved to Mustang Ridge about a year ago, but maybe Travis was the sort who'd let his temper take him to a bad place when Sophie had told him about the fake pregnancy. If so, Travis was going to pay, and pay hard for this.

A bullet slammed into the tree just inches from where Royce and Sophie were, and he pushed her even lower to the ground until her face was right against the snow.

"I'm Deputy Sheriff McCall," Royce shouted out

just on the outside chance those two bullets hadn't been meant for him.

Another shot smacked into the tree.

Well, that cleared up his *outside chance* theory that the shooter wasn't trying to kill him or Sophie. Or both.

"Travis?" Royce tried again. "If that's you, we can settle this without me having to shoot you."

And there was no mistaking, Royce would take out whoever was doing this if he didn't stop. Royce waited for an answer. No shot this time, but he did hear something else. Footsteps.

And he cursed.

Because from the sound of it, there wasn't just one set but two. Hell. Had Sophie been right about those kidnapper–hit men being after her? If so, maybe the shots were meant to pin them in place so the men could sneak up on them, kill Royce and kidnap her.

That wasn't going to happen, either.

"Stay down," Royce growled when Sophie tried to lift her head.

Sophie was shaking, and her teeth were still chattering, but Royce couldn't take the time to reassure her. Not that he could have done that anyway since there was nothing reassuring about this mess. He had to focus every bit of his attention on those footsteps. Not easy to do with the wind rattling the bare tree branches and his own pulse making a crashing noise in his ears.

A fourth shot zinged past Sophie and him.

The angle was different, and using that angle, Royce tried to pinpoint the location of the shooter—directly ahead but moving slightly to the right. He hoped like the devil that it didn't mean the second one was going to the left, but it's what his brother and he would do if they were trying to close in on someone they wanted to capture.

Royce made a quick peek around the cottonwood and saw a blur of motion as the gunman ducked behind another tree. *Mercy,* the guy was getting close, and that probably meant the one on his blind side was, too.

He reached behind him with his left hand and pulled out the Smith & Wesson that he'd gotten away from Sophie earlier. Without taking his attention off the woods, he dragged her to a sitting position and put the gun in her hand.

"Watch that direction," he said, tipping his head to the right. He positioned her so that his body was still shielding her as much as possible. "If you see one of the men, don't hesitate. Shoot."

It wasn't a stellar plan, especially since Royce had no idea if Sophie had any experience with firearms. Plus, she was still shaking, and that wouldn't help her aim.

But he didn't have a choice.

They could both die if one of the gunmen managed to ambush them. Too bad he hadn't told his brother to send out backup, but until that first shot had been fired, Royce hadn't known that things were going from bad to worse.

He didn't have a lot of extra ammunition so he couldn't just start firing warning shots, but Royce waited, trying to time it just right for the best impact. He listened to the sound of that movement on his left. Honed in on it. Aimed.

And fired.

Royce's shot blistered through the winter air, and it slammed into something. Not into a man from the sound of it, but the footsteps and shuffling around stopped.

Royce could have sworn everything stopped because things suddenly became eerily still.

The seconds crawled by, and because Sophie's arm was right against his, he could feel her tense muscles. Her breathing became shallow, too. Royce risked glancing at her just to make sure she was all right. She looked exactly as he'd expected her to look.

Terrified.

But her eyes seemed more focused, and she had a solid grip on the gun.

"McCall?" someone shouted.

Royce didn't answer. He just waited to see what would happen next, but it was a little unnerving to hear this killer wannabe use his name.

"We don't want you," the shooter added a moment later. "We want the woman. Let her go, and we won't hurt you."

Right.

They wouldn't kill a lawman, the only witness to their crime of kidnapping? Plus, there was that whole disturbing part about what these bozos planned to do with Sophie. Royce doubted they had friendly intentions.

But Sophie moved to get up anyway.

Royce cursed and shoved her right back down. He gave her a "what the heck are you doing?" look.

"They want me, not you," she mouthed.

He gave her another look, a scowl, to let her know she was wrong about that. "They shot at *us*," Royce reminded her in a whisper.

And the gunmen no doubt wanted to fire more of those shots at point-blank range. Royce had no intentions of dying in these woods today and allowing Sophie to be taken God knows where so that Travis could do God knows what to her.

Royce risked another peek around the tree, but the gunman he'd seen earlier was nowhere in sight.

"McCall!" the man shouted again. "Hand her over to us. This ain't your fight."

Yeah, it was, and it had become his fight the exact second that first shot had been fired. Or maybe even earlier when he'd walked in on Sophie in the cabin. Either way, Royce wasn't backing down.

The footsteps started again. The guys must have given up on their attempt to lure him into surrendering.

"Get ready," Royce whispered to Sophie.

She did. With every part of her still shaking, she scooted back up and aimed the gun to her right. Royce adjusted his aim, too, and he calculated each of those footsteps. Without warning, he leaned out and fired.

This time, the shot hit human flesh.

Royce was familiar enough with that deadly sounding thud. The man groaned in pain. Then cursed a blue streak. So, he'd been wounded, not killed, and that meant he was still dangerous. Plus, his uninjured partner was out there somewhere, no doubt closing in on them.

"Trade places with me," Royce quietly instructed Sophie.

And despite her shakiness, she managed to work her way beneath him and to the side of the tree where the injured gunman was. Royce was counting on whatever wound he'd given the guy, that it'd be serious enough to affect the guy's shooting ability.

Royce braced himself for whatever was about to happen, and he added a prayer that he could get both Sophie and him out of this alive.

Then he heard another sound.

Not footsteps. It was coming from behind them, and it was the sound of a vehicle driving up on the ranch trail.

Great.

This could be very bad if the gunmen had some kind of backup, which would make sense since they'd need a way of getting Sophie off this ridge. But their backup would also likely be armed and just as dangerous.

Royce turned, adjusting his position so he could try to cover both his right and behind them. He figured there was a high potential to hit one and miss the other, but he didn't have options here. He just had to wait and put his bullets to the best use.

"I'm sorry," Sophie whispered.

Since that sounded like some kind of goodbye, Royce didn't even acknowledge it. "Keep watch," he ordered.

Behind them, he heard the vehicle crunch to a stop on the icy trail, and the driver turned off the engine. The movement from the gunmen was mixed with the sound of the vehicle door opening and closing. That pretty much put Royce's heart right in his throat, but even that wasn't going to make him accept Sophie's goodbye.

"Royce?" he heard someone call out. "Where are you?"

The relief was instant because it was his brother, Jake. Sophie and he had backup, but he didn't want Jake walking into gunfire.

"Here," Royce shouted back. "There are two shooters," he warned his brother.

Just as Royce had expected, that brought on more gunfire. Not one single shot at a time, but blasts from both their right and left. Sophie and he dropped down onto their sides, and back-to-back they both took aim.

And fired.

Royce didn't stop with one shot, either. He sent three bullets in the direction of his gunman, and following his lead, Sophie did the same.

"I'm coming up behind you," Jake called out to them. "And more backup's on the way."

The gunmen probably didn't like the sound of that, and even though they continued firing, Royce caught a glimpse of the guy at his side. He'd turned and was moving back. No doubt trying to get out of there fast since his partner and he were now outgunned.

Royce sent another bullet his way, hoping it would cause him to dive to the ground. He didn't want the goon firing any more bullets in Sophie's direction, but he also wanted the men captured and arrested. That way, Jake and he could get answers about why this fiasco had started in the first place.

"I'm Sheriff Jake McCall," his brother shouted. "Put down your weapons now!"

The warning was standard procedure, but like before, the gunmen just kept firing.

Behind Sophie and Royce a shot rang out.

Jake, no doubt.

And the bullets began to pelt the trees and ground ahead of them. Still, Royce didn't hear the sound he wanted to hear—the gunmen surrendering or at least falling to the ground, wounded and incapable of shooting back.

Sophie kept hold of her gun, but she also put her left hand over her head, maybe because the blasts were deafening. However, it could be because she was about to fall apart. Royce was betting this was the first time in her privileged life that she'd been on the receiving end of gunfire, and he was surprised that she'd been able to handle this much.

Suddenly the shots stopped.

The silence crawled through the woods, and it took Royce a moment to focus on what was happening around him. Jake was there. Behind them and to his right. He'd stopped firing, as well.

Then Jake cursed.

Royce did, too.

"What's wrong?" Sophie asked. There was little sound in her voice, and her eyes were wide with renewed fear when she came up with the answer to her own question.

The gunmen were getting away.

"Get Sophie out of here," Royce told his brother. "I'm going after them."

4

Sophie couldn't sit down. She was too worried to do anything except pace, but she was also exhausted and didn't know how much longer her legs would last. The spent adrenaline and raw nerves were really doing a number on her, and if she sat down, she might collapse.

Or explode.

She'd been pacing in the Mustang Ridge Sheriff's Office for well over an hour now, since Deputy Maggie McCall had arrived at the cabin to drive her back to town. And during that time Royce and his brother, Jake, had been out looking for the men who'd tried to kill them.

Sophie was beyond worried. Those men were kidnappers at best, killers at worst, and now Royce and Jake were in danger because of her.

"The McCall men know how to take care of themselves," Maggie said when she handed Sophie a cup of coffee.

Sophie mumbled her thanks for both the coffee and the reassurance, took the cup and watched the deputy return to the window. Maggie checked her phone, too, as if making sure she hadn't missed a call from her husband. Sophie didn't know Maggie McCall, but the tall blonde seemed just as rattled as Sophie was.

Since it was better than pacing or fidgeting, Sophie checked her own phone for any missed calls and messages. Nothing. She tried again to reach Travis, but again it went straight to voice mail. So did the call she made to Agent Keith Lott. She tried not to read anything into the agent's response.

Or lack of it.

After all, there were plenty of dead spots for reception around Mustang Ridge, and it was possible Lott was somewhere in the area, helping the McCalls with the investigation. But it did bother Sophie that Agent Lott hadn't personally called her or shown up at the sheriff's office. He certainly knew about the danger because he'd been the one to warn her that the two men were on the way to her house to kidnap her.

So where was Lott now?

She prayed that a gunman or two hadn't been sent after him, as well. It was possible. Anything was. Because Sophie had no idea what was going on.

"I didn't mean for any of this to happen," Sophie mumbled

"So you've said." Maggie kept her attention nailed to the window and Main Street. "And you didn't get a good look at either gunman."

It wasn't exactly a question, but judging from her tone, the deputy wasn't pleased that Sophie had kept quiet about the circumstances leading up to the attack. Truth was, there wasn't much more she could tell Maggie other than she had gotten a warning from Agent Lott that she was in danger, and in that frantic, crazy state of mind, she'd run to the cabin where Royce had found her.

Sophie had left out the details of the info she'd been providing to Lott. She also left out the fact that she'd lied about being pregnant with Royce's baby. And the drunken encounter she'd had with Royce the previous month. She'd included bare-bones information in the written statement that Maggie had insisted on taking. But Sophie wasn't sure how long she could keep her secrets.

Or even if keeping secrets was the right thing to do.

Because it might have been her lie that had put Royce in danger in the first place.

"Finally," Maggie said. She practically dropped her coffee cup on her desk, and she raced to throw open the door when the truck came to a stop in front of the office.

Sheriff Jake McCall came in first. Unharmed, thank God. Sophie held her breath waiting for Royce, and when he stepped inside, she knew from his face that the pursuit of the gunmen had not gone well.

"I was worried." Maggie pulled her husband to her and kissed him. Jake took the time to kiss her back before he let go and turned to Sophie.

"The gunmen got away," he informed her.

Sophie had figured as much since they'd returned alone and because Royce was scowling. It was bad news because now they couldn't question the men and find out who'd sent them.

Of course, her money was on Travis.

Royce skimmed his gaze over her, his attention pausing on the jeans and sweater she was wearing.

"Maggie loaned them to me," she explained. And even though it was minor in the grand scheme of things, Sophie was glad she hadn't had to wait around the sheriff's office in her nightgown.

"The Rangers are still out searching for the men, and they have a CSI team in the woods to collect blood samples from the one that Royce wounded," Jake explained. He, too, looked at Sophie. "And on the drive back from town, Royce called your father and brother. They said they were in Amarillo on business and will get here as fast as they can."

"Business," she repeated. Neither had mentioned a trip to Amarillo, but then there wasn't a lot of information being shared at their house these days. She certainly hadn't told them she'd been providing information to an FBI agent.

"Royce called Agent Lott, too," Jake continued. "They're all coming in so we can try to get this straight."

"You actually spoke to Agent Lott?" Sophie hadn't expected to hear that. "Is he all right?"

"Why wouldn't he be?" Jake asked.

"He didn't answer my calls. In fact, I haven't heard a word from him since he warned me of the gunmen who were going to try to kidnap me."

Royce's scowl deepened. "Lott's on the way. But Travis didn't answer his phone so I left a message for him."

It probably wasn't a pleasant message. *Good.* She certainly didn't plan on saying anything nice to him. If he came in, that is. Maybe Travis had realized that the authorities were onto him and had fled.

Royce turned to his brother and Maggie who still had her arm around her husband's waist. "Why don't you head back home?" Royce suggested. "I'll question Sophie's father and brother. And I'll talk to the FBI agent."

Jake shook his head, but before he could say anything, Royce added, "You're on your honeymoon for

Pete's sake. It's bad enough you didn't take a trip, but neither of you should be working." He glanced at Sophie. "They got married just three days ago."

Sophie had heard something about that. She'd also heard the sheriff's young daughter was recovering from leukemia or something similar and that's why there'd been no honeymoon.

"We do need to get ready for Sunny's trip to the hospital," Maggie said to her husband.

"Hospital?" Sophie asked. "I thought her condition was improving."

Jake nodded. "It is. She just needs another treatment, and it'll require a couple of days' stay in the hospital. She'll be admitted first thing in the morning."

"And that's all the more reason for you to leave now," Royce insisted. "I doubt the gunmen will show up here, and if I need help, I can call in Billy."

Billy Kilpatrick, the deputy. While she was pacing, Sophie had seen his nameplate on one of the desks. Sophie hoped the deputy was nearby and capable of providing backup, because she agreed about Jake and Maggie leaving. They obviously had enough to deal with already.

Maggie and Jake exchanged glances before he finally nodded. "Call me if anything comes up," he told Royce.

Royce assured his brother that he would, and Jake and his bride wasted no time getting out of there. Sophie couldn't help but notice they were practically wrapped around each other as they hurried to Maggie's car. A couple in love and hotly attracted to each other.

She envied them.

And then Sophie looked at Royce. Remembered the attraction that she shouldn't be feeling. Or even thinking about. Fortunately, the surly look he was giving her was a different reminder—that he wasn't pleased about any part of their situation other than maybe being alive.

"I'm sorry," Sophie said right off, and she figured she could say it a thousand more times, and it still wouldn't be enough. "I need to make this right."

That deepened his scowl even more. "That's what I'm trying to do."

"But I can do something, too. I called Travis and left a message, telling him we have to talk. I have to let him know I lied about the pregnancy."

"What makes you think he'll believe you?" Royce locked the door, took a magazine clip from his drawer and reloaded. "Travis will probably just think you're lying now, so you won't be kidnapped."

Oh, mercy. Royce might be right. Still, she had to try. "I'll agree to take a pregnancy test."

"Results can be faked." Royce huffed, scrubbed his hand over his face. "Look, if Travis sent these men after us—and I believe he did—then, he's not going to listen to reason. He's riled to the core and wants to get back at you. At us," he amended.

She couldn't argue with that. "But eventually he'll know I've lied."

"Yeah, and by then it might be too late. Just because the two gunmen failed at kidnapping you, it doesn't mean he won't send someone else."

That was a stark reminder that Sophie didn't need. "I have to do something to stop you from being in danger."

"Too late. We're both targets, and despite what the gunman said about wanting only you, I don't believe that for a minute. Any of those shots they fired could have killed either or both of us."

Sophie knew that, of course, but it somehow made it worse to hear the words spoken aloud. "I'm so sorry." Her voice cracked, and she felt the tears burn her eyes.

She hated the tears. And herself. She had made such a mess of things.

"I don't want you talking to Travis," Royce insisted. "Especially not alone. And I don't want another apology," he snapped when she opened her mouth.

Sophie had indeed been about to repeat how sorry she was, but words weren't going to make this all go away.

Royce cursed when his attention landed on the tears she was trying to blink back, and he caught onto her arm and had her sit in the chair next to his desk. He dropped down across from her.

"I don't want tears, either," he grumbled. Then he huffed. "Crying won't help." His voice was softer now, but it was loaded with frustration.

Sophie bit her lip, trying to force herself not to cry. It didn't make it easier that Royce was right in her face, mere inches away. Not only could she see those intense green eyes, she could see every detail of his features.

And she took in his scent, too.

He smelled like the winter woods mixed with his own musky warmth.

That scent, his *warmth,* stirred something in her mind. Just a glimpse of a memory. Of Royce and her falling into bed. For that split second, she could feel the mattress against her back. And more. She could feel Royce's weight on her. The sensation of that hit her hard, and she choked back a sound that was part gasp, part moan.

She shouldn't be reacting or voicing that reaction to

something that was probably just a mixed-up dream. After all, when she'd awakened that morning, Royce hadn't been on top of her.

"Sophie?" she heard Royce say. "Where are you right now? Because, believe me, this conversation is far more important than anything you're thinking about."

True. But it still took her a moment to push the sensations aside. That, and the blasted tears that kept coming to her eyes.

"I'm not usually a crier," she mumbled. There was no way she'd address his comment about what was on her mind. Because *Royce* was what was on her mind.

"Well, you're probably not used to coming so close to dying." He paused. "Most people would cry in your situation. It's just that tears bother me. My mom was a crier," he added so quickly that his words ran together.

Sophie remembered her father saying something about Royce's parents having a bad marriage before Mrs. McCall passed away from breast cancer.

"Tears remind you of your mother's illness?" she speculated.

"No. They just remind me of how unhappy she was. And we're getting off the subject here." He caught onto her shoulders. "What aren't you telling me, Sophie? Are you keeping something secret about the night in the motel? You said we didn't have sex—"

"We didn't." She stopped and stared at him.

"Did we?" he pressed.

Sophie finally had to shake her head. "I honestly don't remember." That required a deep breath. "I have huge gaps in my memory from that night. And that's never happened to me before. I don't get drunk and sleep with people I hardly know."

"Me, either."

She hadn't meant to make a soft yeah-right mumble, but it just popped out. With Royce's hot cowboy looks, she was betting he'd had a one-night stand. Or a dozen.

"I don't sleep with women who aren't my type," he clarified. But then he cursed, waved that off. "It's not an insult. I'm sure I'm not your type, either."

He wasn't. Well, not her usual type anyway, but Sophie could still feel herself go warm when she thought of his kisses. Now *those* she remembered. And his body. That's because he'd been stark naked when she'd woken up in bed with him.

"There's something else you're not telling me," Royce insisted.

Good grief. The man had ESP, or maybe his lawman's instincts were kicking in.

He tapped her right temple. "What is going on in your head? What are you keeping from me? Because I can promise you, it won't help. I need to hear everything that happened. Everything you remember because it could help us figure out how to bring Travis down."

She desperately wanted to stop Travis. But freedom from Travis came with a huge price tag.

"Can I tell you something off the record?" she asked.

Royce looked at her as if her ears were on backward. "Excuse me?"

"Off the record," she repeated. "As in you don't put it in a report, and you don't mention a word of it to anyone, even your brother."

Dead silent, Royce continued to stare at her. "What the hell is going on?"

Sophie didn't back down. Yes, she was still trembling from the attack, but this was critical. "You won't tell anyone," she insisted.

He stared. She waited. And the seconds crawled by before Royce finally nodded.

Sophie searched his eyes for any sign he was lying. She didn't see anything but the renewed anger and frustration. Too bad. She'd rather that than an arrest warrant.

"When I was going through Travis's files," she said, and she had to take another deep breath and give herself some time to choose her words, "I found some papers that could possibly paint my father in a bad light."

Yes, that was sugarcoating it, but she had to be careful with what she said.

He blinked, paused and then cursed. "Bad light? You mean he did something illegal." And it wasn't a question.

Suddenly the tears were gone and she knew what she had to do. Sophie moved closer because she wanted him to see the determination in her own eyes. Determination not to say or confirm anything that would put her father behind bars.

"I love my father," she settled for saying. "And the only reason I just told you about the papers was so you'd have a complete picture."

Royce shook his head and took her by her shoulders again. "There's nothing complete about that. What do these papers have to do with the fact that someone tried to kill us?"

Nothing.

She hoped.

But Sophie didn't get a chance to say that. She heard the doorknob rattle, and her gaze flew in that direction.

And her heart went to her knees.

Travis was standing there, looking right at them through the reinforced glass. Except he was giving them more a glare, and he hadn't missed the close contact between Royce and her. In fact, Royce's hands had been on her.

Royce shoved her behind him. In the same motion, he drew his gun.

"Call off your cowboy, Sophie," Travis said, his voice a dangerous warning. His eyes were narrowed to slits. "Or things are going to get ugly fast."

5

Royce hadn't expected to agree with Travis, but the man was right about one thing—things were about to get ugly.

Travis was clearly upset. Royce was already past that stage, and he glared back at the man who was glaring at him.

"I'll go with him," Sophie insisted. "I don't want a fight."

Well, Royce did. He wanted to beat this moron to a pulp if he was the one who'd hired those gunmen. And Royce was leaning in the direction of that *if* being highly likely.

"You're not going with him," Royce insisted, and he shot her a warning glance over his shoulder. "Stay put. I'll handle this. And then we'll finish that conversation about your father."

Sophie swallowed hard, but he wasn't sure she would actually listen to him. She was turning out to be a lot more stubborn than he'd thought she would be, and his expectations in that area had been pretty darn high.

With his gun drawn and ready, Royce went to the door, unlocked it and threw it open. He gave Travis a quick once-over and didn't see any visible weapons. However, the man was wearing a thick winter coat, and he could hide lots of things under that.

"I heard about the shooting, and I got here as fast as I could," Travis volunteered. "How's Sophie?"

Royce ignored him and his question. "You don't mind if I frisk you for weapons, huh?" Royce asked, and he didn't wait for an answer or permission.

He took Travis by the arm, pulled him inside and practically shoved him against the desk. Royce also kicked the door shut and relocked it. He doubted Travis would turn and run, but he didn't want to risk those gunmen storming the place while he was distracted with Travis.

"This isn't necessary," Travis complained.

"Humor me," Royce fired back. It didn't take him long to locate the gun in the slide holster at Travis's back, and Royce disarmed him.

Travis whirled back around to face him. "I have a permit to carry that concealed."

Royce would check on that to make sure it was true. "Your permit doesn't extend to bringing weapons, concealed or otherwise, in the sheriff's office. Especially since you're a suspect in an attempted-murder investigation."

"What?" Travis's hands went on his hips, and his attention shot to Sophie. "You think I had something to do with this attack?"

"Did you?" Sophie asked.

Travis was breathing through his mouth now, and his face was flushed. In fact, everything about him looked ill-tempered and out of sorts. The wind had chapped his face and mouth and torn through his normally styled reddish-brown hair. He still had on his usual fancy rich clothes—a suit, matching overcoat and shoes that probably cost more than Royce's entire wardrobe—but everything looked askew.

Maybe because his murder-for-hire plot hadn't worked.

"No, of course I didn't have anything to do with the attack," Travis told her. "You're my fiancée, Sophie. I don't have a reason to hurt you."

"Really?" And Royce didn't bother to keep the sarcasm out of that one-word question. "She's your *ex-fiancée,* and you assaulted her when she told you she was carrying another man's child."

A muscle jumped in Travis's jaw, and his narrowed dust-colored eyes shifted from Sophie to Royce. "I was upset. Stunned. You would have reacted the same way if you'd been in my position."

"No. Hell, no, I wouldn't. I don't hit women even when I'm stunned and upset." Royce stepped closer. Since he was a good six inches taller than Travis, Royce hoped he looked as riled and intimidating as he felt. "I especially wouldn't hire two dirt wads to kidnap or kill her."

"I didn't do that!" Travis insisted. He tried to move toward Sophie, but Royce blocked his path. Travis huffed. "I'm here to apologize, Sophie. I love you, and I still want us to get married."

A burst of air left Sophie's mouth. "You slapped me."

"Only because of those pictures." He shifted uneasily. "And because of the pregnancy. Honestly, how did you expect me to react? I know you slept with him before we got engaged, but it still stung."

Royce didn't miss the way Travis said *him.* As if

Royce were something lower than pond scum. Well, Royce didn't think too highly of him, either.

Of course, there was something a whole lot bigger in Travis's weasely justification for his reaction. There was that lying part about Royce and Sophie sleeping together.

Or *maybe* it was a lie.

Sophie had admitted to having blank spots in her memory. Royce had them, too, but he figured even if he was drunk off his butt, he'd remember sleeping with a woman like Sophie.

"Did you hear me, Sophie?" Travis said. "I was jealous that you'd slept with him, and I lost control for just that split second."

Sophie opened her mouth, no doubt to spill the baby lie, but Royce gave a "keep quiet" glare. Travis would learn the truth soon enough, but Royce wanted a few answers first. And he hoped his request for silence in that area didn't have anything to do with tormenting Travis.

Though it probably did.

Even if by some miracle Travis was innocent of hiring those gunmen, Royce still wanted the moron to squirm for slapping Sophie.

"You told Sophie you had pictures of me and her," Royce tossed out there.

Travis nodded. "Someone sent them to me. I don't know who," he said before Royce could ask. "There was no return address on the envelope, and it was postmarked from Amarillo."

"I want to see them." Because seeing them might tell Royce who took them. That was the start to finding out why, and it might shed some light on the attack. It might also prove that Travis was lying about the photos and the hit men.

"They're at my office," Travis explained.

Royce blocked him again when he tried to step around him and get closer to Sophie. "Call someone. Have them brought over."

Travis clearly didn't like that particular order, or maybe his increased scowl was for the body block Royce was putting on him. "There's no one in my office right now. I'll bring them back later today."

"You could do that, *if* I don't arrest you," Royce reminded him. "Right now, I'm thinking your arrest is a given."

The man's shoulders snapped back. "You don't have any proof to make an arrest. Because there's not any evidence against me. Sophie?" Travis mumbled some profanity. "Can you tell this cowboy I wouldn't hurt you? I just want to work things out with you."

"Work out things?" Royce questioned. "What about the pictures and the baby?"

"I forgive her." But Travis's teeth were clenched when he said it, and that wasn't a forgiving look in his eyes.

Before Royce could stop her, Sophie walked closer. She stopped at Royce's side and kept her attention nailed to her scowling ex. "I'm not sure I can trust you, Travis."

"You can't," Royce insisted.

But Sophie and Travis kept their eyes locked. "I can regain your trust," he assured her.

Royce was about to disagree, but something caught his attention. A dark blue car came to a stop directly behind his truck that was parked in front of the office.

He didn't recognize the vehicle, but he knew the two men who stepped from it.

Sophie's half brother and her father, Stanton and Eldon Conway.

"After all," Travis said, his gaze drifting toward the visitors who were making their way to the door. "Look at what I'm doing to help you and your father."

Even though Royce wasn't touching Sophie, he could almost feel her muscles tense. He definitely heard the change in her breathing. Travis's tone had been nonthreatening, but there was indeed a threat just below the surface.

"Yes," Sophie mumbled. She looked up at Royce, and he knew she was about to do something stupid. Or rather she'd try.

"You're not going with him," Royce let her know. "Yeah, I know he agreed to pay off your father's debts, but that's not worth your life."

"Deputy," Travis said. His tone was now placating. "I love Sophie, and her life isn't in danger as long as she's with me."

Royce went with a little placating attitude himself. "Someone hired two men to kidnap her. And those two men then fired a boatload of shots at her. Now, if you didn't hire those men, then who the hell did?"

Travis's mouth quivered, threatening to smile, and he hitched his thumb to the door just as Stanton tested the knob and then knocked.

"Why don't you ask them that question?" Travis insisted. "Because if you want to pin the blame for this on someone, both of them have a much bigger motive for kidnapping Sophie than I do."

Oh, he didn't like that smug look or the sound of this. "What motive?" Royce demanded.

"Ask Eldon." And this time, Travis didn't fight the smile. He grinned like a confident man. "I'm sure if you press Sophie's father as hard as you're pressing me, he'll tell you all about it."

Sweet heaven. This was exactly what Sophie had been trying to avoid, and yet here was her father at the sheriff's office, and he was on a collision course with Royce.

She had to stop it.

Sophie hurried to the door ahead of Royce and unlocked it so she could let in her father and Stanton. Her father immediately pulled her into his arms.

"Are you all right?" he asked. "Were you hurt?" Before Sophie could answer, he eased back and examined her face.

"I'm okay," she assured him.

She was far from okay, but her father was already worried enough without her adding the details of the attack. Still, it would take her a lifetime or two before she stopped hearing the sounds of those bullets and how close they'd come to killing Royce and her.

Her father let go of her, and with his hand extended, he made his way to Royce. "Thank you for saving her."

Royce had his gun in one hand, Travis's in the other so he didn't return the handshake. Didn't look too friendly, either. Probably because of Travis's accusation about her brother and father. An accusation that had to be a lie.

It just had to be.

Stanton had an equally bristled expression on his face. "What exactly happened?" he asked her.

Sophie decided to keep it short and sweet. "Travis and I broke up last night. This morning, an FBI agent called to warn me that someone was going to kidnap me. I ran, and Royce stopped two armed men from taking me. And from killing me," she added in a mumble.

Royce tipped his head to Travis. "He says you know something about those gunmen."

"He doesn't," Sophie argued.

But her father didn't exactly jump to agree with her. In fact, he shook his head and blindly fumbled behind him until he located the chair next to Maggie's desk. He practically dropped down onto the seat.

Oh, God.

Sophie started to go to him, but Royce latched on to her arm and held her back. "Just listen to what he has to say," Royce advised her.

Sophie didn't want to listen, and she didn't want her father to blurt out anything incriminating about those papers she'd found. Royce would have to arrest him then. Besides, she couldn't believe her father actually had anything to do with this.

When her father just sat there, shaking his head, Sophie looked at Stanton for some kind of explanation.

"I don't know what's going on," her brother muttered. But it seemed as if he did know *something*.

Sophie silently cursed. Stanton and she hadn't been close, not since her mother, Diane, had died a year ago in a car accident and had cut Stanton out of the will. Of course, maybe Stanton hadn't been expecting anything since he was Diane's stepson, but he darn well should have expected it since Diane had helped raise him. Stanton had only been five years old when Diane and Eldon had gotten married, and for all and intents and purposes, she'd been his mother.

Sophie returned her attention to her father—someone else her mother hadn't included in her will. She cursed that will now.

And her mother.

Because Diane had ripped the family apart by leaving Sophie everything and then forbidding her to give her father and brother a penny.

Her father finally looked up but not at her. At Royce. "I made some bad investments, and I used the ranch and land as collateral. I was on the verge of losing everything so I got a loan from someone. The *wrong* someone," he confessed.

"A loan shark?" Royce asked.

Eldon nodded, and her mouth went dry. *Mercy.* This was worse than she'd thought.

Royce turned to her, his eyebrow already lifted. "Did you know?"

It took her a moment before Sophie could speak and tamp down some of the wild ideas flying through her head. Or maybe not so wild. After all, a loan shark and the attack could be connected.

"I knew about the debts," she said. "But not about this extra *loan.*"

"That's why Sophie was marrying Travis," Stanton added. "So he'd pay off all our father's debt, including the most recent one."

Sophie's gaze flew to Travis. "You knew about the loan shark?"

He lifted his shoulder. "Not specifically. I just knew your father was in financial hot water."

"And Travis wouldn't give us the money in advance," Stanton volunteered. "He insisted we wait until after the wedding."

Another lift of his shoulder. "A deal's a deal, and the deal was for Sophie."

"Well, that's off now, isn't it?" Stanton snarled. "And this loan shark threatened to get his money one way or another."

Royce jumped right on that. "By kidnapping Sophie?"

The room went completely silent for several long moments. The silence didn't help steady her nerves, that's for sure. Neither did her father's dire expression.

"Maybe," her father finally admitted.

She wanted to scream and pound her fists against the wall. How the heck had her father's finances come to this? And why had he kept something this important from her?

Sophie went to her father, latched on to his chin and forced eye contact. "Did this loan shark actually threaten to come after me?"

Her father didn't answer. Didn't have to. She saw it in his eyes.

"I'm sorry," he said, his voice a hoarse whisper. "He didn't threaten you specifically, but he said I'd be sorry if I didn't pay up. I thought he'd send one of his goons after me." Her father shook his head, groaned. "I didn't know he'd go after one of my kids."

Sophie backed away, and she hadn't realized that she was wobbling until she felt Royce take her arm to steady her.

"I should be the one comforting Sophie," Travis said, and he went to her as well and caught onto her other arm. "I think you and the cowboy can see now that I didn't have any part in the attack."

Sophie couldn't argue with that last part, but she shook off Travis's grip. After everything that had happened, it turned her stomach to have him touch her.

"As far as I'm concerned," Travis continued, "you're still my fiancée, and the wedding is still on. Once we've said our I do's, your father will have the money to pay off the loan shark and his other debts. The threat to your life will stop."

Everyone turned to her. She saw the hope in her father's eyes. The smugness in Travis's. Her brother just looked disgusted by the whole situation, but some of that disgust might be aimed at her since she hadn't been able to find a way around the terms of her mother's will.

But it was Royce's reaction that grabbed her attention.

He was staring at her, waiting, and he seemed to be reminding her of that slap that Travis had given her. Sophie didn't need his reminder, because she could still feel the sting on her cheek. However, she wasn't sure she could let her father face down a loan shark, either.

Royce huffed, as if he knew exactly what she was thinking. "You don't have to marry a jackass to stop a criminal. That's what cops are for." He took a pen and paper from Maggie's desk and pushed it toward her father. "I want the name of the loan shark and any contact information you have."

Her father nodded. "His name is Teddy Bonner, and he's in Amarillo."

"This guy is clearly dangerous," Travis pointed out. "And besides, you're a small-town deputy sheriff. You hardly have the credentials to stop a loan shark."

Royce didn't glare. Just the opposite. He returned the smug expression. "I have a gun and a badge. Pretty good credentials if you ask me. And then there's the whole part about Sophie being here and not in the hands of the kidnapper. I'm pretty sure that means this small-town deputy outsmarted the dangerous loan shark."

Travis's eyes narrowed. "For now."

Royce leaned in. "*For now* is a good start. I plan to keep it that way."

Sophie wanted to cheer. Well, for a few seconds anyway. But then she remembered Royce was paying a very high price for her safety, and after what she'd done to him, she didn't deserve his help.

Her father wrote on the paper, handed it to Royce and then stood. "You'll stop this monster from going after Sophie?"

"I'll do my best," Royce promised.

"Are we free to go then?" Stanton asked.

Her brother was already turning toward the door when Royce answered, "No. Mr. Congeniality here," Royce continued, glancing at Travis, "said he had some photos sent to him anonymously. Know anything about that?" And, with another glance, Royce extended that question to her father.

"What photos?" her father immediately asked.

"Of Royce and me," she clarified when Royce hesitated. Maybe because he didn't want to have to explain anything about the incident in the motel. She certainly wasn't looking forward to explaining it, either, but it might be connected to the attack.

Her father's gaze flew to Travis. "What photos?" he repeated.

"Doctored ones, no doubt," Travis answered. "Unfortunately, I didn't realize that at the time, and it caused Sophie and me to have a little disagreement."

"He slapped her," Royce quickly provided, causing Travis's scowl to return.

"A small fit of temper, that's all," Travis growled. "It won't happen again."

Royce made a sound to indicate he wasn't buying that and looked at her brother again. "What do you know about those photos?"

"Nothing." Stanton dodged Sophie's and Royce's gazes, and he opened the door. "Time to go, Dad."

Her father hugged her and brushed a kiss on her cheek. "I'm so sorry," he whispered. "For everything."

The *for everything* made her freeze, and Sophie wanted to know what he meant by that. The engagement, maybe? But she didn't have time to ask, because Stanton took their father's arm and started to leave.

However, Eldon stopped and turned back to Royce. "This seems minor in light of what happened to Sophie and you, but someone broke into our house."

"When?" Royce and Sophie asked at the same time.

Eldon shook his head. "This morning. Maybe it was the gunmen looking for Sophie."

No doubt. They would have definitely searched the house for her.

"Anything missing?" Royce pressed.

Again, her father shook his head. "Not from what I can tell, but there was some furniture overturned and things out of place."

"I'd take some security precautions if I were you," Royce said. "In case those men return."

That got her moving, and Sophie raced toward the

door where her father and brother were exiting. "Be careful."

"We will," Stanton assured her, and he practically stuffed Eldon into the car.

"Did you see the look on Stanton's face?" Travis remarked. "He doctored those photos so it'd break up you and me."

It was so ridiculous that she nearly laughed. "And why would he do something like that?" Sophie fired back. "Because without your money, my father loses the ranch and everything else. That means my brother loses, too."

His smug look returned. "You think Stanton cares about the ranch when he can get his hands on all that money your mother left you?"

She shook her head. "The only way Stanton could get the money is if I'm dead."

And it chilled her to the bone just to say that.

Travis shrugged. "You just spelled out your brother's motive. I figure he doctored those photos. Or maybe drugged you and the cowboy so he could get you in a compromising position. And then he sent the pictures to me, figuring I'd lose my temper and kill you. Or else hire someone to do it."

Sophie wanted to deny all of that, but her throat clamped shut.

Oh, God.

Had Stanton done that?

"Here's another theory," Royce said. He moved closer, right by her side, so that their arms were touching, and they were facing Travis head-on. "You found out that Sophie and I had been *together,* and you decided a slap wasn't enough punishment. You hired those men to kidnap her. Or kill her."

"I wouldn't do that," Travis argued.

"And then you come here, pretending that you're as innocent as a newborn calf," Royce continued, obviously ignoring Travis's remark. He shook his head. "I'm not buying it."

"You don't have to *buy it*," Travis fired back. "Sophie's opinion is the only one that matters right now."

Both of them looked at her. Waiting. She'd just had an avalanche of information come at her, and she didn't know where to start sorting it all out. One thing was for certain—she trusted Royce.

Well, trusted him to keep her safe anyway.

Travis definitely didn't care for her hesitation. He huffed. "Sophie, here's the bottom line. If you don't leave with me now, the marriage is off, and your father loses everything. Maybe even his life." He looked at his watch. "You've got two minutes to decide."

6

Royce didn't realize he was holding his breath until his lungs began to ache. Hell. He wanted to toss both Travis and his ultimatum out the door, but there was a lot at stake here.

For Sophie.

And for her family.

Travis might indeed save her father from going under financially, but Royce didn't trust the man. He wanted to believe it had nothing to do with Sophie herself. And especially nothing to do with their scalding-hot kissing session the month before. But he figured that his breath-holding wasn't a good sign.

"I'll check up on this loan shark," Royce told her as Travis kept his attention nailed to his watch. "If he sent those kidnappers after you, maybe I can prove it."

That would get the loan shark off the street, but it wouldn't pay off her father's debts. It also might not end the threats to Sophie and anyone else in her family.

"No," Sophie said. "Travis, I'm not going with you."

That was the answer Royce had hoped for, but he sure hadn't expected it. Maybe Sophie had realized just how dangerous Travis could be. Next time, the man might do more than just slap her.

"You know what's at stake," Travis warned her.

She nodded.

Travis waited several moments, maybe to see if she'd change her mind. When Sophie didn't budge, Travis cursed and headed for the door. "You're an idiot to trust that cowboy over me, and you'll be sorry."

Royce nearly gave a smart-mouthed reply, but the truth was, he wanted Travis out of there. He didn't have to wait long for that. Travis slammed the door and headed to his car across the street. Royce kept his eyes on him until the man had driven away.

Sophie was doing the same, and the moment he was out of sight, her breath swooshed out. "I've had more than enough excitement for one day," she mumbled. "I need to go home."

"You can't," Royce reminded her. "Those gunmen are still at large, and they could have your house under surveillance."

The color drained from her face. "I have to get out of here and go somewhere else then," she insisted.

Yeah. Royce knew how she felt. The adrenaline crash was no doubt hitting her pretty hard right now. Him, too. And now that the dust was settling, she was starting to realize just how close they'd come to dying today. Agent Lott was supposed to arrive soon, but they could reschedule their meeting with him. Sophie wasn't in any shape to face the questions he'd no doubt ask.

Her tears didn't return, thank God, but since she looked ready to keel over, he held her up. Sophie took the gesture one step further and leaned into him. Royce upped things too by looping his arm around her waist.

312   *Delores Fossen*

Then she sort of melted against him.

This holding was wrong, and Royce knew it. Sophie was business now. She was the target of hired guns, and that made her someone in his protective custody. Hugging her wasn't exactly crossing the line, but whenever he was close to her like this, his thoughts didn't stay just on hugging. Royce didn't remember everything that happened in the motel, but he sure as hell remembered kissing her.

And touching her.

There was even a blink of an image of him unhooking her black lace bra and having her breasts spill out into his hands.

This wasn't a good time to relive that specific image. Not with her this close and not with Royce dealing with his own adrenaline crash.

"I need to get out of here," she repeated. She stayed melted against his body, and that didn't help clear Royce's head.

"We can go to my place," he heard himself offer.

She looked relieved, as if she wanted to jump at the idea. Royce wasn't jumping, that's for sure. It was a dangerous mix—them, alone at his place. But with this heat simmering between them, maybe there was no place safe. At least he had a security system at his house and the ranch hands could help him keep an eye out for the gunmen. So he rationalized that Sophie would be safer there.

Well, safer from gunmen anyway.

But maybe not from him.

"But what about the office?" she asked. "No one else is here."

"Give me a second." Royce called Billy and asked him to come in.

The deputy said he'd be there in ten minutes, but Royce didn't want to wait. He made a second call to one of the ranch hands, Tommy Rester, and asked him to secure the ranch.

Royce locked up Travis's gun in his desk and stuffed the paper with the loan shark's name and number in his shirt pocket. He hung the Be Back Soon sign in the window that had the emergency contact number. That was the advantage of living in a small town—people didn't expect the sheriff's office to be manned 24/7 as long as someone was on call and responded to 9-1-1.

He locked up and got Sophie moving toward his truck. The snow was light but still coming down, and the icy wind whipped at them. Royce got Sophie inside as quickly as he could, and on the drive to the ranch, he called Sergeant Frank Coulter, a cop in the Amarillo P.D.

Royce didn't put the call on Speaker, even though Sophie no doubt wanted to hear what the sergeant had to say. Still, she might need a toned down version though he had no idea how to tone down the fact that her father might have nearly gotten her killed.

"What do you know about a loan shark named Teddy Bonner?" Royce asked Frank.

"Plenty. Please don't tell me he's in Mustang Ridge."

"Maybe. Or maybe he just hired two goons to come after a local woman. When I intervened, they tried to gun down both of us."

The sergeant made a slight sound of surprise. "You're sure it was Bonner behind that?"

"No, but the woman's father owes Bonner plenty of

money." Royce glanced at Sophie, and she was leaning closer, trying to listen.

"The hired guns don't sound like Bonner," Frank continued. "Neither does the part about going for the guy's daughter. He's real old-school, Royce. Breaking kneecaps is more his style, and he hires muscle to do that. And I've never heard of him using family to get back at someone who owes him money."

Hell. If Bonner wasn't responsible for this, then they were right back to Travis.

"I can bring Bonner in and ask him a few questions," Frank offered. "Who's the fool stupid enough to borrow money from a worm like him?"

"Eldon Conway," Royce answered. "When I get the report done on the shooting, I'll send you a copy. There might be some details of the attack that we might be able to tie back to Bonner."

Royce thanked the sergeant, hung up.

"I heard," Sophie said.

Unlike him, she was no doubt relieved that her father's loan shark might not be the reason she'd nearly died. If it had been Bonner, it would have made this investigation a whole lot easier because he would have had an instant suspect and perhaps even a quick arrest.

Royce turned onto the ranch road, the tires of his truck crunching over the snow and ice. Maybe the weather would slow down the gunmen enough for the Rangers to find them. Maybe. But Royce was guessing the pair already had an escape route planned before they even fired the first shot.

He spotted one of the ranch hands in the doorway of the barn nearest the front of the property. The hand was armed with a rifle. So was the one sitting in a truck by the cattle gate that stretched across the entire road. The moment that Royce drove through, the hand shut the gate.

"You have Angus cows," Sophie mumbled. "I wasn't sure what kind of livestock you raised."

Royce followed her gaze to the cows in the fenced pasture. They were indeed Angus, and since her father didn't raise cattle, only quarter horses, he was surprised she even recognized the breed.

"We have some Charolais, too," Royce explained.

Her attention went from the cows, to the outbuildings and then to the two-story ranch house where his father and sister, Nell, lived. Jake, Maggie and his niece, Sunny, were there, too, for now, but in another month or so they'd be moving to their own house that Jake was having built near the creek.

"It's a big place," she commented.

"Not as big as your father's. And we won't be staying here anyway. We'll be at my house, and it's a lot smaller than this place or yours," he clarified. "It's about a quarter of a mile from here."

"My father has land and the house, not me," she said a moment later. "But he had to sell the livestock because of his money problems."

Yeah. Royce had heard that. And that brought him to something he should probably let lie, but Eldon's money problems were perhaps connected to Sophie's safety. "Why doesn't he sell the ranch and pay off that loan shark?" Instead of trying to marry off Sophie to Travis.

She shook her head. "Even if he got top dollar for the place, it wouldn't be enough, and the ranch isn't worth what it was a few years ago."

Royce had to replay that in his head to make sure

he'd heard her correctly. Maybe the value had gone down, but Eldon still had a lot of land. "How much does your father owe?"

"Honestly, I'm not sure, but from what I can tell he owes about a dozen people close to a million dollars. I don't know exactly how much of that has to be paid to Bonner."

Hell. "That was a lot of cash for Travis to cough up to marry you."

She made a sound of agreement. "But there's a twist," Sophie said as Royce came to a stop in front of his small, wood frame house. "My mother left me nearly ten million, and while there are a dozen or more conditions of her will that prevent me from giving money to my father and brother, there's nothing that prevents my spouse from dipping into it."

"Isn't that what prenups are for?" he immediately asked.

"Travis refused to sign one."

He thought about that. And cursed. "Then Travis could be pressing for this marriage so he can get his hands on your money?"

"Maybe. He said he wouldn't sign a prenup because he has triple the money that I do and doesn't need my inheritance, but I found some things in the papers I sent to Agent Lott that contradicts that. I believe Travis has the million to pay off my father's debts, but I think it would also wipe out his liquid assets."

"Yet you agreed to marry him? Hell's bells, Sophie, Travis could have been planning to kill you—" And his argument came to a halt. "But after the wedding. That's the only way he could have gotten his hands on your money."

She nodded.

"Travis could have sent the kidnappers, though," Royce added.

Another nod. "Maybe he was going to force me into the marriage. Or he's sick enough to stage my rescue so that I'd go running into his arms." She paused, shuddered. "But those men fired shots at us."

"Maybe not on Travis's orders," Royce had to admit. "They could have panicked or even thought they could scare us into surrendering."

Movement in the side mirror caught his eye, and Royce automatically went for his gun. He stopped, though, when he saw his father's truck coming up the road. Royce cursed. He didn't need this today.

"Trouble?" Sophie asked.

"Always," Royce mumbled.

He got out, Sophie did the same, and they went onto his porch, which was scabbed with ice. Sophie's left foot slipped, sliding her right back into Royce's arms, and that's when Chet stepped from his truck.

"Jake told me about the shooting," Chet greeted in his usual snarling tone. "Is that why you brought *her* here?"

Royce opened the door to his house and helped Sophie inside. It was not only warmer there, but it would get them out of the slipping embrace that his father had no doubt noticed.

"Sophie's in danger," Royce informed his father. "And yeah, that's why I brought her here."

Royce braced himself for a scathing reminder of that danger following her to the ranch. Chet had had a few run-ins with Eldon, so Royce figured his father would want her anywhere but there.

Of course, Chet felt that way about most people.

"I've heard talk," Chet said, his attention landing not on Royce but Sophie, "that my son might have gotten you pregnant."

Sophie made a sound of pure surprise, and if Chet's revelation hadn't stunned Royce for several seconds, he might have made that sound, too.

"Where did you hear that?" Royce demanded.

"Around. Is it true?"

"No," Sophie insisted before Royce could tell Chet to mind his own business.

"Good." But there was no relief in Chet's weathered eyes when he looked at Royce. "I didn't think you were that stupid. Best to keep your jeans zipped around her sort."

Royce glanced at Sophie and saw the color rise in her cheeks. What Royce was feeling wasn't embarrassment. It was pure anger.

"Her sort?" Royce repeated. He eased Sophie back so he could step inside and meet his father's gaze. "What? You afraid I'll follow in your footsteps?"

Royce didn't give Chet a chance to answer. He'd made his point, and that point was for his father to back way off, especially when it came to Sophie.

He shut the door. And locked it. While he was at it, Royce set the security system. From the window, he saw his father mumble something and then get back in his truck and drive away. *Good.* He could only take Chet in small doses, and that had been a big enough dose to last him for weeks.

"Your father and you don't get along," Sophie commented. She took off her coat and put it on the peg next to the door.

"No one gets along with Chet." Royce shrugged.

"Well, except my three-year-old niece, Sunny. He doesn't bark and growl at her."

"Then there must be some good underneath that gruff exterior."

Royce took off his coat as well and put it over Sophie's. "If there is, I haven't found it yet. He definitely wouldn't offer me a hug like your old man did you back at the sheriff's office."

"Yes," she said softly. "He loves me. I just wish he were more responsible." She paused. "How do you think your father found out about the pregnancy lie?"

He huffed, tried to rub away his headache. "I don't know, and we won't get the answer from Chet until he's good and ready to spill it. But my guess is that Travis asked around to find out if we were seeing each other. Those kinds of questions wouldn't stay secret long in a small town."

There was also the possibility that someone had seen Sophie and him at the party and had started a rumor about a one-night stand. It wouldn't have been much of a leap to go from that to a pregnancy.

Yeah. That'd be a tasty bit of gossip.

"What was all that 'following in your footsteps' about?" she asked.

Royce didn't huff again, but he wanted to groan. He was hoping Sophie wouldn't mention that, and he was sorry he'd let his temper get the best of him. About that, anyway.

"My mom got pregnant before she and my dad were married. In fact, that's why they got married. Chet had gotten her pregnant and her father forced a shotgun wedding. Mother was a city girl, not at all happy living on a ranch. And even before she got cancer, she was miserable and unhappy."

"I'm sorry." Sophie reached out and touched his arm.

Royce wasn't exactly comfortable with the sympathy. "Your parents don't appear to have had a good marriage, either."

"No," she agreed. "They divorced when I was seven. My mother got full custody of me, and we moved to Chicago. I had to beg her just to see my father and brother."

Well, Royce sure hadn't known that. "I thought you stayed away by choice."

She lifted her shoulder. "Sometimes I did. It was easier than arguing with my mother, something we always did when I wanted to see my dad. And after college, my life and job were in Chicago so I had even more reasons to stay away."

"You ran your mother's charity foundation," he remarked. "Still do."

Sophie blinked as if surprised he'd known that. Royce was surprised, too, but when it came to Sophie, little details about her just seemed to stick in his head. He blamed that on the attraction, but the truth was, he'd found her interesting—in an "opposites attract" sort of way.

"I remember when you moved back here last year," he said. Yeah, definitely opposites, but that hadn't stopped him from noticing her.

"I remember, too. Stanton introduced us at a get-together at the Millers'." She eased her hand from his arm. No longer touching him. "You hated me. Maybe still do."

Royce opened his mouth to deny that.

"I heard you call me Prissy Pants, among other things," she added. "And you made your disapproval crystal clear."

Royce couldn't deny that. He had. "I tend to steer clear of women who aren't comfortable in jeans and boots." He groaned at the sound of that. "Except you look pretty darn comfortable in those jeans."

Hot, too.

Royce especially didn't want to voice that.

Her mouth trembled a little as if threatening to smile. But no smile came. However, she touched him again. Well, not him exactly, but when she scrubbed her hands up and down her arms, she brushed against his sleeve.

"So, you didn't hate me. You hated my clothes," she commented.

Now Royce felt himself smile. And God knows why, because he didn't have anything to smile about. He had a hundred things he should be doing instead of standing there while Sophie sort of touched him. Still, it felt good not to see the fear and worry in her eyes.

Oh, man.

He had that thought a moment too soon because when she looked up at him, the worry was back.

"I've dragged you into a bad mess," she whispered.

He heard the apology coming on, and he didn't want to listen to it. Royce didn't want that worry on her face, either. And for reasons he really didn't care to explore, he didn't want her stepping away from him. He caught onto her arm when she started to move away, and he eased her back to him.

Another hug.

Yet more touching that he shouldn't be doing.

But judging from the way she pulled in her breath,

she needed it. What she didn't need was any other contact with him. Definitely no kissing.

But then Sophie looked up at him at the exact moment that Royce looked down at her.

Their breath met.

The front of her body brushed against his.

And his brain turned to dust.

Royce made things worse by lowering his head, but Sophie lifted hers. Meeting him in the middle. And they met all right.

Mouth to mouth.

This time, the sound she made wasn't one of relief. Nope. That little hitching sound of pleasure went through him like liquid fire because in that sound he heard the need. The heat—and worse, the surrender.

Hell.

One of them needed to stay sane here, and surrendering wasn't a good way to do that.

But the insanity didn't stop with just a touch of their lips. Despite the lecture he was giving himself, Royce's hand went around to the back of her neck, and he snapped her to him. Sophie did some snapping of her own by sliding her arms around his waist. And just like that, the kiss became openmouthed. Hungry.

And very dangerous.

He remembered that taste. One of the few things he did remember about kissing her at the Outlaw Bar. It made his body want more, more, more. So, Royce took more. He deepened the kiss. Pressed harder against her. Until his body wanted more than *more*.

His body wanted sex with Sophie.

Thank goodness they had to break for air because in that split second when they were gulping in breaths,

Royce forced himself to remember that this wasn't just a bad idea, it was crossing a legal line that shouldn't be crossed.

He let go of her. Not easily. But he eased back his hands and stepped away.

Sophie didn't come after him. Good thing, too, or he would have been toast. Instead, she stood there, breathing hard and looking very confused about what had just happened.

She mumbled some profanity. "We don't need this."

Royce couldn't have agreed more. But that didn't do much to cool the heat inside him. In fact, he was already thinking about what it would be like to be with her again. And this time, he would remember, unlike their encounter at the Outlaw Bar.

The sound shot through the room, and because Royce was still fighting the effects of that stupid kiss, it took him a moment to realize it was just his phone ringing. He took the cell from his jeans pocket and saw that the caller was Tommy Rester, one of the ranch hands. Since Tommy was in charge of setting up security, Royce quickly answered it.

"We got a visitor," Tommy greeted. "Special Agent Keith Lott from the FBI. I made him show me his badge, and it looks real."

Because it probably was. "Where is he?"

"At the gate. He said he went by the sheriff's office in town but that Billy told him you'd already left. Billy wouldn't say where you'd gone, but I guess Lott figured you might be here. I didn't confirm that, though."

Good. "Did Agent Lott say what he wanted?"

"Oh, yeah. And he didn't mince his words. He said

he was here to find Sophie Conway and that if we didn't tell him where she was, he'd arrest us all on the spot."

Royce tried not to let his temper get in on this. Lott might be just concerned about Sophie, that's all. And with good reason after that attack. Heck, the agent might believe he was holding Sophie against her will since Sophie herself had thought that Royce might want to do her harm.

"Agent Lott is here?" Sophie asked.

Royce nodded, and he moved closer to Sophie so she could hear what Tommy was saying. He had to decide how to handle this. But really there was only one thing he could do. He had to see the agent and hope that Lott could help him stop the person behind the attack. Also, Lott might be able to fill him in on the FBI investigation that had started all of this in the first place.

"Bring Lott to my house," Royce instructed.

"Will do. One more thing, though," Tommy added. "Agent Lott said he was here because this case wasn't in your jurisdiction and that he'd be putting Sophie into his protective custody. Royce, he's taking her to Amarillo, ASAP."

7

Because Sophie had stepped way back from Royce, she hadn't heard exactly what the caller said about Agent Lott, but judging from Royce's renewed scowl, it wasn't good. She tried to brace herself for another round of bad news and added a silent warning and reminder to herself that she should be focused on finding a way out of the danger.

Instead of kissing Royce.

Later, when her body had cooled down some, she might realize just how bad of a mistake that kiss had been. It had certainly broken down some walls between Royce and her, and it wasn't a good time for that to happen.

"Did they find the gunmen?" she asked. But Royce's scowl didn't offer much hope.

Royce shook his head and pocketed his phone. "Lott wants to take you into protective custody."

Oh. That probably shouldn't have been a surprise. After all, she'd nearly been killed just a few hours earlier, but Sophie hadn't considered leaving Mustang Ridge.

Or Royce.

Yes, he was playing into her decision-making process as well, and he shouldn't. Besides, getting away from him was probably a good idea. It might even get him out of danger.

Might.

Without offering her an opinion on how he felt about protective custody or Lott's arrival, Royce disarmed the security system and opened the door. Just moments later, the black four-door car came to a stop in front of the house, and the bulky, blond-haired man got out. Ducking his head down against the wind, Agent Lott hurried onto the porch.

Sophie had met with the agent at least a half-dozen other times, usually at a coffee shop or café. Never in his office where someone might see her coming and going. And in those meetings he had worn jeans and casual shirts. He hadn't looked much like an agent.

Today, he did.

Lott wore a dark suit and mirrored shades. When the wind flipped back the side of his jacket, she saw the leather shoulder holster and the gun inside it. His badge was clipped onto his belt.

"Sophie," Lott greeted. He tugged off the shades and hooked them on the front of his shirt.

Royce stepped to the side so Lott could enter the house, and he checked around the grounds. Maybe to make sure Lott hadn't been followed. He finally closed the door several seconds later.

"I'm S.A. Keith Lott," he said, and Royce and he exchanged a handshake. "You must be Deputy McCall. I owe you a huge thanks for keeping Sophie safe."

"I was doing my job," Royce answered, and he sounded a little offended that the agent had thanked him.

"Are you okay?" Lott asked her.

She nodded. "You know what happened?"

"I got a full update from the Rangers. They didn't find the gunmen, but the FBI's trying to get a match on the blood taken from the woods." He spared Royce a glance. "We pulled the Rangers off the investigation. The locals, too."

That didn't improve Royce's expression. "I asked the Rangers to come to assist," Royce stated. "I didn't ask you to come, and I damn sure didn't give you permission to interfere in my investigation."

"I didn't need your permission," Lott said. "This is a federal case."

"How'd you figure that? The shooting happened within the Mustang Ridge jurisdiction."

Lott pulled back his shoulders. "Sophie is a protected witness in my investigation."

"But the shooting might not have had anything to do with that investigation," Royce countered. "I haven't determined that yet."

"Investigate all you want, but Sophie's coming with me." Lott latched on to her arm, and Sophie automatically threw off his grip. Maybe she was reacting to the bad day she'd had, but she didn't like this territorial attitude.

Lott looked as if she'd slapped him. "You're siding with this local yokel?"

Now it was her shoulders that came back, and she stepped in front of Royce. Sophie didn't think he'd actually punch the agent, but it was clear he was having to hold on to his temper.

Sophie, too.

She'd never seen Lott act this way, and she didn't like it. He was reminding her too much of Travis.

"Did you hear what Royce said?" she asked Lott. "This attack might not be related to Travis or the papers I've been copying for you."

It could all go back to the loan shark. Of course, Royce and she had already learned that this wasn't Teddy Bonner's usual way to deal with a delinquent payee, but perhaps Bonner had made an exception in her father's case.

"Maybe," Lott conceded, but he didn't sound one bit convinced. "I'm working with two likelihoods, and one is that your ex-fiancé hired those men to kidnap you because he knows we're closing in on him."

"You think Travis got suspicious?" Royce asked.

"It's possible. Heck, he might have even seen Sophie snooping around his office."

Sophie shook her head. "Travis said nothing to me about the investigation."

"But you told me you argued with him and broke things off," Lott said.

"Yes." She didn't want to discuss those alleged photos of Royce and her with Agent Lott. "The argument I had with him was, well, personal."

Lott stared at her, as if waiting for more, but she didn't give it to him.

Royce stepped to Sophie's side so he was facing Lott. "What exactly did Travis do to make you go to Sophie and ask her to help?"

Lott paused so long that Sophie wasn't sure he was going to answer. "Basically, he's money laundering through land deals and using that money to buy illegal arms. Forgive me if I don't give you the specifics, but while Sophie obviously trusts you, I don't."

"You think I'm dirty?" Royce asked.

Lott shrugged. "It's occurred to me that Travis had some help. Maybe from local law enforcement."

"Not from me." Royce leaned in. "And not from my brother."

Sophie agreed. Jake and Royce were taking huge risks to protect her, and there's no way Royce would help a man like Travis.

She silently groaned. Her objectivity was shot. And that wasn't a good sign. Obviously, that lecture she'd given herself earlier had failed big-time.

Sophie blew out a weary breath. "You said there were *two* likelihoods," she reminded Lott. Maybe the second one wouldn't involve revealing compromising photos of her and Royce.

The agent hesitated, dodged her gaze. Definitely not a good sign.

"What?" Sophie pressed.

"Your father could have hired those men." Lott's attention whipped to Royce. "And before you say that makes it a local case, it doesn't. Sophie's father is under federal investigation, too."

It felt as if her heart skipped a beat. Royce no doubt knew what this was doing to her because he caught her arm to steady her.

"I didn't tell you," Lott said to her, his voice just barely above a whisper now. "I *couldn't*. But it's possible your father participated in some of those illegal land deals with Travis."

He had. Sophie had hidden the papers that would prove it, though. But she had no plans to admit that to

Lott. So the agent had two likelihoods to explain the attack, and she was withholding possible evidence for both of them.

Mercy.

"Are you saying Sophie's father sent those kidnappers after her?" Royce asked.

"I'm saying it's possible."

"It's not," Sophie argued. She still trusted her father. Had to. Because she loved him. And that meant this had to go back to Travis.

Lott turned to her again. "I don't think your father tried to kill you. Not exactly, anyway. But he might have sent those kidnappers to force you to go through with the marriage."

That had already crossed her mind. But Sophie had dismissed it, too. Or rather she'd tried to do that. However, she couldn't dismiss the fact that her father was desperate.

"My father borrowed money from a loan shark," Sophie admitted.

Lott certainly didn't look surprised. In fact, he nodded. "Teddy Bonner. Yeah. He didn't hire those men, either. I wouldn't want this to get around, but Bonner's an FBI criminal informant. He might be responsible for an assault every now and then, but he's not a killer."

And that meshed with what the cop in Amarillo had said. Still, Sophie could hold out hope that the culprit was anyone but her father—even if it was related to something he'd done, like borrowing money from a loan shark.

"You're not stupid," Lott said to Sophie. "You must know I can do a better job protecting you than the deputy can. Plus, there's *his* safety to consider. He's already been under fire because of you. Now he's brought you, and therefore the danger, to his family's home."

It was true.

She had known that, of course, but it was a powerful reminder to hear it spoken aloud.

Lott reached for her hand, and this time Sophie didn't push him away. "We need to leave now," he insisted. "It's the safest thing for everyone."

"Maybe we should wait for a blood match on the gunman I shot," Royce interrupted. "His identity could connect us to the person who hired him."

"We might not get a match," Lott countered, dropping his grip on her hand.

Royce gave him a flat stare. "If he's a hired gun, he's probably in the system. Just knowing who he is could tell us a lot about him and maybe his associates, too."

"And while we're waiting on results, the danger doesn't stop for you or your family." Lott mumbled a profanity. "Sophie doesn't need your death on her hands."

Her heart was racing now. Breath, too. And she nodded in agreement. "I'll go with you." She looked up at Royce. "Think of your family," she added in a whisper.

"I have," Royce insisted. "And those gunmen might show up whether you're here or not. They know my name, and it wouldn't be hard to figure out where I live. That's why I took security measures by having the hands armed and on the lookout."

"But this ranch will never be as secure as an FBI safe house." Lott huffed. "Look, I know Sophie and you had a fling or something, and that's probably why you feel the need to interject yourself into this."

Sophie went still. "A fling?" she repeated at the same moment that Royce said, "Who told you that?"

She hadn't mentioned a word to Lott about her encounter with Royce at the Outlaw Bar.

Lott shoved his hands in his pockets, and he shook his head. "I can't say."

"You mean you won't," Royce accused.

Every muscle in Lott's face tightened. "All right, *I won't*. I got the information from a confidential source."

"My brother?" she blurted out.

Lott didn't deny it, but she thought she saw something go through his eyes. A confirmation, maybe. *Mercy.* She really needed to have a talk with Stanton. If he'd sent those pictures to Travis, maybe he'd also told Lott.

But there was a problem with that theory.

Stanton didn't know about the investigation. Or if he did, he hadn't said anything about it. Was her brother in on the investigation, too? And if so, why hadn't he said a word about it to her?

"What did your informant tell you about the *fling?*" Royce asked, and he didn't ask nicely, either.

"He told me enough." And with that vague bit of information, Lott's narrowed gaze cut to Sophie. "I can't believe with everything going on, you had unprotected sex with this guy. If you'd just pretended to be the doting fiancée a little bit longer, we could have arrested Travis before he got suspicious."

Sophie wasn't sure what hit her the hardest—the surprise that Lott knew about the pregnancy lie, Lott's unprofessional attitude or that someone, this confidential source, had talked about her to a federal agent. She opened her mouth to explain to Lott that she wasn't pregnant, but Royce stepped in front of her again.

"What happened between us is none of Lott's business," Royce assured her. "And it's damn sure not the business of this so-called confidential informant."

Sophie agreed with that, but she thought maybe Royce, too, would like to have her straighten out the lie she'd told. His father had already given him grief about it, and it was only a matter of time before it was all over town.

Or maybe it already was.

Even though it was an old-fashioned notion that Royce's reputation might be hurt, it was possible for that to happen in a small town like Mustang Ridge. After all, he was the deputy sheriff, and it might be harder to do his job if the more conservative residents thought he had drunken one-night stands.

"None of my business?" Lott repeated, punctuating with some profanity. He opened his mouth to say more, but his phone rang, cutting him off.

The agent answered the call but stepped away from them. Not that he could step away far. The front part of the house wasn't that large—a living room on one side, a dining area on the other. But to put some distance between them, Lott moved to the fireplace on the far side of the wall and turned his back to them. He also spoke in a whisper.

"You trust him?" Royce asked her, whispering as well. Sophie wanted to say yes. After all, Lott was a federal agent, and she'd put herself and others in possible jeopardy by providing him with those incriminating papers about Travis's land deals. Still, there was something about him that she hadn't seen before today.

Desperation, maybe?

Perhaps he really just wanted Travis arrested and her safe, but Sophie suddenly didn't feel very safe with him. Just the opposite. She felt as if Lott was trying to bully her into doing what he wanted. That might or might not be the safest thing for her to do.

"I'd like to stay with you," she said, her offer tentative. "But I don't want to put you or your family in any more danger."

Royce shook his head. "My niece, Sunny, has some treatments starting first thing tomorrow morning at a hospital in Amarillo. Jake, Maggie and she'll be up there for a couple of days."

Yes, she remembered them talking about it at the sheriff's office. "But what about your sister, Nell, and your father?"

"Nell will go to the hospital with the others."

So all but his father would be away from the ranch. Away from her. Where they'd be a heck of a lot safer. Still, she didn't like the idea of Chet being in the possible line of fire. He'd already made it clear that he wasn't comfortable with her being there.

"Any chance your father will go to the hospital with the others?" she asked.

"Possibly." Royce lifted his shoulder. "Chet and Sunny are close, so he'll want to be there for at least part of the procedure." He stared at her. "My advice— don't insist he leave for safety's sake. He's a stubborn man, and that would make him only dig in his heels and stay put."

Sophie was afraid of that.

"Chet can take care of himself," Royce added. "Don't let any part of your decision be about him."

Hard to do that. Chet might not be likable, but she didn't want him hurt. But she remembered something else Royce had said. Even if she left, the gunmen might still come to the McCall ranch looking for her.

She hated that this was yet another situation of being between a rock and a hard place.

Lott finished his call and turned back toward them. "They found one of the gunmen, wounded but alive."

Sophie had braced herself for more bad news, but this was better than she'd expected. "Is he talking?"

Lott slipped on his mirrored shades and headed for the door. "That's what I'm about to find out."

Royce reached for his coat. "We'll go with you."

"No." Lott didn't look back when he opened the door. "The gunman's in FBI custody, and they have orders not to let you near the place."

"Whose orders?" Royce challenged.

"Mine." Lott glanced over his shoulder at Sophie. "Are you coming with me? I figured you'd want to find out why this guy tried to kidnap you."

Oh, she wanted to know that, but that little niggling feeling in the back of her head got worse. And Sophie hoped she wasn't about to make this decision—maybe the most important one of her life—because Royce's kisses had clouded her judgment.

However, Sophie decided to go with the niggling feeling about Lott. And with trusting Royce.

"I'm staying here," she said.

Because of the shades, she couldn't see the reaction in Lott's eyes, but his mouth certainly tightened. "Suit yourself," he grumbled. "And I hope to hell you don't get the deputy here killed."

Yes. Sophie was hoping the same thing.

But Sophie thought of something else. Another factor in her decision to stay here at Royce's house.

Royce himself and the heat between them.

Sophie looked at him and figured he was thinking the same thing. Just because she wanted the attraction to go away, it didn't mean it would. In fact, it was getting stronger. And she'd just agreed to stay under the same roof with the man she couldn't resist.

But a man she had to resist.

Their situation was already dangerous enough without adding more of this fire to the mix. Besides, the fire could also end up being a deadly distraction. Like her, Royce's attention needed to be on solving this case and making the danger go away. That wouldn't happen if the kissing started again.

And kissing wasn't even the worst of it.

She wanted him, bad, and she was afraid *that* need would overrule common sense. If she let it. The trick was to stop that from happening.

"I need to get some rest," she told Royce. Not a lie exactly. She was exhausted, but rest would give her more than just, well, rest.

He tipped his head to the room off the right of the kitchen. "The spare bedroom," he explained.

Sophie mumbled a thanks and she practically ran there and shut the door. She needed space and time to think. But most of all, she had to put—and keep—some distance between Royce and her.

8

Royce pressed the end call button on his phone and cursed. This was not the start to the day that he wanted. A double dose of bad news.

Triple, he corrected when he looked at the email that popped into the in-box on his laptop. The investigation hadn't just stalled, it was going backward.

He got up from the kitchen table where he'd been working and poured himself another cup of coffee. There'd likely be more cups, too, since he was nursing a wicked headache from the spent adrenaline and the lack of sleep. He'd caught a couple of hours' sleep. Catnaps, really. But that's all he'd been able to manage, what with listening for an attack and trying to figure out who wanted Sophie dead.

There was no shortage of suspects, either—Travis, Stanton, her father. Maybe even the loan shark Teddy Bonner. Royce didn't want to add Agent Lott to that mental list, but he didn't trust the man.

With reason.

The second bit of bad news Royce had gotten confirmed his suspicions about the agent. Now, the question was—what was he going to do about it?

He automatically reached for his gun when he heard the hurried footsteps. It took Royce a split second to remember that he wasn't alone. And that he had a house-guest.

Sophie.

The main reason he hadn't slept well.

She hurried into the kitchen and came to a sliding stop on the tiled floor. She had on a pair of black socks and pajamas. *His* clothing items. The pj's practically swallowed her but somehow managed to skim her body, too.

Royce forced himself not to notice that.

"Sorry. I don't usually sleep this late." Sophie pushed her hair from her face, but it tumbled right back into a sexy heap that pooled on the tops of her shoulders. "You should have woke me up."

"No reason. You needed to rest." He took out another cup and poured her some coffee.

"But you've been working, and I should be helping you." She tipped her head to the laptop and made a sound of approval when she drank some of the coffee. "Any updates on the investigation?"

Royce had hoped she wouldn't ask about that until at least she'd had her coffee, because she might need a clear head to process everything he needed to tell her—especially since it was all bad. He decided to start with the easiest item of bad news, but then stopped when he saw the SUV drive away from the main ranch house.

Sophie hurried to the window, her gaze following his. "Your brother?" she asked.

He nodded. "Nell, Maggie and he are leaving for Sunny's appointment at the hospital."

And that meant Jake was unable to help with the investigation. Not that Royce wanted Jake here, because his brother already had enough to keep him busy. Still, Royce wouldn't have minded having another pair of eyes and ears on the information he'd just learned.

"You said they wouldn't be back for several days?" Sophie moved next to him, her arm against his. A reminder of the day before. A reminder of the kiss, too.

Royce didn't move. He stood there, knowing full well that it wasn't a good idea to be this close to Sophie. She had bedroom hair, bedroom eyes and a mouth he wanted in his bedroom. The rest of her, too.

"That's right," he answered.

"Days," she repeated in a mumble, and she slid her gaze over their touching arms and to his face.

Yes, as in days Sophie and he would be alone. Well, except for his father and the ranch hands. Maybe her brother, too. Stanton had already called twice and requested a visit. So perhaps their alone time wouldn't be so alone after all.

Royce tried to remind himself that was a good thing.

Of course, the weather could work against them, as well. The second wave of the snowstorm was moving in, and it might be worse than the first. Sophie and he didn't need the weather trapping them, just in case he decided to move her elsewhere.

Or in case he needed a break from her and all those bedroom reminders.

"Amarillo P.D. questioned the loan shark Teddy Bonner," Royce said, forcing his mind back on his triple bad news he had to tell her. "They found no evidence that he was connected to the attack on us."

Sophie blew out a long breath, and he heard the frustration in that simple gesture. Yeah, this would have been so much easier if Bonner had been the culprit because the loan shark could have been arrested and off the street. Of course, Sophie would have still had to contend with Travis, but that would be much easier if he wasn't a would-be kidnapper or killer.

"Lott was right about Bonner being a criminal informant. Amarillo P.D. doesn't use him often, but they've found him 'reliable in certain situations.'" That was the cop's exact wording. Which was no doubt code for Bonner being a snitch to help Amarillo P.D. nab someone much worse than the loan shark himself.

"What about the wounded gunman?" she continued. "Did Lott get anything from him?"

Here was the second dose of bad news. "The guy died before Lott could even question him."

No long breath this time. She groaned.

"They did get an ID with his fingerprints," Royce explained. Which could have potentially been good news if he'd lived and hadn't had such a long criminal past. "He was a low-life thug who's worked for a lot of people over the years. *A lot,*" he emphasized.

"But not Travis?" she pressed.

Royce shook his head. "There's no obvious connection to Travis." Nor to any of their other suspects except for her father, and Royce figured Eldon wasn't even on Sophie's suspect list. However, her father was on Royce's.

"We'll keep looking for a money trail," Royce continued. "Someone paid him to attack you, and there'll be a record of it." *Maybe.* "Plus, we might catch the second gunman."

Sophie didn't look very hopeful about that. With reason. It'd been twenty-four hours since the attack, and the guy could be out of the country by now.

Of course, that was better than the alternative.

That the gunman was nearby and planning to come after them again.

Royce glanced out of the corner of his eye and realized she was studying him. "Something else is wrong," Sophie concluded.

Bingo. And it was this something else that troubled him more than the other bad news he'd already delivered to her.

"I have a friend in the FBI, Kade Ryland. And I called him yesterday and asked him to quietly look at Lott's investigation into Travis's criminal activity." He paused. "There is no official investigation."

Sophie blinked. "Maybe it's classified or something?"

"Ryland has the authority to check for that sort of thing." He turned so they were facing each other. "In fact, there weren't even any flags or files on Travis that would have triggered a federal investigation."

"But Travis was doing illegal stuff," she quickly pointed out. "I saw the papers for two illegal land deals, and I copied them and gave them to Lott."

Now here's where things could get sticky. "Did Lott ever say why he suspected Travis of those deals?"

Sophie hesitated again before she shook her head. "Lott only said that Travis was under investigation and that he was a dangerous man. I think it was the dangerous part that convinced me to get those papers. I sensed something was wrong, that Travis couldn't be trusted, so I wanted to see what he was up to."

"And you were maybe looking for a way out of the engagement?" Royce asked.

"That, too." She groaned softly and stepped away from him. "I knew marrying him would help my father, but I didn't trust Travis. I wasn't sure he'd actually pay my father the money if I went through with the marriage."

And he might not have. The marriage might have been Travis's way of getting his hands on Sophie's money. "You were right not to trust him."

"But maybe wrong to trust Lott," Sophie finished for him.

There it was in a nutshell. Lott's unauthorized investigation was bad news number three, but Royce didn't know just what level of bad it was. Maybe Lott was a dirty agent. Or maybe he had someway found out about Travis's illegal activity and had bent some big rules to go after him. Either way, the agent had put Sophie in danger, and in Royce's book, that made Lott *bad*.

"So what do we do about Lott?" she asked.

"We don't trust him." That was the obvious part. The next would take a little time, and during that time, they'd just have to do their best to avoid Lott. "Agent Ryland is going to do some more checking and talk with Lott's supervisor."

"Lott won't like that," she mumbled.

No. And Royce was sure he'd hear from the agent as soon as he found out that Royce had gone behind his back to get answers about the investigation.

"Good thing I didn't leave with Lott yesterday when he was here," Sophie added.

Royce shrugged. "It's hard to argue with that, but I can see why a peace officer would want to stop a guy like Travis. Hell, I want to beat him to a pulp for hitting you."

Sophie's hand went to her cheek, and he could tell she was reliving that particular bad memory. "You were right. I should have filed charges against him for assault."

"It's not too late. Maybe we can tack it on to the other charges against him."

Before the last word left his mouth, his phone rang. Royce put his coffee aside and looked at the screen, bracing himself for more bad news. And maybe it was. Stanton's name was there, and Royce showed her the screen before he answered the call on Speaker.

"Royce," Stanton immediately said. "Where's Sophie? I need to speak to her."

Royce looked at her to see if she wanted to respond. She huffed softly and moved closer to the phone. "Stanton, is something wrong?" she asked.

He didn't answer right away, and that tightened Royce's stomach. "I have to tell you some things," Stanton finally said.

"I'm listening," Sophie assured him.

"I can't talk about this over the phone. I need to see you. You need to know what I did."

The tightening in Royce's stomach turned to a big knot. "What'd you do, Stanton?" he demanded.

"I'll tell you when I see Sophie."

Royce figured that wasn't the best option here. "It's not safe for Sophie to be out and about. If you're worried about someone eavesdropping, then call me back on my landline."

"No. This has to be done face-to-face. Can you meet me at the sheriff's office in two hours?"

Royce checked his watch, though time wasn't the

issue. Sophie's safety was. "You're positive this is worth risking your sister's life?"

Stanton cursed. "What I have to tell you might be the reason Sophie's in danger. So you decide. If it's worth the risk, be at the sheriff's office."

And with that, Stanton hung up.

"Any idea what that's about?" Royce asked her as he put his phone back in his pocket.

"The pictures, maybe?" Sophie didn't hesitate, either. "Travis seemed to believe that Stanton had something to do with that."

Maybe he did. After all, Stanton had been at the Outlaw Bar that night. But Royce couldn't see how that would be so critical that Stanton had to tell Sophie in person. Maybe it was something more. Something that pertained to the investigation.

Or it could be a trap.

Royce hated to think that, but Sophie's brother could want her dead so that Eldon and he could inherit all the money. Sophie was worth millions, more than enough to pay off Eldon's debts and get the Conway ranch back on track. People had killed for a lot less, and if Stanton was as devoted to Eldon as Sophie was, he might be willing to sacrifice his sister for their father.

Yeah. This could definitely be a trap.

"I don't think it's a good idea for us to meet him," Royce let her know.

The surprise flashed through Sophie's eyes, and she opened her mouth. No doubt to defend Stanton as she'd been doing with her father. But she closed her mouth and stared at him.

"It's too risky," she whispered, and it wasn't exactly a question.

Royce made a sound of agreement. "If it's as important as Stanton seems to think it is, we'll make other arrangements to hear what he has to say. A video call, maybe. But I really don't want you leaving the house and going into town where you could easily be spotted by someone."

Like the surviving gunman.

She nodded, eased her cup to the table and leaned her head against the window. "I don't want to believe my brother would harm me."

Royce understood. "He's not our primary suspect," he reminded her.

But Stanton *was* a suspect.

And Sophie's heavy sigh let him know that she was well aware of that. Good. At least she was starting to see her brother through a cop's eyes. Maybe soon she'd do the same for her father. Royce wasn't convinced there was a solid reason to distrust either Stanton or Eldon, but until he knew who was behind the attack, he didn't want to take any unnecessary risks.

She turned and eased right into his arms. Royce didn't back away. Just the opposite. And that caused huge alarms to go off in his head.

He ignored them.

Royce also ignored the lecture he'd been giving himself for the past twenty-four hours—the one that insisted he should avoid getting any closer to Sophie. Heck, he ignored everything he shouldn't ignore and brushed a kiss on her forehead.

She groaned softly, probably because she'd been telling herself the same thing—stay away. Run. Don't get too close. But since she didn't budge, it was clear her body was having the same stubborn reaction that his was.

"I've been trying to avoid this," she mumbled.

"Yeah. So have I." He was failing so badly that he might have to give *failure* a whole new name. Worse, he wanted to fail even harder.

She looked up at him, shook her head. "What are we going to do about this?"

Since the answer on the tip of his tongue was *have sex,* Royce didn't say it out loud. Though judging from the heated look she was giving him, maybe it was on the tip of her tongue, too.

He'd never really had a type of woman he preferred. Hair and eye color didn't matter, and he'd dated both thin and those with curves, but now looking down at Sophie, he knew he'd finally found his type. Maybe it was that tumbled hair. That face. Or those curves hidden in his clothes. Whatever it was, Sophie was it.

Man, he was toast.

Royce fought the urge to kiss her and felt himself losing that battle, too. "When this is over, maybe we can have dinner or something."

She blinked. "You mean like a date?"

"Exactly like a date." It seemed like a good place to start, anyway, and it was something he could put off until Sophie was no longer "the job."

Well. He could put it off if he kept his hands and mouth to himself. That was a big *if* since she was already in his arms.

"We seem a little past the first-date stage," she pointed out.

"We are." Especially after making out at the Outlaw Bar. "But I'm figuring we can backtrack." It seemed more sensible that going full steam ahead, something his body was encouraging him to do.

Sophie nodded hesitantly. "I'm not your type," she reminded him. "I'm a city girl, like your mother."

"Yeah," he settled for saying. "I didn't say a date was a good idea."

And neither was the kiss he pressed on her mouth.

It wasn't quite the same as having her for breakfast, but it felt like a good start. Even when Royce knew he shouldn't be starting anything sexual with her.

He pulled back, enjoying the nice little buzz of heat that went through the middle of his body. Royce enjoyed the flash of surprise in her eyes, too. Not from fear or hearing bad news. This was surprise of a sexual nature. Maybe Sophie had gotten a buzz, as well.

"Yes," she mumbled.

She moved away, nervously sliding her hands down the sides of the pajamas, and the motion stretched the thin fabric over her breasts. No bra. Because he could clearly see the outline of her nipples.

That buzz got stronger.

Royce felt his resolve get weaker. Of course, that always seemed to happen whenever he was around Sophie.

Yeah, she was his type, all right.

Their gazes met again. Held. There was a split second of time when Royce thought he could put a choke hold on the ache burning in his body. That split second came and went. And Royce moved toward her at the same time she moved toward him. It wasn't slow. Certainly not tentative. They moved like two people who seemed to know exactly what they were doing.

That couldn't have been further from the truth.

This time, there was no restraint, no holding back. Willpower and common sense vanished, and Royce helped keep those things at bay when he hooked his arm around Sophie's waist and hauled her to him.

They collided—too crazy from the need to give this make-out session much finesse. But they adjusted, automatically, as if they'd done this so many times that they knew exactly how and where to move. Not a comforting thought.

The kiss was instant and hot. Openmouthed, hungry. It felt as if they were starved for each other and even as the sensations roared through him, a little voice inside Royce's head kept telling him this was a bad idea.

It was.

But that didn't stop him from pulling her body against his. He'd been right about that no bra part. Equally right about how she'd feel in his arms with her braless breasts pressed against his chest.

Sophie made a sound. Part moan, part shiver. She sort of melted against him, every part of her seemingly touching every part of him. Well, except one part that was suddenly whining for attention. So Royce did something about that. He dropped his left hand to her bottom, lifting her so that her sex was aligned with his.

Her moan got louder.

Her grip on his back tightened.

And the kiss got deeper and hotter.

Her taste was so familiar, like something he'd had but still wanted. The little voice got quieter, maybe because of the roar in his head now. Also because his body was already moving onto other things.

Like touching her.

Royce slid his hand beneath the loose pajama top and eased his fingers over her right nipple. It was already tight and puckered, ready for him to do a little exploring.

And tasting.

Yeah, he apparently intended to make that particular mistake, too. He shoved up the pajama top and looked at her for a moment. Just to see if she was going to stop this.

She wasn't.

There was only the welcoming heat in her sizzling blue eyes. Not an ounce of hesitation. And it was Sophie who caught onto the back of his neck and pushed his mouth toward her breast.

The buzz became a full roar.

Sophie's moan became intense.

Everything did. The need, the pressure from the contact of their bodies. The taste of her in his mouth. Especially that. He hadn't remembered kissing her breasts before, but maybe he had, because that seemed like familiar territory, too. Of course, with the way they were grinding against each other, maybe he must want it to feel familiar.

While he tongue-kissed her breasts, Sophie didn't stay put. She pulled him closer and closer, until Royce figured there was only one place left to go. He dropped lower, kissing her stomach. Touching her. And going lower until he kissed her through the flimsy cotton panties.

She mumbled something he didn't catch, and almost frantically, Sophie grabbed on to his shoulders and pulled him back up to face her. She kissed him again. Also frantic, and she slid her hand between them and over the front of his zipper.

Royce saw stars and damn near lost his breath.

Because Sophie didn't just touch him, she started to lower his zipper.

That little voice in his head returned with a big, loud vengeance. He could *not* have sex with her. Not like this when she was so vulnerable. It would be taking advantage of her, and he wouldn't forgive himself for that.

That thought vanished for a second when she managed to get his zipper down and put her hand in his boxers.

Oh, man.

He was already rock hard, and that only made it worse. Her touch was like lightning and speared through him until every nerve in his body was zinging.

It took every ounce of his willpower to push her hand away, and he had a fleeting thought that maybe it'd been this way that night in the motel. Maybe she'd touched him. Just like this. And maybe he'd touched her, too.

And maybe he hadn't resisted her.

Considering how they made each other feel, he was beginning to see just how probable that could be.

Royce knew if he didn't do something fast, then this would go well beyond the touching and kissing stage. They'd land in bed. Or on the floor or kitchen table. The sex would be hot, incredible and mindless.

But not without consequences.

And that's what he forced himself to remember.

Still, this had to go somewhere because Sophie was trying to get her hands back into his pants. If that happened, there wasn't enough resolve in the state to make him stop.

Royce turned the tables on her, and he took her wrists, gathering them in his left grip so he could put his right hand in her panties. She was hot, wet and ready, too, and that hardened him to the point of being painful.

"Don't think," she mumbled.

Bad advice. *Real* bad. It was that wet heat talking, and it wasn't making any more sense than his own heat and need.

Sophie made a sound so perfect, so feminine that it made his erection beg. Royce ignored it, again, and stroked her with his fingers. It was a special kind of torture for him, but Sophie's reaction was worth any price. Her eyelids fluttered down, half closed. Her mouth slightly opened.

She said his name. "Royce," she purred.

And she opened herself to him. She tore away from the grip he had on her wrists and latched on to the counter behind her, pushing her hips forward so that his fingers could go deeper, harder and faster.

It didn't take much so Royce didn't have to keep up the sweet torture for long. She came in a flash, her body pulsing around his fingers. That didn't help his erection, either, but Royce forced himself not to put his sex any closer to hers. He just put his arms around her and held her while her breath gutted and her body trembled.

Her eyes opened slowly, and he could still see the heat there. Well, for a few seconds, anyway.

And then the shock came, draining the color from her cheeks.

Her breath stalled, and the heat was quickly replaced with the stark realization of what they'd just done.

"No harm, no foul," he managed to say. It was stupid. Yeah, there'd been no harm all right, but plenty of foul. He'd had no right to touch Sophie that way.

"Oh, mercy," she mumbled, and she kept repeating it.

Fixing her clothes, she moved away from him and hurried to the sink to splash some water on her face. Her cheeks were flushed, and the glance she spared him was short and filled with regret.

"It would have been worse if we'd had sex," Royce assured her. His erection didn't buy that, but that brainless part of him had no say in this.

She glanced at the front of his jeans. Winced a little. "I'm sorry. I guess it won't do any good to tell you again I don't do this sort of thing." She waved off any response he might have had to that. "But twice we've been together now, and twice we've ended up, well, here." Sophie tipped her head to his zipper area.

He had to do something to break this tension—she looked ready to burst into tears. "You think this qualifies as our first date?"

She stared at him. Blinked. And then gave a dry laugh. "You don't want to date me." Any trace of the laugh faded just as quickly as it had come.

He shrugged. *Dating* probably wasn't the right word, but every inch of him wanted to haul her off to bed.

She went to the fridge, far enough away from him that it should have helped. It didn't. Because he couldn't seem to take his eyes off her.

Sophie, on the other hand, was looking at everything but him. She reached to open the fridge, but her hand froze for a moment before it dropped to her stomach.

"What's wrong?" Royce hurried to her, and when he saw the stark look on her face, that took care of any remnants of what was going on behind his zipper.

She shook her head and slapped her hand onto the fridge. "I'm just dizzy. And a little queasy." As soon as she said that, her eyes widened, and her mouth didn't drop open, but it was close.

"Maybe you need to eat something?" he suggested.

But judging from her reaction, that was the last thing she wanted. Another head shake. "What's today's date?"

Hell.

Royce didn't want to jump to conclusions. There were plenty of reasons for a person to get dizzy and feel queasy. But it was the look of near shock on her face that had him wondering if these symptoms were caused by something else.

"It's the fourth," he managed to say. And he waited, afraid to ask what he knew was on both their minds. It had been five weeks since the party at the Outlaw.

"You said we didn't have sex," he reminded her.

She leaned against the fridge and looked up at him. "I said I didn't remember having sex with you. But—" Sophie groaned and turned away from him.

Royce wasn't feeling dizzy or queasy, but he was feeling things he didn't want to feel—like some major concern. "But what?"

The same emotions were in Sophie's eyes when she finally looked at him again. "When I woke up in the motel room, I was naked. We both were."

He thought about that a moment. "You were partly dressed when I saw you." Definitely. He would have remembered a stark-naked Sophie.

"I put on my underwear and was putting on the rest of my clothes when you woke up."

Oh, man. He did not like the direction this was going in. "Uh, did you feel any different?" *Stupid question.* Royce tried again. "Were there any signs on your body that we'd had sex?"

She didn't answer. For a long time. "Yes." Sophie squeezed her eyes shut, and she groaned even louder than Royce. "I didn't remember that, not until just now, but I was a little tender. And please don't make me explain that."

He wouldn't. In fact, he didn't want to be having this discussion at all, but it was necessary. "Any signs that you might be, uh, pregnant? Other than the stuff you're feeling right now, that is."

She dropped the back of her head against the fridge and scrubbed her hands over her face. "A missed period. Things have been so crazy that I didn't notice I was late."

Royce couldn't dispute that, but a feeling that he thought might be panic started to crawl through him. Still, he tried not to show Sophie just how bad that panic was.

She pulled in her breath, looked at him again. "I never slept with Travis. Never. And whether you believe me or not, I don't have one-night stands. In fact, I haven't been with a man in over a year."

Sophie winced as if she hadn't intended to reveal that, and she pushed herself from the fridge and would have stormed off, but Royce got hold of her arm.

"Why wouldn't I believe you?" he asked.

"Because I lied about being pregnant." Tears sprang to her eyes. "And now it might not be a lie at all."

She shook off his grip and practically ran out of the kitchen. Royce went after her and caught up with her just as she ducked into the guest room. She would have shut the door in his face if he hadn't caught onto it. He didn't go to her and pull her into his arms, though that's what he wanted to do. Despite everything he was feeling—and he was feeling a boatload of stuff—he wanted to reassure her that everything would be okay.

All right, maybe not okay, but he really wanted to stop those damn tears spilling down her cheeks.

"Think back to that night," he said, hoping to get her to focus. Even though it probably wasn't a good idea to focus on what was making her cry. Still, they needed to know the truth. "What's the last thing you remember before waking up at the motel?"

She sank down onto the edge of the bed and smeared away the tears with her hand. "Kissing you in your truck."

"Okay." Royce tried to pick through his own memories. Yeah, that was there. French kissing, and he had his hand up her shirt and in her bra.

"I unzipped your jeans," Sophie mumbled.

That particular memory came back at him hard and fast. Especially hard. And he had to fight off the effects of remembering how Sophie had slid her hands into his jeans. And over his erection.

"Think back," he repeated, not easily. "We were in the truck when that happened, but where was it parked? Because all I remember is, well, nothing about the location."

"Yes." And there was enough heat in her voice to let him know that she remembered some of that non-location stuff, too.

"We were in the side parking lot of the Lone Star Motel," Sophie explained. "I'd already gotten a room before the party because I knew I'd be drinking, and I didn't want to have to drive back out to the ranch." She paused. "Plus, Travis was there at the ranch, staying the night in the guest room next to mine. I didn't want to see him."

"And I'd left my truck in the motel parking lot because there weren't any spaces at the Outlaw Bar."

So they were filling in bits and pieces, but the biggest piece of all was still blank.

Or was it?

Sophie stood slowly. "I need to get dressed so I can go into town and buy a pregnancy test." But she paused. "No. Scratch that. I need to go somewhere other than Mustang Ridge to buy it."

Yeah. Because she'd be seen, and something like that probably wouldn't stay a secret. "Half the town thinks you're pregnant anyway," he pointed out.

"And the other half has heard that I said it was a lie." She blinked back more tears. "I just don't want to feed the gossips."

Well, it would do that, and besides it might be safer if they headed away from Mustang Ridge. He really needed to be working on the investigation, but Royce figured his focus would seriously be lacking in that area. Best to get this pregnancy question settled once and for all, and then he could, well, figure out the next step.

A baby.

Man, he hadn't seen this one coming, and he couldn't even wrap his mind around it.

"Just wait for the test result before you get upset," Sophie mumbled. And he wasn't sure if she was talking to him or herself.

She picked up her clothes from the dresser and motioned for him to turn around. "I know. At this point, modesty seems too little, too late."

Yeah, it did, but with the heat and confusion rifling through his body, it wasn't a good idea to see Sophie strip down.

Royce turned away, but he could still hear her dress. Could feel her, too. And maybe it was that combination of sensations that triggered something in his head. He whirled back around.

Not the best idea he'd ever had.

Sophie was standing there in just her bra and panties while she reached for her jeans. She froze. "What's wrong?"

Nothing was wrong, but he realized that response was coming from the brainless part of him reacting to Sophie's nearly naked body. Her bra and panties weren't skimpy. In fact, they appeared to be cotton with no peekaboo lace, but he had memories of what was beneath that underwear.

"You have a tattoo," he said, though he didn't know how he managed to speak. His mouth was suddenly bone-dry.

She got that "deer caught in the headlights" look and nodded. When she turned, she eased down her bra strap, and he spotted the tiny flower tattoo on her shoulder blade.

"My father and brother don't even know it's there," she whispered. "It's a relic from a college trip to Scotland, and it's not in a place that many people can see."

"No," he mumbled. But he'd known it was there, just as he'd known the sounds of pleasure she made in bed.

Yeah. Those popped into his head, too.

"We need to get that test done," she insisted.

Hurrying now, she pulled on the jeans and sweater, and Sophie sat on the edge of the bed to put on the shoes she'd borrowed from Maggie. She went to the adjoining bathroom to wash her face and groaned when she looked in the mirror. Maybe because she thought she didn't look good without her usual makeup and perfectly styled hair.

She looked *good,* Royce silently argued.

Damn good.

That thought collided with the reminder of why she was rushing to leave. The test. And the possible pregnancy that might or might not be a lie. Later, Royce was sure he'd have to deal with that. One way or another. But he forced everything out of his head except making this trip. He went back to the kitchen to close down his laptop, and he grabbed his coat and keys. However, before Sophie and he could make it out the door, his house phone rang. Royce hurried to answer it, hoping it wasn't trouble.

Or his father.

He didn't want to answer questions about where Sophie and he were going.

"It's me, Tommy," the ranch hand said. "We got a problem."

The young man sounded frantic and out of breath, and Royce was a hundred percent sure that this was not going to be good news.

"I got word from one of the hands who was putting out in the back pasture," Tommy continued. "Two men just came over the fence. And, Royce, they're carrying guns."

9

Sophie waited by the front door for Royce to finish his call, but she stepped back when she saw the stark expression on his face.

"There's been a change of plans." Royce threw open the cupboard over the fridge and took out a handgun and some ammo. "There are two armed men on the property, and they're headed this way."

Her breath vanished, and Sophie couldn't even utter the *Oh, God* that started racing through her head.

Royce put the gun he'd retrieved in her hand and took out another one from the wall unit in the living room. He didn't waste any time, and Sophie was glad he caught hold of her to get her moving, because her feet seemed anchored in place.

He took her through his bedroom and into the bathroom at the back of the house, and Royce put her in the tiled shower stall.

"How close are they?" she asked, and even though her hands were trembling, Sophie got the gun ready just in case she had to fire.

"They crossed the back fence about five minutes ago." He hurried to the sole window in the room and shoved back the edge of the curtain. "That puts them about a half mile away from the house."

Not far at all. Just minutes for someone determined to get to them. And she figured these two were determined if they'd chosen to trespass on a ranch in broad daylight. Sophie could see the pasture and one of the barns, but she didn't see anyone, including ranch hands or gunmen.

"Will your hands try to shoot them?" she asked.

"Yeah." And that's all Royce said for several seconds. "Tommy's trying to get into position to stop them, but he might not have an easy shot. The two aren't making a beeline across the pasture. They're staying along the fence line where there are a lot of trees they can use for cover."

"Two of them," she repeated. "Whoever's behind this hired someone else to replace the dead gunman."

Royce made a sound of agreement and glanced at her from over his shoulder. "There might be more than two."

That caused her heart to slam against her chest, and even though she already had a death grip on the gun, Sophie's fingers clamped harder around it.

"I can't call the deputy," Royce said. "It'd leave the sheriff's office unmanned. But the ranch hands are all armed and are good shots."

Royce's cell rang, and without taking his attention from the window, he yanked out the phone, placed it on the sill and put the call on Speaker. Probably to free up his hands in case of attack.

"Royce, I lost them," she heard the man say. Tommy, no doubt. "They went back over the fence by the west barn and disappeared into the woods."

Royce mumbled some profanity. "Come back closer to the houses. You said you've warned my father?"

"Chet knows. I told him to stay inside like you said, but I doubt he'll listen."

"He *won't* listen," Royce verified. "Just watch out for him because he'll be out there somewhere."

Royce punched the button to end the call, shoved the phone back into his pocket and grabbed her hand again. "I need to be at the west side of the house, to keep watch and back up Tommy. And I don't want to leave you in here alone. Not with the window so close to the shower."

Sophie couldn't agree fast enough. She definitely didn't want to be alone, and besides she might be able to provide some backup, too. She wasn't a marksman by any means, but she had fired a gun before on one of the visits to the ranch when she was a teenager.

Shutting the bathroom door, Royce led her back into his bedroom and positioned her on the side of the dresser before he hurried to the window. He pulled up the blinds and stood to the side so he could look out.

"Stay down," Royce warned her.

She did. Sophie could no longer see the outside, but she could see Royce, and if he spotted the men, she'd be able to tell from his body language.

The seconds crawled, but her thoughts didn't. They were racing through her head. She wanted to catch these men and demand to know if it was indeed Travis behind all of this. It was sickening to know that someone wanted to harm Royce and her.

And for what reason?

It certainly seemed an extreme reaction for a man scorned, but then Travis was often an extreme person. A dangerous one, too, she added. Maybe the scorned feelings had mixed with his need for revenge for her encounter with Royce and it had brought them to this. Now it wasn't just Royce and her. Chet and the ranch hands were in the middle of this.

Even though Sophie had braced herself for an attack, the sound still sent her heart to her knees.

A gunshot.

It was deafening. And that caused her breath to gust because the shot had been fired very close to the house.

Royce didn't get down or duck out of sight. He threw open the window and pushed out the screen. She started to yell for him to get down, but she couldn't. If the gunmen didn't already see Royce, then her voice might give away their position in the house.

There was another shot.

Then another.

Both were thick blasts that seemed to shake the entire house. They definitely didn't seem like shots fired from a handgun but rather a rifle. That could mean the gunmen were far enough away from the house to possibly be out of Royce's shooting range.

But maybe not out of the ranch hands'.

Of course, anyone out there was in danger of being killed.

Royce took aim and fired. His shot rattled the panes in the window. Rattled her, too, because the men were likely converging on the house.

Another shot came flying through the window, and glass flew across the room, some of it landing on the bed and clattering onto the floor next to her.

"Stay back," Royce repeated.

She did, but Sophie caught a glimpse of the movement in the yard. A man wearing camo and a black baseball cap ducked behind a tree, and that put him much too close to the bedroom.

Much too close to Royce, too.

Royce leaned out again, directly in front of the window, fired and ducked back behind cover.

The gunmen returned fire, the bullets pelting into the window and the side of the house. Sophie saw the spray of drywall and wood and realized some of the shots were tearing through the exterior wall and coming into the room. But they weren't just coming from the direction of the bedroom window, they were also coming from the back of the house and ripping through the bathroom, as well—where Royce and she had been just minutes earlier.

"We have to move," Royce insisted. "Get down as low as you can and crawl into the living room to the side of the sofa."

Sophie dropped to her belly and started making her way there. The shots didn't stop. In fact, they were coming at them even faster.

Her heart was in her throat now. Racing out of control. And even though her hands were shaking, she tried to keep a firm grip on the gun in case she had to help Royce return fire.

It seemed to take hours for her to get from the bedroom to the sofa, and she pressed herself against it, making room for Royce. He didn't come right away, something that didn't help her racing heart, but he finally scampered out of the bedroom and slammed the door behind him. He'd barely gotten to her when his phone buzzed.

Volleying his attention between the doors and windows, he took the call on Speaker.

"We got a problem."

Not Tommy, but it was a voice she recognized. It was Royce's father, Chet. "Just got a call from one of the hands. Tommy's been shot, and he's pinned down by the side of your truck."

Sophie's breath vanished. *Oh, God.* The man trying to protect her had been hurt. Maybe worse.

"I've already called for an ambulance," Chet said, "but you know those medics can't get to him with all this shooting going on. I'll see what I can do to get to Tommy and help him."

"No." Royce glanced at her, took her by the shoulder and pushed her flat on the floor. "Stay put," he insisted. "I need you to make sure neither of the gunmen gets into the house with Sophie."

"You gonna help Tommy?" Chet asked.

"Yeah. Just make sure you watch the house." And with that, he ended the call.

Sophie frantically shook her head. "It's too dangerous for you to go out there."

"It's too dangerous for Tommy if I don't help," he countered. Royce didn't give her a chance to disagree. "Lock the door behind me and then get back down. If anyone you don't recognize comes through a window or door, shoot him. And don't even think about following me."

The warning had barely left his mouth when Royce raced toward the door and hurried out.

Royce hated the idea of leaving Sophie alone in the house, but there was no other option. It was too dangerous for his father to try to cover the distance between the main ranch house and Royce's truck. There was too much open space where Chet could easily be gunned down. Plus, the gunmen had the upper hand. They'd clearly established position where they could pick off anyone and everyone who tried to make it to the wounded ranch hand.

But maybe the gunmen wouldn't count on someone coming from the front of Royce's house.

And that's exactly what Royce planned to do.

He only hoped his father could manage to stop anyone from getting inside. Chet still had a good aim. Good eye, too. So maybe Chet could keep these would-be killers away from Sophie. And there was no doubt in his mind now that they'd come here to kill rather than kidnap. If they'd wanted her alive, they wouldn't have fired all those dozens of rounds directly into the house.

Royce paused a moment on his front porch until he heard Sophie lock the door as he'd ordered her to do. He wished he could have taken the time to reassure her, but any reassurance at this point might be a lie. Yeah, they had more ranch hands than gunmen, but the hands weren't hired assassins.

He went to the end of the porch and peered around the side of the house. Royce immediately spotted his truck that had been riddled with bullets.

And he spotted Tommy.

The ranch hand was on the ground between the house and vehicle, and Tommy had his left hand clutched to his shoulder. There were blood on both his hand and jacket.

Hell.

He had to do something fast or Tommy might bleed to death. It wouldn't take the ambulance that long to respond, but Chet was right about the medics not being able to come in with bullets flying.

Keeping low, Royce eased over the porch railing, his boots landing without sound in the snow. Of course, being heard wasn't a huge concern since the din of non-stop shooting was deafening. The shots gave him another advantage, too.

Royce was able to pinpoint the location of the shooters.

One was still behind the massive oak only twenty yards or so from his house. The other was farther toward the back and was firing into the bathroom.

Keeping close to the house, Royce inched his way toward the truck. He had to do something about the shooter behind the tree to stop any other bullets from slamming into Tommy.

But how?

How could he draw the SOB out into the open so he could stop him?

A noise distraction wouldn't work, so Royce pushed aside some snow and located a rock. Using his left hand, he hurled it in the direction of the tree and immediately took aim. The moment the rock hit, he saw the movement.

The gunman pivoted out from the tree.

And fired.

Directly at Royce.

Royce fired, too, and he dove to the side so he could use the front of the truck for cover. His shot smacked into the tree, but as soon as he could, he fired another shot. And another. He knew from the sound of that one, that it hadn't hit the tree.

The gunman dropped forward, collapsing onto the snowy ground.

One down. One to go. But Royce hoped that he could at least keep one of them alive so he could question the moron and confirm who was behind this assassination attempt.

Royce shifted his attention to the back of the house where the sounds were still coming from, and he hurried to Tommy. He'd been right about the blood loss.

Way too much.

And Royce had to rethink his plan to keep the second one alive. The sooner the gunman was eliminated, the sooner he could get that ambulance on the grounds.

"I'll get you some help," Royce promised Tommy.

Tommy nodded, and Royce moved away from the injured man to the back of the truck. When he peered around the corner of the house, he immediately spotted the gunman in the doorway of the barn. That meant he was literally dead center of Royce's house. Worse, the man would see Chet if he came from the main house, and he'd see Royce if he ducked out of cover.

They needed some kind of diversion, and with the guy's position, a rock toss wouldn't get the job done.

Royce took out his phone and called his father. "I need you to open your front door," Royce instructed, "and start firing into the ground at the front of the barn. Don't take any chances and don't lean out too far." He didn't want anyone else shot today.

"What you thinking of doing?" Chet asked.

"I need to get from my truck to the left side of the barn and then to the back." It wasn't much of a plan, but it would end this situation the fastest.

"You planning on sneaking up behind this bastard?"

"Yeah." The barn had a back entrance, and once he had it open, Royce would have a direct shot at the gunman. "Just keep the gunman turned in your direction until I can get to the side of the barn."

"Will do."

Within seconds of ending the call, Royce heard the first shot come from his father's rifle. It slammed into the snow just a few feet in front of the gunman. As expected, the guy whirled in Chet's direction and returned fire.

Royce didn't waste any time. He bolted from the corner of his house and ran toward the barn. He saw when the gunman spotted him. The man turned. Fired.

Just as Royce dove to the side of the barn.

He quickly got to his feet and started running. He tried to clear his mind and just focus on the task at hand. But that was almost impossible to do. Royce couldn't forget that Sophie was inside his house, much too close to all this gunfire. She was no doubt terrified and worried about Tommy.

Sophie would see this as her fault, and he didn't want her doing anything stupid to try to put an end to it. He damn sure didn't want her to try to surrender because this gunman clearly wasn't looking for that. He wanted her dead.

Royce rounded the corner to the back of the barn, and, staying low, he hurried to the back entrance. The shots came, piercing through the thin wood walls of the barn.

Out front, he heard his father continue with the shooting diversion, but obviously the gunman had realized that the real danger was coming from behind because that's where he was aiming now. Royce reached for the door, but he had to drop to the ground when a bullet skimmed across his jacket sleeve.

"You coward!" Royce heard his father shout. "Show yourself and quit hiding in the barn."

Royce groaned because judging from the sound of his father's voice, Chet was no longer inside the house. He was coming toward the barn where he'd be a sitting duck.

The gunman's shots changed, but bullets continued to come at Royce. The gunman must be shooting with a weapon in each hand. That would throw off his aim, but it wouldn't take much to shoot a man like Chet in the open.

"It's me that you want!" Sophie shouted.

This time Royce didn't just groan, he cursed a blue streak. He'd told her to stay put, but she hadn't listened any better than his father. Sophie was out of the house.

And right in the middle of this hellish mess.

Because he couldn't risk either Sophie or his father being killed, Royce threw open the barn door. He came in low but ready to fire.

But that wasn't necessary.

The gunman volleyed glances between Royce and the front of the barn, and Royce saw the look in the man's eyes.

Surrender.

He dropped both guns on the ground and lifted his hands in the air. "Don't shoot," the gunman said. "Let me talk to my lawyer first, and I'll tell you everything you want to know."

10

"You shouldn't have come out of the house," Royce said to Sophie *again*. "I told you to stay inside."

"I'm okay," she reminded him *again*. "And so is your father. You, too. It all worked out."

Well, except for Tommy, but according to the medic who'd taken him away in the ambulance, his injuries didn't appear to be life threatening. Sophie was more than thankful for that since Tommy had been shot trying to protect her.

"It worked out because we got lucky," Royce snapped. "Same for you," he snarled to his father who was in the backseat of the SUV where he was guarding the handcuffed gunman they were driving to the sheriff's office.

Clearly, she'd upset Royce by going into the yard, but there was no way she could have stayed tucked safely inside while he took all the risks. Sophie would have reminded him of that, again, if his phone hadn't buzzed, something it had been doing nearly the entire trip from the ranch and into town.

It wasn't a pleasant drive.

The snow had started to fall again, making the roads

slick, and they were literally inches from the man who'd tried to kill them.

She listened to the phone conversation to see if it was an update about Tommy, but apparently it was about the gunman's body the police would have to retrieve from the ranch. It was necessary since that shooting would involve reports and such, but she figured Royce's mind was racing too much to deal with the details.

Hers certainly was.

Chet, however, seemed to have his attention honed in on the man next to him.

"I want the name of the dirtbag who hired you," Chet demanded. It wasn't his first demand. He'd repeated it from the moment Royce had handcuffed the guy and stuffed him into the SUV.

"I have to see my lawyer first," the gunman mumbled.

That only hardened Chet's glare, and even though Sophie didn't believe in breaking the law, she almost wished Chet could smack the man around and force him to talk. Especially since his lawyer would almost certainly tell him not to say anything incriminating. Judging from Royce's stern expression, he felt the same way.

Royce brought the SUV to a stop in front of the sheriff's office, and Billy, the deputy, threw open the front door for them. With Chet on one side of the gunman and Royce on the other, they practically dragged him into the building. They made a beeline for the holding cell and dumped him inside. Royce had already called the assailant's lawyer, so now it was just a matter of waiting.

Sophie hoped that *waiting* didn't include her falling apart.

Her hands were trembling, and now that the immediate danger had passed, she was reliving every moment of the attack and was painfully aware of just how close Royce had come to dying.

But it wasn't just their own dilemma.

There was the injured ranch hand and the fact that Royce's truck and house were now riddled with bullet holes. He'd also killed one of their attackers and would mentally have to deal with taking a man's life. The only saving grace was that the rest of Royce's family hadn't been at the ranch to be caught in the middle of the gunfight.

Both Chet's and Royce's phones buzzed at the same time, so while they took their calls, Sophie busied herself by going to the small break room to make a fresh pot of coffee. They probably didn't need anything to keep them alert, since they were all already on edge, but it gave her restless hands something to do. However, busy hands didn't do anything to calm her mind.

The past two days had been a whirl of attacks and interrogations. So much for her to process and come to terms with.

Too much.

Despite the aftermath of the danger, there was something else darting through her thoughts. She glanced down at her stomach and wondered if she was pregnant. The timing certainly sucked, but then maybe there was no ideal time for news like this. Either way, she would have to deal with it.

And unfortunately so would Royce.

If she wasn't pregnant, then she'd be able to give Royce a big out. One that he no doubt wanted. He'd already made it clear with the story about his mother that he didn't want a relationship of convenience. Heck, he might not want to be involved, period. It wasn't as if there was something between them. Only a possible one-night stand that neither of them could even remember. Hardly the basis for raising a child together.

Sophie frowned at the disappointment she felt. She certainly hadn't planned on motherhood until she'd found Mr. Right and had gotten married. She was thirty, and there was plenty of time for marriage and motherhood.

So why did it suddenly seem as if this baby was exactly what she wanted?

She pushed that puzzling thought aside, blaming it on adrenaline and the fact she had just come close to dying. She'd been using that excuse a lot lately. But there was no sense being disappointed and worrying about a situation that might not even exist.

"Jake's on the way," she heard Chet relay to Royce when he'd finished his call.

She glanced up, but instead of Chet, she saw Royce in the doorway of the break room. He had his shoulder propped against the jamb and had followed her gaze to her stomach. Sophie groaned softly. He had enough on his mind without worrying about *that*.

"A problem?" he asked.

"No." She couldn't say it quickly enough, and even if there had been something wrong, like queasiness, she wouldn't have mentioned it to him. "Any news about Tommy?"

Royce shook his head, pushed himself away from the jamb and walked closer. When he got to her, he took a paper towel from the roll on the small counter and dabbed it to her forehead. Sophie was shocked to see the blood he swiped away.

"Probably a cut from the broken window," he said, his voice as tight as his expression. He wet the paper towel and wiped it again.

"It doesn't hurt," she insisted, and since there was no mirror, she glanced at her reflection on the glass front of the microwave. Sophie couldn't see any other injuries.

"It could have been much worse than a few cuts." Royce mumbled some profanity and tossed the paper towel into the trash bin. "I should have done a better job keeping you safe."

Sophie huffed. "I brought the danger to you. Not the other way around. You did everything humanly possible to keep me alive."

Nothing about his expression changed, and he leaned against the counter and stared at her.

Before his gaze dropped back to her stomach.

Sophie was afraid this was about to turn into a what-if chat so she diffused it. She slipped her arms around Royce and pulled him to her.

He made a sound, deep within his throat. A sort of rumble that she felt in his chest. He certainly didn't move away from her, and he even brushed a kiss on her forehead. Not exactly the hot kiss they'd shared at his place, but it still seemed intimate. As if they were so comfortable with each other that a kiss was a given.

"When we get a name from the gunman," he said almost in a whisper, "I can make an arrest. Then, we can see about getting that test done."

She nodded, causing her face to brush against his mouth. Again, not a kiss, but Sophie felt it deep in her blood. That seemed to be a problem for her whenever she was around Royce. She could always feel him even when he wasn't actually touching her.

Sophie heard the bell jangle and knew someone had just entered the sheriff's office. She stepped away from Royce but not before Chet saw them standing together. That was twice he'd seen them like that. And judging from his sour expression, he didn't like it any better now than he had the day before.

"Agent Lott just arrived," Chet told them.

Royce drew in a weary breath and walked out ahead of her. Agent Lott was still by the front entrance and was removing his coat and gloves, but his attention zoomed right to Sophie.

"I warned you something like this would happen," Lott snarled.

"It could have happened no matter where I was," she argued.

Lott's eyes narrowed to slits. "Not with me, not in my protective custody. I hope you'll do the right thing now and leave with me."

Royce walked closer, his boots thudding on the tiled floor. "You pulled Sophie into a dangerous, unauthorized investigation. If you hadn't done that, she probably wouldn't have been attacked in the first place."

Lott snapped back his shoulders. "Who told you it wasn't authorized?"

"Does it matter?" Royce didn't wait for an answer. "The only thing that matters is your rogue investigation nearly got Sophie killed."

"And Royce," she added. "One of his ranch hands was shot, too."

"You're blaming that on me?" Lott huffed. "The danger would be here with or without me because of Travis's dirty dealings. It doesn't matter how or why the investigation started, but things have come to light now, and there'll be arrests."

"Then make the arrests," Royce said.

"I can't." Lott didn't seem pleased about that, either. "I needed a specific set of papers to tie Travis to all of this, and Sophie claims she didn't find them." Lott's gaze froze on her.

"I don't know what you mean," Sophie lied.

Maybe it was a guilty conscience, but Lott seemed to see right through the lie. "You're not helping yourself by hiding them. And you're not helping your father."

"What papers?" Royce asked.

Sophie tried not to react, was sure she failed, and gave Royce a look that she hoped he would understand—a silent promise to tell him the truth when Lott wasn't around.

Or at least the semitruth.

Of course, she'd already mentioned to Royce that she'd found something that wouldn't paint her father in a good light, so this wasn't a total surprise. Except that Royce had no idea how important those papers were to Lott's investigation.

The silence that settled over the room was long and uncomfortable. She prayed that Lott didn't press for those papers. Prayed, too, that Royce didn't press her for an immediate explanation.

Lott pushed his thumb against his chest. "I'm in charge of this investigation, and withholding evidence is a crime."

"A crime," Royce repeated before she could respond and tell Lott to take a hike for threatening her. "Yeah. There's been quite a few of those on your watch. So, since you're in charge, you can tell me who hired that goon in there." He hitched his thumb in the direction of the holding cell up the hall.

"Oh, I will, as soon as I know," Lott insisted. "As soon as Sophie starts cooperating. And if necessary, I'll get a court order to take Sophie into custody as a material witness."

Her stomach dropped, and she whipped toward Royce. "Can he do that?"

Royce glared at the agent. "Not without a fight, and trust me, I'll fight it."

"So will I," Chet said, stepping to her other side.

Sophie didn't know who looked more surprised by that—Royce, Lott or her. She hadn't expected Royce's father to back her up.

"I'm not going to let some pissant federal agent come in here and ride roughshod over us," Chet added.

"Like father, like son, I see," Lott grumbled.

She felt Royce's arm stiffen and knew that was a major insult, but he didn't say anything. Maybe that's because some movement outside the building caught everyone's attention. A familiar car came to a stop behind Royce's SUV, and her brother, Stanton, stepped out.

Sophie didn't care for the timing of Stanton's visit. She wasn't up to chatting with anyone, but her brother had made it clear earlier that they needed to talk, so it was no surprise that he'd come.

The surprise, however, was Agent Lott's reaction.

Lott mumbled some profanity and looked at Sophie. "You might want to rethink that protective custody."

She shook her head. "Why, because of my brother?"

"Yeah," Lott warned. "You'd be stupid to trust him."

"What the heck does that mean?" Royce asked the agent just as Stanton stepped inside.

Lott turned so that he could volley glances at both Stanton and her, and he reached in his pocket and handed Sophie a business card. It was for an Amarillo attorney that she'd never heard of.

"Who is this?" she asked. She gave the card to Royce, but he, too, only shook his head.

"Someone you'll want to call first chance you get," Lott answered. "Because Stanton did more than just take pictures of you and Royce last month. A lot more."

"Care to explain that?" Royce insisted.

But Lott ignored him. He shot Stanton a glare, grabbed his coat and gloves and headed for the door. "I'll be back with that court order to take Sophie into custody."

11

Royce didn't know what to react to first—the fact that Lott was still threatening that court order, the lawyer's business card or the bombshell the agent had dropped about Stanton.

Stanton did more than just take pictures of you and Royce last month. A lot more.

Since Lott hurried out the door and Stanton was making a beeline for Sophie and him, Royce decided he couldn't delay dealing with her brother. Later, though, he'd need to make some calls to see how to stop Lott.

But there was also the issue of those *papers*.

The ones that Lott had accused Sophie of withholding. She certainly hadn't denied it. Which meant those papers were more important than she'd led him to believe.

The papers went on the back burner, and while Stanton was still making his way inside, Royce punched in the numbers on the card Lott had given him. The female assistant for Ellen Burkhart answered. Royce identified himself and told her that he needed to speak to the lawyer about an investigation he was conducting. The assistant told him that Ms. Burkhart was in a meeting but would call him back shortly.

With that out of the way, Royce turned to Stanton, who was now standing directly in front of him. "What did Lott mean about the pictures?"

Stanton didn't have much of a reaction. It was as if he'd expected the question. Probably had. He glanced at Billy and then tipped his head to the sheriff's office. "We should discuss this in private."

Sophie groaned, but inside Royce was having a more serious reaction. *Mercy.* What the devil had Stanton done and had it nearly gotten Sophie killed?

"I'll head back to the ranch," Chet said to them when they started out of the reception area.

Royce glanced back at him, nodded and made brief eye contact to thank his father. Later, he'd make that a real thanks for Chet's part in staving off the attack. Royce led Sophie and Stanton to Jake's office just off the reception area, and he shut the door.

"Start talking," Royce ordered Stanton.

Sophie's brother didn't exactly jump into an explanation. He first helped himself to a drink of water from the cooler in the corner. "I drugged you," Stanton said, still with his back to Sophie and him.

Even though it was just three little words—not much to process at all—it took a few moments to sink in.

It didn't sink in well.

"You did what?" Royce took a step toward him.

"I drugged both of you," Stanton repeated. "I put some Rohypnol—roofies—in your drinks when you were at the Outlaw Bar."

"My God." And Sophie repeated it several times. Her

voice was all breath now, and she, too, walked closer to Stanton. "Why?"

Royce didn't want to wait for the *why* because there was no reasonable explanation for this. *Mercy.* Now he knew why he couldn't remember anything.

"Have you lost your mind?" Royce charged forward, ready to beat him senseless, but Sophie reached him first and held him back. "What you did was stupid, reckless. Hell, even dangerous."

"I want to hear what he has to say," Sophie insisted. "And then you can punch him."

Good. Sophie and he were on the same page there. Of course, he hadn't figured she'd be happy about her brother drugging them. There could be no good reason for that.

Stanton wiped his forehead with the back of his hand and leaned against the desk. "I wanted to break up Travis and you. I didn't want you to have to marry that SOB." And that was it, apparently what Stanton considered to be a reasonable explanation for what he'd done.

"So your solution was to drug me and a deputy sheriff?" Sophie's voice wasn't a shout, but it was close.

"I needed a way to get those pictures so I could show Travis. I figured if he saw them, he'd break things off with you."

"Or kill us." Sophie huffed, cursed and let go of Royce. This time, he caught her since she seemed ready to slap her brother. Stanton deserved a slap, maybe more, but Royce didn't want Sophie to have to be the one to deliver the blow.

"Why me?" Royce asked. "There were others at the party that night."

Stanton lifted his shoulder. "I saw you looking at

Sophie a couple of times. I thought you were interested in her. Besides, you weren't in a relationship with anyone else, and based on those looks, I didn't think you'd mind making out with my sister."

Sophie went back to repeating some *Oh, God*'s. "Stanton, Royce and I didn't just make out. We ended up in the motel. Did you plan that, too?"

His eyes widened, and the color drained from his face. "No, of course not. I didn't intend for things to go that far."

Sophie's hands went on her hips. "Then explain how far you meant it to go."

Stanton nodded, swallowed hard. "I took the pictures of you kissing while you two were in Royce's truck, and the plan was for me to get Sophie out of there. But when I went to my car to put away the camera, there were some deputies doing Breathalyzer tests. I flunked, and they took my keys."

Sophie looked at Royce to verify if that could have happened. He had to nod. "Jake had a couple of deputies from nearby towns come in and do the tests so we could cut back on DUIs and accidents."

Stanton made a sound of agreement. "They wouldn't let me leave, and by the time I passed the test an hour later, I couldn't find either of you."

"Because we were in the motel," Sophie informed him through clenched teeth.

Her brother squeezed his eyes shut a moment. "God, I'm so sorry. What happened? I mean, did you…"

That was one apology Royce wasn't about to accept. "I have a vague recollection of us walking over to the motel. Or rather staggering there. But I don't remember what happened once we were inside, because you drugged us."

That hung in the air between them for several long moments. "I didn't mean for things to go this far. I just didn't want Sophie to have to marry Travis."

"Neither did I," Sophie said. "But this wasn't the way to make that happen."

Stanton paused, studied her face. "You're not still marrying Travis, are you?"

"No," she snapped. "I prefer not to say 'I do' to someone who's possibly trying to kill me."

"Then I stopped it," Stanton concluded, suddenly not sounding so apologetic after all.

"Yes, you did," Sophie agreed. "But as plans go, this one sucked. For heaven's sake, Stanton, did you even think it through? I mean, without the marriage you and Dad lose everything. How were you planning to fix that, huh?"

"I'm trying to work out a deal with some, uh, loans of sorts so I can expand the ranch and bring in more livestock."

Royce glanced at Sophie, but she clearly didn't know anything about this.

"Your father's credit is shot," Royce reminded him. "Probably yours, too. Just who's willing to lend you that kind of money?"

Stanton dodged his gaze. "I'd rather not say, not until the details have been worked out."

Sophie groaned again. "You're not going to a loan shark?" She didn't wait for him to answer. "Because that hasn't worked out well so far for the family." She stopped, stared at Stanton. "Does this deal involve anything illegal?"

The knock at the door stopped Stanton from answering, not that he would have anyway. Before Royce could tell the person knocking that they didn't want to be disturbed, the door flew open, and Eldon hurried in as if there were some kind of emergency.

"What's going on here?" Eldon asked. "What's happened?"

Royce wasn't sure he wanted to get into Stanton's drug confession, especially when there were so many other things to discuss.

"Someone tried to kill Sophie and me *again,*" Royce explained to Eldon.

Eldon immediately looked past Royce and at Sophie. He went to her and pulled her into his arms. "Travis did this?"

She shook her head and eased back so she could face him. "We're not sure, but Royce does have one of the gunmen in custody, and he says he'll tell us who hired him when his lawyer shows up."

Royce was glad he was watching Eldon's expression because he didn't miss the man's blink. It was just a split-second change of expression before Eldon became the loving father again. He gave Sophie's arm a pat, and then he hugged her again.

"I need to talk to this gunman," her father insisted, turning his attention to Royce. "I need to find out if, well, if the loan shark hired him to come after Sophie."

Maybe that explained the blink, but Royce wasn't feeling very generous about taking anyone, including Eldon, off his list of suspects.

"I can't let you question him," Royce explained. "He's already made it clear that he won't talk without his lawyer, and besides, this is an official investigation.

I can't let civilians go in there and question a suspect. I've already called in the Rangers to assist me with the interrogation."

Not because Royce didn't think he could do the job, he could, but he wanted a Ranger present. There was a clear conflict of interest here since Royce himself had been one of the gunman's targets and therefore couldn't be impartial. He didn't want the gunman's lawyer to use that in some way to get his client out of the charges that would be filed against him.

Eldon nodded as if that was the answer he expected. However, there was also fear in his eyes. "Ask him if he's working for Teddy Bonner, the loan shark."

"Oh, I will," Royce assured him. In fact, he would ask that right after demanding to know if the man worked for Travis.

Eldon turned, looked at Stanton. "Why are you here?"

"I had to talk to Royce and Sophie." Stanton paused and groaned softly. "Last month, I drugged them and took some compromising pictures to show Travis."

That reaction was much more than a blink. Eldon moved fast. He shoved Stanton against the wall. "You did what?" he snarled.

Sophie got between them and maneuvered her father away. Royce made sure Eldon stayed back by latching on to him.

"Stanton didn't want me to marry Travis," Sophie explained. "And he thought this was the way to prevent it."

Eldon opened his mouth, closed it. Every muscle in his body went board stiff, and he seemed too outraged to speak.

"I couldn't let her marry Travis," Stanton added. "I had to do something."

"You had to do *this?*" Eldon cursed and turned away from his son. "The attacks hadn't even happened yet. There was no reason to do anything this extreme. Besides, I still think the attacks are tied to the loan shark, not Travis."

Royce didn't like the sound of that. "Are you saying you think Sophie should go through with a marriage to Travis?"

It took several long moments for Eldon to answer. "No." But his tone said yes. So did his body language. "He hit her. I don't want her to be with a man like that. But I have to see this from the other side, too. If Sophie could have married him, just for a month or two, then the family wouldn't lose everything."

Royce hadn't been wrong about those body language cues. Eldon still wanted this marriage. And while he didn't agree with Stanton's drug plan, Royce was glad it had succeeded in ending Sophie's engagement.

Of course, it might have created another situation if she was indeed pregnant. Despite everything going on, Royce was beyond anxious for her to have that test done.

Stanton moved away from the wall, fixed his clothes that had gotten askew when his father grabbed him. "There's no guarantee that Travis would have given us the money. You can't trust him. He could have married Sophie, murdered her and claimed all her money as his."

"We could have forced Travis to sign a prenup," Eldon pointed out.

"Again, no guarantees," Stanton reminded him. "Besides, you and I created this financial mess. Not Sophie. She shouldn't have to pay for what we did." He looked at Royce and his sister. "I'm really sorry about what happened."

Stanton didn't wait to see if his apology would be accepted, and he turned and walked out. And Royce let him go. For now. He might still arrest Stanton for slipping Sophie and him that drug, but that was minor considering everything else that was going on.

Eldon didn't waste any time going back to Sophie and pulling her into his arms. "Your brother's right about one thing," Eldon said softly. "I shouldn't have asked you to get me out of this financial mess."

Royce saw her grimace, and he figured she was feeling a lot of things right now. Anger for what Stanton did. Fear from the attack. But she also clearly loved her father and maybe saw this as a failure on her part.

"Stanton said he's trying to work out something to have the debts paid off," Sophie told her father. "Any idea what?"

Eldon eased away from her, and like Sophie, there was a boatload of concern in his eyes. "No. But I'll find out and let you know." He kissed her cheek. "I love both Stanton and you, and I know you were just trying to help me by marrying Travis. I'm so sorry it's all come to this."

There was nothing but fatherly love in Eldon's tone and in the last look he gave Sophie before he walked out. It didn't take Sophie long to react to that fatherly love, either. She groaned, made a sound of pure frustration and rubbed her hands over her face.

"I hate to see him like this," she mumbled.

Yeah. Fatherly love could create a lot of guilt. Royce didn't have that problem because Chet wasn't loving. Well, not like Eldon, anyway. And it made Royce wonder. Eldon hadn't begged and pleaded with Sophie to go through with the marriage to Travis, but maybe he thought that fatherly love/guilt was enough to push Sophie back in Travis's direction.

"Do you trust him?" Royce came right out and asked.

Sophie opened her mouth as if she might jump to say yes, but she only shook her head. "I want to trust him. Stanton, too." She paused. "But Stanton drugged us, and my father, well, he hasn't been a saint, either."

Royce thought about that a moment. "You're not just talking about his bad financial decisions, are you?"

"No." And she paused again. "I have papers that prove my father's involvement in one of the illegal land deals with Travis."

"Papers," Royce repeated. "The ones that Lott mentioned?"

"Yes." She said it so softly that he didn't actually hear the response. Royce only saw it form on her mouth.

"I want to see them," he insisted.

She shook her head. "If you do, you'll have to arrest my father."

Hell. Definitely not good. Royce hated to put Sophie in this position. Hated to put himself there, too. But as a lawman, he had to demand to see those papers. However, before he could do just that, his phone buzzed, and when he saw the name Ellen Burkhart on the screen, he knew it was a call he needed to take because the attorney might have information that Sophie and he needed.

Or at least info that Lott felt they needed, anyway.

"Deputy McCall," the woman said when he answered the call. Royce put her on Speaker so that Sophie could hear.

"Ms. Burkhart, I got your card from Agent Keith Lott, and he seemed to think you could help me with an investigation." That was a generous interpretation of why Lott had given Sophie the attorney's card, but he wasn't even sure what questions he should ask the woman.

"Yes. Agent Lott said you might be calling."

Sophie's eyebrow lifted, probably wondering why Lott would do that or open this proverbial door, but Royce didn't have the answer to that, either.

"I can't break attorney-client privilege," the woman went on, "so I'm not sure how I can help you."

Royce took a moment to figure out how to phrase what he was going to say. "I need info about Sophie Conway. What can you tell me about her?"

"Not much," she immediately answered. "The information I have probably isn't connected to your investigation."

"Anything you can tell us will be helpful." Royce hoped.

The woman cleared her throat. "Well, I won't give you the name of my client. You'll have to hear that from him. But soon it'll be part of court documents and Ms. Conway will find out anyway."

Sophie's eyes widened. "Not the papers about the land deal," she mouthed.

Yeah, Sophie definitely wouldn't want those in the court system since she'd said they could lead to her father's arrest.

"What will be part of court documents?" Royce came out and asked.

"My client is challenging the terms of Diane Conway's will." She paused a heartbeat. "And that's all I can tell you, Deputy McCall."

The attorney ended the call, and Royce and Sophie

stood there, staring at each other. She didn't exactly seem shocked by the news.

Sophie shook her head. "I tried to challenge it, but I failed. I wanted to share the estate with my father and brother."

"So, you think Eldon or Stanton are challenging it again?" he asked.

"Yes." She wearily scrubbed her hand over her face. "Probably Stanton. That must have been what he meant when he said he was looking at other ways to get the money."

Yeah. But it did make Royce wonder why Stanton hadn't just admitted that.

He looked at Sophie and saw her blink back the tears. Royce immediately went to her and pulled her into his arms.

"My brother's desperate," she whispered. "And if I'm dead, then he and my father will inherit. Stanton wouldn't do that for himself, but he might be willing to do that for our father."

Royce couldn't argue with that. Nor could he dismiss the fact that Eldon might have something up his sleeve, too. Maybe Eldon didn't have outright plans to kill Sophie, but he could have used the kidnapping to fake her death or something. Of course, any of those bullets could have killed Sophie so it was possible the plan—if it existed—had failed.

Sophie looked up at him, and the fatigue was all over her face. It didn't take away from her good looks. Nothing could do that. But it was a reminder for Royce to put something else on his to-do list.

"When the gunman's lawyer arrives," he said, kissing the small nick on her forehead, "I'll question the guy so we can turn him over to the Rangers, and then I'll get you out of here."

Sophie didn't fight him on that, probably because she was as eager to leave as he was. Soon, though, he'd have to bring up the papers again. But not now. For now, Royce just held her close and wondered why the heck this should feel so natural.

And right.

Even though there were at least a dozen things wrong with this.

"You must hate me," she mumbled. "Your life is a mess, thanks to me."

Royce frowned and pulled back just enough to make eye contact. "I don't hug people I hate."

"Well, you should hate me." She tried to pull away from him, but Royce held on.

"It'd be easier if I did," he confessed. He groaned. Cursed. "Let's just get past some of these obstacles, and then we can, well, talk."

"Talk?" She stared at him and slid her hand over his chest.

He felt that hand slide not just on his chest. But lower. It didn't help that her breath was meeting his, and that he could practically taste her. To cool himself down a little, he did slip his hands over her body, too.

Over her stomach.

It was meant to be a reminder of some very important details they had to learn and maybe even work out. But the only reminder Royce got was that he wanted to touch her, and this time he wanted to remember every last detail of it.

And that would be a mistake.

He repeated that to himself several times and forced

himself away from her. Sophie backed up, too. She stuffed her hands in the back pockets of her jeans as if to make sure she didn't intend to touch him, but the look on her face said the opposite.

Royce was certain his face was saying the same.

The staring match continued until he heard the bell over the front door jangle again. *Good.* Maybe it was the gunman's lawyer or the Rangers. Either way, it would get this situation out of the waiting stage.

"Royce?" Billy called out. "You better get out here right now."

That got Royce moving fast, and he automatically drew his gun and pushed Sophie behind him. He braced himself for another attack. For more gunmen.

But it was Travis.

The man was in the doorway, his left hand covered with blood and pressed against his head.

"Someone just tried to kill me," Travis said. And he collapsed into a heap on the floor.

12

"Call an ambulance," Sophie heard Royce say to Billy.

That sent her heart racing, and she hurried to Royce's side so she could see what was going on.

Oh, mercy.

The last thing she'd expected was for Travis to be on the floor of the sheriff's office, but there he was, and judging from the blood on his hand and clothes, he'd been injured.

She and Royce went to Travis, and Sophie knelt down and put her fingers to his neck. His pulse was strong so she eased back his hand and spotted the gash on his forehead.

"Someone ran me off the road," Travis grumbled. His eyelids twitched and finally opened.

"The ambulance is on the way," Royce told him. He grabbed a handful of tissues from one of the desks, stooped and pressed them to Travis's head. "Who did this to you?"

Sophie didn't miss the skeptical edge in Royce's voice. Yes, there was concern, too, but he probably had the same thoughts as Sophie—was this injury for real or some kind of act?

The blood was real, that's for sure, but when Royce wiped it away, she saw that the cut wasn't very big at all, and there didn't appear to be any other trauma. Still, she was glad there was an ambulance on the way.

Royce stood, and with his gun still in his right hand, he went to the window and looked out. "How did you get here?" he asked Travis.

"Walked. My car's in a ditch on Pearson Road, about a quarter of a mile outside of town."

It was a long way to walk with a real head injury, which only increased her suspicions.

"And you're sure this wasn't an accident and that someone purposely ran you off the road?" Royce pressed.

"Yes," Travis snapped. Cursing, he sat up and pushed Sophie's hands away so he could hold the wad of tissues to his head. "It was a big-rig truck. It hit my car from behind and didn't stop until it pushed me into the ditch."

Royce glanced down at him. "Then, there'll be tire marks on the asphalt from where you tried to brake." His skepticism went up a significant notch.

With reason.

Travis could be doing this to throw suspicion off himself. Of course, hurting himself was an extreme measure, but so were the things they'd suspected Travis of doing. He might be desperate to avoid an arrest.

"I heard you have one of the gunmen locked up here," Travis said. He wobbled, or else pretended to, and he eventually got to his feet.

"Yeah," Royce confirmed. "He says he's willing to give up the name of the person who hired him. Does that make you nervous? Is that why you're really here?"

Travis's eyes narrowed. "I'm *really* here because

someone tried to kill me, and you're a deputy sheriff. I want an investigation, and I want that SOB driver of the truck caught and thrown into jail."

Outside, she heard the wail of the ambulance siren, and it pulled to a stop in front of the building.

"Once the doctor checks you out," Royce said, "come back and fill out a report. I'll get out to the crash site first chance I get."

"Do that," Travis snarled.

The door flew open, and two medics rushed in, but they weren't alone. A tall sixtysomething man wearing a suit stepped in behind them.

"Alfred Davis," the man announced. "I'm here to see my client, Jimmy Haggard. I understand you have him in custody."

Good. That meant they might finally have some answers. Well, from the gunman, anyway. They might not know the truth about Travis until the doctors examined him. And even then they might not know if he'd managed to fake this.

The two medics led Travis to the ambulance, but Travis kept his attention on Sophie. "I'm not the one who wants you dead," he told her.

He waited as if he expected her to say she believed him. She didn't. And after several moments, Travis added more profanity and walked out with the medics.

"Call me when you know his condition," Royce said to one of the medics just as the phone on Billy's desk rang. "And get me an update on Tommy Rester. He's in surgery to remove a bullet that this guy's *client* put in his shoulder."

"Busy day," the lawyer mumbled, and he kept his eyes on Travis until the man was in the ambulance.

Sophie followed the lawyer's gaze. "You know Travis Bullock?" she asked.

"No. Why should I?" Davis looked past her and at Royce. "I need to see my *client*," the lawyer crisply reminded him in the same tone Royce had used earlier.

Royce headed toward the holding cell, but Billy called out to him. "That was your brother on the line. Jake said he's on his way here."

Royce groaned. Jake had too much on his mind right now to be dealing with this, but Sophie welcomed the help.

"You can't go into the interview room," Royce said to her. He unlocked the cell and moved the handcuffed gunman into the interrogation room. "But there's a two-way mirror, and you can watch from Jake's office."

Once Royce had Haggard and his lawyer in the interrogation room, he stepped inside Jake's office with her. He pulled out the chair and had her sit.

"I'll see about getting you something to eat. You look ready to fall flat on your face," Royce remarked.

She felt it, too, but Sophie kept that to herself. Besides, Royce had had just as tough a day as she had, and he still had an interview to conduct.

"We'll get to the bottom of this, I swear." And he brushed a kiss on her cheek. However, he didn't leave. While he called the diner and asked for sandwiches to be delivered, Royce watched the lawyer and gunman as they whispered to each other.

"Whispering's not a good sign," she said to Royce when he finished his call. "Davis is no doubt advising his client to stay quiet."

"They're cooking up something," Royce agreed. "You think Davis recognized Travis?"

"Maybe. He was certainly giving Travis the once-over." Perhaps because Travis had been the one to hire his client, but what they needed was proof of that.

"I'll tell Davis that the interview will start as soon as the Rangers arrive," Royce said.

He gave her another quick kiss, this one on the mouth, before he clicked on the intercom mounted on the wall and strolled out as if nothing out of the ordinary had just happened. There was nothing ordinary about his kisses.

Nothing ordinary about the man, either.

Sophie sat there, the feel of his kisses still going through her, and she groaned. She was in real trouble here, and it wasn't just from the danger. She was falling for him. Hard.

She watched as Royce went back into the interrogation room, but he'd hardly made it through the door before the lawyer stood. *Uh-oh.* Sophie figured the man was about to put a quick end to any interview.

"We want a plea deal," Davis said, surprising her. But Sophie figured without a deal, the gunman wouldn't volunteer anything, putting them right back to square one.

Royce's hands went on his hips. "Your client took shots at several people, including me. I'm not exactly in a charitable mood."

"He wasn't there to kill anyone," Davis argued.

"Coulda fooled me. My ranch hand, too. He's the one who got shot."

"An accident, I assure you. My client was hired to find Sophie Conway and talk to her, that's all."

Sophie jumped to her feet. The comment was so ludicrous that it was insulting. There'd been no attempt to talk, only the attack with a hail of bullets.

"Talk?" Royce repeated. She heard the raw anger in his voice. Saw it even more in his body language.

Haggard, who was seated at the table, calmly nodded as if he didn't have a care in the world. "I got written instructions to talk to the woman and give her a phone number. The man who hired me wanted to speak to her."

Royce walked forward, practically pushing the lawyer aside so he could get in the gunman's face.

"What number and who gave it to you?" Royce asked, slapping his fists onto the metal table and getting right in Haggard's face.

"You didn't agree to the plea deal."

That didn't help ease the tension in Royce's expression. "I'll tell the D.A. you cooperated and see what can be worked out. And that's the best offer I can give you."

Haggard hesitated, then shrugged. "The whole deal was brokered through a third party. And before you ask, you can't speak to him because you shot and killed him."

No, no, no! That was not what she wanted to hear.

Sophie moved closer to the window, until she was so close to it that her breath fogged the glass. She wanted to get a good look at Haggard's face so she could see any signs that he might be lying. But the man was no doubt a good poker player, because he wasn't revealing anything.

"When you surrendered back at the ranch, you said you'd tell me the name of the person who hired you," Royce reminded Haggard.

Another shrug. "The man's name is Lucky Monroe, and like I said, he's dead."

Royce groaned, stepped back, but his hands stayed balled up into fists. "So, this Lucky Monroe hired you?"

Haggard nodded, and his carefree expression turned smug. "I guess you're sorry now that you killed him, huh?"

Royce's gaze sliced back to the man. "No. The only thing I'm sorry about is that I didn't take you out, too."

"Deputy," the lawyer warned.

"Your client is scum," Royce informed him right back without taking his glare off Haggard. "Where's this so-called phone number you were supposed to give Ms. Conway?"

Haggard lifted his hands, the cuffs clanging against the table, and he spread his fingers to reveal the writing on his left index finger.

Royce took out his phone and pressed in the numbers. Sophie waited, her lungs aching because she was holding her breath. She prayed it wasn't her brother or father who would answer that call.

The seconds crawled by, and she finally heard Royce curse. He jabbed a button on the phone and shoved it back in his pocket. "I got a recording. The number is no longer in service."

Both relief and disappointment flooded through her. This would have been so much easier if Travis had been on the other end of that line. Of course, it didn't make any of their suspects innocent. It only meant the person after them had covered his tracks.

"Since Lucky Monroe couldn't have disconnected that number," Royce said, "any idea who did?"

Haggard shrugged again but didn't say a word.

Sophie tore her attention from the man when she

heard the front door open, and she went to the doorway to make sure it wasn't another visitor they didn't want.

However, it was Jake.

Royce's brother glanced down at the blood drops on the floor. "From Travis Bullock?" he asked Billy, and the deputy verified that it was.

Jake stepped around them and made a beeline toward her. "Are you okay?" he asked.

"We're alive," she settled for saying and tipped her head to the interrogation room. "Royce is in there with the gunman and his lawyer, but they're not saying much."

"Figures," Jake grumbled. "I'll see what I can do about getting Royce and you out of here."

Sophie shook her head. "But what about your daughter?"

"She's fine. Maggie and my sister are with her, and none of us will be going back to the ranch until we're sure the danger has passed."

Which might not be for weeks.

It sickened her to think of that. Jake's little girl should be home, recovering from her ordeal, but there was no way that could happen with the gunman's boss still calling the shots.

"I'm sorry," she said to Jake.

He nodded. "Not your fault."

Jake walked away and into the interview room. She couldn't tell from Royce's face if he was glad to see his brother or not.

The two brothers stepped out into the hall, and even though Sophie couldn't hear what they said, the end result was that Jake went back into the interview room and Royce came to her. Sophie expected him to say they were leaving, but he stood in front of her, not moving.

"I need those papers," he said.

Her breath stalled a moment. She certainly hadn't forgotten about the papers that would incriminate Travis. And her father. But with everything else going on, she'd pushed them to the back of her mind.

Royce obviously hadn't done the same.

With reason. Those papers could perhaps put Travis behind bars and stop the attacks, and even though it could cause her father's arrest, too, she couldn't put that above the safety of Royce and his family.

Sophie nodded. "They're in a safety-deposit box in Corner's Lake." It wasn't far, less than ten miles from Mustang Ridge, but she stepped into the hall so she could glance out the front window. "How bad do you think the roads will be?"

"We can get there," he assured her. Royce blew out a long breath. "I'm sorry you have to do this. Sorry that I couldn't find another way."

Yes, so was she.

They started toward the front, with Royce grabbing their coats that he'd dropped onto his desk, but before they could even put them on, Royce's phone buzzed. He took it out, glanced at the screen.

"It's Special Agent Kade Ryland," he let her know. "My friend at the FBI." As Royce had done before, he put the call on Speaker.

"Royce," the agent said. "This is a heads-up. Lott managed to get a court order to put Sophie Conway into protective custody."

Her breath didn't just stall, it stopped for several seconds.

"How the hell did Lott get that?" Royce asked. His voice was tight, the emotion barely under control.

"I'm not sure," Ryland answered. "He pulled some strings, that's for sure. Oh, and get this. The investigation is all aboveboard now. Well, as aboveboard as the paperwork says it is."

Oh, mercy. Normally, a legal investigation wouldn't have caused her heart to race out of control, but she didn't trust Lott. And besides, he was a suspect in these attempts on their lives.

"Any way you can stop the court order?" Royce asked. She hadn't thought it possible, but his jaw muscles tightened even more.

"Sorry, no. It's too late for that," Agent Ryland answered. "Lott's on his way to the sheriff's office now to take Sophie into his custody. I figure you've got ten minutes at most to get her the heck out of there."

13

This was not how Royce wanted things to play out.

He didn't want to be on the run with Sophie, especially with the snow coming down, an FBI agent on their tails and no answers to help them stop another attack.

Still, they had no choice. He couldn't let Lott take her into custody, because Royce wasn't sure he could trust the man. Of course, there were several people on his do-not-trust list, including Sophie's own father and brother.

Royce checked his watch again. Only a few minutes since the last time he'd looked, but time seemed to have stopped while Sophie was inside the secure area of the Corner's Lake Bank where the safety-deposit boxes were kept. He hadn't gone into the room with her because he'd wanted to keep watch. It was the least he could do since he was already having second and third thoughts about taking her there. But he couldn't get past his gut feeling that those papers were critical to their staying alive.

Still waiting, he stayed near the window so he could see the traffic trickling down Main Street. He'd parked in the back, just in case Lott took this route to get to Mustang Ridge, and Royce had made sure they hadn't been followed. Still, he wouldn't rest easy until he had Sophie out of there and safely tucked away somewhere.

If somewhere safe was even possible.

They'd been lucky that the bank wasn't crowded. Luckier still that it hadn't yet closed because of the weather. Maybe their luck would hold up, and the snowy roads would stop Lott or anyone else from finding them.

Royce heard the footsteps and spotted Sophie walking back toward him. She handed him the manila envelope she'd had tucked beneath her arm, and without making it too obvious that they were hurrying, they got out of there.

"Where now?" she asked as they made their way to the parking lot.

"A motel."

She slowed a little and gave him a questioning look. Maybe she was asking if that was a good idea, but Royce had no idea how to answer that. Even if a motel turned out to be perfectly safe, Sophie and he would still be alone there. And with the attraction simmering hot and fast between them, *alone* probably wasn't a good thing. Better, though, than having bullets fired at them.

They got into the SUV that he'd borrowed from Billy and drove out onto Main Street. Sophie tipped her head to the grocery store just up the block from the bank.

"We could get the test," she reminded him.

Royce certainly hadn't forgotten about the possible pregnancy, but unlike the bank, the grocery store was packed. Probably because people were stocking up on food in case the snow closed the roads.

"Too risky," he explained.

If someone recognized them, the word might get back to the person behind the attacks. Or to Lott. Either way, that wouldn't be good for Sophie and him. It was best if they kept their location as secret as possible.

Sophie didn't argue and kept her attention on the side mirror. Royce kept watch, too, and headed out of town and toward the highway that would eventually lead to the interstate. He didn't want to go too far in case Jake needed him, but he wanted to be far enough away from Mustang Ridge that he wouldn't immediately be recognized when he checked into a motel.

In the few minutes before he'd gotten Sophie out of the sheriff's office and away from Lott, Royce had managed to grab a few supplies. Definitely no pregnancy tests. But Billy had given them some sandwiches and soft drinks he'd brought for his lunch and dinner. Royce had even grabbed some cash and a change of clothes from his locker. Not that the extra jeans and shirt would fit Sophie, but she might be able to use the shirt as a pajama top.

It certainly beat the alternative of her sleeping naked.

Okay. Royce amended that.

Her sleeping naked greatly appealed to certain parts of his body, but it wasn't a good idea. Nor was thinking about her wearing only his shirt. However, he might be able to get a room with two beds. Separate rooms were out, because he didn't want her out of his sight, but separate beds might help him get through the night without going crazy.

He looked around the cab of the SUV to see if there was anything they could use while hiding out. Royce had to push away Billy's stash of cigarettes and disposable lighters, and he found something he hoped they wouldn't need.

A handgun and some extra ammo.

It wasn't much, but with everything going on, Royce would take every little bit of help he could get.

He heard the unfamiliar buzzing sound and realized it was the prepaid cell he'd taken from the sheriff's office. Jake and he used the phones sometimes to issue to temporary-hire deputies, but Royce had snagged one so he could leave his own phone behind. With Lott's FBI resources, he'd easily be able to trace Royce's phone, but he couldn't do that with a prepaid cell.

Royce shut the glove compartment and answered the call, but he didn't say anything in case it wasn't Jake or Billy. However, it was Billy, so Royce put the call on Speaker.

"Lott finally left a few minutes ago," Billy explained. "And yeah, he was madder than a hornet when he found out Sophie wasn't here and that we couldn't tell him where she was. He's threatening to bring charges against us for obstruction of justice."

Royce groaned. He didn't need this. Neither did Jake or Billy, but there wasn't a good alternative for keeping her safe.

Sophie cleared her throat, causing Royce to glance at her. "I don't want anyone getting in trouble because of me," she said. "I can call Lott, talk to him."

He shook his head. "Not a good idea. I don't want any communication with him because we might inadvertently give him clues to our location."

Plus, he didn't want to put Sophie through Lott's intimidation tactics, especially since she might be giving in to them.

She squeezed her eyes shut a moment. "But maybe I should go with him."

"Hell, no." And Royce didn't have to think about that. "Not until we're sure we can trust Lott."

Maybe not even then.

"Jake's still tied up, questioning that gunman," Billy added. "But he said he'd handle Lott if he comes back."

Royce didn't doubt his brother's abilities. Jake was a good lawman, but he also didn't want Jake to get in trouble over this. The problem was that Royce wasn't sure how to prevent that and keep Sophie safe. What he needed was to figure out who was responsible for the attacks, stop them, and then there'd be no reason for Lott to place Sophie in federal protective custody.

"Thought you'd also want to know," Billy continued, "that the doc checked out Travis and said it wasn't much of an injury. All he needed was a couple of stitches."

"Was it self-inflicted?" Sophie asked just as Royce turned onto the interstate. He wanted to know the same thing.

"Possibly. The doc couldn't say for sure, and Travis walked out of the hospital when the doc hinted that's what might have happened."

So Travis was out and about somewhere. But so were their other suspects.

"What about the site where Travis said he was run off the road?" Royce asked Billy.

"The road's covered with ice and snow. Can't tell much until this storm passes through. Oh, and Agent Kade Ryland from the FBI called, too," Billy added. "Should I give him your number?"

Royce considered it, and while he trusted Ryland, he didn't know if there'd be some way that Travis could get the information. "Better not risk it. What did Ryland want?"

"He found out who's trying to contest Sophie's mother's will," Billy answered.

"Who?" Royce and she asked in unison. But he didn't miss the fact that Sophie held her breath, obviously bracing herself to hear the answer that would implicate her father or her brother.

"It's Travis," Billy said.

Now *that* was an answer that Royce hadn't anticipated. Apparently, neither had Sophie because with her mouth open she moved closer to the phone.

"How could Travis challenge the will?" she asked. "My mother didn't even mention him in it."

"It's a long legal explanation, one I didn't fully understand, but it seems as if Travis believes he has a claim to the Conway ranch because Eldon owes him a boatload of money. Travis's lawyers are saying Diane Conway *arranged* her assets so they couldn't be used to pay off debts incurred before her death."

Royce thought about that a moment and looked at Sophie. "Is it true? Did your father get some money from Travis before your mother died?"

She stayed silent a moment, too. "Maybe. You think Travis has a claim?"

"Who knows," Billy answered. "The guy could be just grabbing at straws."

Yeah. But if there was some basis to it, then perhaps Travis could get his money and back off from Sophie. Maybe that would end the threats.

Unless Travis was hell-bent on getting revenge for their possible one-night stand after Stanton drugged them.

Of course, if Travis got his hands on that money,

Sophie and her family would probably be broke, but at least they'd all be alive.

If Stanton, Eldon or both were innocent, that is.

"Call me if anything else comes up," Royce instructed Billy.

He ended the call, hoping that would be the last of the bad news, and he took the ramp to exit the interstate. There were three buildings on the access road—a hotel, restaurant and a motel. He chose the latter since it would mean Sophie and he wouldn't have to go traipsing through a lobby to get to a room.

"There are a lot of cars in the parking lot," Sophie pointed out.

Royce knew the concerns; she didn't have to voice them. More cars meant more people who could possibly see them. But it also might mean the place was already full. At least he could see the registration desk through the large front windows, which meant Sophie wouldn't have to go in, yet wouldn't be out of his sight.

"Get down on the seat," Royce instructed, "and lock the doors." He got out, waited until she'd done that before he hurried inside.

"You're in luck," the clerk immediately said. "One room left."

Finally, something had gone their way. Royce used his cash to pay for a deposit and the room, and he gave the clerk a fake name. Maybe that would stop Lott from pinpointing their location.

Once he had the key to the second-floor room, Royce parked in the back, gathered their things and got Sophie into the room as fast as possible. Royce did a quick check of the room, though there wasn't much to check. Just the bedroom and a small bath. No one was inside, lurking, ready to attack, so he double locked the door and even put on the chain.

"You should eat," he said, depositing the bag of supplies on the small table.

Since the table was directly in front of a window, he closed the blinds and took a sandwich and a bottle of water to Sophie who sank down onto the foot of the bed.

"Thanks," she mumbled, and took the items from him.

But it was obvious her attention wasn't on eating. She glanced first at the envelope of papers that he'd put next to the bag. Then she looked back at the sole queen-size bed before her attention returned to him.

"There were no rooms with two beds," Royce volunteered.

Sophie shrugged. "It probably wouldn't have mattered anyway."

He knew exactly what she meant. They'd been alone two other times before—in the Mustang Ridge motel and in the kitchen at his house, and both times they'd made out.

Maybe more.

Even if nothing had happened at the motel a month earlier, plenty had happened in his kitchen.

"So we, um…wait?" she asked.

That sounded a little sexual to him, probably because his mind kept drifting in that direction whenever he was around Sophie.

Royce nodded. "Jake might get something from the gunman." He motioned toward the papers. "There might be something in those, too." Anything that would give him the name of the person responsible so he could make an arrest.

Then they could deal with the pregnancy test.

Royce hadn't realized he'd been staring at her stomach until Sophie cleared her throat. She'd obviously noticed what had gotten his attention.

"No symptoms," she reminded him. "And the odds are slim since it was just that one time."

True. And Royce didn't want to speculate on how he would feel if that test came back positive or negative. Besides, it just didn't seem real that a drugged or drunken encounter could have resulted in a baby.

She stood, placing the sandwich and water on the dresser just a few feet in front of her. "Are you going to file charges against Stanton for drugging you?"

Royce shook his head. "I haven't made up my mind about that yet. But if I get proof that he's involved in these attacks, he's going to jail."

Sophie didn't argue. She just gave a resigned nod and walked closer to him. Her arm brushed against his when she went to the table and retrieved the envelope with the papers. Even though she didn't open it or say anything, Royce knew what she was feeling.

"I'll do everything within my power to keep your father out of this," he said.

"Unless he's the one trying to kill us." Her voice was a hoarse whisper, and he couldn't just see the fatigue and worry in her eyes, he could feel it.

Even though he knew he shouldn't do it, Royce reached out, put his arm around Sophie and pulled her to him. There was nothing he could say to make things better. Nothing he could do, either. So he just stood there and held her. It might have stayed a simple hug if Sophie hadn't slipped her arms around him, too.

And worse.

She pulled back just a little, met his gaze.

The fatigue was definitely there in all those swirls of blue in her eyes, but there was a spark of something else. Again, he knew exactly what because the spark was also there inside him.

The corner of her mouth lifted. "Does this qualify as our second date?" she asked.

Royce laughed before he could stop himself. He didn't know how Sophie had managed to find any humor in this mess, but he was glad she had.

He pushed the hair away from her cheek and brushed a kiss there. That was all he intended to do because even a chaste kiss between them had an edge to it. Touching her in any way always seemed like foreplay. But he didn't pull away after the cheek kiss.

Sophie turned a little at a time until her mouth was against his. Royce felt the groan rumble in his chest. Felt the heat start to rise. With all that heat, it was hard to believe there was a snowstorm outside.

"I think we both know what'll happen if this kiss continues," Sophie said, her breath brushing against his lips.

Yeah, he did know. For some reason it no longer seemed like such a bad idea.

Even though it was.

Their situation hadn't changed, and if he got her in that bed, he'd lose the focus that he needed to keep her safe. And alive.

"I should take a shower," she whispered.

It sounded like yet more foreplay, and Royce felt himself go rock hard. She waited, maybe to see if he intended to join her. He wanted that. Man, did he. He wanted nothing more than to do something about this constant ache that he had for her.

Sophie studied his eyes a moment before she gave a slight nod. "You're stronger than I am," she said. And with that totally inaccurate observation, she walked away and into the bathroom.

Hell.

He'd known this would be difficult, but he hadn't braced himself nearly enough for being here alone with Sophie.

Royce stood there, debating if he should go after her. He had a dozen reasons why he shouldn't, and he forced himself to remember each and every one of them. He needed to go through those papers. He needed to keep watch.

And keeping watch wouldn't happen if he was having sex with Sophie.

Royce cursed again and wished that he had zero willpower so he could go into that shower with her. But instead, he grabbed the papers and got to work.

14

The water spraying on her was too hot, but Sophie didn't turn down the temperature in the shower. She wanted the heat and the steam. Because if that heat seeped into her, she might forget the other kind of fire that was roaring through her.

Royce's kiss was responsible for it.

But Sophie rethought that. She'd been burning for Royce for over a month now, and the recent kisses had just been a reminder of the obvious.

She pressed her forehead against the warm glass shower door so the water could massage the back of her neck. It, too, became a quick reminder of Royce's touch. So did the water sliding down her breasts, belly and well, lower. She had just fragments of memories of Royce touching her at the motel a month ago, but there had been that incident in his kitchen.

The one where they'd practically had sex on the counter.

Now *that* touching she remembered.

And still felt it.

The sliding water only helped her feel it more. Made her ache more, too.

Sophie moaned, cursed and slapped off the shower.

The heat and water caressing her definitely weren't helping. Cold probably wouldn't, either. In fact, she was afraid there was only one cure for what ailed her, and that cure was in the bedroom.

Maybe even on the bed they'd have to share.

Sophie got a clear image of that, too, and felt even more heat. She'd walked away from him earlier, but she wasn't sure she'd have much luck doing that again. Her willpower was shot, and even worse, she didn't want to get it back.

She stepped from the shower, dried off, but she stopped when the towel was on her stomach.

There.

That was a reminder she did need—that she might be pregnant. Sophie managed to keep that pressed into her mind until she spotted Royce's shirt that she'd draped over the towel rack. He'd taken it from the sheriff's office since she had no other change of clothing there.

His shirt made her think of the man who owned it. If it carried his scent, then she was a lost cause.

She brought it to her face and sniffed.

Lost cause, all right.

Even though it was clean, it had no doubt been in his locker at work with other clothing, and the scent had transferred. Just a trace. Just enough to remind her of that blasted heat.

Sophie got dressed in the shirt and yet another item of Royce's clothes—a pair of his boxers. She had no other clean underwear with her so she washed her own panties and bra and hoped they'd dry soon. Until they did, she would literally be clothed in reminders of a man she couldn't seem to forget anyway.

With her nerves zinging, she eased open the bathroom door and spotted Royce. Yes, on the bed. He'd taken off his boots and had his legs stretched out in front of him. His dark hair was rumpled, probably because he was idly scrubbing his hand through it while he had his attention plastered to the papers he was reading.

Everything about him was hot. That bedroom hair. His rugged face with the sexy stubble. That sensual mouth that made her crazy with heat. His hands.

Yes, those were plenty capable of creating heat, too.

He looked up and seemed to do a double take. That didn't help with her nerves, and she glanced down to make sure everything important was covered. It was. His shirt went to her midthigh, and the boxers covered far more than her panties would have.

Royce's gaze slid from her face, to her breasts and all the way to her legs. By the time he'd finished, Sophie felt as if he'd undressed her.

Worse, she felt as if she wanted him to undress her.

"They look better on you than on me," he commented.

There seemed to be something unspoken at the end of that. Maybe something along the lines of she'd look better with nothing at all. But perhaps the ache in her body was filling in the blanks for her. This had to stop.

Had to.

And Sophie repeated that to herself.

"Find anything?" she asked, forcing herself to speak. Her nerves kicked in for a different reason. Those were the papers that could get her father arrested.

"Maybe." His attention stayed on her for several more seconds before going back to the paper. "According to this, three people signed the land deal that was used to launder money. Your father, Travis and someone named Milton Wells. Any idea who he is?"

She shook her head and walked closer. "I didn't find out much about him. I did an internet search and learned he's the head of some company."

"Investacorp," Royce provided. He glanced at the phone on the bed next to him. "I made some calls while you were in the shower."

And judging from the way his forehead was furrowed, he hadn't been pleased with what he'd learned. "This Milton Wells is dirty, too?"

"Maybe not just dirty but bogus. The company no longer exists, and according to Agent Ryland at the FBI, it was likely an offshore dummy company set up to launder money and do other illegal things."

Oh, mercy. Nothing about that sounded good. "And yet my father got involved with them."

"He might not have known it was a dummy company or that they were involved in anything illegal. I need to talk to him and find out where he met this Milton Wells and how much he knows about him."

"I could call him," she suggested. It would get her mind off Royce and back on to things that could actually help them out of their situation.

"No. I'd like to keep you out of this. Ryland's working on it, and he's also working on getting the court order canceled for your protective custody."

"Agent Ryland can do that?" Sophie asked.

"He's trying."

And if Ryland managed it, Royce and she could go back to Mustang Ridge. Well, maybe. They could if they managed to neutralize the danger.

"So what happens with my father and those documents?" she asked.

"If Eldon knows anything that can be used to arrest this Milton Wells, then we might be able to work out a deal to keep your father out of jail."

Sophie hated to get her hopes up, but she did anyway. "Thank you. After everything that's happened, it's generous of you to do this for him. For me."

Royce tilted his head, stared at her. "Hey, I said I'd do everything to keep your father out of jail, and I will."

"I know."

Her words hung between them. Their gazes stayed locked. And something changed in the air.

Without taking his attention off her, Royce dropped the papers on the bed next to his phone, and he eased across the mattress toward her. Even though they weren't officially lovers, Sophie knew that look he was giving her. She saw the subtle changes in him. This was no longer about the papers and the promise he'd made to her.

This was about *them*.

She didn't go closer. Couldn't. Her feet seemed anchored to the carpeted floor, but Royce had no trouble moving. He got to the edge of the bed, swung his legs off the side. However, he didn't get up. He caught her by the waist and inched her toward him.

"Just so you know," he said, "I don't usually do reckless things."

She nearly laughed. Nearly. "So, I'm reckless?"

"No." His cool green eyes were no longer cool. They were sizzling, like the rest of him. "You're the woman I apparently can't resist. Not resisting you is the reckless part."

He didn't seem happy about that. Neither was she because she couldn't seem to resist him, either. That didn't make things even. Or right. So, yeah, this was reckless. But Sophie didn't pull away when Royce leaned in and pressed his mouth to the front of her shirt.

To her right breast.

She had no trouble feeling his kiss through the fabric of the shirt. It was just as hot and arousing as if his mouth had touched her bare skin.

Royce didn't stop with just the breast kiss. His grip on her waist tightened just slightly, and he eased her forward. The next kiss he gave her was on her stomach. Then, lower. To her right hip bone.

Sophie's eyes fluttered down. She felt herself go from warm to hot. And she slid her hand around the back of his neck to bring him even closer. Not that she needed to do that. Royce was already moving in that direction anyway.

He kissed her. Still through the clothes. And he touched her, too. His hand slid lower, over the small of her back and to her bottom, and using that same gentle pressure, his fingers lit some new fires along the way.

"You can say no," he whispered. "You *should* say no."

His words and breath created an interesting sensation through the cotton boxers, and the sensation speared through her.

"I don't want to say no," she answered.

Sophie wanted to shout *Yes!,* grab on to him and put his clever mouth right in the center of all that heat. Better yet, she wanted their clothes off and them both on the bed. She wanted Royce to send her flying.

Royce pushed up the shirt so he could kiss her exactly the way she wanted. He went lower, shoving down the boxers and using his mouth to rev up the heat even more. But soon, it wasn't enough. Her body was burning for him, and Sophie wanted more.

He seemed to sense that, too, and as if they were in sync in both body and mind, his grip around her backside tightened, and he pulled her forward. Wrapped in each other's arms, they dropped back onto the mattress.

The kisses didn't stop, though he moved them back to her mouth and neck, all the while adjusting their positions until the center of her body was aligned with his erection pressing hard against his jeans.

Her breath caught in her throat. Her head went light, and it got even lighter when he pulled off her shirt. His, too, and his bare chest landed against her breasts. Another mind-blowing sensation.

Sophie had guessed that Royce pretty much had a perfect body, and she hadn't been wrong about that. Not overly muscled, but he was toned and tight. Yes, perfect.

The kisses got deeper, and he used his tongue on her nipples until Sophie was arching her back and begging for more. Royce gave her more. He stripped off her boxers and made his way down her body for some of those kisses she'd been fantasizing about.

Oh, mercy.

Perfect, indeed.

It didn't take long, just a few of those well-placed kisses before Sophie wanted this to go to the next level. She wanted Royce, naked and inside her.

She caught on to his shoulders and pulled him up to go after his zipper. He didn't help, and for a moment she couldn't figure out why. Then she realized he was taking his wallet from his back pocket.

Royce pulled out a foil-wrapped condom.

Great. She was so hot and ready for this that she'd forgotten all about the basics of safe sex. Thankfully, Royce hadn't, and he put on the condom as soon as he'd taken off his jeans and boxers.

He looked at her, as if checking one last time to make sure she was okay with this. Sophie was more than okay, and she hooked her arm around his waist and brought him down to her. Exactly where he should be.

Royce entered her slowly, but there was nothing slow about her response. The sensations exploded through her. So hard, so fast. That Sophie lost her breath. She couldn't speak—her throat had clamped shut. Couldn't hear because of her heartbeat crashing in her ears. But she could feel. Oh, yes.

Even though Royce started out gently, it didn't stay that way, and Sophie was thankful for it. This wasn't the time for gentle. She needed him. Needed this to be finished.

Royce did his part.

He moved deep and hard inside her, and Sophie wrapped her legs around his waist allowing him to lift her hips toward each of those thrusts. Royce had already given her a climax in his kitchen so she knew something about how he could make her feel.

But this was more.

The pleasure was blinding and soon unbearable.

Royce's gaze stayed locked on her, and he didn't waver. Not with the look in her eyes nor with the intensity. Sophie wanted to tell him this was perfect.

Too perfect, maybe.

She wanted to tell him to finish her. But that wasn't necessary, either. Royce moved his hand between them, touching her where they were already so intimately joined, and just like that, Sophie felt herself shatter.

The raw pleasure and relief roared through her, and the only thing she could do was hold on to Royce and let him finish her off.

15

Royce tried not to make a sound when he used the small coffeemaker in the motel room to brew a strong cup. Sophie was still asleep, and he wanted her to stay that way awhile longer, but he also needed the caffeine to clear the cobwebs in his head.

He sat at the desk where he'd left the papers and tried to study them again. Royce could see all the details of the sale. Could see that Eldon, Travis and this third man, Milton Wells, had clearly broken the law, but even after several whispered conversations with Agent Ryland, Royce still didn't know who Wells was.

Of course, the same could be said for the entire investigation. Despite the dozen phone calls and emails he'd exchanged, there'd been no breaks or new developments in the case overnight.

Unlike his relationship with Sophie.

Oh, yeah. There'd been a break there all right.

Before he'd even landed in bed with her, Royce had known it would be a mistake. That hadn't stopped him, of course, and sadly it wouldn't stop him from making the same mistake again. He still wanted her, and having sex with her had only fueled that need. It hadn't satisfied it at all.

Now, the question was—what was he going to do about it?

"Nothing" would be the right answer. With Sophie's safety and this investigation hanging over his head, there's no way he should be thinking about extending this affair.

Or whatever it was.

But it was almost impossible to push it aside when they still didn't have the results of a pregnancy test. That was a result that could change everything.

He hadn't planned on fatherhood, but he wouldn't run from it, either. No. Just the opposite. If Sophie was carrying his child, then they would need to work out something. Shared custody. A relationship of convenience. Whatever it took to put and keep him in the child's life. No way would he be a bitter, emotionally absent father like his own.

However, this did give Royce a little insight into how Chet had felt about an unplanned pregnancy. It wasn't an easy matter.

Sophie didn't make a sound, but she jackknifed to a sitting position. Her eyes were wild, unfocused, and her gaze darted around the room until it landed on him. Even then, it seemed to take several seconds for her to recognize him and breathe a sigh of relief.

"A dream," she mumbled.

More like a nightmare. Royce had had a couple of those, too, during the night. Some about the investigation. Another about potential fatherhood.

Sophie threw back the covers, but then immediately threw them back on when she glanced down at her naked body. "Sorry."

His eyebrow went up. "I'm a guy. Trust me, seeing you like that isn't cause for an apology."

She made a soft sound of agreement and eased back the covers again. However, this time she grabbed her clothes and quickly started to dress.

"If you're hungry, they're plowing the roads now," Royce told her. "We could go to a drive-through fast-food place and get something."

"Maybe later." She paused and glanced at him from the corner of her eye. "How many second and third thoughts are you having this morning?"

Part of him admired her direct approach. Another part of him dreaded the answer. He wouldn't lie, that's for sure. "A few. But not for the reasons you're thinking."

This time Sophie made a sound of disagreement. "You're thinking you crossed a line by sleeping with someone you're protecting. A law enforcement no-no. You're probably also thinking this complicates things. Plus, there's that whole part about you believing I'm totally wrong for you."

Okay. So, maybe she did know the reasons for his second and third thoughts.

"I'm wrong for you," he corrected. Then shrugged. "That doesn't stop me from wanting you."

The corner of her mouth lifted, and she pushed her tousled hair from her face. Sexy hair, he noticed. Actually, everything about her fell into that category, including her generous curves and that welcoming smile that she no doubt hadn't meant to be so welcoming.

She stood, went closer, took the cup from him and

had a huge sip of his coffee. "What do you want me to say? That I can be content living in a place like Mustang Ridge? That I'm not a city girl?"

"Nothing wrong with being those things," Royce admitted. "But if we were looking for something long-term, it might be a problem."

She stared at him. "Long-term?"

He let his gaze drift to her stomach. "Oh. That kind of long-term." She shook her head. "I don't want you to feel trapped."

Like your father.

She didn't say the words, but it was there in her tone and the look she gave him. "What? You don't think I'd be a good dad?" he asked.

"No. You would be," she quickly answered. "I'm just not sure it'd be fair to put you in that position."

"Fair?" For some reason, that riled him. "Sophie, none of this was fair. Your brother drugged us, and if he hadn't done that, we probably wouldn't have had unprotected sex."

"If that's what happened." Sophie dropped a kiss on his forehead.

Sophie had another sip of his coffee before she tipped her head to the papers.

"Anything?" she asked.

So sex, possible future sex and long-term plans were no longer the topic of discussion. Royce figured he should feel relieved, but he knew it was just delaying the inevitable. Eventually, they'd have those test results, and even if they were negative, the attraction sure wasn't going to dim.

"According to Agent Ryland at the FBI," he explained after he collected his thoughts, "Milton Wells from Investacorp doesn't exist. A dummy name for a dummy company."

She stared at the papers a moment and then huffed. "So, he could be anyone?"

"Yeah. But he'd still have to be someone your father knows since they signed the papers together. By the way, I tried to call him this morning, but the call went straight to voice mail."

That in itself wasn't suspicious. After all, it was early. But there was something about her father that bothered him.

"I talked to Billy this morning, too," Royce continued. "Neither your father nor brother has called the sheriff's office to find out where you are."

Royce was about to ask if that was out of the ordinary, but he could tell from the concern in her eyes that it was.

She shook her head. "Maybe Lott is with them, and they don't want to call because he might learn where I am."

That was possible. Lott would definitely go to her family or Travis to find out where she was. Still, if Sophie was his family member and essentially missing, he'd be out looking for her.

Blowing out a long, weary breath, she sank down onto the foot of the bed. "I have to at least consider my father and brother are suspects."

Royce settled for a nod. He was doing more than considering it because they both had strong motives.

Money, and lots of it.

If Sophie was dead and out of the way, Eldon would have the money to pay off the loan shark and revive the ranch. Stanton and he might also be nursing some ill feelings about being completely cut out of Diane Conway's will. But what didn't fit in that scenario was the fact that Stanton had drugged Sophie and him.

His phone buzzed, cutting off that thought, and Royce recognized the number when he glanced at the screen.

Special Agent Kade Ryland.

Royce had already spoken to the man twice this morning, but he was anxious to hear if the agent had found anything out about Milton Wells. Sophie was clearly anxious, too, because she moved closer to the phone, and Royce put the call on Speaker.

"Deputy McCall," Ryland greeted. "Hope you're sitting down for this, but the order to take Ms. Conway into protective custody has been pulled."

Royce could see the relief go through her. It went through him, too. "Thank you," he said to the agent.

"Don't thank me. Lott pulled the order himself."

That took away a little of Royce's relief. "Why?" he asked suspiciously.

"Lott says it's no longer necessary. He said he found proof of who's been trying to kill you and Ms. Conway, and he's on his way now to Mustang Ridge to make an arrest."

Sophie leaned on the desk and sank down onto the edge of it. "Who is Lott arresting?" Since her voice had little sound, Royce repeated the question so the agent could hear it.

Agent Ryland cleared his throat first. "Sophie's father, Eldon Conway. Lott's picking him up at the ranch and taking him to the Mustang Ridge jail."

Sophie tried to tamp down the feeling of panic, but she was failing big-time.

Not long before Agent Ryland's call, she'd accepted that her father and brother could be suspects. Or so she thought she had. But it cut her to the core to know that Lott claimed to have proof of her father's guilt when her father had been the one person she'd tried to protect.

"We'll get to the bottom of this," Royce said to her. He'd already given her various assurances of that as they'd thrown their things into the SUV and started the drive back to Mustang Ridge.

Sophie hoped that was possible. "Even if Lott found the incriminating papers for the land deal, what kind of proof could there be that my father tried to kill us?"

Royce glanced at her, and Sophie saw the sympathy in his eyes. A stark contrast to the look he'd given her the night before. He also didn't hesitate, which meant he'd given this some thought.

"Jimmy Haggard, the gunman I questioned, could have named your father," Royce offered.

"But wouldn't Jake have told you?" she asked.

He shook his head. "The Rangers took him into custody late yesterday. Haggard could have worked out some kind of plea deal with them."

"And Haggard could have lied to save his own skin."

Royce reached across the seat, caught her hand and gave it a gentle squeeze.

It helped.

Well, it helped as much as something like that could. But what would help even more was speaking to her father and hearing him say he had nothing to do with this. So far, she'd had zero luck with that, since her father wasn't answering his phone. That wasn't so unusual, though, since he often forgot to carry his cell with him and the snowstorm might have interfered with service.

"Maybe it wasn't a deal that Haggard struck," she said, more to herself than Royce. She was thinking out loud, trying to make sense of this. "Maybe it was Travis. Or Stanton."

Royce squeezed her hand again. "You'll drive yourself crazy by guessing like this. In a half hour or so, we'll know for sure."

That was an optimistic timetable because the snowy roads would certainly slow them down. Sophie refused to think of what would happen if they couldn't get through.

There was little traffic on the interstate, probably because the snowplows were still out, but Royce kept glancing at the side mirrors. No doubt to make sure they weren't being followed. Maybe that meant he didn't believe her father was guilty.

Royce took out his phone and pressed in some numbers. Since it was on Speaker, a few seconds later Sophie heard Billy answer.

"Any sign of Lott yet?" Royce asked the deputy.

"None, but then the roads are still pretty bad here. Might take him a while to get out to the Conway ranch and then back here to the sheriff's office." Billy paused. "You had a chance to talk to Eldon?"

"Not yet. Sophie's tried to call him a couple of times."

Yes, and she'd try again when Royce finished this call. She didn't want her father to try to run from Lott, but she didn't want the agent to spring an arrest on her father, either.

"I'll let you know the minute they arrive," Billy assured him. Royce clicked the end call button, handed the phone to her and took the turn off the interstate.

The ramp was mostly clear of the snow, but Royce had to slow down the moment he got onto the two lane road that would take them back to town. It would be slow going, and that didn't do much to steady her nerves.

Sophie tried to call her father again but got the same results. It went to voice mail. It was the same when she tried to contact Stanton. Like before, she left messages for them to call her and she gave the number of the pre-paid cell phone.

"Nothing," she relayed to Royce.

She took a deep breath, trying to concentrate on keeping watch, but the dizziness hit her. Not an overwhelming sensation, but Sophie did touch her hand to her head.

"What's wrong?" Royce immediately asked.

Thankfully, the dizziness went as quickly as it came. "I'm okay," she assured him. "I'll get something to eat when we get to Mustang Ridge."

Royce gave her another concerned glance, but he didn't voice what they were both thinking. She really needed to get her hands on a pregnancy test—soon. But for now, Sophie had more immediate concerns.

She looked down at the phone that she still had in her hand and groaned when she saw they no longer had service. A dead zone. So, even if her father got her message, he might not be able to call her back right away.

Even though Royce didn't make a sound, Sophie heard the change in his breathing, and her gaze snapped to him. He was volleying glances into the side and rearview mirrors, and she looked behind them to see what had garnered his attention.

A semitruck.

It wasn't unusual for commercial trucks to be traveling here since the road led to several small towns, but it was obvious that Royce had an uneasy feeling about it.

"A problem?" she asked.

Royce shook his head. "I'm not sure."

He kept watch. So did Sophie. And she soon saw what had put the concern on Royce's face. The truck was going too fast, and the road was icy and narrow. Passing them wouldn't be safe.

Royce tapped his brakes, no doubt to make sure the driver of the semi saw them. But the driver didn't slow down. He continued to barrel at them. Closer. And closer.

"Hell," Royce growled. "Make sure your seat belt is on."

The warning barely had time to register in Sophie's mind when she felt the jolt that slung her body forward.

The truck plowed right into the back of their SUV.

16

Royce tried to brace himself for the impact, but there was no way to do that with the huge truck crashing into them. Their SUV was much smaller, and the snowy road didn't help. Royce had to fight the steering wheel just to keep the SUV from going into the ditch.

"Oh, God." Sophie grabbed on to the dash with both hands.

And Royce knew why. The semi came at them again, bashing into them and sending the SUV into a skid.

Royce turned the steering wheel into the skid and tapped the brakes. However, he'd barely gotten control when the truck slammed into them again. He saw the back bumper fly off, and the rear-lift door flew up.

The bitter cold air immediately rushed into the cab of the SUV. So did the roaring sounds of the semi. It was like some monster bearing down on them for another attack.

Because the semi was so high off the ground, Royce couldn't see the driver or if it was just one person in on this attack. He suspected there were others since this seemed to be an attempt to kill them.

So, who was behind this?

One of their suspects, no doubt, because the odds were sky-high that this was connected to their investigation.

The semi crashed into them again and ripped off the entire rear door. Even if Royce managed to keep the SUV on the road, it wouldn't be long before the semi literally tore their vehicle apart. Then Sophie and he would either be killed in the impact or else would have to face down whoever was doing this.

Royce risked glancing at her. There was no color in her cheeks, but she was no longer holding on to the dash. Sophie was rifling through the glove compartment, and she took out the extra gun and ammo that Royce had seen the day before. Maybe, just maybe, they'd live long enough to use that ammo on the SOB who was doing this.

"Grab one of the lighters, too," he told her.

She probably had no idea why he'd want that, but if this truck managed to get them off the road and they had to escape into the woods, the lighter might come in handy to build a fire.

Another hit from the semi, and Royce felt the back tires give way. Thank God there was no other traffic on the road, because the SUV shot straight out into the opposite lane, and they headed for the ditch.

"Hold on," Royce warned Sophie as she crammed the gun, ammo and lighter into her jacket pockets.

The adrenaline was pumping through him. His heart racing out of control. But Royce forced himself to do a split-second assessment of their situation. Yeah, they were going to crash. No way to stop that. But they would hit the ditch and beyond that there were some trees.

And even a small wood-frame farmhouse.

Maybe there was someone inside who would see what was going on and use a landline to call 9-1-1.

Royce was certain they'd need backup.

If they survived, that is.

The semi slammed into them again, clipping the back of the driver's side of the SUV. The impact completely dislodged the tire, and it flew through the air, bouncing off the semi. Royce did what he could to keep control of the SUV—it wasn't much—but he put a death grip on the steering wheel and tried to keep them on the road.

He failed.

The SUV plowed nose-first into the snow- and ice-filled ditch.

The airbags deployed, slapping into them and knocking the breath out of Royce. He immediately looked at Sophie to make sure she was alive. She was, thank God. Not only alive but able to move.

Royce moved, too. Fighting for air, he slapped down the bag and drew the gun from his shoulder holster.

Beside him, Sophie did the same and then threw open the door. Or rather she tried to do that. She only got it open a few inches before the bottom edge of the door jammed against the frozen ditch.

Royce looked out his side window and saw both doors of the semi fly open. That upped the urgency for Sophie and him, and he twisted his body so he could kick the passenger's door. With the critical seconds ticking off in his head, he gave it another kick. And another.

Before it finally flew open.

"Move!" he said to Sophie, though she no doubt understood the need to do exactly that.

She practically spilled out of the SUV and landed on the side of the ditch. Royce pushed her out of the way so he could get out, too, and then he grabbed her by the arm so they could start running. He didn't look back because he figured whoever had been in that semi was armed.

He was right.

A shot flew by them just as Royce shoved Sophie behind a tree.

Royce cursed for putting her in this situation again. And then he cursed the person responsible for this attack. He was sick and tired of Sophie being in danger and not even knowing the reason why.

Another shot came, tearing through a chunk of the tree trunk and showering them with splinters. Royce didn't return fire. Sophie had a handful of extra ammo, plus the backup weapon, but he didn't know how long this fight would go on. Best not to use any bullets until it became absolutely necessary.

He figured that wouldn't be long from now.

"How many?" she asked.

Since Sophie was about to peer out from the tree, Royce pulled her to the ground and looked for himself. "There are three."

All of them were wearing ski masks and camouflage clothes just like the other two gunmen who'd attacked them at his house. Now the new trio was using the wrecked SUV for cover, but only two of them were poised to fire.

The other appeared to be searching through the SUV.

For what, though?

Royce tried to keep an eye on him, but that was hard to do with the other two continuing to fire shots at them. Each bullet tore away more of the tree, and Sophie and he couldn't just sit there and wait to be gunned down.

He needed to put some distance between the shooters and them and then get into a better position to return fire.

"There's no service out here," he heard Sophie say, and it took him a moment to realize that she was looking at the cell phone.

Royce hadn't even known that she had managed to hang on to it. It might come in handy if they could get out of this dead spot for service. Of course, even if they could call, help wouldn't get there for *a while,* but a while was better than nothing. Royce would take all the help he could get to keep Sophie safe.

With the shots still coming fast and furious, Royce glanced behind them at the pair of oaks. They were much wider than the cottonwood they were using for cover now, and it would give Sophie and him several extra feet of breathing room. Plus, it had the added bonus of being even closer to the house. He didn't want anyone inside being hurt from the gunfire, but a house would give them much better protection than the trees.

"Stay on your stomach," Royce instructed her, though he had to shout over the roar of the gunfire. "And crawl there." He tipped his head to the oak.

"What are you going to do?" she asked.

"Try to give you a diversion. It'll be okay," he quickly added when he saw that she was about to argue with him. "Hurry."

He left no room for doubt in his voice, and thankfully, Sophie stayed low and inched her way toward the oaks. Royce darted out from the cottonwood and fired. He didn't see where his shot landed because he immediately went back behind cover, but he heard the bullet strike metal. Probably one of the vehicles.

He checked to make sure Sophie was behind the oak. She was. Royce glanced out again. Not at the shooters but at the guy going through the SUV. And Royce cursed when he saw what the man had in his hand.

The manila envelope with the land papers.

Hell. How the devil had they known the papers were there? And why were they so important to retrieve during a gunfight?

Royce figured he wouldn't like the answer to either question, but both Travis and Eldon had some serious reasons for those papers to be destroyed. It was going to hurt Sophie bad if her father was wearing one of those ski masks. However, Royce couldn't let that play into this.

Sophie came first.

And if her father was behind the attacks, then they'd have to deal with that later. For now, Royce just tried to even the odds.

Staying low, he moved to his left and took aim at the gunman positioned at the front end of the SUV. The one with the papers had already headed back to the semi. Out of range. But Royce figured his best chance to pick one of them off was the guy on the front end.

It was a risk, but everything about their situation was risky.

Royce leaned out from behind cover. And fired.

He double tapped the trigger and saw the man he'd targeted jerk back from the impact of the shots that Royce had just fired into his chest. For a moment, Royce thought the guy might be wearing Kevlar, but he wasn't. The man dropped to the ground.

One down.

That thought barely had time to register in Royce's head when he heard the sound. Felt it, too.

The pain seared into his shoulder as the bullet slammed into him.

"Watch out!" Sophie shouted to Royce.

But she was already too late.

She'd seen the movement from the corner of her left eye. Another gunman. Not the one who'd taken the papers from the SUV—he was inside the semi now. This one had no doubt made his way from the back of the semi and toward them. Sophie could only watch in horror as the man fired a shot.

One that hit Royce.

"Stay down!" Royce told her just as she started to race toward him.

He was right, of course. If she moved out from the cover of the oak, the gunmen would just shoot her, too, but it took every bit of her willpower to force herself to stay put and not hurry to Royce.

Sophie levered herself up a little so she could get a better look at Royce. She prayed that he'd manage to survive that shot, and she was more than relieved to see him moving around. He was staying behind the tree, thank goodness, but she didn't miss the blood on his jacket. She had no idea how badly he'd been hurt, but she had to do something to get them out of there.

She looked around and saw the gunman still at the rear of the SUV. The other one, the bastard who'd shot Royce, was no longer in sight. Maybe he'd ducked behind a tree, too, or he could have even headed back to the semi. There were some shrubs and even the ditch that he could be using to conceal himself.

So, there were three attackers still alive.

With Royce's normally good aim, that wouldn't have been such bad odds, but there was nothing normal about their situation.

The shots started to come again. Nonstop. Deafening. But they all seemed to be coming from the shooter at the rear of the SUV. Sophie didn't have Royce's shooting skills, but she fired a shot that guy's way. He ducked down behind the SUV.

It was a temporary lull, but Royce used it to crawl his way to her. Even though Royce was cursing and telling her to stay down, Sophie fired another shot at the gunman, to keep the attention on her. And that meant she had to keep her attention on them, to make sure they didn't try to come after Royce and her from a different direction. She considered calling for backup, and would, once she no longer had to fire shots to keep the men at bay.

Royce finally made it to her and pulled her back to the frozen ground.

"How bad are you hurt?" she asked, but Sophie was terrified to hear the answer.

"I'm okay."

It sounded like a lie and probably was. While Royce kept watch, Sophie pulled open his jacket and looked for herself. There was blood. Too much of it. Of course, any amount was too much when it came to Royce. She wadded up some of his shirt and put some pressure on the wound, hoping it would slow the bleeding.

"We need to get to the house," he said.

She looked back at the place. Not far. But every step would be dangerous, especially with those shots coming at them. Plus, she saw something she hadn't seen from the road.

The weathered For Sale sign.

Oh, mercy. That meant there might not be anyone inside to help them.

"I need the lighter," Royce added. "And any paper you might have in your pockets."

He used his hands to rake together some dead leaves and small sticks from the ground.

"They're too wet," she reminded him.

"We don't need a fire. Just smoke. And the wind is working in our favor. It'll carry the smoke toward the gunmen."

Yes. It might shield them from the shooters.

Might.

Sophie helped Royce scoop up as much debris as she could safely reach and then she rummaged through her pockets. She had a wadded up tissue and a receipt from a coffee shop. Royce pulled out his wallet and added some twenty dollar bills to the stash.

She lit the tissue and held her breath.

The shots didn't stop. In fact, they seemed to come at them even faster. The oaks were old and thick, and thankfully the bullets couldn't get through, but the gunmen could easily change positions and try to come at them from a different angle. Both Royce and she kept watch to make sure that didn't happen.

It didn't take long, just a few seconds for the bills and paper to catch fire, and Royce gently placed some of the damp leaves on top. He'd been right about the direction of the wind. It carried the smoke away from them.

"You have the gun with the backup ammo. So stay down and fire a shot to your left," Royce instructed. He added even more leaves to the now billowing smoke. "The gunman's moving."

Oh, God.

She'd taken her eyes off him for just a moment, but he had indeed moved and was trying to make his way closer toward them.

Sophie fired.

The gunman ducked back down just as a gust of wind caught the cloud of ashy-gray smoke and sent it coiling out in front of them.

She and Royce added the last of the debris they'd collected, and they waited for the smoke to thicken. Time seemed to stop. The only thing that did. Because the fear inside was going at lightning speed. Not for herself.

But for Royce.

They needed to get to safety so she could call an ambulance, maybe from a landline inside the house— if there was one.

"Now," Royce said.

And that was all the warning Sophie got before he latched on to her hand and got them moving. They stayed as low as possible but started running toward the house. Even over the sound of her own heartbeat roaring in her ears, Sophie heard the footsteps of the gunmen running straight toward them.

17

Royce knew the smoke wouldn't give Sophie and him much cover for long. That's why he hurried, pushing Sophie to go as fast as she could go. They had to make it inside the house so she'd have some protection.

And so he'd have position to take out these SOBs.

The shots returned, just as Royce had expected, though he figured the gunmen still didn't have a clear line of sight because of the smoke. They were no doubt just randomly firing and hoping to get lucky.

That might happen.

Royce didn't take Sophie onto the front porch. Everything about the place told him there was no one inside, that the farmhouse had been empty for months or longer. Part of the roof had caved in, the front steps, too.

So he headed for the barn.

It wasn't in much better shape than the house, but at least there'd be no floor for them to fall through.

The barn door was wide-open, and heaps of snow-dusted hay were scattered everywhere. Royce pushed Sophie inside, and they managed to slam the door shut. There was no lock, and Royce knew they only had seconds before the shooters would catch up.

"Go over there," he told Sophie, and he motioned toward the side wall.

That way, she wouldn't be directly in front of the door. Royce took cover behind what was left of a stall. It wasn't much protection, but he might not need it because he checked the back door, and it was indeed closed tight with a thick board lock. Old-fashioned, but it looked rock solid. That meant if the gunmen tried to get inside, they'd have to go through the front.

And get by him to reach Sophie.

Royce looked over at her and hated what he saw. The fear in her eyes. And more. She was terrified for him. He wanted to reassure her that his injury wasn't that bad.

He hoped.

Yeah, he was bleeding. The warm blood was trickling down his chest from his left shoulder. There was pain, too. Lots of it. But Royce pushed that pain as far back in his mind as he could and kept repeating to himself that they had to get out of this alive.

And then he'd learn the identity of every man hiding behind those ski masks.

Because this was going to stop.

The footsteps got closer, and despite the wind, Royce thought he might have heard whispers. The gunmen were no doubt trying to figure out the best way in. Royce hoped there wasn't one.

Sophie and he waited, but as time closed in around him, Royce began to think of some worst-case scenarios. Maybe the gunmen would try to use smoke or fire to draw them out. Just as Royce had done. He didn't have long to dwell on that thought, though.

There was a sharp cracking sound.

And a split second later, the door flew open.

Royce fired. But it was too late. The guy who'd kicked in the door dove to the right side of the barn, and the shot missed him.

Royce mumbled some profanity, and though he wanted to check on Sophie again, he didn't. He staked his attention on the now-open barn door and kept it there. He listened, trying to pick through the sound of the wind, his heartbeat and their breathing, so he could detect any movement.

He did.

Royce turned, took aim at the side of the barn where the gunman had landed. And he fired.

Royce's shot blistered through the air, the sound echoing through the barn, and he heard the groan of pain. And then the thud of a body hitting the ground. Royce waited, hoping the hit hadn't been faked, but then he heard something that confirmed it. One of the other gunmen cursed, and judging from his footsteps, he hurried toward his dead or injured partner.

"Stay down," he mouthed to Sophie in case the men tried to rush in. Or return fire.

Part of Royce hoped they'd just run away so that Sophie and he could escape, but that would mean this wouldn't end here. Until he had the person responsible, the attacks would just continue.

The phone in his pocket buzzed. Bad timing. Royce couldn't risk taking his attention off the front door to look at the screen and see who was calling, but this meant they now had cell service. Good to know if he managed to eliminate the two that were left, then he could call for help.

He kept listening, but Royce no longer heard the

mumbles or profanity of the gunmen. No movement, either. And without the shots being fired, the silence closed in around them.

Royce didn't exactly get comfortable with the silence, but a jolt went through his body when he heard the crashing sound. He automatically glanced at the rear door, figuring their attackers were trying to get through there.

But there was no one.

His gaze slashed back to the front just as a gunman jumped out from cover. Royce fired at the same time there was more of that crashing noise. He pivoted, frantically looking around him, and he saw Sophie trying to scramble away from the gaping hole that was now in the side of the barn.

Someone had pulled off several of the rotting wooden planks.

And Royce got just a glimpse of the terror on Sophie's face as the person yanked her through the opening and out of the barn.

One second Sophie was on the barn floor, and the next she was being pulled outside.

Oh, God.

What was happening?

Yelling and kicking, she fought the person who was dragging her across the broken wood siding, but he was a lot stronger than she was. Plus, he'd had the element of surprise. By the time she'd realized what was happening to her, he had her out of the barn.

It was one of their attackers, but she couldn't see his face because of the ski mask.

Sophie landed hard on the cold ground, but she immediately tried to turn and aim the gun at her attacker. Again, he had the advantage of size and position, and he kicked the weapon from her hand. It went flying into the snow, and the pain screamed through her hand. At a minimum she would have bruises, but Sophie was afraid she might have broken bones. That wouldn't help her fight.

She didn't give up, though. Couldn't. Clearly her life was on the line here. Royce's, too, since he was already injured. She could hear him calling out to her, but she couldn't take the time to answer. She was in a fight for her life.

Sophie tried to scramble away from the gunman, toward the weapon he'd knocked from her hand. If she could get it, then at least she'd have some way to defend herself. But before she could even get close to it, the man latched on to her hair and dragged her to her feet.

"Sophie!" Royce shouted.

"Stay down," she warned him, and prayed he would listen.

Her attacker put her in front of him. Like a shield. And he shoved the gun against her head.

"Move and you die," he growled.

His voice was a hoarse whisper. One that she didn't recognize. Part of her was actually relieved that it wasn't her father or brother who'd launched this attack. Of course, that didn't mean one of them hadn't hired these men.

That hurt far more than the throbbing ache in her hand.

She shoved aside the physical pain and the thought. Right now it didn't matter who'd hired these men. It only mattered that Royce and she got out of this alive.

Sophie had some hope that it might be possible.

After all, the gunman hadn't immediately killed her when he pulled her out of the barn. He could have. Easily. In fact, he'd obviously known where she was, maybe because he'd heard her breathing or moving around inside, so he could have just fired through the rickety wall and ended her life. But he hadn't.

Why?

What did he want from Royce and her?

"McCall, make this easy on yourself and the woman," someone shouted. The other gunman, she realized. Judging from the sound of his voice, he was still somewhere near the front side of the barn.

"I've called for backup," Royce answered. "In a few minutes, cops will be crawling all over this place."

She figured that was a bluff, but it did seem to unnerve the man who was holding her. He jammed the gun even harder against her head and started dragging her toward the front where she figured the other gunman was waiting.

"Let Sophie go," Royce said. "There's no reason for you to hold her."

"Yeah, there is," the man behind her yelled. He paused, and she heard the whispered voice then.

Sophie glanced around, expecting to see yet another attacker, but she noticed the tiny communication device hooked into the ski mask near his ear.

"Will do," the man mumbled to that whispered voice.

So, there was someone else. *No.* The two gunmen were bad enough, but there was another culprit. One no doubt calling the shots. Maybe literally. Because while the gunman hadn't immediately put a bullet in her, she didn't think the same would be true for Royce.

"We have to leave with the woman now," the man holding her shouted to his partner. "Deputy McCall, that means you either surrender now or we start shooting. We got a lot of ammo, and those barn walls ain't gonna hold back many bullets. You want another shot in you, McCall?"

Royce didn't answer, but she could hear him moving around inside. *Mercy.* He wasn't surrendering, and she had no doubt that these men would do as they'd threatened.

"What do you want with Sophie?" Royce finally shouted.

She heard the whispered voice again.

"Business," her captor answered, no doubt repeating what he'd been told to say by the person on the other end of that communicator.

"Business that has to do with those papers you took from our SUV?" Royce added.

Yes, the papers. The ones that implicated her father, Travis and the other man in an illegal land deal. Was that what this was all about?

"I'm guessing Milton Wells is your boss," Royce continued. She could hear him moving inside, but she had no idea what he was doing. "I'm also guessing that Wells doesn't want anyone to find out who he really is."

The person on the communicator said something that Sophie wished she could hear because Royce seemed to be on the right track. Well, the right track for unnerving the man with the gun to her head.

"I have other copies of those papers," she tossed out there. It, too, was a bluff. There were no duplicates because she hadn't wanted other copies of the incriminating documents that could send her father to jail.

But her captor obviously didn't know that.

"We're taking her now," he shouted to his comrade after getting yet more whispered orders.

So that was it. The papers were the key to all of this, and if the duplicates actually existed, they would no doubt force her to hand them over.

And then they'd kill her.

"This is your last chance, McCall," the other gunman warned. "Surrender, and you'll live."

Sophie figured that was a lie, especially since the man holding her moved the gun and lifted it toward the barn.

Sweet heaven. They were going to start shooting.

She had to do something. She couldn't just stand there and let Royce be killed. Sophie adjusted her footing, preparing herself to drop down. She'd also try to elbow the man in the stomach. It wasn't much of a distraction, but maybe it would be enough for her to try to wrestle that gun away from him.

Sophie got ready, drew her elbow.

But before she could move an inch, she heard the movement behind them. Someone was running, and she saw the blur of motion from the corner of her eye.

Royce.

He came from the back of the barn and slammed his gun against her captor's head. He went down like a bag of rocks.

Royce immediately caught on to her. "Let's get out of here," he whispered.

They turned to run toward the house.

But they didn't get far.

18

Royce cursed when he saw the man step out from the back of the barn. The guy hadn't been there just seconds earlier when Royce had gone through the door to get to Sophie. But he was there now.

And he had a gun pointed right at Sophie and him.

Royce fired even though he was certain he didn't have a steady shot, and in the same motion, he dragged Sophie to the ground so she wouldn't be in the direct path if the guy returned fire.

He didn't.

It didn't take Royce long to realize why. The other gunman who'd been at the front of the barn now raced around the corner, behind Sophie and him. He was still armed, and he pointed his weapon at them.

Sophie and he were trapped.

Hell.

Royce had known it wasn't much of a plan for him to try to get her out of there, but he'd had to try. He couldn't just stand by while these goons kidnapped her.

And he was certain that's what they were planning to do.

Kidnap her and force her to tell them where those

duplicate papers were that she'd hidden. Except he was pretty sure that the only copy of that land deal was now in the hands of the attacker who'd come from the back of the barn.

Royce covered Sophie's body with his. Trying to protect her. And he studied the man who was now making his way toward them. He didn't walk with the same air as the others. There was a confidence. No, make that arrogance.

This guy was the boss.

Too bad Royce couldn't see his face. Also too bad it could be any of their suspects. If he could pinpoint which one, he might have a better chance of negotiating their way out of this dangerous mess.

Especially if it was Eldon or Stanton.

Royce could maybe play the family card and remind them that Sophie was blood. It might also mean her life wasn't in as much danger as he'd thought it was since either Eldon or Stanton would probably indeed let her go once they made sure there were no other copies of those papers.

Other than an out-and-out escape, that was the best-case scenario here. For Sophie, anyway. The gunmen had already made it clear that they'd planned to kill him. Royce didn't think they would automatically change their minds about that, either. He was a loose end they couldn't afford to keep around.

The man in front of them aimed his gun. Not at Royce. But at Sophie, and he tipped his head to the gunman behind them.

"Put down your weapon," the lackey ordered Royce. "If not, I'll blow a hole in your lady friend's arm. It won't kill her, but it won't feel too good, either."

Royce glanced at both men, and there was nothing in their body language to indicate that was a bluff. They would indeed shoot Sophie. He had no choice but to toss his gun onto the ground, but he kept it close.

Still within reach.

Of course, either of those men could get off a shot before Royce could get his gun back in his hands, but maybe he could create some kind of distraction.

"Let Royce go," he heard Sophie say. "And I'll take you to the papers."

Royce cursed again and shot her a "stay quiet" glare. Which she ignored.

"If you hurt him," she said to the man who stopped directly in front of them, "then I'll never give you those papers."

The man said nothing, but he did look at the other gunman who was behind Sophie and him.

"Want me to go ahead and take care of him?" the man asked his boss.

"No!" Sophie practically shouted. She pushed herself away from Royce, wriggling out from the meager cover that his body was providing for her, and she got to her feet. "I meant it. If Royce dies, you don't get what you want."

She looked back at Royce as he, too, got to his feet. There was worry etched on every part of her face and in her eyes, and that worry went up a huge notch when her attention landed on the blood on the jacket. The blood flow had slowed down significantly, thank God, but he was sure he looked like a man in need of serious medical attention.

"I'm so sorry," Sophie whispered to him, probably because she was still blaming herself for all of this.

But Royce was blaming the man in front of them.

"Let me guess," Royce said to that man. "You're Milton Wells, the guy who signed that illegal land deal. Of course Milton Wells is just an alias, isn't it?"

That wasn't exactly speculation since neither Kade Ryland nor Royce had been able to locate any info about the man.

"You're probably guessing—rightfully so—that eventually I'll figure out who Milton Wells really is," Royce added. "And that's why you want to kill me."

Sophie's eyes widened, and she tossed glances at all three of them. Hopefully, she realized now that it wouldn't do any good for her to go with them. If she did, it would just make it easier for them to kill her once they figured out that she couldn't give them what they wanted.

She turned back to the man in front of them, her gaze traveling from his head to his boots. No doubt trying to figure out if it was her brother behind that mask.

"It's either Stanton or Agent Lott," Royce said, going with his theory that this was someone who'd posed as Milton Wells. "Because your father and Travis had already signed the document."

Of course, it could still be one of them, but Royce thought he saw a slight change in the boss's body language. Just a hint of movement that made Royce believe he'd hit the proverbial nail on the head.

"Lott," Royce said. "I know it's you."

The man certainly didn't confirm it. Neither did his hired gun that still had a Glock pointed right at Sophie's arm. The seconds crawled by.

And the man finally cursed.

"This shouldn't have been this hard," he mumbled,

adding more profanity. It was enough for Royce to recognize the speaker.

Agent Lott pulled off the mask, stuffing it into his
jacket pocket. "If you think that knowing my identity
will save you," Lott growled, "then think again. One
way or another, I will get those papers from Sophie."

"Oh, mercy," she murmured.

She didn't sound relieved that it wasn't a family
member trying to kill them, probably because she knew
just how dangerous a rogue agent could be. Lott had the
shooting skills and the backup to gun them both down.
And Sophie and he didn't exactly have a lot going for
them. No gun, and his shoulder was practically numb
from the pain and blood loss.

But Royce had something Lott didn't.

The will to keep Sophie alive. The agent was doing
this to cover his butt and his illegal activity, but Royce
was fighting for Sophie's life.

"Sophie will go with you," Royce said to Lott.

It was a lie. Well, hopefully. Royce didn't want Lott
to get Sophie out of his sight, but he needed some kind
of diversion. Better yet, he needed one or both of those
guns aimed away from them.

Sophie shook her head and caught on to Royce's arm.
"They'll kill you," she whispered.

They'd try. Royce would try to stop that, too.

He moved closer to Sophie, brushing his mouth over
hers. "Play along," Royce whispered.

"Touching," Lott complained. "But I don't have time
for a lovers' goodbye." He motioned with his gun for
Sophie to follow him. "Come on."

She looked at Royce again, her eyes silently asking him what to do, and he glanced toward the side of

the barn to that gaping hole. If possible, he wanted her through there. No, it wouldn't be much protection, but it might keep her out of the line of fire when he went for his gun on the ground.

Sophie gave a shaky nod, hopefully understanding what he wanted her to do. While he was hoping, Royce added that she would duck inside the barn for cover and not try to save him.

"Goodbye," she whispered. And then she turned as if she might indeed leave with Lott.

The agent reached out to take her arm. But he missed. Because Sophie screamed at the top of her voice and lunged toward the opening in the barn.

Royce dropped to the ground just as the shot blasted through the air.

Sophie didn't have time to make it through the hole in the barn. She'd tried to create a distraction by screaming, but it hadn't worked.

Lott had fired.

At Royce.

Without thinking, she turned and dove at the agent. Even though he was a lot larger than she was, she had speed and fury on her side. Sophie slammed into him, catching him off balance, and sending them both crashing to the ground.

Lott cursed, calling her a vile name, and he flipped her onto her back as if she weighed nothing. But Sophie didn't give up. She latched on to his right wrist with both of her hands and held on, digging her fingernails into his bare flesh.

She heard the movement. The scuffle. And she

prayed that Royce hadn't been hit, that he was able to fight off the other gunman. But Royce was already hurt.

Maybe worse.

The thought of that broke her heart into a million little pieces. Royce had done so much to keep her safe, and here he was risking everything for her. That only made Sophie fight harder.

Lott fought harder, too. Probably because he knew if he didn't stop her and Royce that he'd spend the rest of his life in jail. Not a good outcome for a federal agent. He pinned her legs to the ground. Her body, as well. And he punched her in the jaw with his left hand.

The pain shot through her, and Sophie could have sworn she saw stars.

Somehow, despite the pain, she managed to hang on to Lott's wrist, and she clamped on the back of his hand with her teeth. Lott howled in pain and tried to bash her away from him.

Even over the roaring in her ears, Sophie heard Royce. He was cursing, too. And then she heard something she didn't want to hear.

A cracking sound.

And someone yelled in pain.

Because the adrenaline and the pain were pumping through her, it took her several moments to figure out that it wasn't Royce who had yelled but the other gunman.

She looked past Lott, not easy to do with him trying to wrestle his shooting hand away from her, and she saw Royce coming directly toward them. He had his gun in his hand, and in addition to his shoulder, his head was bleeding.

"Stay back!" Lott yelled.

Until he said that, Sophie hadn't known that Lott had seen Royce, too. But he had. Lott bashed her in the face again, and when her head flopped back, he snapped his left arm around her and dragged them to a standing position. Even though she kept hold of his wrist, that didn't stop Lott from twisting the gun until it was pointed at Royce.

"If you keep struggling, Sophie," Lott said. "Royce dies here and now."

Lott left no room for doubt in his voice, so Sophie's grip melted off his wrist.

Now that she was facing Royce, she had no trouble seeing all the nicks and cuts on his face—no doubt from the fight with the gunman. She hadn't heard a shot, so Royce had probably knocked the guy unconscious. That was good except for the fact that Lott still controlled the situation. As long as he had Royce in the crosshairs of his gun, she couldn't do anything to risk him shooting.

Royce was just a few feet in front of them.

There was no way Lott could miss.

"It doesn't have to be this way," Royce said. He kept his gun aimed at Lott, but she doubted he had a clean shot because she was literally in his line of fire.

"It does," Lott argued. He tightened his grip on Sophie and started to back away. He was trying to escape with her.

No!

That couldn't happen. She might be able to stall him for a little while, but eventually he'd kill her. Of course, her more immediate concern was for Royce.

He followed Lott and her.

"You'll get some jail time," Royce tried again. "And with a good lawyer, maybe not even much of that."

She felt Lott shake his head. "Travis is dead. I killed him, but I haven't had time to set up the evidence to frame you."

"Travis is dead?" Sophie asked.

"Yeah. He was blackmailing me about that land deal. Not a good idea."

That robbed her of her breath. Not because Sophie cared for Travis. No, he was scum. But it meant Lott was a killer now. First-degree murder, and he would no doubt do anything to make sure he wasn't arrested for something that would get him the death penalty. It let her know just how desperate, and dangerous, this man was.

"Hard to set me up for a murder when I'm dead," Royce reminded him.

"Hard, yes, but it's doable," Lott argued. "When those two men regain consciousness, they'll clean up the mess and plant your body where it needs to be. It'll look as if you got into a gunfight with Travis."

Royce shook his head. "If Travis is already dead, that'll be a tough sell. A good CSI will be able to determine that the times of death don't match."

"Yeah, if it weren't for this cold weather."

God, that was probably true. Besides, as a federal agent, Lott knew how to stage the evidence. That's why Sophie had to do something.

But what?

She'd already lost one scuffle with Lott, and while Royce was still armed, he was hurt and didn't look too steady on his feet. And then Sophie saw something that made their situation go from bad to worse.

One of the gunmen on the ground groaned and

stirred. It wouldn't be long before he got up, ready to help his boss commit another murder or two.

"Plus, you have other loose ends," Royce said. He, too, was keeping an eye on those men. "That confidential informant you told us about. What if he gets scared and tells all?"

"He won't know to tell," Lott answered. "Because he didn't know he was an informant. It was Stanton, and I had him followed. That's how I knew he'd drugged Sophie and you."

"And I guess it didn't occur to you to stop him?" Sophie asked.

Lott lifted his shoulder. "Sometimes, those things play out in a man's favor. I figured if Stanton accidentally killed one of you with a drug overdose, I could blackmail him into doing whatever I wanted—including getting me those papers."

He was beyond sick. Their lives were nothing to him. And with his two goons stirring and ready to get up, Lott would no doubt unleash them first on Royce.

Then, her.

Sophie didn't think. Without warning, she dropped down, jerking Lott down with her. They didn't hit the ground like before, but he wobbled.

Royce dove at them.

He pushed Sophie out of the way and rammed right into Lott. They fell onto the ground, and the fight started instantly. Both of them were jockeying for position and trying to disarm the other.

Sophie hated the thought of Royce being injured further, but she had to do something to stop that gunman who was already trying to sit up. She raced to her gun, scooped it up and pointed it right at him.

"Move and I'll shoot," she warned, and it wasn't a bluff. She would indeed shoot the man rather than let him try to help his boss.

Sophie gathered both of the gunmen's weapons and tossed them inside the hole in the barn wall. That freed up her hands so that she could keep her own gun aimed and maybe help Royce.

Lott and he were delivering punches. Hard ones. And Sophie nearly screamed when she saw blood fly through the air and land on the snow. Royce already had too many injuries, and God knows what this was doing to his gunshot wound.

It could be killing him.

She stood there, volleying glances between the gunmen and the fight. Trying to decide what to do. Her heart was pounding. Her head racing with the worst thoughts possible.

She couldn't lose Royce.

Sophie was ready to dive into the fray, but the sound stopped her cold.

A thick blast.

It echoed through the air. Through her. And it made her blood turn to ice.

That's because someone, either Lott or Royce, had fired the shot.

Her breath vanished, and it took every ounce of her willpower just to stay on her feet. She prayed. Waited. And she saw Royce roll off Lott and to the side. He landed hard on his back on the ground.

She kept her gun pointed at the gunmen, but she ran to him, terrified of what she might see. There was more blood. Too much. And for several horrifying moments, she thought he'd been shot again.

"I'm okay," Royce said, his breath gusting.

Sophie shook her head, not believing him. He couldn't be okay, not with all that blood on his jacket.

Royce got to his feet, not easily, but she latched on to his arm and helped him get up. That's when she realized Lott hadn't moved. She looked down at the agent and spotted the source of the blood.

On Lott's chest.

He wasn't moving, and his eyes were fixed in a blank, dead stare.

"It's all right," Royce whispered to her. He took the gun from her, aimed it at the gunmen, and with his left arm he pulled her to him. "It's all right," he repeated.

And Sophie was on the verge of believing him.

Until she felt Royce collapse against her.

19

Royce tried not to make any sounds of pain or discomfort while the nurse stitched him up. That's because he knew Sophie was in the exam room next to him, and he didn't want her to hear anything else today that would add to her already raw nerves.

His nerves were certainly raw, too. Partly because of the attack that could have easily left Sophie and him dead. Also because he was berating himself for falling for the stupid ruse that Lott had created. The dirty agent had said he was going to arrest Sophie's father because he'd known it would send them racing back to town on the only road they could have used to get to Mustang Ridge.

It had turned out to be a bad mistake.

And it had nearly cost him Sophie.

That in itself was bad enough, but now Royce's nerves were raw for a different reason. When Dr. Amos Jenkins had taken Sophie into the adjoining room to examine her, Royce had been able to hear them talking. He hadn't heard exactly what they were saying, but just the sound of Sophie's murmurings had given Royce some reassurance that even though she was shaken up, she was okay.

But he could no longer hear her.

Royce tried to assure himself that's because the exam had gone well and there was nothing else for Dr. Jenkins to say to her. However, his thoughts were moving in a different direction, too. That something was wrong. That she'd had an injury that he hadn't noticed on the way to the hospital. There'd been plenty of chances for that to happen.

"Can you hurry?" he asked the nurse, Alice Wilkins. It wasn't his first request but his third, and he made it clear he would keep asking until she'd finished.

Maybe that's why she made a sound of disapproval. "Hold your horses. I'm working as fast as I can." She added another stitch. "You were lucky."

Yeah, the doctor and X-ray tech had already said the same thing. The shot to his shoulder had been a through and through. But Royce didn't feel lucky, and he wouldn't until he'd made sure that Sophie was okay.

It seemed to take hours, but the nurse finally finished with his shoulder and started in on the cuts on his head. Those would have to wait. He'd used up all the patience he had, and Royce eased the nurse aside, got off the table and headed for the door.

"I'll be back," he told her, but that might not be the truth. He'd be back only after he saw Sophie.

Royce bolted out the door and nearly ran smack-dab into his brother. "Whoa," Jake said, backing up. "In a hurry?"

"Where's Sophie?" But Royce didn't wait for an answer. He went to the examining room and threw open the door.

Empty.

"She went to the bathroom," Jake supplied. "She's all right."

Yeah, and Royce might believe that once he saw her for himself.

Jake caught on to him when Royce started down the hall. "Dr. Amos told Sophie and me that you were okay, that your injuries weren't too bad and you were just getting stitched up."

"They aren't bad," Royce agreed. "What did he say about Sophie's injuries?"

"They're minor. Just a few cuts and bruises. She was a little queasy, though, and that's why she wanted to go to the bathroom."

Hell. Queasy didn't sound good for several reasons. Maybe the pregnancy. Maybe an injury the doctor hadn't detected. Even if it was simply because she was upset—and she had a right to feel that—Royce didn't want her going through that alone.

"Hey." Jake stopped him again when he started to leave. "What's going on? Did something happen that you didn't tell me about?"

Nothing that had to do with the investigation. Royce had filled in his brother when Jake had arrived at the vacant farm and driven them back to Mustang Ridge. In turn, Jake had taken over tying up a few loose ends, like charging the surviving gunmen and starting the paperwork.

"I'm not blind," Jake said, keeping a grip on Royce's arm. "I saw the way you were holding Sophie in the truck."

He'd done some holding all right. In fact, Royce hadn't wanted to let go of her. It might take a lifetime or two for him to forget the bullets flying past her and the way the SOB Lott had punched her in the face.

"You care for her," Jake added.

"I do," Royce admitted. And it was a relief to say it aloud.

However, his relief was cut short when he heard the hurried footsteps and he saw Stanton making a beeline toward them.

"I heard," Stanton said. "Is Sophie hurt?"

Royce was about to say he didn't know and head out to find her, but he saw the movement at the end of the hall and spotted her coming out of the bathroom.

His breath of relief was a lot louder than he'd anticipated, and it caused both Jake and Stanton to give him a funny look. Royce ignored them and went to her. Sophie moved quickly toward him, too, and they pulled each other into their arms.

She held him gently, mindful of his wounded shoulder, but Royce brought her even closer to him.

"The doctor said you'd be okay." Her voice was all breath, and she was trembling. She held him so gently that he figured she was terrified of hurting him.

But nothing hurt now.

Well, except for seeing those bruises on her face and chin. Royce wished he could give Lott another beating for those. It took a special kind of scum to hit a woman.

He pushed her hair from her face so he could examine every nick, every scrape, and yeah, those godawful bruises.

"Nothing serious," she assured him but frowned when her attention landed on his bandaged shoulder. "You shouldn't be on your feet."

Royce ignored that. "Jake said you were queasy."

She nodded, glanced around, nodded again and looked as if she might say something. And then Sophie's attention landed on her brother who was making his way toward them.

"Stanton." She eased away from Royce and hugged him.

"I heard what Lott did to you." Stanton cursed. "I'm glad the bastard's dead." He lifted her chin, examining the bruises, and had a reaction similar to Royce's.

Even though Royce still wasn't happy about Stanton drugging them, it seemed as if he really did care for Sophie. And that meant Royce would figure out a way to forgive him. Sophie could no doubt do the same since he was family and she loved him.

"Royce is the one who's hurt," she said, stepping away from her brother. "He saved my life. Several times," she added, her voice breaking now.

Royce pulled her back in his arms. "She saved mine a couple of times, too."

"I'm thankful for that," Stanton said, and he glanced back at Jake. "Your brother doesn't know yet, but our father turned himself in for the illegal land deal." He paused, met Sophie's gaze. "He'll no doubt have to do some jail time."

Royce braced himself for her reaction. She didn't burst into tears, maybe because of the spent adrenaline and bone-weary fatigue but she gave a heavy sigh and ran her hand down her brother's arm.

"I can hire a lawyer for him." Sophie shook her head. "But I can't save the ranch."

Stanton's sigh was heavy, too. "I didn't expect you to." He gently kissed her cheek. "And maybe that's not such a bad thing. Don't know about you, but I'm looking forward to a clean start."

Yeah. So was Royce. But he wasn't sure Sophie and he had a shot at that. Too much old baggage. Maybe too much new baggage, as well.

"I'll go to the sheriff's office and check on Dad," Stanton said. "I'll let him know you're okay."

"Thanks. I'll be there later myself."

"Are you sure you're up for that?" Royce asked.

She nodded but waited until her brother had walked away before she added anything. "I love my father. Always will. But I can't undo what he's done, and he needs to pay for that."

Maybe her change of heart had come because she'd seen firsthand just what illegal activity could do. After all, Lott wouldn't have had a reason to try to kill them if it hadn't been for her father's land deal.

"I'll see my father," she explained. "But then I think he and I need some space."

Royce figured that wouldn't be a pleasant meeting, and he intended to be there. Well, after he got something else out of the way.

"What about the queasiness?" Royce asked.

Sophie glanced around as if to make sure no one was close by. No one was. Even Jake was still waiting up the hall, probably to give them some time alone. She took the small pen from her pocket. At least Royce thought it was a pen, but then he had a closer look.

"A pregnancy test?" he asked.

"I got it from one of the nurses I know." She dodged his gaze. "It only takes two minutes, she said."

Two minutes. Not long at all.

Royce reminded himself that they needed to know

and they would have already had it done if it hadn't been for the attacks. But suddenly a big knot formed in his stomach.

"I can take you somewhere so you can do the test," he offered.

She tipped her head to the ladies' room just a few doors down. "Or I can do it here."

Yeah. *Here.* Which would mean that two minutes was actually two minutes and wouldn't include a trip that would delay the results.

"Let me tell Jake that it's okay for him to leave," Royce said.

She nodded. And Royce saw it then. Her nerves just beneath the surface. He wasn't the only one with a stomach in knots.

He went back to Jake, trying not to look as if his entire world was suddenly up in the air. "Why don't you go on back to the office, and I'll join you there?"

Jake glanced at Sophie and then at him. "No, you won't. Whatever's going on between you two, you need to settle it."

He thought of the pregnancy test. Well, that would settle it.

Or would it?

Even if Sophie was pregnant, that didn't mean she'd want him in her life. Hell, she might not want him, *period.* He'd told her she wasn't his type. Had harped on the fact of his own parents' bad marriage. Yeah, she was attracted to him.

He was attracted to her.

But that didn't mean anything was *settled.*

"Take some time off," Jake insisted. "And before you kiss her again, you might want to wash the blood off your face. Most women don't find a bloody cheek very romantic."

It was exactly the kind of lighthearted brotherly ribbing he needed. Jake hadn't had to say he would support him no matter what—Royce knew that he would.

Drawing in a long breath, Royce headed back down the hall, and he caught Sophie by the arm as they walked to the ladies' room. "I'm going in with you," he insisted.

She stopped so fast he nearly tripped over her. "It's the *ladies'* room," she emphasized. "And you know what I have to do on this thing, right?"

"That's what I figured." He saw her point then. Most women wouldn't have wanted a man around for that. "I'll wait right outside the door."

Sophie nodded, seemed relieved. "The nurse said if we get a plus sign, I'm pregnant. A negative sign means I'm not."

Simple enough. The makers of the test probably made it that way because they figured some people might be crazy in this situation.

Sophie turned to go inside the bathroom. Royce stopped her and kissed her. Not one of those gentle pecks he'd given her earlier. Not a kiss of relief, either. The kiss he would give his lover.

Because Sophie was.

She had a slight smile when she eased back and ran her tongue over her bottom lip. The concern quickly returned, but before he could kiss it away again, she ducked inside.

Royce considered a quick trip to the men's room to wash his face as Jake had suggested, but the next few seconds suddenly seemed a lot more than two minutes.

He paced. Checked his watch. And then put his ear to the door to listen.

"I need you to time this," he heard her say.

Royce cursed. Heck, the two minutes hadn't even started yet. He fastened his attention to his watch. Or rather tried. And he gave up and opened the door.

Sophie was there standing by the sink where she'd placed the little white stick.

"Anyone else in here?" he asked.

She shook her head, and Royce stepped inside with her. He glanced at the test. The screen was still blank. A clean slate, so to speak.

And that's when it hit him.

He didn't want a clean slate on either the test or his life. He wanted Sophie. Royce caught on to her and turned her to face him so he could tell her that.

"It'll be okay," she whispered.

"Yeah." Maybe it would be. Their gazes connected, and he pulled her into his arm for another kiss. "Sophie, I'm in love with you."

She blinked and made a sound a drunk person might make. "W-what?"

Royce tried not to panic, but he'd hoped she would jump into his arms and tell him that she loved him, too. Well, she wasn't jumping. She was staring at him with her mouth open.

"I know, it's sudden," he tried.

But she pressed her fingers over his lips. "No. It's not. We've lived a few lifetimes in the last few days. It's not sudden at all." She swallowed hard. "And I'm in love with you, too."

At first, it felt as if someone had slugged him. The air sort of swooshed out of him. Hardly a manly reaction. But the breath returned. So did the relief. And he hauled her into his arms. Gently, of course. Because of their injuries. And the kiss he gave her was gentle, too.

"Marry me," he said with his mouth against hers.

She pulled back again. "If you're doing this because of the test—"

"I'm not. In fact, I don't want you to look at that test until you've answered me. Will you marry me, Sophie?"

Tears sprang to her eyes.

The door sprang open, too.

"Sorry," Royce said to the woman who was about to come in. "Official police business."

He shut the door, held it closed with his foot and turned back to Sophie. "Well?"

"You said I wasn't right for you." She didn't wait for him to correct that falsehood. "But I am. And you're the right man for me."

Yeah. That was the response he wanted, and the kiss she gave him wasn't too shabby, either.

"Well?" he pressed. "I need an answer to my proposal."

"Yes," she said before he even finished. And she repeated her yes a couple of times.

Royce couldn't help himself. He whooped for joy and probably scared some folks out in the hall. He didn't care. Right now, the only thing that mattered was that Sophie loved him and she'd said multiple yeses.

The next kiss was considerably longer and hotter than it should have been, considering they weren't close enough to a bed to finish it off the right away. They pulled back, breathless and revved up.

"We should celebrate," he suggested, "in bed."

"Are you up to that?" She glanced at his shoulder, at his sly smile, and gave him a smile of her own.

"Always," Royce assured her.

First, though, they had to look at the test stick on the sink. It no longer seemed as life altering as it had been just ten minutes ago. In fact, either way it went, Royce would be happy because if Sophie wasn't pregnant, he'd do something about getting her that way real quick.

Without looking at the little screen, she scooped up the test and held it for him to see. Sophie kept her gaze nailed to his.

And this time Royce didn't just smile. He laughed.

The little pink plus sign was crystal clear.

Royce pulled her back to him. "I need to get you to the altar right away," he said. He turned the test so she could see it.

Sophie blinked, but the smile came just as quickly. The laugh, too. "Are you ready for this?" she asked, blinking back happy tears.

"Oh, yeah," he drawled. Royce figured Sophie and he were in for one heck of a good life.

* * * * *

We hope you enjoyed reading
ANGEL OF MERCY
by *New York Times* bestselling author
HEATHER GRAHAM
and
**STANDOFF AT
MUSTANG RIDGE**
by *USA TODAY* bestselling author
DELORES FOSSEN
Both were originally Harlequin® series stories!

You crave excitement!
Harlequin Intrigue® stories deal in serious
romantic suspense, keeping you on the edge
of your seat as resourceful, true-to-life women
and strong, fearless men fight for survival.

C.J. hated to admit that the cowboy might be right. Before
Boone McGraw had walked into this office, she'd been sure
Hank's death had something to do with one of his older
cases. All of his newer cases that he'd told her about were
nothing that could get a man killed.

Now she had to adjust her thinking. Could this be about
the kidnapping? Her mind balked because Hank loved
nothing better than to talk about his cases. He wouldn't have
been able not to talk about his one unless… Unless he did
know something, something that he thought could put her
in danger…

"Why do you think the hit-and-run wasn't an accident?"
the cowboy asked.

It took her a moment to get her thoughts together. "This
ransacked office for one. Clearly someone was looking for
something in the old files."

"You're that sure it involved a case?"

She waved a hand through the air. "Why tear up the office unless the killer is looking for the case file—and whatever incriminating evidence might be in it?"

He nodded as if that made sense to him. "But if it was here, don't you think that whoever did this took the file with him?"

"Actually, I don't. Look at this place. I'd say the person got frustrated when he didn't find it. Otherwise, why trash the place?"

"You have a point. But let's say the file you're looking for is about the McGraw kidnapping. It wouldn't be an old file since he called only a few weeks ago. When did he turn off his phone and electricity here at the office?"

C.J. hated to admit that she didn't know. "We've both been busy on separate cases. But he would have told me if he knew anything about the case." He wouldn't have kept something like that from her. And yet he hadn't mentioned talking to the McGraw lawyer and her instincts told her that Boone McGraw wasn't lying about that.

That Hank now wouldn't have the opportunity to tell her hit her hard. Hank had been like family, her only family, and now he was gone. And she was only starting to realize how much Hank had been keeping from her.

She had to look away, not wanting Boone to see the shine of tears that burned her eyes. She wouldn't break down. Especially not in front of this cowboy.

Don't miss
ROUGH RIDER by B.J. Daniels,
available October 2017 wherever
Harlequin® Intrigue books and ebooks are sold.

www.Harlequin.com

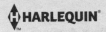

INTRIGUE

EDGE-OF-YOUR-SEAT INTRIGUE, FEARLESS ROMANCE.

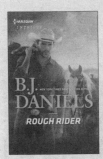

Save **$1.00**

on the purchase of ANY Harlequin® Intrigue book.

Available wherever books are sold, including most bookstores, supermarkets, drugstores and discount stores.

Save $1.00

on the purchase of any Harlequin® Intrigue book.

Coupon valid until November 30, 2017.
Redeemable at participating outlets in the U.S. and Canada only.
Not redeemable at Barnes & Noble stores. Limit one coupon per customer.

Canadian Retailers: Harlequin Enterprises Limited will pay the face value of this coupon plus 10.25¢ if submitted by customer for this product only. Any other use constitutes fraud. Coupon is nonassignable. Void if taxed, prohibited or restricted by law. Consumer must pay any government taxes. Void if copied. Inmar Promotional Services ("IPS") customers submit coupons and proof of sales to Harlequin Enterprises Limited, P.O. Box 3000, Saint John, NB E2L 4L3, Canada. Non-IPS retailer—for reimbursement submit coupons and proof of sales directly to Harlequin Enterprises Limited, Retail Marketing Department, 225 Duncan Mill Rd., Don Mills, ON M3B 3K9, Canada.

U.S. Retailers: Harlequin Enterprises Limited will pay the face value of this coupon plus 8¢ if submitted by customer for this product only. Any other use constitutes fraud. Coupon is nonassignable. Void if taxed, prohibited or restricted by law. Consumer must pay any government taxes. Void if copied. For reimbursement submit coupons and proof of sales directly to Harlequin Enterprises, Ltd 482, NCH Marketing Services, P.O. Box 880001, El Paso, TX 88588-0001, U.S.A. Cash value 1/100 cents.

® and ™ are trademarks owned and used by the trademark owner and/or its licensee.

© 2017 Harlequin Enterprises Limited

HIBJDCOUP0917

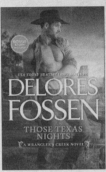  

Need an adrenaline rush from nail-biting tales
(and irresistible males)?

Check out **Harlequin® Intrigue®**
and **Harlequin® Romantic Suspense** books!

New books available every month!

CONNECT WITH US AT:

Harlequin.com/Community

 Facebook.com/HarlequinBooks

 Twitter.com/HarlequinBooks

 Instagram.com/HarlequinBooks

 Pinterest.com/HarlequinBooks

ReaderService.com

**ROMANCE WHEN
YOU NEED IT**

SGENRE2017